The
Flower
Girl

Maggie FORD

The Flower Girl

EBURY
PRESS

1

Ebury Press, an imprint of Ebury Publishing,
20 Vauxhall Bridge Road,
London SW1V 2SA

Penguin
Random House
UK

Ebury Press is part of the Penguin Random House group of companies
whose addresses can be found at global.penguinrandomhouse.com

First published by Ebury Press in 2021

www.penguin.co.uk

A CIP catalogue record for this book is available from the British Library

ISBN 9781529105582

Typeset in 11.5/13.5 pt Times New Roman
by Integra Software Services Pvt. Ltd, Pondicherry

Printed and bound in Great Britain by Clays Ltd, Elcograf S.p.A.

The authorised representative in the EEA is Penguin Random House Ireland,
Morrison Chambers, 32 Nassau Street, Dublin D02 YH68.

Penguin Random House is committed to a sustainable future for our
business, our readers and our planet. This book is made from
Forest Stewardship Council® certified paper.

MIX
Paper from
responsible sources
FSC
www.fsc.org   FSC® C018179

To my friend Rosalie Howe

Also my thanks to James Sacre for his most valued information on magic and magicians

Do I own the days I walk through?
Do I dare to choose my way?
And where you lead should I just follow?
I'll never walk this path again.
You draw the world that I must live in.
Are you the writer, and I the pen?

'*The Pattern Maker*' *by Brian Bedford of Artisan*

Chapter One

The tray was empty. All that was left were four tiny posies, their paper leaves and petals limp and soggy from the damp air.

As Christmas shoppers passed along London's opulent Oxford Street, hurrying with a mid-December fog beginning to descend, Emma Beech took the tray from around her slim neck and dropped the spoiled bunches into the gutter. No point taking them home. Her mother would have made a fresh batch for tomorrow.

Tomorrow, Saturday, the fog hopefully having lifted, she'd try the theatre queues. The wealthy who never queued but hurried straight into the foyer from their carriages preferred real flowers, a lady fluttering her eyes at being presented with a posy or a corsage. It was ordinary folk who bought paper ones for a penny or two. They didn't wilt and could be used as fire-stove ornaments, lasting for ages and gathering dust, but perfect imitations of the real thing. Mum was clever with her fingers.

The fog was closing in rapidly. With the tray under her arm, Emma made for a horse-bus pulling up a few yards away. It went from Oxford Street to Shoreditch. To save the fare, she would be walking the rest of the way along Commercial Road to Stepney, where she lived with Mum and her elder brother Ben.

Clutching her ticket and half listening to the conversation around her, the plod of the horses' hooves and the driver's throaty warning to others partly blinded by the thickening fog, she gazed through the window.

Mum would be pleased to see an empty tray. She worked hard, did Mum. As well as paper flowers she did silk work, tassels for ladies' mantles, antimacassars and mantelpiece runners for an employer who, like all his kind, paid an insult of a wage to outworkers. Nor was it regular, so the paper blooms helped keep her just clear of poverty's cold clutches.

Emma helped, twisting stems, cutting leaves and petals. She'd left school two years ago, at thirteen, to work at Bell & Co. the match people in Bow, but after a year of repetitious work with its stink of phosphorous and hot wax, she'd been laid off. She wasn't sorry. She'd hated dipping sticks in the thick paste from which, despite the match girls' protest fourteen years ago in 1888, it was still possible to get that disease that rotted the jaw bone, called phossy jaw.

By the time she got to Shoreditch, visibility was down to a yard or two. One hand clutching her tray, the other holding her skirt clear of the pavement, she tucked her head into the narrow collar of her flimsy jacket. Already drops of moisture were gathering on her lashes, her long, auburn hair under the inadequate straw boater now damp and heavy.

At six-thirty and completely dark, this pea souper meant feeling her way at a snail's pace. She could hear the detonation of fog signals from the railway, nearer at hand muffled warnings of cab and cart drivers, a wheel easily mounting the kerb in a fog to endanger pedestrians.

The air had become acrid with the stink of thousands of London's domestic and industrial chimneys, but one smell assailed her as she blindly passed one point. Hot tar. It brought back childhood memories of standing beside the warm, glowing brazier as workmen raked the shiny, smooth-flowing tar to the puff and rumble of the ponderous steamroller.

The odour lingering in her nostrils, Emma looked for the glow of the next gas lamp. It was easy to become disorientated. All she had to tell her she was still in Commercial Road was the occasional dull clip-clop of hooves or the muffled rumble of cart or carriage wheels. Once or twice a figure, head sunk into a scarf, breath hanging on the air, sidestepped a near collision with her in the fog, grunting an apology, to be swallowed up again in passing.

The landmark she'd been looking out for, St Anne's Church, loomed up like an apparition. Church Row ran beside it. Down there was home.

She was preparing to turn the corner, cautiously feeling the railings, when a tall figure came out of the fog, cannoning into her with some force.

She gave a little cry of annoyance. The cry became a shriek of alarm as the man grabbed her arm, his face, half hidden in a thick muffler, inches from hers, the eyes pale and staring. Certain she was about to be molested and not a soul nearby to run to her aid, Emma hit out with both hands, her tray tumbling from her grip.

Her cry must have startled him because he instantly leaped back. Unable to save himself or the heavy object

3

he held in both arms, together with a long stick, he hit the ground, still clutching the thing he held as though it were a baby, though the stick clattered a short way off.

With an impulse to run vanishing, Emma went over to him, now full of apologies. In an effort to make amends she bent to help him up but was surprised to have him cringe away.

'Oh, I didn't mean to scare yer,' she blurted. Silly, it was he who had scared her. 'Let me 'elp you up.' Silly again – he was tall, thick-set and she was slim, with little weight to her.

She stood back uncertain as he waved her away, at the same time pulling his muffler higher over the lower part of his face. She watched him get awkwardly to his feet, still refusing to let go of the thing he clutched so protectively.

'I'm ever so sorry,' she began.

He appeared embarrassed. 'It is I who should apologise.'

The voice was cultured, in the pronounced way actors on the stage spoke, every syllable clear and clipped, and she wasn't sure whether to feel amused or belittled by it.

'Clumsy of me,' he continued. 'I should have taken care in weather such as this. I must have given you quite a turn, my dear. I do apologise.'

'Don't think nothing of it,' she began. 'It was ...' She stopped, as in putting his weight on both feet, he sucked in a painful hiss.

'Oh, yer've 'urt yerself!' she burst out. 'Is it yer ankle?'

He tried the injured foot again. 'I must have twisted it. Stupid of me.'

'No it ain't,' she countered. 'Look, sit down fer a bit on the concrete edge of them church railings till the pain goes. I'll 'elp yer over to them.'

She made to take his arm but again he drew back from her as though insulted and hobbled over the railings. Taken aback by his almost aggressive reaction, she was about to leave him to himself when he spoke.

'Would you kindly retrieve my pole before someone trips over it?'

He pointed to the stick just about visible in the murk. It was more an order than a request, the voice deep and commanding, one accustomed to being obeyed, like a regimental sergeant major. She now noticed that his clothes, though shabby, had the look of having once been expensive. If they were his own and not given to him, then perhaps he was someone who had recently come down in the world, hence his tone.

Annoyed, she moved to obey, but only because it was sensible to move an object that could be dangerous to anyone walking by and not seeing it. It was a strange-looking thing, one end pointed, the other end carved like a blunt screw.

'What is it?' she queried, handing it to him. 'It's funny-looking fer a walking stick.'

'It is not a walking stick.' Again the sharp and commanding tone.

'Oh! Then what is it?' She was determined to have him speak civil to her. After all, none of this was her fault. To her surprise his tone moderated.

'To support this.' He looked down at the object he still held. 'This is a hurdy-gurdy in case you are wondering. Some date back eight hundred years. This isn't so old, maybe around thirty years. I bought it nearly a year ago from a pawn shop. When I still had a little money left to spend.' His low chuckle held a bitter ring.

'Can you play it?' she asked.

'Of course I can play it.'

'Is it easy?'

'That depends. One needs nimble fingers. And mine are very nimble – or were once.' He leaned over to examine his ankle, twisting it this way and that, the pain obviously now diminishing.

Emma knew she ought to be on her way. Mum would have supper ready, eager to see how much she'd made today. But she was intrigued.

'Where do yer play?'

He looked up sharply. Although she couldn't see much of him between the scarf and the hat he wore she felt instantly intimidated. She wasn't one to be easily put down. Life, especially these last three years, had made her strong-minded even at fifteen, sixteen come February, and where poverty often bowed some people, she had always fought it tooth and nail with some vague belief that one day it must all change, that somehow she'd make it change. This unfamiliar feeling made her angry with herself.

'What I mean is,' she forged on as the scrutiny threatened to put her even further on edge, 'do yer play it for yer own amusement or fer money?'

He didn't reply but she guessed he must be a street musician, one of the many of such down and outs trudging the gutters for a pitying penny or two. If he was a street entertainer he seemed painfully ashamed of it – like someone who may have known easier times, even genteel times, but was now forced to beg for a living. This fact seemed obvious from his speech.

She'd known better times too, maybe not so grand, but comfortable enough. Her father had been a stevedore in the docks with a good gang who got the plum jobs while hundreds of others had to line up 'on the stones' as it was called, in hope of a week's or even a day's work. Three years ago he'd been killed falling into a ship's hold. There were no more wages, and his colleagues, hard up as they were, putting a few pence into the hat to help tide the widow over for a week or two.

Mum had tried to keep body and soul together with nothing coming in. Emma's elder sister Molly had died of influenza. Not long after, they'd lost Ernie, only eight years old, of meningitis. It left just her and Ben. How Mum had got through those years didn't stand thinking about.

Emma had never seen her weep though she was sure she did inside. Missing her sister terribly, Molly so lively and animated and kind, she'd often given way until a sharp reprimand from Mum to pull herself together made her force back the tears. Mum was tough. And thank goodness. But for her they'd have ended up in the workhouse, because Ben was no bloody use.

His temper, which had always been short, had become insufferable, and he never once took into consideration how Mum struggled on. Evicted from the little rented house in Leonard Street, with most of their belongings taken and sold by the landlord to help pay the back rent, she still remembered helping push a borrowed old handcart with what little Mum had managed to keep hold of through the wet streets to the two rooms in Stepney she'd finally found while Ben instantly pronounced it a slum. As if it were Mum's fault.

Life would have been so different if Dad hadn't got killed. Yes, she knew all about coming down in the world and the bitterness she could detect in this man touched a spot in her heart.

'I sell flowers,' she said, affecting cheerfulness so as to let him see that trying to earn an honest penny from selling wares or making music was not begging, if that was what he was thinking. 'Paper flowers – in the West End – but not to the toffs. They buy real ones. Just to ordinary people. I was on me way 'ome when you blundered into me.'

'I have apologised for that.' Above the muffler, the eyes didn't look a bit apologetic. They seemed to pierce into her with an intensity she was finding almost alarming.

Against her better judgement, Emma subdued an urge to hurry away. She wasn't going to let him intimidate her. And let him get the best of it? No.

'D'you busk round 'ere, then?' she continued with more cheeriness than she felt. 'I expect you work the pubs. You get the best pickings from them coming out after a good evening's boozing.'

'Why should that interest you?' The sharp retort should have warned her away but she was now determined to stand her ground.

'Do you? I mean busk round 'ere?'

He stood up abruptly, startling her. 'That is none of your business.'

He was looming over her now, making her back away a fraction. What if he wasn't as harmless as he'd first appeared, sitting by the parapet with his twisted ankle?

She saw his hand come towards her. It might have been a gesture of apology but looked more like a threat. Worse, as he reached out, the muffler slipped to reveal a deep scar stretching from the point of the chin almost to the left ear, the scar new and still livid. In this eerie fog it looked as though half his chin had once been cleft.

She let out a shriek and made to run, but the hand caught hold of her arm. 'Let me go!' she screamed. 'I'll call someone.'

'I mean no harm.' His raised voice certainly sounded as if it did.

'Let go of me! I'll scream for the police!' she cried out as she fought the unyielding grip.

'Please,' boomed the voice. 'Don't be afraid of me.'

But already she had pulled free. Clinging to her tray, her other hand holding up her skirts for more freedom of movement, she ran blindly into the fog, putting distance between him and her, praying that she was heading down Church Row in the direction of home. If not, she would be hopelessly lost. There was panic in the thought as she ran.

After a while with no pursuing footsteps, Emma calmed. What had made her tarry so long with a total stranger? She'd felt sorry for him at first, reluctant to leave someone who'd been hurt, but why had he turned so odd? Still, it was over now. She was safe. What mattered now was not to lose her way. Too easy to lose all sense of direction in this weather, you could walk right past a familiar place and not even know.

Emma turned her mind to gauging where she was, sensing rather than seeing landmarks. Coming up against the iron bollard at the corner of the alley crossing Church

Row that led to St Anne's churchyard, she felt the unforgiving coldness of the cast iron before she saw it, black as black in a black world.

A few cautious steps into empty space, hand outstretched like a blind person, took her to the bollard's companion on the other corner. All that was needed now was to proceed straight on, one hand exploring the wall, doors set at intervals, a faint smudge of light from a window or two for comfort.

Too occupied now to think of the narrow escape she'd just had, she counted the doors. One. Two. Three. The broken pavements were barely eighteen inches in width with a cobbled road hardly wide enough for a horse and cart to pass, yet this evening it was like moving through a black chasm. The only indication of the houses opposite was the indistinct glow from an uncurtained window or two, blurred by vapour, the gas lamp at the end of the street affording no light this far down. All was so quiet now, quiet like the grave. Quieter, knowing it wasn't, yet a dead feel to the air around her.

She thought again of the man who'd accosted her. What if he'd gone down another street and was already ahead of her waiting for her? Emma's heart began to beat against her ribs with sickening thuds.

Ahead loomed a broad, darker patch in the fog – the arch under the Blackwall Railway line. The fifth door of the eight houses between the alley and the Mitre Street Bridge was where she lived.

She all but fell through the front door, so warped as to be incapable of being locked. This was the hovel she called home, but never had it been so welcome. The dark hall smelled of stale cooking. A door on her right led to a tenanted room. The two rooms her mother rented from a scrimping landlord were up one flight of bare wood stairs that went on up to a top floor.

Hardly had she got in when her mother's voice called from the bedroom where she did her work. 'That you, Em? How'd it go terday?'

Before she could reply, Mum was there, her satisfied gaze trained on the empty tray. 'Sold 'em all then, did yer?'

Emma put the tray down behind the door. She must still have looked a little flustered for Mum eyed her suspiciously. 'Yer did sell 'em all, didn't yer? Yer didn't throw any away just ter make me feel pleased?'

'There were four ...'

'Four!' Anger was in the voice, her hard work tossed in the gutter. 'It takes me ages ter make just one bunch and you sling 'em ...'

'They was all wet and soggy. It's pea soup out there. I was lucky to keep what I sold dry in this weather.'

Even as she retaliated, she kept a fine distance between herself and Mum, whose hand could be hard on a girl only just out of her fifteenth year. 'No use bringing 'em 'ome again with me. They weren't no good any more. Yer couldn't of done nothink with 'em.'

The anger faded. She even shrugged. 'Ah, well, don't s'pose so. But it's a waste. I got yer supper keepin' warm on the trivet.'

'What is it?' asked Emma, gazing towards the two plates balanced on a gently steaming, black saucepan of water standing on a small iron platform hooked on to the grate to the meagre fire.

11

'Scrag-end. Got it yesterday from the butcher just before he closed, in time ter stop 'im throwin' it out. Said I could 'ave it for tuppence because it was all dried up. But it soon plumped out with a drop of water. With a bit of onion and potato an' a bit of salt, it's made a nice meal, all in all.'

Maud watched with satisfaction as her daughter ate with relish. She'd had hers around midday, just a little to keep her going. Money didn't stretch all that far. Now she contented herself with bread and a scrape of plum jam.

'I 'ad mine earlier,' she said when Emma looked concerned. 'After yer being out all day in this weather, yer need all the nourishment yer can get.'

Ben, if he noticed at all, would think only of himself. After scrimping and scraping to give him a decent meal, he'd gaze at it as though she'd given him a plate of horse droppings. She knew just what he'd say. 'What's this muck?' and if he saw her bread and jam, 'Do yer 'ave ter eat that when I'm 'avin' me tea? You tryin' ter make me feel guilty or somethink?'

Her explanation of having had hers earlier would earn a sneer.

'Yeah, the one what cooks ends up with the biggest share – a little taste 'ere, a little taste there, and before yer know it, they've 'ad enough ter feed a regiment!'

No point arguing. It would lead to a row and Ben going off half-cocked could be a bit too nippy with his hands. She might be his mother but there'd been times when he'd landed her one. Sorry after, but a bucketful of sorries didn't get rid of a smarting cheek.

Emma was so different, caring, hardworking. The money she was now handing over from selling would help pay next week's rent. It was hard work keeping this roof over their heads, miserable as it was. What little was left would go on food, scrounged cheaply from market stalls.

These past years she'd learned to become very alert to what could be got for next to nothing, she who'd once received Jack's pay packet before ever he'd opened it. A good man he'd been, never off into the pub to drink it all away like some did. Heavy-handed, true. She'd dodged a few of his swings during the odd quarrel or two. Sad, thinking back, unable to remember any cause for quarrelling, just married life. But he'd always been fair. Wouldn't stand no nonsense, but fair. They had lived moderately well until …

Now she was reduced to scrounging and it went against the grain. She'd learned to swallow her pride as she ducked under market stalls when they were closed down for the night for a few cabbage leaves, a couple of potatoes, a manky onion or a carrot that had fallen underneath or been thrown down. A marrow bone from the butchers or, like today, a couple of bits of scrag-end of mutton the butcher might have thrown to his dog. Last night she'd hung about watching him clear his counter, dropping the unsaleable bits in a bucket before bringing down his shutters.

'Do you want them?' she'd asked as she always did, as did all the women in her straits. It was up to her to keep an eagle eye out and get in first. Sometimes it was a fight.

He had grinned. He knew the rules, and sometimes even dropped a bit of good stuff in the bin. It was the same with the bakers, for a farthing or so, two or three-day-old bread was still eatable if not saleable to those well off enough to expect fresh bread each morning, or even others who would take yesterday's loaf for a penny while the truly poor waited and watched like hungry rats in a cellar – hungrier, for that clever vermin got its food free, always. The scurry for bits and pieces as shops closed was degrading. But she was thin and agile and sharp-eyed and could by now swallow her pride.

'Did Ben get work today?' Emma asked as she ate.

Emma had gone out this morning on two slices of bread and dripping. She had become used to only two meals a day, maybe a penny cup of dark brown tea in a workmen's café around midday.

'Ben? Work?' queried Maud. 'Came back around nine this morning. Said there weren't nothing to be 'ad at West India Docks, then slouched off ter meet some of them bone-idle mates he loafs around with.'

Her reference to Ben's mates was scathing, deeming every one of them as bone-idle as him. All right, so dock work had always been irregular, but Ben gave up too easily, lazy more like it, preferred hanging around the boxing booths, betting on the winner, or even going up against some prize-fighter himself. If he won, he'd treat everyone in sight; if he lost, he'd borrow off a chum.

He was big and well muscled like his dad, but there the resemblance ended. Jack, never a betting man, would lay his pay packet in her lap. But not Ben; yet with his father gone, he now saw himself as the man of the house. It was a pity he didn't think to take on the responsibilites

14

that should go with the title. Nineteen, he was, soon to be twenty, a man in years, yet not a drop of responsibility in his veins.

Emma pushed away her empty plate. Mum could make a banquet out of virtually nothing. Ben hadn't yet come home, and she was thankful. There had never been much love lost between them as far as she was concerned. He was all bluster and there'd been many a row. But it upset their mother.

He still wasn't home by the time she and Mum went to bed. 'I'll keep his supper hot for him,' Maud said, putting what was left in the stewpot on the trivet over the fire, refraining from raking the few coals with a little water on them to stop them burning through so that tomorrow they'd only need a bit of paper and splintered wood to light them again. 'Miserable night like this, he'll need something warm inside him,' she said. 'We can spare a few coals for once.'

Emma felt rancour stir. Why did Mum indulge him? He wasn't worth it. Unkindly, she felt it was him Mum favoured, allowing him to lounge about while she went selling Mum's flowers for her in all weathers. Tonight Mum was ready to keep the fire in and his supper hot, yet all day on her own she'd freeze rather than light it for her own benefit, to save fuel.

In bed beside her, Emma listened to Mum's soft, regular breathing and thought of her day, the man she had encountered on her way home. What if he'd become suddenly violent? He had been strange. Whether he'd hurt himself falling or not, she should have hurried away. But she hadn't exactly been scared then, only later. She wasn't usually jittery, she who stood up to the local louts, giving as good as she got, even Ben, big bully though he was. Like the other day when he had caught her a back-hander during some row they'd had, sending her flying, she had refused to be cowed, spitting at him and calling him all the names under the sun before she fled. There were times when she had defended Mum against him too.

No, she wasn't scared of anyone. But someone blundering into you in the fog could be startling and that livid scar had been a bit alarming.

Thinking back on it now, but for that scar he'd seemed a passable-looking man. In his early forties maybe, maybe less. What she'd seen of his eyes, even in the fog, she'd had the impression of them being a clear, sharp blue. She kept seeing those eyes and that straight nose.

While Mum began snoring gently beside her, she fell to wondering where he lived, what sort of conditions he lived in. Finally she gave up. She probably would never see him again, anyway.

Chapter Two

Still thinking of the girl who had blundered into him, Theodore Barrington collected himself with a tot of brandy in a pub called The Flying Swan, glad to rest his painful ankle before going on to where he lived nearby.

It wasn't much of a place, set in an alley which was as squalid as his room, each side lined by smoke-blackened walls, with doors that hadn't seen a lick of paint in years, and bare, dusty windows, many with cracked and broken panes. This is what he'd come down to. He wondered how much longer he could keep this up. Twelve months ago he had been living in luxury. Yet he'd deliberately chosen this life. No one else had made him do it. Now it was too late to go back.

Closing the door on the stink of poverty outside, he set the hurdy-gurdy down on a small table in the far corner, laying his bowler hat down beside it. His overcoat, once expensive, he hung on a peg along with the muffler, and limped the five steps to the empty fire grate, lit the single candle on the bare mantelshelf above it and picked up a battered, blackened kettle.

He had to feel his way down the pitch-dark passage leading to a scullery and a tap in the yard beyond. The one in the scullery had long ago been cut off, but there was a gas ring, covered in the greasy fluff of ages. The scullery was littered with the rubbish of a dozen or more tenants crammed in the other four rooms – screwed-up newspaper, mouldering paper bags, tins with their residue clinging to the sides and stinking to high heaven.

The tap in the yard dripped continuously, forming a permanent pond of stagnant water over which he cautiously stepped. Dripping was all it was capable of; turn it though he might, the kettle filled at a snail's pace. The gas ring was every bit as bad, a tiny flame that took ages to heat a drop of water.

Eventually the mug of tea was warming his hands. The room was stone-cold, the fog seeping in under the ill-fitting door. It was too late to light a fire from the small pile of splintered wood sitting beside it. He'd have tea, sweetened with a drop of condensed milk, and go to bed. The only way to keep warm.

He sat on its edge and gazed around the seven-foot-square room by the light of the single candle. One peeling wall was completely obscured by cardboard boxes full of magician's paraphernalia. He'd not looked in any of them these twelve months. Nor were they anyone's business but his own.

That girl had been far too curious. Precocious. How old was she? Sixteen? Seventeen? Around here, people aged quickly. Maybe she was only fifteen, who could tell? Yet she'd been quite beautiful. Confident too.

Putting down the empty mug, Barrington sighed and eased out of his shoes, shabby enough to make him

18

cringe: they too had been expensive. He reached forward, pinched out the candle and sank back down on to his bed.

In the dark, visions began moving through his mind. Bright lights, applauding audiences, performances before the mighty and privileged, on one occasion royalty when their new King Edward had been Prince of Wales. All gone, gone from the moment when he'd regained consciousness in a hospital bed, his face bandaged, his eyes and nose swollen. His assailant hadn't broken his nose but the scar across his face would remain as a reminder of a fine career ended so abruptly.

That girl he'd cannoned into had been so apologetic. She hadn't deserved the rough edge of his tongue – he'd been quite rude to her, but she hadn't turned a hair. Time was when people fled from his roaring temper if a thing didn't please. He'd been someone to reckon with then, commanding respect from the lowliest stagehand to the stage manager himself.

Shattered by the loss of his wife, her death entirely his fault, this need to do penance for what had happened had reduced him to this. Now even that had been shattered by a slip of a girl he couldn't get out of his mind.

He was angered yet intrigued by her fearlessness. Eleanor had been fearless, standing up to that unnerving anger of his that would floor others. In the dark, the girl reminded him so much of Eleanor.

Saturday had been another good day. Christmas near and the fog gone, she'd successfully plied the theatre queues outside the Hippodrome just off Leicester Square. Opened two years ago in 1900 its circus acts and aquatic

19

dramas pulled in rich and poor alike. She now had a pocket full of money.

'Yer do better than I ever could,' Mum said, the smoothing iron she was using poised above one of Ben's shirts as Emma spread the money out on the cloth.

'It's a pretty face what does it. So long as yer don't look miserable. No one looks at a pitiful face. Pinch yer cheeks 'ard now and again ter bring up the colour. That's what people want. They like ter buy from rosy cheeks.'

'Rosy bloody cheeks be buggered!' came a growl from the ancient sofa Ben slept on at night.

There was nowhere else for him to sleep, but it suited him, coming home well after the others had gone to bed. He made full use of it during the day as well, as he had been today while she and Mum had been working.

He rolled over to glare at the money Emma had brought in. 'That ain't gonna last us. A few bloody pennies!'

Emma was at him immediately. 'So what d'you bring in? I don't see no money of yours on the table.'

Ben came upright. 'You shut yer mouth!'

'And you shut yours!'

She caught Mum's look for her to hold her peace, but she was sick of Ben and his bullying ways. 'Yer can bellow as much as yer like when yer start bringing a proper wage into the 'ouse. Until then ...'

Ben up on his feet, his roar cut short her words. 'Who d'yer think yer talkin' to, you bloody cheeky little cow?'

'You, that's who!' she shot back at him.

Mum, still holding on to the fire-heated flat-iron, was between them, parrying the blow with her arm. 'Get in the bedroom, Em.'

There came a shriek of pain from Ben. 'Christ! Yer silly cow, yer burned me arm!'

Mum stepped back from the offended arm, now raised in anger at her, but Emma, stepping in, pushed him away.

'Fer Lord's sake, Ben! You ain't 'ardly touched.'

But he was already cowed, his mother still holding the iron aloft as if in defence. If he went for her now, the still hot iron would get the better of him. Instead, he pushed past the pair of them.

'I'm bloody off out,' he announced, grabbing his jacket and flat cap from the hook on the door. Yanking the door open with a force that threatened to have it off its hinges, he left it open as he made off down the stairs to the street. Emma looked at her mother. The woman looked suddenly exhausted.

'You sit down. I'll do the ironing.' As if with no will of her own, her mother sank down on one of two wooden chairs they possessed. Taking the iron from her, Emma replaced it on the trivet. 'You need a pick-me-up. I'll pop down to the pub first and get you a drop of stout. You like stout.'

Without waiting for a reply, she grabbed the one jug they possessed from the shelf by the fireplace. The white glaze was cracked, the handle stained, the lip chipped, but it held a comfortable pint. Many a household had such a jug, and many a relief it brought back from a pub for twopence. Making off in the wake of Ben, she closed the door behind her, quietly.

Saturday night, The Flying Swan on the corner of Mitre Street and Three Colt Street was crowded and thick with tobacco smoke, beer fumes and sweat. Elbowing her way to the counter, she put tuppence down for her jug to be filled before fighting her way out again.

Once outside she took great gulps of fresh air. It was then she heard the music, but such strange music, the tune only just discernible over a continuous, monotonous drone. Glancing towards it, she became aware of a sense of recognition. Wasn't the man playing that odd-looking instrument the same who had cannoned into her last night?

Emma realised with a tiny shock that he had seen her too. He stopped turning the small handle on the instrument. The little girls who had been dancing to his music paused while onlookers shot him a glance of irritation. Seconds later he'd resumed playing and the children their dancing.

Emma hesitated. She could hardly walk on by. There had to be some acknowledgment of him, if only out of politeness. She moved towards him through the few people watching the children. In the glow from the pub's swing doors and window he didn't seem so large or scary as last night.

She put on a smile as she approached. 'What are you doing here?'

The smile was not being returned, making it look as though she had sought him out on purpose.

Emma kept a tight grip on her sunny mien. 'I didn't expect ter see you. The Swan's our local. I've been getting me mum a jug of beer.'

He still hadn't smiled. Not that she'd have seen it for the muffler over the lower part of his face, but his eyes would have crinkled a little if he had. In the pub's glow the rest of the face was handsome, in a stern, commanding way.

22

A voice rasped from close by. 'Come on, mate, give us some more toons. We was enjoyin' that.'

Again he had stopped playing, and seeing she was spoiling his chance of making money, Emma said, 'I'd better be off. Glad I saw you again. How's the ankle?'

'Recovered,' he said curtly, resuming playing, almost like a hint for her to leave. Emma nodded.

'Hope to see you again then,' she said, retreating.

He did not reply.

While his nimble fingers sped over the keys controlling one of the strings to produce a merry tune at the demand of his audience, Theodore Barrington followed her with his eyes. He watched until the figure became swallowed up in the darkness, reappearing briefly under the light of a gas lamp. She had a graceful walk, and the sort of carriage that proclaimed her as being quite able to take care of herself in any circumstances.

For a moment his heart raced. He didn't know her name or where she lived, and there came an odd sadness that he'd probably not see her again. The onlookers were clapping in time to the prancing children, one or two of the adults joining in, trousered legs going, heavy boots stomping, a middle-aged woman waving her skirts, hat bobbing. This could bring in a few more coppers. On a Saturday night, beer brought careless generosity. It should have been gratifying, but all he could think of was the girl.

'Come on, guv'nor, give us anuvver one.'

Quickly he obliged. No need to think of the tunes he played. Think instead of the girl who had just left.

After a year of this instrument, there was little need to concentrate. Much as it had been when performing magic, sleight of hand and illusions so meticulously rehearsed over years of practice that they were to him second nature, leaving him to charm the audience with patter to set them laughing or shivering as he paced the stage. Smooth movements and deft misdirection took eyes away from playing cards plucked from thin air or doves from an empty box, billiard balls appearing between fingers, and so on.

His act had had a darker side, the reading of minds that thrilled and terrified. Eleanor, his wife, had also been his assistant. After her death he'd been unable to carry on. No one else could have matched her – until now.

Mind-reading? Trickery. He'd been a past master. That girl, he could have taught her everything he knew had he but known her in his heyday. His heyday? Theodore smiled grimly beneath the muffler that hid the scar from others. One minute the toast of the town, the next, hiding, shunning social life, a recluse.

It had been so sudden, that knife attack by a demented drunk. The man being consigned to a lunatic asylum had been of little consolation.

Three months previously, Eleanor had fled to her death from one of his dark rages, rages he now fought to curb. Theirs had never been a smooth marriage, constant argument stemming from his suspicion of her having eyes for others, and much later for just one other. He'd sacked that *one other* the same day that last row had had her fleeing from the dressing room and out along the alley, himself in hot pursuit. She'd run out into the main road, under the hooves of a team of dray-horses, the wheels of the heavily laden brewer's cart all but cutting her in two.

24

The sight had torn at him in sleep, plagued his wakening moments, robbing him of his concentration. It also awakened memories he'd thought erased, that once, long ago in his youth, he'd been instrumental in another death, that of a college chum.

By the third month he knew he was slipping, his temper even shorter and fiercer. Theatre managers were soon shaking their heads.

The day he'd failed to cope with a restless audience of common fools, having in desperation taken a booking at a second-rate, East End theatre so as to keep up an extravagant lifestyle, he'd fumbled an easy trick, and had then made the error of rising to the jeers of a drunken group in the audience, ordering them to leave. Worse, he'd unwisely included the rest of the audience, saying that he was above performing before fools. It had been unforgivable. He'd been booed off the stage.

Having stormed at the theatre manager, who had rightly upbraided him, he strode out of the stage door into the alley. Seconds later a figure had materialised from the shadows to confront him, demanding to know just who he thought he was calling him a fool in front of everyone? A blow full in the face had knocked him to the ground. A knife had whipped across his chin, perhaps intended for his throat. The scar from that knife had ended his career. His self-assurance fled. It had never returned.

Discovering the hurdy-gurdy had given him a lifeline. He could never have seen himself labouring, for all this need to do penance. Even so, it was punishment in itself to feel his shame that for days on end he would huddle in his room until hunger drove him out, the lower part of his face hidden from others.

Even in summer he had kept the muffler on. He was becoming known by it, decrying the expensive clothes that although by now well worn brought curious glances from those who had never known any but the cheapest of garments. He was sure people often speculated about him. Had that pretty young girl also wondered about him? In an odd way he found himself hoping that she had as he continued playing; that he would linger in her mind for a while longer.

Chapter Three

What Emma was really thinking about come the next morning was Ben and how angry with him she was. Not so much for coming home so late, gone twelve-thirty in fact, or even waking the neighbours who lived above them – a voice calling down for him to shut up and let them sleep, accompanied by a few ripe expletives, and Ben bellowing back with even choicer ones – but the way he'd spoken to Mum when she'd got up to see if he wanted some stew, telling her to bugger off back to bed.

Emma hadn't interfered. It would have caused a worse scene that time in the night, with Ben drunk, of course. Instead, she saved it up for this morning to give him a piece of her mind, any thoughts she might have had of the man who played the hurdy-gurdy swept clean away.

Ben glared up at his sister from the couch from where she had awoken him. It was Sunday, his head felt as fat as a full-sized boxing glove and all he asked was to lie in. But what chance was there with her and their mother bustling around? No escape for a man in this one room with two women who insisted on rising early, even on a Sunday.

'I come in when I like!' he growled dangerously as Emma stood over him. He saw her lips compress, a fifteen-year-old acting like she was fifty!

'I ain't talking about the time yer came in,' she retorted. 'What I'm talking about is the way yer spoke ter Mum, and after she'd kept yer supper warm for yer an' all. Yer ungrateful, that's what you are. Yer treat me and 'er like dirt! I don't care about me but yer can't talk to Mum like that.'

He was up on his feet, his head banging with the effort. He groaned.

'I didn't want no supper.' He saw her sneer, hands on hips, tall for her years.

'No, I suppose you'd 'ad all yer wanted somewhere else.'

The broad hint that he'd been well attended to elsewhere, alluding to his masculine needs, brought a roar from him, the effort again making his head thump. He was in no state to retaliate. His mother was looking edgy as well and he didn't think he could take on the two of them just now. Instead, he shoved past Emma, grabbed a faded towel from the hook beside the unlit fireplace and stumbled out. In the back yard he would put his head under the outside tap and wash away his thick head.

Last night had been good; money in his pocket after betting on a fight in one of the boxing booths around Stepney and Limehouse, the girl on his arm gazing adoringly up at him, and him saying he could have knocked the champ down with a single blow. 'And don't think I couldn't,' he'd boasted.

The champ flexing his huge pectorals and biceps had looked a bit too professional for his liking, but he'd have loved to have Clara see what he could do. There would be other times. He rather fancied Clara.

'I'm pretty good, y'know,' he told her. 'Feel them muscles.' And she had gently explored the offered arm, giving out an awed 'ooh!' as her finger felt the movement under his jacket sleeve. 'I bet you're good.'

He *was* good. Big, strong, well built, boxing was one thing he really excelled at. He wished Dad were alive to see it. There still lurked a sense of failure, remembering him, as a youth resenting his ability to stand up for himself, Dad's confidence that brooked no interference in looking out for his family, not even from Ben. Dad had taught him to box yet had regarded his efforts with exasperation, and he'd hated the sense of inferiority it gave.

He missed his father, of course. On his death he'd tried to take over, but Mum, having idealised her husband's forcefulness, saw his own efforts as mere bullying. Didn't she realise they were lucky to still have a man around the house, two women alone in the world? He could have gone and left them to it, but instead she accused him of being idle, bringing in hardly any money, though he did, sometimes, and having no control over his temper, always looking for a fight. Of course he had fights. It went with living in the East End. He'd fight anyone who crossed him, no matter how big the bloke, and that took courage, an echo of his father's bull-headedness, who'd fought many a bloke in the docks. If ever he made the big time boxing, he'd show them, show everyone he was as good as Dad any day. He'd bring in more money than Dad ever dreamed of.

It certainly beat dock work, humping bloody great sacks of sugar, shoulders sore, sugar grains sticking through the sacking to rasp the skin, or shovelling coal that filled lungs with black dust, or shouldering cow hides that could give a bloke anthrax and often did, and all for lousy wages.

He had promised to put himself forward for a bout on Wednesday and Clara had cooed, 'Ooh, lovely!' and could she come and watch him.

She obviously saw him as her hero and he was determined to prove himself in front of her. He'd been going out with her for just over a week and when she learned he was a boxer, her adoration had known no bounds, and already she'd let him have a feel of her tidy-sized breasts.

She'd popped a toffee into her mouth and sat contentedly chewing while he stood up with legs splayed and fists punching the air as though it were he in the ring, bawling encouragement to the champ amid the roars of those around him as the loser staggered and bled.

'Go on, mate! Knock 'im down! Slaughter 'im! Finish 'im!'

The loser carted off between two chums, the champion circling in a slow walk of triumph to encompass the sea of faces below him, gloved fists clasped above his head in casual, self-opinionated triumph, it had been a short but exciting bout and though Ben's florin bet had reaped only five shillings, it was enough for a beer for himself and something stronger to impress Clara.

'I'll go and collect me winnings,' he told her, his interest in the next bout waning. He had something far more pleasurable in mind, if his luck held. 'I'm goin' ter treat yer, OK?' he said.

His arm was squeezed in appreciation. 'Will yer buy me a gin, Ben, instead of a beer?'

'I'll buy yer two gins. Doubles if yer like.'

He had felt generous and had thought he might even put a few pence Mum's way. That was until this morning with Emma having a go at him and Mum looking as if she was ready to take her side. Well, sod 'em! Mum could go for a run before he offered any of his hard-won money. It would be better used on Clara, who'd been very generous after her two double gins, showing her thanks by letting him have a little kiss an' a cuddle as he put it, but it became more than that, of course.

Her hand wandering to rest against his leg had told him just how much more it could become. After her couple of doubles and not quite in possession of herself any more, he'd quite enjoyed that little kiss and cuddle he'd given her up against an alley wall.

'There yer go.' Ben threw eight silver half-crowns down on the table before his astonished mother on Thursday morning.

'There y'are – two quid! An' don't say I don't bring no money 'ome.'

'Where d'yer get all this?' queried his mother. 'You ain't workin'. I know that fer a fact. Yer've spent the last two days loafing around indoors.'

'Getting in trim,' he said proudly. 'I won it, boxing. Won the purse.'

She shrugged. 'What about you? You left yerself short?'

Ben guffawed. 'Me, I've got twice that in me pocket. 'Ad a win on a card game too.'

After taking the purse last night for winning that bout he'd boasted on Saturday of taking on, he felt good. The so-called champ last night had been no match for him, big though the man was. Called himself a champ? Where had the manager got him from? The man had been totally out of condition. He'd sized that up even as he'd climbed into the ring. But it had still taken ten rounds to put the bloke down for the count, and though he'd come away with a face like a lump of beef pudding, he'd kept his feet. The loud, coarse approval of the crowd had been like music from heaven as he collected his prize-winnings.

Clara had been all over him, kissing his cuts and bruises, her arms around his neck as they celebrated. He was king. And like a king, he'd taken command of her, twice.

Emma surveyed the scattered coins with derision. 'If I know you, yer stole it more likely. Yer just telling us a tale.'

Ben glared at her. 'Oo you callin' a thief.'

'Well, yer didn't come by it honestly.'

'I bleed'n won it fair an' square, so don't you go calling me a tea leaf.'

'Em, let it drop!' cried her mother. 'It don't matter where it came from. It's a Gawdsend. This week 'as been so poor, snowing on an' off, you ain't been able ter stay out long enough ter do much sellin'.'

That was true. She'd been forced to come home early day after day, chilled to the bone, her thin jacket and skirt white with snow or soaked from driving sleet. How had the hurdy-gurdy man coped?

She hadn't seen him since the day he'd snubbed her, yet she found herself wondering about him. He probably hadn't fared much better than she. Despite Christmas being only two weeks away, in this sort of weather people stayed indoors or rushed out and back again, certainly not stopping to buy paper flowers or drop a coin into a street musician's tin. On Monday evening she did brave the elements to see if he was outside the Swan, which was in the next street, telling Mum she was seeing her friend Lizzy, who lived just a couple of streets away.

'In this weather?' Mum had queried, her tone suggesting she thought that if Emma could face being out after dark in such weather just to see a friend, she could face going out selling during the day.

It had been a wasted trip – he hadn't been there, nor on Tuesday or yesterday. He might be there tonight; the snow had turned to rain and more people were about, trying to make up for the several wasted days. She didn't know why she wanted to find him but told herself it was just curiosity. It would only take a few minutes' detour on her way home, or after tea.

Minutes after Ben's money falling on the table, Mum had grabbed her hat and coat and made off to the shops to buy legitimately. Ten minutes she was back with tripe and onion, carrots and hot green peas in a teacup. In no time at all, the three were sitting around the table like a proper family, Emma even feeling better towards Ben. With everything so comfortable afterwards, just her and Mum, with him sloping out for the evening, she thought better of leaving all this warmth to brave the evening on some wild-goose chase.

Thursday was a fine day if still chilly. Her wares sold, she made her way to the Swan before going home, but again no sign. Perhaps he was only there on Saturdays, working elsewhere during the week. But Saturday brought more disappointment, and a determination to stop being silly. After all, the man had been twice her age, if not more. Why bother with him?

There was snow again on Monday and Emma hurried straight home to huddle appreciatively by the fire. Ben had got himself a few days' casual dock work, his first day of back-breaking unloading leaving him stretched out after tea. Monday evenings had little to offer for entertainment and he was again broke.

Lying flat on his shabby old sofa like some ancient Roman emperor, he waved a finger towards the white jug on the shelf. 'Pop out, Em, an' get that jug filled for us.'

Emma glowered at him from the chair where she sat warming her feet by the fire. 'Get it yerself, yer lazy bugger!'

For an answer he leaped up, agile enough now, and grabbed the thing down, shoving it in her face. 'Mind yer bleed'n mouth. I've bin working me guts out all day while you stand around in the street doin' bugger all.'

'And where's the money coming from?' she demanded.

He paused. 'Mum, give us tuppence. I'm skint.'

'What 'appened to all the money yer won last week?' Mum asked.

He glared. 'None of your business.'

'Gambled and drunk it all away,' she concluded in low tones.

'My business what I do,' he retorted, his blue eyes, so much like his father's, threatening trouble. Mum said no more, but Emma did.

'I ain't getting yer any beer with Mum's money. Go an' buy it yerself.'

The blow, though not hard, took her by surprise. With a cry more of anger than pain, she leaped up and grabbed the jug from him, raising it high above her head. It was Mum who stopped her bringing it down on his skull, snatching it from her. 'Look, I'll pop down there for it.'

'No, you won't.' Emma swung viciously back to her brother, hazel eyes wide and blazing, her voice low and deliberate. 'Hit me again, Ben, and I'll scratch yer eyes out if that's the last thing I ever do.'

'You what?' But he did look somewhat shaken. Turning her back on him, Emma went over to winkle tuppence from the tiny pile of takings she'd put on the shelf for Mum to keep them in food for another few days.

'That's Mum's money,' she stated as she made for the door. He didn't know that what was left from his earlier generosity had been secreted away to buy a bit of pork for Christmas Day. He'd soon have made short work of it. Already he'd been eyeing what she had on the shelf.

'Keep yer thieving 'ands off it,' she warned, and before he could go after her, she was off.

She still felt the slap and she was angry. 'It's me what protects yer both,' he'd said after Dad died. If this was his idea of protection, she was a monkey's uncle. Emma put him out of mind as she went towards The Flying Swan. Would the man with the hurdy-gurdy be there? But what bothered her more was why she should be interested at all.

Barrington groaned and turned painfully on his narrow bed from which he hadn't risen for three days. God knows how he'd come by this flu.

Huddled under a single blanket over which he'd spread his top coat for extra warmth, he lay staring at the hurdy-gurdy on the small, thin-legged table, his only chair pushed well underneath for more room.

He'd have to force himself out soon if only to buy food. Despite feeling so ill, he'd had to crawl out of bed on several occasions to get water, had managed to make a drink of tea for himself, but the tea was running out and the condensed milk was no more than a few spoonfuls at the bottom of the tin and developing a sugary crust.

At least he wasn't eating. He'd lost all appetite, shuddering under the covers, trying to sleep off aching limbs and pounding head. With no handy coins to feed the gas meter and one candle left, he lay with only the distant street lamp to see by.

The wood for a fire was running out too, and if he were not to end up dead from cold or starvation, he'd have to shift himself soon. He thought the flu pains were not quite so bad as they had been yesterday and perhaps if he wrapped up well and went out, he might feel better. Once on his feet ...

Forcing himself up, still dressed in his top clothes for extra warmth, he took his coat off the bed and put it on. Something made him pick the instrument up from the table. The touch of it against his hands seemed to bring back a little strength. Tentatively trying the handle that turned the carborundum wheel against the strings, he gently pressed the keys, played a bar or two. Yes, he could do it, he'd go out.

There came an instant thumping on the floor above his head, a faint but furious voice demanding, 'Shut up that bloody row!'

He ceased instantly; with a rueful smile replaced the instrument. Taking a sip of water from a chipped mug, he reached for his bowler and his muffler. He had no incentive to shave, he who had once been so meticulous about his appearance. The muffler would hide the stubble as well as the scar. He grimaced as he thought of the scar.

The wind caught him a mighty swipe as he stepped out into the street, making him gasp. But it had its compensation in that it would help to clear his muzzy head. He'd take up that pitch outside the Swan. It wasn't too far, just a few hundred yards from here. He'd stay there just long enough to feel better with himself.

The Swan was all bright and welcoming after her short but cold traipse. As she neared, Emma caught the familiar thrum of the hurdy-gurdy and felt her heart race. Strange, why it should. Taking control of the feelings the sound prompted, she turned into the noisy pub without looking in the direction of the music. She was getting Ben his beer. That was all. Yet there were things she'd have liked to know about the hurdy-gurdy man: why he struck her as being different from the usual run of street musicians, why he behaved as though used to being obeyed. People in his station were never commanding, bullying maybe, shouting and hollering, but this quiet authority wasn't what she was used to. She yearned to find out more, but this wasn't what she was here for, she told herself as she carried on into the pub without looking his way.

Neither the public nor the private bar was crowded, and outside only two or three people had paused to hear what the street musician was playing, but mostly heads were bent against the stiff wind, eager only to seek the warmth inside. No children danced this evening, though three or four ill-clad urchins stood huddled against the pub porch out of the wind, grateful for any warm air issuing from the opening and closing of the swing doors as customers went in or out. Should an urchin be fool-hardy enough to seek the warmth of the pub's brightly lit entrance, he'd be sworn at and cuffed aside.

Her jug full, Emma could no longer resist crossing the few feet of uneven pavement to where the player stood in the kerb. He looked chilled to the bone. His muffler was wound about his ears to come well up over his nose, so that only his eyes were visible beneath the worn bowler. It was the eyes that arrested her attention and took the smile from her lips, replacing it with a look of concern.

She too had her ears covered against the raking cold, but even that knitted shawl couldn't quite combat the December weather. The man was shivering. He looked ill. Emma was instantly full of concern.

'You shouldn't be out in this weather,' she blurted.

'Go away, child. Mind your own business,' came the deep growl, the voice cultured despite its irascibility and being smothered by the muffler.

She ignored the reprimand. 'You ought ter go 'ome. Yer look ill.'

She glanced down at the cloth bag at his feet. In it were two pennies, a couple of ha'pennies and a button. How long had he been here in order to reap threepence and a contemptuously thrown coat button? For some time, by the looks of him. The tips of his fingers protruding from a cut-down pair of once fine leather gloves to leave them free to manipulate the hurdy-gurdy's keys were blue. He was shivering and his eyes were inflamed and puffy.

He had ceased playing though no one now was even bothering to listen. He seemed near to collapse.

'Please go home,' she begged, but his only response was to order her to leave him alone, that he could look after himself well enough.

'No yer can't,' she said as she saw him stagger slightly. Perhaps she was sticking her nose in but it was all too obvious that he needed help despite what he'd said. 'I think you should go home. I'll help you.'

Almost aggressively the arm she offered was shrugged off. 'I need no one's help. I have never needed ...'

His voice died away and for a moment he gazed at her, then slowly inclined his head. It was all she needed.

'Come on!' she ordered, picking up the bag with its pitiful contents and stuffing it into his coat pocket.

While he clung to his hurdy-gurdy and she to the pole and her full jug of beer, she held his arm as best she could. No one appeared even to have noticed them leaving, everyone too cold to care, they too looking for warmth somewhere, either at home or in the pub. The urchins huddled by its door shivered on – no one to see *them* home, if indeed they had a home.

Emma asked where he lived, in sudden dismay that it could be miles away. She was relieved to find it was only a step. Of course, he couldn't have come any distance in this weather. Even so, he moved so slowly, so painfully that it took a while, the wind whistling through the arch under the railway, before they reached one of several creosoted doors in an alley, one that connected Three Colts Street to her own street. In fact, her friend Lizzie lived just round the corner in Grenade Street. Quite fortunate, came the thought. Perhaps she could look in on him tomorrow on her way to Lizzy's and see how he was. The way he looked he'd not be going far.

What Emma hadn't realised was that someone leaving the pub had seen her leading the musician away. He stood for a moment, then dashed back into the pub where he'd left his mate, Ben Beech, to say what he had seen.

'Thought I ought ter tell yer,' he gabbled excitedly. 'Clinging to 'is arm, she was, like they was lovers. Street musician, he was, twice 'er age.'

Ben glared. 'What makes yer think it was 'er?' Moments after Emma left for the pub, Ben had gone too, preferring to drink with mates. Seeing her waiting for her jug to be filled, he'd crept by to sit in a corner until she'd gone, then went over to some faces he knew at the bar. He'd been surprised to see Reg, who had just departed, come rushing back, full of what he'd apparently witnessed.

'I'd know yer sister's flaming 'air anywhere, even with an 'at and scarf on.'

Em had lots of lads lusting after her looks and the way she had of carrying herself. Lots would have liked to know her better, but always fussy, she never let them get far. But Reg had said this bloke looked twice her age, and a street player at that. 'You *sure* it was 'er?' he pushed.

The smaller man nodded. 'Sure as I'm standing 'ere. I just thought you ought ter know.'

Yes, of course. He was the only one in the family left to protect her. His face twisted suddenly. He glowered at his informant. 'If yer right, I'll 'ave 'is guts fer garters. If yer wrong, I'll 'ave yours!'

Reg paled. 'I'm tellin' yer the truth. I saw 'em, wiv me own eyes.'

Ben's half-empty tankard was slammed down on the wet counter, and with heavy shoulders hunched and big fists clenched, Ben made for the door, thrusting aside groups of drinkers as he went. Even so, by the time he got outside there was no sign of her or the man Reg had been so sure he'd seen her with.

Chapter Four

Reaching his door, Barrington shakily turned his key in the lock before glancing at Emma. 'Thank you for your help, my dear. I can manage now.'

She would have let it go at that except that she could feel his arm shaking beneath her hand. The fact that he'd gone out on such a night in his state convinced her that he probably had little or nothing to eat or any warmth. Neglected, he could so easily go down with pneumonia.

'I really ought to 'elp yer indoors,' she offered. 'Make yer a cup of tea or something. To warm you up.' He looked to be on the point of collapse and before he could make any objection she had guided him inside, away from the bitter cold.

'Where d'yer keep yer matches?' she enquired, needing to light the gas mantle on the wall. She was told there was no gas but there was a candle. In the feeble light as the wick spluttered then strengthened, she bit her lip at seeing the state of the place.

This room was what he called home? Where she lived was poor, with its flaking and smoke-darkened ceiling and plaster, but Mum had made it into a home, with a welcoming if small fire; sweeping, scrubbing the floors, fighting the bugs that crept from behind peeling and discoloured wallpaper. With no money for luxuries like new wallpaper and paint, she at least tried to cheer it up with pictures cut from old magazines she found. But this place was sheer squalor, no fight put up against a landlord's neglect, no care to improve on what it was. How could anyone live in such a place?

Emma glanced at the cardboard boxes stacked up against one wall, leaving hardly space for the narrow bed, a chair and small table on which stood a tin kettle, a mug and an open tin of condensed milk. She looked back at the boxes. What on earth did he want all those for?

She lifted the kettle and heard the water slop inside it. ''Ave yer got any tea?' she queried. 'They do say tea's a medicine, yer know.'

'There is nothing I need.' The cultured voice, vying strangely with its surroundings, was terse. 'Thank you for your help. Now you must go.'

Despite the weary tone, it was a command. Command or not, he was in no state to be left. Emma stood her ground.

'Let me light a fire for yer before I go. It's freezing in 'ere. Yer too ill ter be ...'

'I said leave me alone. Please.' The sudden strength in his voice startled her. But he could die if left to his own devices.

'I'm lighting a fire,' she said firmly, 'and making you a cup of tea before I go, if I can find it.'

'There is none left. There is nothing.'

His earlier commanding tone had deserted him, and for a moment she stared at him. This was the sound of a man defeated, who'd lost heart and was about to give up. Illness did that to a person already at rock bottom, hope of any future allowed to die. Perhaps he too preferred to die, have whatever had brought him to this depart with him.

It seemed to her such a terrible end, all alone on a wretched bed in a freezing room surrounded by all these cardboard boxes. What were they for? He could have used them to keep himself warm at least. But a man without a woman to care for him, be she mother, sister or wife, was a lost soul. A woman with the natural instinct for self-preservation made the home, caring for her man, seeing his children fed. Likewise a woman should have a man to fend for her. Even if he beat her or drank away his wages, it was better than being at the mercy of an unkind world. Emma felt a cynical smile touch her lips. She and her mother might as well be alone against that world for all the help and protection they got from Ben.

Pushing the thought aside, she glanced again at the boxes, each held together with string. 'Yer could make a nice warm fire with them.'

He shot to his feet. 'Leave them alone! Go home! I can ... can see to myself ...'

The effort must have drained him and he sank back on to the edge of the bed, his back to the tiny, dusty, bare window with its surrounding wall of broken plaster. All he could manage was, 'They are all I have.'

Emma remained glaring at him. 'What's in them?' She wanted to add, 'that's so precious,' but thought better of it.

'My work,' came the reply. 'My lifeline. Were I to sell what they contain, I might as well expire.'

'Yer might well expire if yer don't get something warm inside yer,' she warned. Already she had reached out and was ripping the top off one of the smaller boxes while her patient sank back, too weak to resist.

It ripped easily, being damp from the air of the room. Would it burn? There were some sticks of wood beside the grate. Quickly she laid the bits of cardboard in the rusty grate, laying the sticks crisscross on top. Not much of a fire, but certainly better than nothing.

There was probably a kitchen at the back of this house, and a tap where she could fill his kettle. What about tea? He said he had none. There came another thought. The beer she'd bought. She had put the jug down on the table. Beer was food as well as drink.

The contents of the small box, exposed when she'd torn off the top, now halted her as she reached for the jug. Inside the box were several packs of brand new cards. Questions immediately began to race through her head. A gambler. Had he gambled all his money away, reducing him, an obviously cultured man, to penury?

There were also a lot of coloured handkerchiefs. They looked like silk. A red one was wrapped around a metal box. But she was here to help, not pry. Emma poured some of the beer into a mug she found on the table. Ben would be furious finding a half-empty jug. She wouldn't think about Ben just now. But she would have to leave soon or he'd be doubly furious.

As she handed the mug to her charge, her elbow caught the edge of the box, knocking it to the floor. The metal one tumbled out, the lid popping open, strewing silver coins across the floorboards.

Emma stared at them in disbelief. What was there was enough to feed a whole regiment for weeks, or someone like her for months. All sympathy vanished. Here she'd been sacrificing Ben's beer as well as delaying getting home, and what for?

She frowned at him. 'What's these?'

He had slipped his muffler down to drink. The scar no longer alarmed her, but the wealth of stubble on his cheeks and his moustache uncut and ragged only increased her newly found contempt.

'Well?' she repeated when he did not reply. 'There's me 'elping you 'ome, thinking you was starving, and 'ere is all this money. Who are you?'

His broad mouth beneath the moustache was working as though with indecision as he gazed down at the spilled coins.

'I suppose I should be honest with you,' he said at last.

'So I should think,' she blazed. 'There's me putting meself out for yer, and probably getting meself inter trouble with me brother fer giving you 'is beer. He's going ter be in a proper rage when he finds 'is jug only 'alf full.'

'I'm sorry. I'll pay for the beer,' he said.

'And so you ought,' she snapped, still unforgiving, still stunned by the sight of all those gleaming coins, more than she'd ever earned in her life. Several half-crowns, quite a few florins, a good sprinkling of shilling pieces and even some five-shilling pieces, there had to be at least five or six pounds lying on that floor. It was only right he should pay for the beer. With it she could refill the jug. Ben would be none the wiser.

'I think you must 'ave a nerve, living in these conditions when you ain't even poor. And leading me on ter thinking you was.'

That he was far older than her, and as such should be respected by someone her age, didn't occur to her in the frame of mind she was in. As far as she was concerned, he didn't deserve her respect. People she knew had to skimp and scrape, clinging to their bit of pride usually by a thread, and here he was, rolling in money, with the cheek to go out begging.

All this she blurted out as with an effort he bent to pick up the fallen coins, slowly and painfully returning them to the tin to put it back into the cardboard box, which he placed beside him on the bed. Emma felt that she could have been talking to herself for all the attention he was paying her and it made her feel even angrier.

'You ain't even listening ter me,' she raged. He looked up at her.

'You think me nothing less than a fraud. I have my reasons. Ones you could never comprehend, my dear. You are young, so young. You think you have seen much of life, but you haven't. Not yet. What is your name, child?'

He seemed to have been unruffled by her outburst, and in fact, it was an effort for him to talk, his breathing so harsh. But the question took her by surprise. After all she'd said to him, he hadn't even turned a hair.

'Why should you care?' she challenged.

'You have been very kind. I merely feel that I would like to know.'

His continuing mildness mollified her a little. 'Emma Beech,' she said in a tone intended to convey that she still hadn't forgiven him.

'Emma,' he repeated slowly. He was wheezing less, the beer probably helping a little. 'Is that a shortened version of your full name?' As she stared in confusion, he elucidated. 'Is it short for Amelia?'

She understood. 'No, Emily.'

'Amelia is prettier. Amelia Beech. It has a nice ring to it.'

She didn't care what sort of ring it had or what he thought pretty. Her name was none of his blessed business anyway.

'What's your name, then?' If her demand was audacious, she wasn't repentant, but it prompted the hint of a smile that for a moment made him appear younger than she suspected him to be.

'My name is Theodore Barrington. The Great Theodore. Perhaps you have heard of me.' When she shook her head, his smile became wry.

'I *was* famous, you know. I am … was, a magician. I have appeared before royalty.' The smile deserted him and his voice became deep and sad. 'But no more. That was nearly a year ago. Ah, how one's life can so quickly change!'

'But you've got money,' she reminded him. 'So why live like this?'

She swept out an arm to encompass the degradation around him, but his gaze was vacant, as though he were somewhere else.

'When my wife was killed,' he murmured, 'the fine reputation I had so carefully acquired over the years went with her.'

'What happened to your wife?' asked Emma as he lapsed into silence. 'You said she got killed?'

'Beneath the wheels of a brewer's dray.'

He ignored the horror Emma registered at the vision, continuing as though rambling in feverishness, recalling aloud the events of some terrible night after appearing before an elite audience, seeing his wife exchange glances with an assistant of his and instantly accusing her of being too free with the young man. The ensuing argument, one of many, had her running out in a temper, into the path of the heavily laden brewer's dray.

Emma listened in awe as he spoke of trying to put it from his mind by drinking, by spending recklessly and falling into financial debt, how it had affected his skill as a magician, with bookings no longer forthcoming, even his name spoken with disdain.

Her sympathy began slowly to return. She had little idea what it must be like to be wealthy, to move in upper-class circles, have beautiful clothes and eat mounds of fine foods. She saw the wealthy passing her by every day she stood selling her flowers and had often wondered about their lives, what their homes were like, what they did other than going to theatres and parties, what they thought about.

This man who'd moved in such circles must now be poorer than the meanest beggar in having known better things. She felt suddenly and strangely superior to him. It would be nice to have money – lots of money, but to have fame and then lose it must be awful.

'I last performed at the Empress in Brixton, my lowest ebb,' he was saying, almost musing. 'I who appeared in the finest of London's theatres, the Alhambra, the Empire, the Tivoli, the Palace Theatre, so many, and many of the best in other cities. I was known and toasted by everyone.'

His voice had grown throaty. 'I dismissed my assistant and continued working alone but my act was therefore limited. I was drinking. On stage I told myself I had to have been mistaken about he and my wife together. One can think of other things when performing – illusions so well rehearsed over years of practice that the hands alone can go through the procedure, leaving the brain to concentrate on showmanship and patter, while one is free to exercise power over the audience. But with me, I couldn't get the pair of them out of my mind, and couldn't concentrate. In a way I regret dismissing him as I did, since I have often wondered if my suspicions might have been unfounded.'

Emma watched him take another sip of beer. It seemed to strengthen his voice, which began to develop a bitter edge.

'I was in such a state, however, that one day I fumbled quite a simple trick. They were a rough lot. I heard myself being hooted at by some drunken louts and I committed the unforgivable – I bellowed back at them, told them they were not worthy of my time, and left the stage.'

He drained the mug. 'In my dressing room I lit a cigar, had a brandy to quiet my nerves. One brandy became another, I who had upbraided those drunkards. When the stage manager entered to tell me he had cancelled my booking, I flew at him in a rage and left. Outside the stage door one of those I had insulted had been waiting for me, and attacked me with a knife.'

Ruefully, he fingered the scar. 'I never returned to the stage.

He fell silent and Emma for the first time ever found nothing to say. She knew about violence. It could be found in every corner of the East End. She and her friend Lizzie had several times backed away on coming upon a street fight, and knives were as common apparel to a lout as his own cap, and most carried a scar or two. Dark alleys, and there were plenty of them, were places from which a thief with a ready cosh could leap out on an innocent passer-by. A girl in this area needed eyes at the back of her head. Being raped was horrible enough, and usually kept to herself out of shame, but being found to be carrying a baby out of wedlock, rape or no, could be an even worse disgrace.

She had a feeling that this man was really using his scarred face as an excuse to shun the life he'd known, the death of his wife having set him on a downward course long before the knife attack.

Needing to change the subject, Emma found her voice again, giving it a bright edge.

'Are they all your tricks and things in them boxes?'

He looked at her like a man coming out of a dream. His lips even curled into a smile, but again a bitter one. 'Tricks and things,' he repeated. 'That's all they are. Nothing magical, nothing mystical, just cheap illusions.'

'I've been ter watch magicians and it looks real enough ter me.'

She became aware that he was studying her closely. 'Were you my assistant, you'd learn quickly enough that nothing about it is real.' The gaze became a scrutiny, appraising, making her squirm and blush. 'You would make an ideal assistant. You have beauty, grace, height, and already a good figure. And you are quite charming, even at your age.'

Now she really was squirming. 'I ain't nothink of the sort.'

'You are, my dear. You should be in the theatre. I could teach you so much. Had I but known you a year ago, it could all have been so different.'

He was being too familiar. 'I've got ter go,' she burst out. 'Me brother will be waiting for 'is beer. I'll be late 'ome, and with only half a jug left.'

Barrington reached into the cardboard box beside him, and taking out the tin, opened the lid to extract a two-shilling piece. Before she knew what he intended, he caught hold of her hand and pressed the coin into it.

'I can't take that,' she gasped. 'I only need a penny to fill it again.'

'For your kindness. You are a good girl.' He gave her arm a weary push. 'Go home now.'

Despite her protest, her hand had closed greedily over the florin. You didn't come across generosity like this very often. At the door, she paused.

'You sure yer'll be orright?' As he nodded, she tilted her head and gave him a speculative look. 'Yer know, if yer was to grow a proper beard, no one would ever see that scar and I believe yer'd look just like our new King Edward. Impressive. I bet yer'd get yer confidence back if yer did that, and yer could go back on ter …'

Her observations were cut short. 'I have asked you to go.' He seemed to be fast succumbing to his illness again. 'Please oblige me by doing so.'

Outside, with snow flurrying around her, Emma gazed down at the florin. What had possessed her to accept such an amount? She was assailed by conflicting thoughts. They could live well for days on this, but she should have made more protest. Even so, he wasn't poor, as she had thought. But if he wasn't poor, then why hadn't he bought medicine to make himself better? Was he so filled with remorse that he'd intended to leave himself to die?

Emma grew suddenly determined that he shouldn't die. Along by St Mary's Church in Commercial Road were a few shops, still open, even on a Monday. There was an oil shop that sold everything from oil, vinegar, boot polish, washing boards, pails, to onions and open sacks of split peas, lentils, dried fruit, tea, and whatever else a housewife needed.

From shelves stacked with bottles and tins, she bought a bottle of soothing linctus for his chest, another tin of condensed milk and a few ounces of tea – after what he'd given her, the least she could do.

Bending her head before another snow shower, Emma retraced her steps, stopping off at the Swan to top up her jug, briefly impeded by a couple of belligerent drunks being thrown bodily out by a burly landlord.

Mr Barrington opened the door to her knock, taking so long to answer that she wondered if he'd fallen asleep or even collapsed. She thrust the things at him. 'Ter 'elp yer get better,' she blurted, and before he could argue, turned and ran off, jug held out to prevent any of it spilling.

Her mother was waiting for her, but Ben wasn't. 'Said he was fed up waiting, and went off out. Said he'd get 'is own beer with 'is mates. That means if he's got any money at all, we won't be seeing any of it. Probably borrowing off them and he'll 'ave ter pay them back before I ever get a sniff of any from 'im. I do hate debt. It's a killer.'

'Yer don't 'ave ter worry,' Emma told her. 'Look what I found, lying in the road outside the Swan.'

On the way home she'd rehearsed her story. The florin now broken by buying medicine and tea, she held out a shilling, keeping back the rest for some rainy day. That way, saying she'd found it made it seem authentic.

It did her good to see Mum's faded hazel eyes light up. Yet she looked sorrowful.

'Some poor blighter could of done without losing that,' was her comment but Emma detected that it was said without too much sympathy. Someone else's loss was her gain, and a shilling was a fortune when come by unexpected. It meant a bit of extra meat, a loaf of bread, vegetables, a bit of coal for the fire. With what she'd hidden away out of Ben's sudden burst of generosity last week, it was going to be a grand Christmas.

Chapter Five

'I'm off ter see Lizzie,' Emma said after a supper of potato and carrot stew, washing up while Mum went back to her work. Ben had already gone out, not even bothering to say he was off.

It was Monday and Emma hadn't gone near that Mr Barrington for over a week, resisting the temptation to see how he was, while repeatedly telling herself that he wasn't her concern. But staying indoors got her brooding and restless and glad when Tuesday came for her to spend it with her friend.

Lizzie was a year older than herself. They usually met each other on Monday, Tuesday and Thursday evenings when they could, though this Thursday was Christmas Day, a day for family. Sometimes she went to Lizzie's, sometimes Lizzie came to her. If Ben happened to be in, they'd pop off down Commercial Road out of his way. It had coffee stalls and pubs and street entertainers; they'd meet other friends to chat with under the street lamps, giggling and swapping naughty stories and weighing up the lads.

She was comfortable with these sorts of people. Unlike the man she'd helped home who had, she felt, become just a little too familiar for her taste. Yet she couldn't get him out of her mind.

For a whole week she hadn't even been to the Swan for Ben's beer, daring his wrath with excuses, in case she bumped into the man. After all, it was up to the fellow to look after himself. Anyway, it wasn't proper, a girl her age visiting a man of his age.

'If you and Lizzie Wallis go out ternight,' Mum said, her head still bent over her silk work, 'don't get too free with the boys. I know what they're like. Yer don't want no trouble. Yer only fifteen, remember.'

'I'll be sixteen come the end of February,' Emma reminded her. 'I know what I'm doing.'

A girl grew up quickly in the East End, not like pampered daughters of the rich with their private tutors and girls' colleges, not knowing the facts of life but merely expected to become good little wives to wealthy husbands.

'Well, you just be careful if you and 'er goes out,' Mum was saying. 'Be 'ome by ten before the pubs get too rowdy, you 'ear me?'

Yes, she heard her. Pubs stayed open all day from early morning until the early hours of next morning, depending on the whim of the publican.

She let herself out with Mum's last snippet ringing in her ears. 'Keep away from drunks. Pretty young gels like you can draw too much attention from the wrong sort.'

Was Mr Barrington the wrong sort? He'd sipped that mug as genteel as a gentleman might a glass of wine, not swilling it like some vulgar ruffian. Yet he'd overstepped the mark in taking hold of her hand without her permission, and had looked at her in a way she'd rather he hadn't, saying she was a beauty, admiring her figure, then giving her money as though, now that she thought back on it, he saw her as one of those to whom men did pay money.

Mum obviously knew all about a girl drawing attention. Had she ever been innocently lured when young?

At forty-odd, there were still traces of her having been pretty, though hard work and want these last two years had put lines on her face that shouldn't have been there yet. She'd probably been a real heart-stopper at sixteen, and married at nineteen. Her hair was faded and dry now and dragged back into a convenient bun, but it still retained a touch or two of that vibrant auburn Emma herself had inherited from her.

She had Mum's hazel eyes too, though Mum's were faded. But it was probably their natural glint of fun that bothered Mum in case they could attract the opposite sex before Emma was ready to cope with them.

From the window Lizzie saw her coming and her lips tightened with mild envy at those swaying hips that even petticoat and skirt couldn't hide. She wasn't jealous of Emma, but she couldn't help wishing she were the one who caught the eye of all the boys. She merely stood in the background, ignored by all except for some pimply, skinny lout who couldn't find anyone else.

As Emma came in through the downstairs door that like all those in this row was too warped to lock, Lizzie turned and hurried to her own door.

'Em's 'ere,' she said over her shoulder to her mother, sitting by the small fire. Her mum did little around the place and it was a shambles, not like her friend's tidy little home. Her mum was always scrubbing and cleaning. But the bugs and mice and rats got in just the same. Her own mum never even tried to fight the constant fifth of these places. Who could blame her?

Emma Beech burst in through the door and reverting automatically to her old way of talking, chirped, ''Ello, Mrs Wallis. 'Elio, you lot,' to the five younger children playing on the floor around the fire. 'Evenin'', Mr Wallis,' who'd lumbered down from the bedroom where he'd been sleeping all day.

He was temporary night watchman for a gang of navvies, keeping an eye on abandoned machinery and tools. He was usually gone by dusk, but they were working late to get as much done before Christmas as possible.

He barely nodded as she entered. The children didn't even look up. Emma took up position in the middle of the shabby room with its bed in one corner where the children and Lizzie slept top to tail, but still in each other's way.

Without looking at her, Lizzie's mother muttered, 'You two gels can go inter our bedroom to 'ave yer little chats, if yer like.' But Lizzie looked at Emma, her tongue playing with her top lip in indecision.

'Did yer want ter go out instead?'

Emma shook her head. There was something she needed to ask Lizzie's advice on. The look in her eyes must have conveyed itself to Lizzie, who without another word led the way into the one bedroom.

Sitting on the bed Lizzie's dad had just vacated, still warm under Emma's bottom and acceptable on a cold night with no fire in here, they chatted about this and that. Lizzie still worked at the match factory and had a long moan about the grind and the conditions. Emma spoke of how cold it was standing at the kerbside selling to people who more often than not hurried by without a glance in her direction and how she trudged up and down theatre queues on Fridays and Saturdays, other days stamping her feet outside Liverpool Street Station or plying the queues at bus stops or hanging about the hackney carriage ranks. In a lighter vein they discussed lads they knew, giggling over some of their antics to get noticed, but all the time Emma's mind was on something far more important. She finally seized her chance as there came a lull in the talk.

'I met someone the other day,' she blurted.

Lizzie's interest rose. 'Some boy? Do I know 'im?'

'Not really a boy.' Emma took a deep breath. 'A man, I'd 'ave ter say.'

'You mean a proper man, like over twenty-five.'

This was difficult. 'Older than that.' Now she'd begun, she'd have to continue. Lizzie wouldn't let it rest until she heard the lot. 'It was a bloke what plays outside The Flying Swan sometimes. You might of seen 'im.'

'I've seen lots of 'em playing outside the Swan,' came the arch reply. 'An organ grinder, a bloke singing ditties. Lots, like they do everywhere.'

'What really 'appened,' Emma went on, 'was that I stumbled into 'im in that fog around the end of November. I knocked 'im over ...' She stopped as her friend let out a peel of laughter. 'No, really. I 'elped him up. Then I saw him the next day playing this hurdy-gurdy thing outside the pub.'

Lizzie stopped laughing to listen as Emma went on to say how offhanded he'd been on that second occasion, how, after disappearing, he had shown up terribly ill and how out of the goodness of her heart she'd assisted him to where he lived, and what had transpired after helping him into his room.

Lizzie's eyes were like saucers. 'You went in 'is room with 'im?'

'Well, what else could I do?' Emma said. 'I couldn't leave him there on 'is doorstep. He's only got one room ter live in and he was ever so ill.'

'Not so ill as ter 'old yer hand without asking.'

'It was only me hand,' Emma reminded. But she needed to get everything that was bothering her off her chest. 'That's not what's worrying me. It was what he said ter me, what's made me feel peculiar.'

'What did 'e say to yer?'

'Like he thought I was nice.'

She didn't want to go into detail and make Lizzie aware of her own plainness, the thin, pinched face, the pale blue eyes, the straight, mousy hair straggling in stringy strands down her back whereas her own curled in a thick auburn mass. 'Things what blokes shouldn't be saying to someone they've just met and who's bin good enough to 'elp them 'ome.'

'Oo,' said Lizzie, her tone full of uncertainty and warning, reading more into it than Emma intended.

'Nothink improper went on,' she hastened. 'But I didn't think I ought ter go back since ter see how he is.'

'I shouldn't think so,' Lizzie said emphatically.

'The trouble is, I can't stop thinking about 'im.'

'Blimey, yer ain't started fancying 'im, 'ave yer?'

'No, of course not!' Emma fiddled with the ragged edge of the washed-out blue coverlet. 'He's twice my age. Maybe more. I don't know. But he was very handsome in a sort of commanding way. Sure of himself. He was once a magician on the stage.' She proceeded to tell Lizzie what Barrington had told her of his life.

'He's bin married,' Lizzie reminded her at one stage, to which she returned huffily,

'Anyone his age is bound to have been married. I said his wife was dead.'

'That's what he told you,' Lizzie warned.

'I believe him.'

'Some men can get yer ter believe anything.'

Emma felt her back go up. She didn't know what she wanted from Lizzie. Certainly not advice to keep away from him or be told she was being a fool, nor even to be told to carry on seeing him. What she needed was to talk about it. Keeping this secret was tying her in knots. 'Me mum or Ben must never know. Ben would kill me. He thinks it's his job ter keep an eye on me, like as if he was me dad.'

What she didn't know was that Ben already had his eye on her, was watching her like a hawk.

More in defiance of what Lizzie had said than anything, the following evening on her way home Emma made a quick detour to see how Mr Barrington was. As the door closed, the furtive shadow at the far end of the alley materialised into the large figure of a man. Hugging the wall, he flitted towards his goal with an agility at odds with his well-muscled frame. At the door, he paused and surveyed it balefully as though expecting the wood itself to cringe before his gaze.

'Caught yer, my gel!' he hissed. 'Creeping inter a geezer's 'ouse. If it's the same bloke what Reg saw, he's got me ter reckon wiv now.'

He'd catch them red-handed and bust the geezer's boko for him. He'd been in the Swan and had caught a glimpse of her passing by, just the head and shoulders above the frosted glass of the lower half. He'd leaped up from the pint he'd been drinking, and without pausing to tell his mates what he was up to, had barged out in time to see her go out of sight under the dark railway arch. Following, he'd seen her go in through this door. How long, he wondered testily, before she came out again.

He'd intended to wait and confront her but now he wasn't so sure. The beer he'd been enjoying had been from his own bloody round and he was buggered if he was going miss out on the next bloke's call by hanging about here in the cold. There'd be plenty of other times to catch 'em at it.

'I'll bide me time,' he muttered to the door. 'Give 'em enough rope and the pair of 'em will 'ang themselves wiv it.'

Letting out an contemptuous hiss, he turned on his heel and trudged back the way he'd come, hands in his trouser pockets, his chin jutting out in his decision to bust that geezer's nose for him, later. At the moment the uppermost thing in his mind was the beer he'd left and the free one to come.

Having let her in, the young man went and stood by the table, looking to Barrington to do the introductions.

'Amelia, my dear,' obliged Barrington, though he didn't smile, in fact looked ill at ease and glowering. 'This is Martin Page, my one-time assistant before I gave up my profession as a magician. Martin, this is Amelia Beech, who so kindly helped me home when I was taken desperately ill. I consider her a most kind-hearted young girl.'

As Page nodded, Emma said, 'Me name's really Emily. Most people call me Emma, or Em.'

She heard Barrington cough, not from illness because he was looking much better, but a short and sharp one to bring Page back to whatever he had been talking about. Emma glanced from one to the other and now saw that neither seemed at ease. In fact there was hostility in the air, making her wish she hadn't come in here. She found herself ignored as Page turned abruptly to Barrington.

'Listen, Theo, you can't go on like this.' He spread his arms to encompass the miserable room. 'Not even a decent fire in the grate. There's nothing to eat. And where the hell do you wash? The place stinks. The whole district stinks! I can't believe you've let yourself sink this low. It's taken me nearly a year to find you. You simply slipped out of sight. I know it's been bad for you, but to disappear without a trace.'

'He's been ill,' Emma ventured.

Page glanced at her. 'So I noticed,' he said, using a gentler tone towards her. He turned back to Barrington.

'You were such a damned good teacher, Theo. I enjoyed being your assistant.'

'I can well imagine you did!' Barrington muttered slowly, the depth of sarcasm in the remark making Emma frown, but if Page noticed, he gave no sign.

'Since you vanished, I've been at a loose end. My father insists I work with him in his business as managing director, but I can't settle. The stage got into my blood because of you. And then you go and walk out on me.'

'P'raps I should go,' Emma ventured awkwardly, and again the young man turned his eyes to her.

They were wide set and dark velvety brown. His hair was dark and glossy with a slight wave to it. He wore a good quality, single-breasted ulster, open to reveal a casual, dark brown tweed lounge suit. On the table beside him lay a brown bowler hat. What she most noticed, with a small shock, was the way he was regarding her so that she turned away quickly to avoid blushing.

'I'd better go,' she said to Barrington. 'I only came ter see if you was all right.'

'Well, my dear, you see I am.'

It was terse, rude, and she felt her cheeks colour. She'd already avoided a blush at the young man's scrutiny, but this was from anger. How dare he brush her off like this? She'd done nothing to upset him apart from coming, and he hadn't seemed to mind. It was then that she noticed the tight-lipped way he was regarding Page. Perhaps he'd seen the look Page had given her and was feeling protective towards her. He needn't have worried. She could take care of herself well enough.

Page had turned back to him. 'So why didn't you let me know where you were? I know full well why you took off, but not to say you were going.'

'Why should it concern you?'

Barrington's tone was harsh. Both seemed to have forgotten her but she could hardly leave without observing the common formalities of leaving.

'I was hardly six months with you,' Page was saying.

'And in that time I taught you well,' Barrington sighed. 'You were the best assistant I'd ever had. You had talent beyond my expectations. I have to admit, it was because of you that my act became second to none.'

'Then why dismiss me? I know you were grieving, but why didn't you tell me where you were?'

'What I decided had nothing to do with you. I had my reasons. You were handsomely paid off at the time.'

'Who cares!' Page exploded. 'When I heard what happened, I visited you in hospital, but I didn't come to pester you for the money.'

Barrington glared. 'I suppose your father provides well for you now.'

'Indeed. He merely disapproved of my wish to go my own way, I was a disappointment to him and could sing for my allowance, but I didn't need his help while I was with you. Then one day I came to visit you in the hospital and you'd gone. Not a word. What was I supposed to do?'

Barrington's manner melted a little. 'I am sorry, Martin, I wasn't in my right mind. My wife, the incident, it built up in me. I wasn't sure myself what I was doing. I simply could not go back to my old life.'

'So you let yourself go completely downhill. Look at this place. You had money, fame, influential friends, a fine house – I was proud to be your assistant, proud of the trouble and patience it took you to teach me. You and Eleanor.'

Barrington's ill humour returned like a stroke of lightning. The vivid blue eyes seemed to blaze.

'I would thank you not to speak of my wife in front of me! Do not even utter her name!'

Page's brown eyes flared too. 'I know what you think, Theo. But your jealousy wasn't justified. She was friendly and …'

'Friendly! Is that what you called it?'

'Yes, friendly, and helpful. I respected her, but we never …' He broke off, apparently thinking better of it, and for a moment or two they fell silent.

Emma was about to make her excuses and leave when Page spoke again. 'If you had to become a recluse, Theo, why didn't you go off and hide yourself in that fine house of yours?'

Barrington seemed to wilt a little. 'Because people would visit and pester me, as you are doing now, and I didn't want that.'

Emma had been switching her gaze from one to the other. Now she focused it on Barrington with a hard stare. Not because he'd been offhand with her after all she'd done for him, but that her sympathy and attempts to help him had proved to be a waste.

The man had money. He owned property, according to Page. Ever since those coins had spilled out on to the floor, she'd felt something wasn't quite right. These boxes of magician's props – why was he hanging on to them?

'What 'appened to your house, Mr Barrington?' she asked

He merely shrugged, but it was Page who spoke, in a monotone. 'Empty – deserted – almost every window broken and cracked – paintwork peeling – garden unattended – weeds waist high. It's now as sad as he is!'

This last was said with some venom and there was bitterness in his expression. 'This, would you believe,' he continued, extending a dramatic arm towards the older man, 'is the most talented illusionist you ever saw. And he threw it all away.'

In this stance he looked every inch the theatrical pro. Slim, handsome, upright, young, he was about five or six years older than her. Emma felt a small thrill run through her. 'He probably 'ad 'is reason,' she said in Barrington's defence, needing to say something, anything, to smother the sensation.

'Many people hit a bad spot in life,' said Page as though he'd been on earth sixty years instead of twenty. 'They pick themselves up and carry on.'

Yes, her mother had done exactly that, even now struggled to make ends meet, sometimes at her wits' end to do so.

'The show must go on,' Page said. 'Yet this one walks off the stage in the middle of his act because a few drunks harass him. That's no excuse for anyone to leave the stage.'

Barrington stiffened. 'Now look here, Martin ...'

'And now he's lying here, making himself ill, feeling sorry for himself and giving up on everything.'

'You would too,' she leaped in, 'if you'd lost your wife.'

'I'm not married.'

'Well then,' she pointed out succinctly, and again there descended a short silence.

Martin Page glared at Barrington for a moment, then drew a wallet and pencil from the inside pocket of his ulster, fished out a piece of paper and using the wallet as a rest, scribbled something on it. He held the paper out to Barrington, not taking his eyes off him as he replaced the wallet.

'I'm staying with my people. My address, if you wish to get in touch. I've had enough of being stuck in an office, my father calling the tunes.'

Barrington ignored the piece of paper. 'Then this visit is purely for selfish reasons.'

'Not at all. I just hate to see you wasting yourself like this.'

'What I do is no concern of yours, Martin. If you need so desperately to get back into the theatre, then get back into it. You don't need me. There are plenty of magicians out there looking for an assistant.'

'No one like you. I told you, you were the best.'

Barrington flicked a dismissive hand. 'If you are worth your salt and long for the stage so much, you will find someone else. But stop bothering me.'

'I've never bothered you before.'

A mocking smile made the other man's moustache twitch. 'Having found me, I suppose you will be plaguing me endlessly.'

'All I want is for you to come to your senses. No one could touch your illusions, not even Devant, and he's one of the best magicians around, and that mind-reading act of yours was unique.'

Again Barrington smiled, this time at the flattery, the threatened row being smoothed away. 'Thanks to you and your fine memory,' he conceded. 'I couldn't have done it as well without you.'

But Page was still angry. 'Then get yourself out of this place and let's get back together again and make some money.'

The offer was met with a shake of the head. 'I've no interest in money. This is what I am now.'

'So why are you hanging on to all this?' Page swept an arm towards the boxes. 'If you don't intend going back on the stage, why keep them?' His challenge met with silence; he let out an exasperated breath. 'You're lying to yourself, you know that, Theo. Very well, sink into your stupid morass of despondency. If that's what you want. I don't care.'

Barrington's temper rose. His spine straightening, he glared at his visitor, Emma entirely forgotten.

'I never asked you to come here, Martin. I have not asked for your opinion, your help or sympathy or even your anger, so please, kindly go.'

'If that's the way you feel,' Martin shot back at him, 'then do what you like to yourself. But you might as well take this.'

He flung the piece of paper on to the floor and grabbing up his hat, crammed it on his head.

'I'm sorry you had to hear all this,' he said in a milder tone as he eased past Emma to get to the door. Then he was gone. Emma was left gazing anxiously at the man who once more slumped on the bed.

'You all right, Mr Barrington?' was all she could think to say. When he didn't reply, she retrieved the piece of paper from the floor and held it out to him. When he didn't take it, she laid it down beside him on the bed.

'I'd better go,' she mumbled. 'Is there anything yer want? I could go and get yer something to eat or some more medicine if yer like.'

When he shook his head, she quietly let herself out. After all, he and his peculiar need to punish himself was none of her business, was it?

Chapter Six

Emma hurried back home, seething with indignation, hardly aware of the cold for the anger she felt with Barrington, and with herself. How could she have been such a fool?

Had it not been for that Martin Page she'd never have even known about Barrington's house. He'd have gone on letting her think that all he had in the world was the money she'd seen in that tin box. Having the wool pulled over one's eyes was enough to make a saint's blood boil. How dare he act as though he hardly had a penny to bless himself with. She had come to a decision – she would never go back there again.

Still incensed, she pushed open the main door to where she lived without even noticing that the door to the downstairs room was open. As she made to go upstairs, a woman's rough voice hailed her.

''Scuse me, luv, if yer don' mind. Can I 'ave a minute?'

Glancing towards it, Emma saw the gross figure of Mrs Lovell, who occupied the room, standing in the doorway. Emma had met her once or twice, the woman going out as she was coming in, or the other way around, nodding the time of day to each other. She'd usually have a babe in arms, a boy, pasty-faced, wrapped in a grubby shawl. Very often a waif-like little girl no more than three years old would be clinging to her skirt. Emma would hurry by them, overwhelmed by a sour body odour. Now, with that same smell assailing her, the woman was calling to her, compelling her to pause.

Rolls of fat trembled under her chin. It hung from her arms exposed by the rolled-up sleeves of a stained, striped blouse whose bodice strained against a huge and sagging bosom. A bit of sacking covered the black skirt, though still unable to hide the immense belly and hips. This time she had her young daughter in her arms while just behind her, lying in a wooden drawer on the floor beside a splay-legged kitchen chair, was the baby, covered by a few bits of linen. On the other side of the chair was a chipped enamel basin. Having caught her attention the woman bent sideways and picked it up, holding it out to Emma.

'Couldn't get me a drop o'water, could yer, love? I've got me 'ands full. Me kiddie's being sick and I can't leave 'er an' get it meself.'

Unable to ignore the plea, Emma moved towards the room to be met by the smell of vomit and urine. Holding her breath she took the basin.

'Thanks, luv. Yer a good gel.'

Yes, wasn't she? Running about for everyone else but herself. That rogue, Barrington, had said she was a good girl after she'd given him half of Ben's beer before trotting all the way back to Commercial Road in a snow shower to get that medicine for him. True, he'd given her money for going, and rewarded or not, she never minded helping people, but with him she felt cheated.

Emma gave the woman a brief nod and hurried off with the basin to fill it from a tap in the back yard where tenants got their water for washing and cooking. The tap could sometimes be a mere dribble. Other times it came out in a gush, soaking those using it. Tonight it was behaving itself.

Trying not to slop the contents, Emma returned with the basin. It was an effort not to heave as she put the basin on a bare wooden table by the wall, above which hung two lines of washing. Mrs Lovell took in other's washing, so Mum said, but none came even quarter-way to Mum's whiteness. Perhaps those Mrs Lovell did for couldn't afford enough to be fussy.

Emma tried not to ask if she could do anything else for her, longing to escape this all-pervading odour. The child might have a catching illness and the last thing Emma wanted was to be ill and unable to sell Mum's flowers. Mum would have to go out in her stead on top of having to make them. But there was no fire in the rusty iron grate.

'You ain't got no fire,' she said, stating the obvious.

'Can't get out ter find no wood,' came the reply.

'Shall I try and find yer some?' Warning bells rang in Emma's head. She'd really let herself in for it when all she wanted to do was get out of here and flee upstairs to her own rooms, smelling so fresh and clean as only Mum could get them. But the sick child needed warmth of some sort.

There was an open yard down the road where people would fling their unwanted rubbish. There might be a few sticks of wood if others hadn't got there first. She'd get a fire going, then leave. Mum would be wondering where she was and getting anxious.

She was soon back with half an old crate stinking of rotten cabbage. She'd stamped it into splinters to make carrying easier. With that and a few bits of paper she'd found she quickly got a fire going, igniting the paper with a candle that was all the woman had for light, the gas lamp on the wall unlit, probably with no coin for the meter.

All the time Mrs Lovell was saying, 'Yer a good gel, luv. Yer an angel, yer really are.'

While she'd been out, the woman had sat the girl on the floor beside her and now held the baby whom she was suckling, her breast looking like some huge, pasty half-deflated football. Emma averted her eyes, not because she was a prude, but that the size and shape was almost offensive to look at, and as Mrs Lovell grinned her thanks, revealing a gap in her not too clean front teeth, Emma nodded.

'I'll be away then,' she said.

The little girl was beginning to retch again. Mrs Lovell hastily put her baby back into its wooden drawer, the little mouth jerked off her breast with a sucking sound. Bending over the girl, she pushed her head down over the basin. Emma again averted her eyes as yellow bile spewed into the bowl of water. Her own bile rising, she fled.

Mum had heard her coming up the stairs. 'Yer a bit late, Em. I was getting worried. Just as well Ben ain't in yet.'

Rebellion caught hold of Emma. 'Why? Should it worry 'im? I was with Mrs Lovell – her girl's sick. Anyway, he ain't 'ome.'

'If he was, he could turn awkward.'

'So can I.'

Struggling out of her short coat, grown tighter around a bust that in the last six months had developed quite nicely, she yanked the hatpin from her boater, took it off and viciously jabbed the pin back, dropping it on the sofa and sinking down beside it. 'Why should you worry about him?'

'I don't like rows, luv. Everyone around 'ere listening to it.'

'There's enough noise and arguments go on round 'ere for no one ter notice ours,' Emma retorted.

'We never 'ad rows when yer dad was alive. Now Ben's taken over ...'

Emma stiffened as if she'd sat on the hatpin. 'Ben ain't *taken over*, and he never will. He only thinks he 'as. He's only me brother no matter what he says. I can give back as good as what he can dish out.'

'Please don't, luv.' Mum wasn't normally one to plead. She was as strong-willed as any and had always had her pride, but life had dealt her so many blows these last few years that it was whittling away her spirit. It worried Emma the way she was beginning to flag.

'All right, I won't say nothing. But if he raises his 'and to me, mine'll be raised to 'im, no matter what. I'm sorry, Mum, but I ain't going ter be browbeaten by the likes of 'im.'

But by the time he got home they were in bed so he had no idea how long she'd been out, not that it was his business anyway. She was still awake at midnight when he finally fell in through the door, cursing and swearing at something that was in his way. She'd been thinking about Barrington and how she had been so fooled by him. She would go there to see him one last time, maybe in January, and give him a piece of her mind.

She heard Ben stumble into another obstruction, swear vilely before throwing himself down on his creaky sofa. He was muttering away to himself and she caught the words, 'I'll get 'er, yer see if I don't,' as he made himself comfortable. After that all went quiet but for his stentorian snoring.

It wasn't such a bad Christmas after all. Mum, having religiously sacrificed a penny each week despite all other hardships, had been given a somewhat scrawny goose from the Goose Club Dad used to pay into when he was alive and doing well. A typical survivor, she made that carcass last for days.

Nothing from Ben, who was mostly out with his mates, but Mum still had that money from his fight and she knew how to make it last as January bought its hardships. The rest of the meal came from the Watney Street and Crisp Street markets, vegetables too suspect to sell at proper prices. With coins in the gas meter and a bit of coal on the fire, all warm and cosy, Emma put aside thoughts of Barrington, though being duped like that still rankled.

It was three weeks into January before she finally succumbed, even though she knew she ought not to. 'I can't 'ave 'im get away with it,' she told Lizzie. 'The cheek, him having me on like that. It's no use, if I don't 'ave it out with him, I'll go potty.'

They sat toasting their toes by Lizzie's fire, her parents down the pub and the younger children amusing themselves on their bed in the corner. Lizzie was the eldest, the others ranging from seven to thirteen years, the gap explained by two others dying between times.

Lizzie held her hands out to the warmth, not looking at Emma. 'I think yer'd be an idiot ter go back there. Yer don't know what designs he might 'ave on yer.'

Emma had told her about the money he'd given her, and the visitor he'd had and the hostility there'd been between them.

'What made yer *go* after a bloke like that?' Lizzie said, making it sound as though Emma was down to scraping the bottom of the barrel where lads were concerned. But Emma knew Lizzie's tendency to nurse envy. If only she'd smarten herself up, pull her hair back, put a smile on her lips, the boys would be interested in her. She could make herself quite pretty if she tried.

'I've not *gone* after 'im!' she retorted and saw Lizzie smile. 'I just lent an 'elping 'and to 'im that one time,' she said defensively.

'And then went back the second time. If that ain't going after a bloke, I don't know what is.'

'Well, perhaps I did get a bit too involved,' Emma conceded, staring into the fire. 'But nothing wrong went on.'

'Except ter earwig into 'is private business with that friend what had come visiting 'im.' She looked away from the fire to train a judgemental gaze on her friend. 'Yer should of left when yer realised it was private.'

'Yer can't just walk out.'

'And then find he's got money after all. He was leading you on, Em.'

It was Emma's turn to look at her, sharply. 'He wasn't leading me on. It wasn't none of my business anyway. He didn't boast at all about what he'd got and what he hadn't got, so he wasn't leading me on. Anyway, it's done with now.'

'Except that you want ter go there and give 'im a piece of yer mind. Why should you worry? He's forgotten all about yer.'

Perhaps he had. The talk drifted to other things, and she came away determined to forget Mr Barrington and his strange existence. It was all too complicated to bother her head about.

Lizzie felt pleased with herself after Emma left. Em always got the boys while she stood in the background, overlooked, ignored. It did her heart good to hear about this old man – he was an old man compared to the two of them – and money or not, Emma must be hard up for boys all of a sudden to go running after someone like that. And a street musician! Still, Em peddled her wares in much the same way, so she should feel at ease with the likes of that sort. Lizzie felt suddenly superior. Her own family was poor, everyone was poor around here, but at least what she did was honest work, working in a factory for proper wages, such as they were.

What had Em been thinking, wanting to go round to see him again? Perhaps she had her eye on the hidden wealth he was supposed to have. Lizzie could just see her batting her eyelids and sticking out her threepenny bits to make herself look older. For as long as she'd known her, Em had daydreamed of one day being rich; talked about the well-off who passed by her tray of paper flowers as if she was on speaking terms with them. Stupid. No one around here ever got rich. That was how life was. When you were poor you stayed poor unless you were a thief, and they nearly always got caught.

But a street musician! Tempting her with money. Blimey! The next thing, she'd be in the club! Even so, she didn't want Em to come a cropper. She'd have to warn her again, and keep warning her, about the dangers.

From The Flying Swan with its gaslight piercing the wintry darkness, came laughter and the raucous, musical plea for 'Bill Bailey to please come home'.

In the gutter outside came the jangling, ringing, disjointed strains of 'In The Good Old Summertime'. But it wasn't the hurdy-gurdy playing, but a barrel organ.

Emma hurried on, her heart beginning to thud in the knowledge that she was going to visit Mr Barrington in his room. She knew it was wrong and Lizzie Wallis's warning buzzed in her head. But he might be ill again. What if he lay inside that miserable room, stone-dead and not a soul there to find him? She glanced at the barrel organ. The hurdy-gurdy man could be somewhere else. Buskers moved around. But if he was ill …

No light was coming from his window. Lights from others, blurry with dust, made his look as though it indeed harboured death. Emma stretched up and put her face to the tiny pane of dirty glass. Pitch-black inside. Then for a moment the snowy clouds parted and a full moon threw brief light into the room. No hurdy-gurdy lay on the table. He was out. He was all right. She could go home with an easy heart.

She was glad he wasn't there. Mum was under the weather with an awful cold. She should have gone straight home after selling what paper flowers Mum had managed to make, struggling through her tightened chest to do so. Sneezing and sniffling and continually wiping her nose with a hanky sewn from old sheeting, she'd stoically waved away Emma's concern that she was straining her streaming eyes making the delicate petals.

'It's only a blessed cold. Don't wonder, the winter we're 'aving. But yer got ter keep going. The last thing I want,' she said through a blocked nose, 'is ter end up 'aving ter stuff mattresses or glue matchboxes tergether fer starvation wages. I've still got me silk work, and when it comes in, the wages is still better than stuffing blessed rotten mattresses.'

Emma was doing the shopping, after a style. Juggling with pennies but without Mum's instincts to find food others had overlooked. Wood could be got from the council rubbish heap, scores of other women doing the same, picking it over like crows.

Burying her pride, Emma dedicated herself to collecting up bits of coal fallen off coal carts; the place had to be kept warm, especially with Mum's cold. The money Ben had given her before Christmas was down to the last few pennies. Since then he'd brought in virtually nothing, and there was still the rent to be met or it would be out on their ear from this place too. Their only salvation was what she earned selling, but with Christmas behind them, few people were interested in buying. After stamping her feet for hours in bitter cold, she'd return home with just a handful of coppers.

She did the cooking, Mum protesting that if only she felt well enough she'd rather do it. Not that there was a lot to cook, really, with only her money coming in. Ben too had a cold, and that for him meant being ill enough to huddle in front of the fire and not work. He'd not been near the docks for over a week, any job he might have got was leaped on by someone else perhaps equally under the weather but still forced to stand with hundreds of others for whatever job was handed out, meaning a difference between starving and surviving.

He lay on the sofa, sneezing and spitting into a handkerchief. She hated washing those hankies. When they had money, Mum would take their stuff to the public wash-house attached to the bath-house in Bonemakers Row on the far side of the railway arch. It was noisy, steam-laden and full of chatter across the low-sided cubicles, but for Mum it was a chance to meet other people.

She always came back rosy-cheeked, and not only from the heat and steam – but not lately. Washing done at home saved three-ha'pence. The hot water heated on the fire, Emma would grit her teeth as she bent over the fluted wooden scrubbing board and wielded the scrubbing brush on the slimy squares of material Ben had used. They made her heave, even after their soaking in salt water for ages to help get the worst off.

As for washing herself, the public bath-house had to be given a miss. For tuppence, bring your own soap and towel, she'd sink into a bath full of hot water and for an hour feel like a duchess. Lying there, she'd dream of what it must really be like to be one, or at least have money to have your very own bathroom, all warm and steamy.

Such musing brought thoughts of Theodore Barrington, Theo as the young man had called him. How could anyone turn their back on money and profession to walk the dirty streets of the East End? The man had to be mad. She was well rid of him.

It was two weeks before her mother was well enough to do for herself, while Ben with youth on his side was up in a week, finally forced to look for work, missing his pint and game of cards. Mum, for once, was angry enough to refuse him even a few pennies.

'He can borer off 'is mates if he needs a drink that bad,' she said to Emma. 'I ain't goin' ter finance 'im any more.'

To his face she said, 'Find yerself work if yer broke.'

His answer to that was for her to shut her mouth. 'I ain't no bloody kid, so don't try ter tell me what ter do.'

He knew well enough that sooner or later he'd have her dipping into her purse for the odd sixpence or so out of what Emma brought in. Put it on a game of cards, with a bit of luck scooping a decent pot, and when he was properly fit again, a few successful rounds with some so-called prize-fighter, and he'd be back in funds.

'I can make enough dosh without working. I'm bloody nineteen an' I know what I'm about,' he told her, as if nineteen years of age made him the pinnacle of manhood.

Which reminded Emma that she'd be sixteen, next month. Properly grown up. She could hardly wait.

Chapter Seven

It was her birthday, the twenty-seventh of February. Sixteen at last – a world removed from being fifteen. In a single day, it seemed she had leaped from feeling herself a child to being suddenly all grown up.

Not that today was any more special than any other. She still went out selling, returning home by omnibus, but the sun had shone all day as though especially for her. There would be no other celebration, no cake, no special tea. Money didn't stretch to such luxuries. One thing, however, had been out of the ordinary – this morning, quite out of character, Mum had given her a peck on the cheek and said, ''Appy birthday, luv,' as she went on twisting the last few stems to lay in her daughter's tray.

Ben had forgotten altogether. She expected that. But two weeks back Mum had handed her a silver sixpence to spend on herself.

'Better take it now,' she'd said. 'I might not 'ave it by the time yer birthday comes round.'

She had intended to hang on to it in case there'd be need to hand it back if things got tight. Instead she and

Lizzie had gone to see a pantomime at the Queen's Music Hall in Poplar, threepence in the cheapest seats with a good view despite that, and lots of fun. So she could count the sixpence as being a well-spent birthday present.

Now she was sixteen, she dearly wanted it to be seen as special, and as she turned into Church Row, it came to her that she could go and show off to the hurdy-gurdy man. He looked on her as a child, it was time he saw her as an adult. Though he might not even be there any more after all this time. Even so, she made a quick detour to the Swan.

He hadn't gone away. His music floated to her even before she saw him. Jolly music, like a birthday greeting, and it lightened her footsteps. The glow from the pub showed a cheerful ring of onlookers. They were clapping in time to the rhythm. There came a thought that with so many onlookers he must be raking it in. Then she remembered the money he already had, the house he owned, keeping it secret, and the joy she had felt for him immediately turned sour. Shouldering her way through the throng, she planted herself at the front.

'Oy!' A woman with a feather boa gave her a shove. 'What d'yer fink you're at?'

Emma turned on her. 'I've got as much right as you!' she retorted.

The lively music had faltered as the player saw her before resuming his playing. One or two people who'd begun to do a knees-up paused then resumed prancing, and the onlookers gave an appreciative applause while a couple of boys let out a few cat-calls at the sight of women's legs as, their skirts held clear, they stamped up and down. One of the boys was immediately cuffed by a bystander. The boy ducked and made a rude gesture before moving off with his three mates, arms linked across each other's shoulders.

'Oy, you!' A voice suddenly bellowed from the Swan's public bar door.

Barrington didn't stop playing but looked up as the publican waved an arm towards him. 'Yus, you, mate, on yer way! Yer keepin' me customers out o' me pub.'

Barrington ceased playing, his humour light. 'I shall be spending a little in your pub later, so what harm?' he returned calmly.

'Yer won't be spendin' as much as me regulars do, Mr La-di-da wiv yer fancy-talk. A bloomin' busker, like the rest of 'em, yer takes yer money and 'ops orf ter somewheres else. Go on, be orf, an' let me do a bit o' trade too, if yer don' mind.'

The landlord's words reminding them that throats needed quenching, the small audience began to disperse. Barrington didn't appear too put out. Picking up his coin tin, he began gathering up any coins that had missed their mark as Emma approached.

'Not too bad at all,' he remarked as she reached him. 'I would like to buy you a glass of lemonade, if I may, my dear?'

Though the offer was tempting and in its way would have been a sort of birthday treat, at sixteen something stronger like a port and lemon would be more suitable, and she was still a bit irked and she had to get home.

'I can't,' she said tersely. 'I've bin out selling all day and me mum will be waiting for me.'

'I suppose you are right,' he said. 'I will leave as well. I shall not grace his worship's pub after that little show of temperament. I shall take his advice and have my tipple elsewhere.' He was smiling as he unscrewed the stand from the hurdy-gurdy. He straightened up to look at her. 'So, what brings you here this evening?'

Emma thought quickly. 'I just fancied a walk before going 'ome, and I 'appened to 'ear your music.'

'I see.' He was looking straight at her. His eyes were an intense, mesmerising blue. They made her fidget with self-consciousness. He knew she was lying. 'It's me birthday,' she said quickly. 'I'm sixteen.'

There was amusement in his eyes, the lower half of his face still hidden by his scarf. 'Congratulations.' He dropped the tin of money into the pocket of his overcoat. 'And what did you get for your birthday?'

'Nothing.' Emma's head went up in defiance. 'People round 'ere ain't got the money ter throw around on birthday presents.'

'Then here is a present from myself.'

As he dipped a hand back into his pocket, Emma began backing away, embarrassing memories of that first time he'd given her money and what Lizzie had said about that.

'I don't want yer money.'

Even as she stammered her protest, he reached out, caught her wrist and placed a shilling piece hard against the palm of her hand. To her shame, she felt her fingers close over the coin as though with a will of their own, her mind telling her that she needed it more than he did.

'Why do yer do this busking lark?' she burst out in sudden, quite unreasonable temper. 'Yer don't really 'ave to, do yer? That Martin Page I saw at your place said you 'ad yer own 'ouse – said a good magician makes lots of money, and you said yerself yer was good. So why don't yer?'

His amiableness disappeared. 'You must go home, my dear,' he said brusquely.

'I think it's awful,' she went on, brushing aside his advice. 'A man what's already got money doing this sort of thing when there's people like us what ain't got nothing trying 'ard ter make a living.'

'Have nothing.'

'What?' She looked at him in confusion.

'The phrase is, "you have nothing", not, "ain't got nothing".'

Emma glared. 'I talk as I like!' she retorted and saw him shrug.

'As you wish,' he said, turning away as though dismissing her from mind.

She wasn't going to be dismissed that easily. 'What's the matter with you?' she demanded, following him as he began to move off. 'You act like you ain't got two brass farthings ter rub tergether, yet yer've even got an 'ouse of yer own 'idden away.'

For some reason, for the first time she had need to correct her words. She'd heard posh people, passing by her and her flowers. 'Your own house – hidden away,' she corrected. 'That Martin Page said how clever you was as a magician.'

But it was an effort to keep it up, and why should she, just to please him? He was nothing to her. 'Why did yer leave off being a magician?' she asked, trailing after him.

She grasped her empty flower tray more firmly to her side as he stalked ahead, refusing to pause for her to catch up, in fact his already long stride lengthening so that she was forced to trot to keep up.

'What I am or have been is none of your business, young lady,' he said over his shoulder. 'You might be sixteen now, but that gives you no right to be rude.'

She hadn't meant to be rude. She only wanted him to see that he was doing himself an injustice. Putting on a spurt she caught up to him.

'Look, Mr Barrington, I know I shouldn't poke me nose in, but why don't yer do yer magic fer people round 'ere instead of playing that thing.'

'Because I chose not to.'

'Yer'd make a lot more money. But yer've already got money, ain't yer?' she added, unable to help herself.

He ignored the dig. 'I'm sorry, no.'

'Why?'

He did not reply and again anger overtook her. 'Because if yer did,' she exploded, 'yer'd 'ave ter talk to yer audience, and ter do that yer'd 'ave ter get rid of that muffler, an'yer don't want no one ter see that scar, do yer?'

He stopped so abruptly that she almost ran into him. 'You go too far, young lady!' he said, turning on her. 'May I put it this way? As you choose to speak as you do, I choose to be what I am. Do you not agree that that's fair?'

For a moment she was stumped for an answer and he began to move on again, walking swiftly. Stubbornly, she followed.

'I know yer still see me as a child, Mr Barrington. And I suppose to you I am, but I'm sixteen now, and round 'ere that's well grown up. Life's hard around 'ere. It makes yer grow up quick.'

Hurrying and talking at the same time was making her ever so slightly out of breath, young as she was, as she followed behind him into the black depths of the railway arch and on into the alley where he lived. Soon he would gain his door, go in and close it on her. She needed to continue talking fast.

'What I'm trying ter say, Mr Barrington, is that I'm used to this sort of life. I was brought up to it, or something like it, and you weren't. I expect it weren't too bad last spring and summer, or even last autumn, but you only just got through this winter by the skin of yer teeth. Yer've never known what it can be like fer people like us what's got almost nothing. But yer've begun ter find out this winter. So 'ow many winters are yer going ter put up with before it kills yer?'

Words poured from her as they neared his door.

'You 'ave ter be brought up 'ere ter survive. Please, Mr Barrington, listen ter me.' They had reached his door. 'Look, yer've got ter go back ter what yer've been accustomed to, go back to what you was doing.'

She couldn't remember when she'd spoken for so long in one go. But he was regarding her as his hand sought for the key in his pocket.

'I know what I'm talking about, Mr Barrington,' she hurried on, her tone growing even more urgent. 'And I know it ain't just that scar what did for yer. It's everything else, like losing yer wife, like blaming yerself. I know that from what you told me the day I 'elped you 'ome. Yer use that muffler to hide from yerself – not from other people.'

He was looking steadily at her, key poised in the lock. 'You are indeed more grown up than your age tells me. You are quite perceptive.'

87

She wasn't sure what perceptive meant, but she brightened on recalling the solution she'd come up with the evening she had helped him home when he had been unwell.

She began again. 'If yer that conscious of yer scar, why don't yer do what I suggested a while ago, hide it under a beard. Like I said, one like our King Edward wears. All distinguished. Or do yer just *like* torturing yerself?'

He ignored the taunt, his tone sharp. 'I no longer have any interest in appearing distinguished – to anyone!' Any moment he would say a terse goodbye and turn the key, open the door and close it against her. She needed desperately to get out all she wanted to say before that happened.

'Because yer could do yer conjuring and amaze people instead of 'aving them patronise yer, dancing to yer music and walkin' off. Yer could make 'em respect yer, like yer said yer once did.'

He seemed unimpressed. 'Conjuring is an art reserved for the stage.'

'I've seen it done in the streets,' she answered back. 'Along with them what eat fire and jugglers and such. They make lots more money than the ordinary buskers what play old trumpets and violins and such. People watch with their eyes bulging, and even though a lot ain't all that good, people are still caught out trying ter find what cup a ball is under, or where the lady is out of three cards, that sort of thing. You could do that.'

'Simple tricks,' Barrington scoffed. 'Done by amateurs!' He suddenly seemed to grow in stature. 'I'm a master of magic, a conjuror, an illusionist, a reader of minds.' The timbre of his voice deepened as if imparting some pearl of wisdom to a pupil. 'Prestidigitation is a worthy profession. Sleight of hand done by a master can mystify nobility. It is not for the despicable curbside entertainer looking for pennies thrown by gaping onlookers as one would throw a bone to a dog.'

Without warning the imperious tone faded. He appeared to wilt just a little. 'One must practise daily, and I have not practised for over a year now.'

Emma snapped herself from the spell he'd momentarily cast over her on the bit about reading minds. Of course conjurors used trickery. Everyone knew that. But mind-reading, he could do that! That gave her the shivers.

'It's the will ter do it what yer've lost,' she said boldly. 'Not yer touch. Yer could start practising again.'

'For the curbside?' The sneer haughty, but she ignored it.

'Yer've got all them boxes in there.' She jabbed a finger toward the still closed door. 'Yer could pick up again if yer practised.'

'I'm sorry,' he said, turning away from her to twist the key in the lock. 'It's too late.'

The door being opened, Emma grabbed his arm. 'Yer could ...'

He cut short what she was about to say. 'I wish you'd cease uttering that word, "yer".' His expression was one of utter distaste. 'It offends me. How can you bend the King's English so unpalatably? While you are with me, let me get one thing straight – I will thank you to kindly think what you are saying. Now, girl, say YOU. Say it, girl!'

The barked command made her jump. 'You,' she obliged, meekly.

He nodded. 'It takes no more effort to pronounce it properly than to abuse it. And you have a nice voice when you use it as it should be used.'

Anger at having been so uncharacteristically meek melted. 'Do I?'

'In fact,' he went on, 'were I to take up my profession again, you would make an admirable assistant. But I would require you to speak English as it should be spoken.'

They stood at the opened door, she tall but still having to look up at him, her mind in turmoil. Was what she was seeing in his face signs that he was beginning to see her point, almost as if he was coming to some decision about picking up his profession again, maybe if only as a street entertainer? Her heart began to race.

'Do yer ...' she broke off as he frowned at her. 'Do you mean it?'

'Mean what?'

'About doing magic again.'

'I did not say that. I said were I to.'

He came to himself abruptly. 'Look my dear, come in.' Pushing the door open, he stood back for her to enter, she doing so as though under his command. As he began to close the door, first glancing out, maybe to check no one had seen her, thinking of her reputation, she heard him curse.

'Damn the man!'

Before he could close the door fully, it was caught and held ajar by someone who had appeared from the darkness. Barrington's tone was full of anger. 'What the devil do you want?'

'I thought I'd look you up again, Theo,' came the reply, and Emma instantly recognised the light, easy tone of Martin Page. It was a pleasing voice, but she was disturbed to hear it, being found here by him.

'To see how you are,' he answered. 'Being nearby, I thought I'd ...'

'Plague me,' Barrington finished. 'Now that you've traced me.'

Emma had shrank back into the darkened room, hoping he wouldn't come in, reluctant to have him discover her here and see the expression that discovery would bring to his face. But he'd already noticed a presence and she saw the paleness of his teeth as his lips split into a grin.

'Ah, I see you already have company.'

He'd glimpsed the female shape, long skirt, small boater hat. But he couldn't have recognised her. Please, came the silent prayer, don't let him in.

'Well, Martin,' Barrington was saying. 'Now you're here, you had best come out of the cold.'

Prayers gone unanswered – for bad girls in strange men's rooms, they never were – she stayed very still, hugging a corner. Hopefully she'd slip out with a quick excuse to be off before Barrington closed the door and had time to light any candle or gaslight. But the door closed, match struck, and she saw the look of surprise on Page's face as the gas mantle flared.

'How do you do?' His tone was formal, stopping short of her name. He had probably forgotten it anyway.

'I'd better go,' she whispered in reply, her voice small.

'Please, not on my account,' he said. 'I shan't be staying long myself.'

But he'd already turned his back on her, that alone speaking louder than words. Barrington had put the hurdy-gurdy down on the bed, taking off his overcoat and bowler to drop them down beside it.

'So,' he said with a deep breath. 'What is it you want?'

'I want you to pick up where you left off, Theo.'

'We've had all this out. You've had your answer.'

'Not the one I'm looking for. Even in some cheap music hall you could live better. Exactly how long do you intend keeping up this fiasco of yours?'

'What I do is no concern of yours,' came the savage reply.

'I think it is,' Page said passionately. 'You still blame me. No matter what I say or do, I can't seem to convince you that nothing ever happened. Nothing! In spite of what you think, Theo, there was never anything between Eleanor and I ...'

He broke off and glanced at Emma as though aware that he might have said too much. It brought an instant rush of blood to her cheeks, like someone caught out eavesdropping. There was a troubled look in his eyes. Seconds later he'd turned back to Theodore Barrington.

'Theo, I don't know what's between you two, but she is just a kid.'

Indignation swept over Emma, embarrassment forgotten. 'I'm sixteen! You can't be much more than twenty!'

He was gazing at her again, his brown eyes still troubled. 'You would do well to keep away from him,' he said darkly. 'You've no idea what he can be like. There are things you don't know – don't want to know – about him. Take my advice. Leave. Before you get caught up in his web.'

'It's you who needs to leave,' Barrington snapped. 'You'll not change my mind, about the stage or yourself. I shall *never* go back to it.'

Emma had been thinking that Martin Page was only trying to frighten her off so he could wheedle his way back, but on Barrington's statement, she leaped forward.

'You mustn't say that!' she cried out. How could he turn away from such a romantic existence as the stage?

They were both looking at her. But she had to convey her own feeling on this. 'I told yer,' she said. 'If yer 'ad a beard to hide that scar, perhaps all them guilty feelings might go away.'

She knew what she wanted to say, but not *how* to say it. There was perhaps a name for the way a visible scar could be used as an excuse, a cover for something that went far deeper, but she couldn't think of any.

Faltering under their combined stare, she went on in a diminished voice, 'I only thought it might 'elp, that's all.'

Barrington spoke first, his voice surprisingly soft considering both men had seemed at odds with each other. 'My dear, what did I tell you a little while ago? It is "you", not "yer". And there is an aitch in the word "help".'

She couldn't believe what she was hearing. With this going on, he was trying to teach her to speak properly? Woodenly, she repeated the correct pronunciation then felt annoyance flare. Why d'yer *want* me to talk proper?'

'To become a young woman worthy of notice,' he said, Martin now ignored.

'What if I don't want ter be ... to be noticed.'

'With your beauty, my dear, you can become anything you want, but you'd have to work hard and learn to speak well. I couldn't take you on as my assistant if you didn't.'

Emma stared, unable to make sense of those words as Page broke in.

'Theo, what're you up to?'

93

Barrington turned to gaze slowly at him. 'I am saying that were I ever to return to the stage, I would use a female assistant.'

Page frowned. '*I* was your assistant, Theo, a damned good one and you know it. You taught me.'

'That was before ...' Barrington allowed a significant pause, then adopted a more vague note. 'Before those events leading up to my wife's unfortunate demise.'

'There *were* no *events*, as you put it,' Page said tightly. 'But you'd be ready to stake all on some green girl with no training just to have your so-called revenge. Wasn't dismissing me out of hand enough for you?'

'I said were I ever to go back, not that I will.' Barrington said levelly.

'Same thing.' Page went to position himself squarely in front of him like one ready for a fight, but Barrington's gaze remained steady.

'Not the same thing at all, Martin. I need to get one thing straight. The past is behind me. It is not forgotten. But it is behind me.'

Page was eyeing him narrowly. 'So no matter how much I protest, Theo, you're never going to alter your mind about me, so what is the point of my trying?'

'No point at all.'

Emma stood transfixed, one man openly smouldering, the other calm yet with the calmness of a quiet day before a tempest breaks. Whatever there was between them was none of her business. All she was thinking was what Barrington had said about a lady assistant, intimating it was her he had in mind.

'So you mean you might go back on the stage?' she ventured.

It was Page who answered. 'If he does, it will be to spite me – him and his baseless suspicion. But he won't. I know him. He won't.'

'It don't 'ave to be in a theatre.' She couldn't let this golden chance slip. Her mind's eye saw the money she could bring home to Mum, even from helping a street magician with his tricks, if that was what being his assistant meant. She took an enthusiastic step towards Barrington.

'Yer could start with doing your conjuring on the street – see how people take to it.' She was trying hard to speak nicely – her chances depended on it. 'Work the theatre queues, an' I could help you, like you said. I'm very quick to learn and you could teach me.'

Her voice trailed off inadequately as he levelled his eyes at her, and a small shiver ran through her as he continued to hold her gaze. There was something about it that made her feel uncomfortable. Nor had he spoken, but again Martin spoke for him.

'Let it be, my dear.' The words were quiet, friendly, yet there was that same warning there, and bitterness too. 'Best not to believe all he says.' Page's eyes were so gentle, so deep brown, for a moment she felt a person could have easily melted into them.

Barrington's deep voice broke the spell. 'I can see that I may indeed need to sport a beard.'

The interruption tore her away from the younger man. 'What?' she asked in bewilderment.

'The beard,' Barrington repeated.

Martin was immediately forgotten in her returning enthusiasm. 'Yer mean yer'll take my advice an' go back on the stage?'

'Not the stage, young lady. Not yet.'

'Then like I said, yer could do the theatre queues. Yer can make good money playing ter them. People like entertainment what's different when they're 'aving … having ter queue up outside waiting ter go in.'

The eyes studied her. '"That is".'

'That is?' she repeated, bewildered for a moment.

'You said, "what". "What's different". The word is "that".'

She couldn't recall. All she knew was that he was going to take her advice, and that if she was to be his assistant he would be her tutor, not only for the work but to improve her diction. She would be a willing pupil.

There came visions of becoming someone, something she'd yearned for all her life, especially since losing her father, and Mum having to skimp and scrape with no hope of ever getting out of the existence they now endured.

Emma had been so caught up in her visions of the future that she didn't see Martin Page slip quietly out. But Barrington did, and he smiled to himself.

He had kept a perfect control over his fury at Martin's continued professions of innocence. It had been a fine move, the reference to taking on a female assistant. Martin knew it had been directed at him, and it did Theo good to see the shock and anger on the younger man's face.

The only mistake was to foolishly commit to promises, even half promises, to take up his profession again. But having done so, yes, it would serve its purpose admirably, thanks to an innocent young girl. What he would like to see was Martin coming back to him begging as he saw him regain his previous fame, Martin left out in the cold. Ah, the taste of revenge was sweet indeed. The man could protest all he liked against accusations of playing around with Eleanor. And what if Eleanor *had* made the first move?

He had known for a long time of the pleasure Eleanor had derived from making eyes at other men, but they knew better than to cross him. It was Martin who had been the fool, giving in to the temptation, even to being seduced, though sometimes he wondered if it had ever gone that far. He had always been an inherently jealous man and had perhaps read more into it than there had been. But who could say? Was Martin going to let on if there had been anything more?

There had been a time when he had felt very close to Martin, drawing strength from his youth. Then seeing him and Eleanor growing ever closer, ever friendlier, he'd grown suspicious, and even though he had never found them in any compromising situation, his affection for Martin had turned to bitterness. Yet there still remained a shred of that liking he'd once had for the boy, and that annoyed him. If only his suspicions had been founded, he could have hated Martin to his very core instead of being victim of these visions that bounded and rebounded in his brain. If only he could test him now. But it was too late.

Chapter Eight

The moment Emma came in through the door after seeing Barrington, she was greeted by a challenge from her mother.

'Where 'ave yer been? What've yer been up to?' Mum came to stare into her face, her tall, thin frame bent at the waist for fiercer scrutiny. 'Ben says yer've been seeing some bloke.'

'Ben?' Emma tried to appear normal. 'I've got lots of friends and of course some of 'em *are* boys. What's wrong in that?' she asked, taking off her coat and hat to drape them on one of the hooks behind the door that held all their outdoor clothes. 'If I don't look around at the boys I see around 'ere, I could end up bein' left on the shelf, and yer wouldn't be too 'appy with that – yer daughter an old maid.'

She was talking far too fast, rambling on trying to cover herself, she supposed, with the stupid sense that guilt must be practically written on her forehead as plain as chalk on a school blackboard.

'I ain't talking about lads,' Mum was saying. 'I'm talking about some older bloke. Ben said yer've been seein' some older bloke.'

Tiny talons of alarm seemed to be clutching at Emma's heart. 'Don't be so silly, Mum,' she managed to laugh, but her mother stood her ground.

'Don't tell me not ter be silly! Ben saw yer.'

'Saw me, what?' The talons had tightened.

'Going into some bloke's 'ome.' Mum's lips were thin. 'One of Ben's mates saw yer goin' off with some street musician. Yer was on 'is arm.'

'Heaven 'elp us, Mum!' Relief swept away the grip. She couldn't help a ring of sarcasm in her voice. 'You telling me yer've been listening to some soppy tale my brother's been told by someone else what read something into what he thought he saw?'

'Not just that. Ben's followed yer to an 'ouse in Mitre Alley.'

Emma's need to bluster came entirely from new fear. 'Who do he think he is, following me around? Where's he now?'

'Out.'

'That's just like 'im, unable to accuse me ter me face.'

'But did yer? Did yer go inter some bloke's 'ouse?'

Mum was being persistent and she needed to brazen this thing out. 'Did Ben see 'ow long I was supposed ter be in this bloke's 'ouse? Did he hang around ter see if it belonged to one of me friends and not some bloke?' She felt the tension in her muscles relax as her mother moved back to the loaf she'd been sawing before Emma came in.

'As far as I know,' Mum said in a more congenial tone, 'he saw yer go by the Swan, and after what 'is mate told 'im, he left his drink on the bar and went after yer ter see where yer went, but he 'ad ter leave and go back to the pub in case someone else 'elped themselves to 'is beer.'

Relief was a silent sigh. She'd have liked to know who the mate was who'd seen her that first time, but it would have been foolish to ask, though there was a need to explain and vindicate herself.

'I know what Ben's mate must've seen,' she began as though on some sudden recollection. 'It was just before Christmas, a street musician what took ill. It was so cold and no one was bothering to 'elp 'im, so I did. I 'elped back him to where he lived. Anyone would do the same.'

When Mum looked back at her, the half-loaf hugged against her chest, bread knife held ready for slicing, her suspicions had flown, her eyes showing quiet pride. 'There's lots as wouldn't. Yer a good gel, Em. Just like you ter 'elp some poor old devil.'

Emma smothered a bitter smile. Again told she was a good girl. Mum ought to know the excitement that was even now gripping her after what Theodore Barrington had said. The pictures danced in her head of her finally being someone, of getting out of this place. He'd filled her with such hopes and now she yearned for them to come true.

Mum had resumed her cutting of the three-day-old bread into thick slices to toast in front of the fire to go with their supper. 'But yer 'ave ter be careful.' Her tone had grown waspish. 'Trust Ben ter listen ter gossip from mates no better than him.'

The moment was over, but she knew she ought to be well advised to keep away from people like Barrington.

She was out of her depths with the likes of stage folk. That young man, too, who'd so taken her eye. What had he been alluding to with his words of caution? But such a wonderful picture had been painted for her of the sort of life she'd never contemplated but now felt that she had always yearned after.

A magician's assistant. It sounded so wonderfully grand. Maybe it would only be street entertainment, but who could say where it would lead? Visions came of one day having fine dresses, being on stage before an admiring audience.

Why not? She was tall, had a good figure once decent corsets instead of second-hand ones gave her a proper wasp waist. Theodore Barrington had remarked on her pretty face, he'd said beautiful. And he'd even hinted at teaching her how to talk. Yes, it could all come about.

Emma knew she would go back and see him, over and over again, until she was eventually able to persuade him to go back to the profession that had once made his name.

Martin Page had done his best to warn her against him, and of course he would – from what she'd gathered this evening, he and Barrington weren't on too friendly terms, and of course Page would be jealous at being dropped in favour of her.

Of course nothing was certain, but she could dream.

Lizzie's gaze was riveted on the pavement just ahead as she and Emma wandered back home along Commercial Road, arm in arm, after saying goodbye to a knot of half a dozen girls and lads around their own age.

They'd hang around one of the street lamps by a tea-shop or a pub. With the girls ogling the boys who came out, and the boys ogling the girls who passed by, they'd indulge in amiable backchat and jostling until time to go home around ten or ten-thirty.

'I still fink yer should ferget about 'im, yer know,' Lizzie said, tightening her arm in Emma's to add weight to her bit of wisdom. 'I think yer've gone a bit soppy over this bloke.'

'I've not gone soppy over 'im,' said Emma. 'I was just saying I can't 'elp thinking of what he said, like teaching me ter talk proper, and about he might go back ter being a conjuror, and me 'elping.'

'I told yer before,' Lizzie said, turning her head to look earnestly at her friend. 'Blokes like that can spin enough tales ter turn any gel's head. But you ain't never normally been one ter let yours be turned.'

'I've been telling meself that fer a week,' came the admission.

'There you are,' said Lizzie, but with Emma bent on pouring her heart out to her, she was a willing listener.

'I've been keepin' all this ter meself for over a week now. But I'm a bit worried. Ben's been following me. If he really do find out that Mr Barrington is more than twice my age, Mum'll kill me.'

'And so will he,' Lizzie said, 'knowing what your brother's like.'

Ben Beech's reputation was unsavoury in an area full of unsavoury characters. Louts between fourteen and nineteen lurked on street corners for any likely passer-by not guarding his purse, or to keep an eye out for any nosy copper when an illegal game of pitch and toss was going on in a back alley. There was always a street fight somewhere around, belts, buckles, sticks, coshes, with

Ben Beech often in the thick of it. He preferred his fists and not just in the boxing booth. Big and beefy, head and shoulders taller than most of the undersized, underfed East End lads, he was a battler, a bruiser, and if a bloke didn't have two or three mates with him, it was better to cross over to the other side of the street when Ben Beech came along. Yet girls threw themselves at him. Lizzie too would feel her heart go pit-a-pat when she saw him, though he never once looked her way, much less twice.

'I ain't told a soul except you,' Emma was saying. 'I still ain't sure I'm doing the right thing.'

'Well, yer know what I think,' Lizzie said.

Two young lads passed, lurching along, shoulders hunched, hands in trouser pockets, necks deep in turned-up jacket collars against a breezy March evening. As they approached, their necks lengthened considerably and one lad let out an appraising whistle, the other asking, 'Yer muvver's let yer out, then?' A common salutation that usually drew the retort, 'An' do yer own muvver know yer out?' quite often leading to conversation and eventually a consent to go for a 'cuppa tea', so as to get to know each other.

Lizzie merely stuck her tongue out at them and they laughed as they lurched by, tugging threadbare caps to a jaunty angle over their foreheads in defiance of being spurned. There were plenty of other fish in the sea.

'I think,' Lizzie went on, 'that yer'd be advised ter think twice about all that what he told yer. Especially after what this other geezer said about 'im, the one yer said was a nice-looking young man.'

Emma had touched on him on their way out to meet their friends in Commercial Road, but she hadn't had time to expand before being greeted by everyone. The way she'd described him had made him sound quite romantic, like Prince Charming in the pantomime, but Emma hadn't appeared smitten by him, more like she was being hypnotised by this conjuror chap and his talk of her being his assistant.

It wouldn't happen, of course, just a lot of rubbish. Things like that didn't happen to ordinary girls from around here. The man was leading her on and Em, who usually knew her own mind, for once needed to be warned. Lizzie no longer felt envy, only concern.

'It all sounds fishy ter me,' she said as they neared home. 'Yer don't know what blokes like that 'ave got in mind fer young gels, especially pretty ones. It could even 'ave something ter do with the white slave trade we 'ear about. Don't want ter find yerself smuggled off ter some 'ot Arab land and never ter return. It do 'appen. More often than yer think.'

She'd read about it in the penny romances she sometimes bought. Being laid off from the match factory after Christmas had done her a bit of good. She'd been taken on at Edward Cook and Company soapworks, not as clean as the match factory, but she was earning one shilling and sixpence more. Her father didn't bring in a lot but at least he was now in work as a casual crossing sweeper so she could afford to splash out on the occasional penny romance she so loved reading, with no long words to get stumped over.

'Them Arab potentates is always ready ter pay a lot of money fer pretty girls fer their slaves. 'Ow der you know this conjuror bloke ain't got you in mind fer somethink like that?'

But she could see by Em's face as they parted company that she was set on having her own way. Emma had always been a stubborn one. Lizzie didn't want to think of what awful things could happen to her best friend because of this silly notion of hers, so she put it out of her mind. It was Emma's look-out and there was nothing she could do about it.

No passers-by had paused to listen to him today. People hurrying out from The Flying Swan would glance at him then walk on. Nor did any children dance, though beyond the arches boys were playing a noisy game of ball down the street and a group of girls had a washing line for a skipping rope stretched across Mitre Street a little way off.

He couldn't blame the weather for his lack of success, a spring-like Friday buoying the spirit. His mind wasn't on his playing. He'd pause every now and again, thinking of a beautiful young girl who had come to haunt his thoughts. She'd not been nigh or by for over a week and he was certain he and Martin between them had frightened her off. Damn Martin!

Darkness was descending, later now that March was giving way to April. When she came this way it was usually around half seven, but with the lengthening days she could stay out selling her mother's flowers for longer, taking advantage of the better weather.

Positioned as he was on the corner, Theodore could see along both Three Colt Street and Mitre Street. She could come from either direction. When she did, if she did, he must not appear too welcoming. It would give her airs. He'd made that mistake with Eleanor, had allowed her too much rope, and look what she had done to him in return.

This girl reminded him of Eleanor, self-assured but without any of the spitefulness. Eleanor had been tall and beautiful, and hard. This girl, for all her independent nature, struck him as being more pliable, where Eleanor had stood up to his moods and fought back, tooth and nail.

He knew he could be moody. Strange moods when they were upon him, when he'd grow silent, drink more than he ought, become sombre and brooding. He'd been like this all his life, making few friends for all he was sometimes capable of indulging in uproarious bouts of socialising.

Maybe it was being an only child, sent to boarding school by parents who spent most of their lives in India, his father in the diplomatic corps, a chargé d'affaires. Growing up lonely amid a crowd of contemporaries, he'd studied alone, sought individualism; magic had lured him naturally. So had hypnotism, wielding power over any who might mock his hobby. He became very good at it, would practise on college companions to their amazement, and he loved seeing them in awe of him. Thus the magic and the pull of the stage. But the hypnotism was something best forgotten.

He turned from it now as it started to invade his peace of mind, and thought of the girl who, whether she'd meant to or not, had begun to give him new hope, something he'd been dead to for over a year.

She'd been so persuasive, so certain of his return to life. Her words of encouragement coupled with a sudden desire to let Page see that he hadn't fallen by the wayside, had done its job. He'd even begun to grow that beard she'd suggested. The long, stark white cicatrice, once so noticeable, was being slowly hidden. He could have done this long ago, but it would have been too easy. After a year of self-recrimination and mental self-flagellation, was it time it was all put behind him? Maybe. Pausing yet again in his playing, he glanced once more along Mitre Street.

And there she was.

Emma came to stand several feet away, but sullenly, he not having taken the slightest notice of her. Her sullenness, however, gave way a little as she saw that at least he'd taken notice of the suggestion she'd made the last time she had seen him. Even though the early April evening was cold, he was no longer wearing his muffler and that there were definite signs of a beard, not just a mere stubble from neglect. It was fair and just thick enough to lessen the indent the scar made across his chin.

Emma began to move towards him and at last he ceased turning the hurdy-gurdy's handle, the underlying low whine dying.

'So you have come, as I expected you would,' he said quietly.

As he'd expected she would? Annoyance flooded through her. 'I just thought I'd take it into me mind ter see if yer was 'ere, that's all,' she said sharply.

'Dear girl!' His voice was filled with exasperation. 'Listen to yourself. How can you assault the ear with such vile abominations? If you've decided on being my assistant, it's time I began teaching you how to speak.'

Emma stood dumbfounded as he bent to pack away the hurdy-gurdy. It all sounded so outlandish that she burst out laughing. The sound made him look up to regard her with slow deliberation so that she squirmed.

'You have a most delightful laugh, Amelia, do you know that?' he said quietly, without a semblance of a smile on his own lips. 'You also have quite a pleasing voice when you bother yourself to use it properly.'

Laughter had died the instant it began, seemingly inappropriate, but she was flattered by his remarks and she liked the way he called her Amelia.

'Why are yer … Why are you doing this?' she asked as they walked off, she with one eye on her surroundings after what she'd learned about Ben. 'Why have yer … have you changed your mind about going back to conjuring? And why choose me to be your assistant if you're not going to?'

Already she was becoming aware of what she was saying and the way it should be said. She wasn't stupid, and it wasn't hard to put on the posh talk when she wanted, even if it didn't flow naturally as it did with the toffs who passed her on their way into theatres. It had always been fun to mimic them, making her friends laugh. But she'd never tried incorporating it into everyday conversation. She'd have had everyone laughing at *her* if she had. Now of course, there could be another goal in sight, and it was imperative to let him see that she could do it.

Reaching the place where he lived, she hurried inside behind him, with a prior glance around lest she was being spied on. Closing the door, he put the hurdy-gurdy on the table and her empty flower tray beside it.

'Sit down, Amelia.' He indicated the one rickety chair.

She did as ordered, thinking that every request of his seemed like a command. But she liked being called Amelia. It made her feel special.

He was looking at her, his blue eyes steady and unblinking, holding her attention almost against her will.

He'd seen her consternation, for he relaxed his gaze and allowed a smile to touch his lips.

'Don't be alarmed, Amelia,' he said, his tone soft. 'I am not about to hypnotise you. I will never do that – never take away another's will, although I know from past experience that I am capable of it. Now, my dear, as I have already explained to you, everything a conjuror does is trickery. There is no mystery about it. Even mind-reading is a trick, although I regret hypnotism is not. That is something not to be taken lightly. I am telling you all this because if you are willing to learn, I can teach secrets such as others could never believe are mere tricks. But first, you must learn to speak properly.'

'I know how to speak properly,' she said, immediately mimicking the tones of the elite as she described their mannerisms and the haughty way they conducted themselves.

He did not smile now. 'That is not you, that is someone else.'

Emma frowned. She thought she'd done it well. 'What d'you mean, someone else?'

'You are aping what you have heard. I want you to find your own voice, your own mannerisms, to move naturally as becomes you. You must be yourself, so please do not copy those you hear, the foolish, empty-headed creatures prattling on their way into a theatre or a party. The gift you will find will be your own.'

She sat very still as he moved closer to her. 'I have it in mind to take your advice and try my skills first on those in the street, to entertain them with magic instead of playing that thing.' He waved a dismissive hand at the instrument on the table, but his expression had grown wistful.

'However, after all this time I will require an inordinate amount of practice, months perhaps, for my fingers to again become supple enough to manipulate the simplest moves.'

He made small rippling movements with fingers that she'd never truly noticed before as being amazingly slim for a person of his build. They appeared as dainty as any woman's, yet somehow possessed power.

'I cannot do it alone, however,' he continued, his voice a monotone. 'This is a huge step for me, you understand. I had vowed never to go back to it. Now, thanks to you and your charming presence, I have decided it is time to put behind me all that has happened in the past.'

He paused, giving her a long, searching look. 'But to do this, I shall need the support of someone I can trust. You, Amelia. I would like you to be my assistant. I would never contemplate taking on someone with whom I am not familiar for such an intense profession. Martin, of course, knows my work implicitly, but I cannot bring myself to consider him, even though as time has gone on I've often wondered, was I mistaken about him and my ...' He broke off and began again. 'With you I'd have no qualms.'

'But I don't know nothing about conjuring.'

'I will teach you.' His lips broke into an indulgent smile. 'And the phrase is, "I don't know anything", or "I know nothing". You understand?'

She nodded obediently, but it didn't matter. Her heart was pounding with excitement. To be with him, entertaining in the street; if he was as good as Martin said he was, who knows, she could end up on a proper stage with him, in a proper theatre, she who'd stood outside so many, wishing she were one of those elegant ladies alighting from a carriage on the arm of an escort in opera hat and cape, white gloves and silver-topped cane.

If this man succeeded, she'd certainly benefit, far better than selling flowers and being looked down on by toffs. Yet though every fibre of her cried out, yes please, it needed thinking about. It was all too good to be true.

Then there was her mother. And Ben. She knew how they'd receive it. And if it all came to nothing, she'd be on the receiving end, looking a fool; worse still, having reaped their anger all for nothing, find her every move watched, never trusted again, her freedom curtailed. No, it wasn't worth it.

'Mr Barrington, I've got ter go. Me mum'll be wondering where I am.' Her attempt at fine vocabulary all went in her confusion, but if it jarred on him, he made no sign.

'Will you think about what I have said?'

No, it was too good to be true. She was just dreaming, and so was he. 'You'd have to practise too much,' she said as an excuse. 'I don't think you'd ever make it work, not after all this time.'

Why had she said that, she who wanted so much to get out of this deprivation all around her?

Grabbing up her tray, she wrenched open the door to the alley and fled as fast as boots and skirts allowed, one hand holding her straw boater down on her head. Unaware of the looks her flight brought from passers-by and even children playing in the street, she didn't stop until she reached home all breathless, and it wasn't just from running. What if all he'd said did come true? What a wonderful life could be lying in store for her.

Chapter Nine

Why was it taking so long? Mr Barrington had warned that it could be some while before he felt ready. But nine weeks? It was already June and Emma could feel her patience beginning to wear thin. All those expectations of something exciting happening were melting away, and here she was, still selling Mum's paper flowers.

Just talk. He hadn't meant a word of it. Or perhaps he had, dreaming like her. And that's all it had been. To have something like that dangled before her eyes and then to have it dissipate into thin air, made it all the more galling. Yet he continued to keep her on tenterhooks, dangling on a piece of string.

'Come here on the Wednesday of each week,' he'd said imperiously in April. 'Without fail. But no more than that, for I shall be working and not wish to be disturbed. I shall inform you how I am progressing.'

She like a fool had done as he'd asked, glancing over her shoulder in case Ben, beginning to wonder about these regular outings, decided to follow her. Ben seemed to have forgotten those earlier intentions of his, for which she was grateful, but she had no wish to awaken his curiosity, which hopefully she wouldn't, because she was usually back home inside of ten minutes at the most.

It was an odd situation. She sometimes wondered why she bothered when all that Barrington ever did was to open his door to her knock, never letting her in, but telling her that he was not ready yet, that he'd see her next week, and then close the door in her face. Nine weeks of this and she was getting thoroughly fed up and frustrated. Yet somehow, she felt unable to not go, ever on alert that on one of those visits he might invite her in and there it would all be, his conjuring tricks laid out before her, he in his magician's clothing, saying he was ready to teach her how to be his assistant.

At the end of the second week of June, Theodore knew this was the time he had been waiting for. He had known it for the past fortnight as his fingers began to go through their manipulations no longer with need for him to think about it, every movement having now become instinctive. But he'd had to be certain. And now he was.

There were two more days of practice until Amelia knocked once more on his door. Never again would she need to keep rigidly to that command. On Wednesday he waited. And there was her knock. Drawing in a deep breath, he stiffened his back, drew up his shoulders until his full six feet one inch of controlled muscle was reached. Then he went slowly to open the door to her.

Emma found herself brought into the room. It was the most bizarre of any invitation she could have imagined. He hadn't spoken, hadn't held out a hand for her, not

even any movement of the head, but the faintest alteration of expression in those penetrating blue eyes, and
she just knew she was being asked to enter.

The evening June sunshine seemed to leap about the
room as he spoke in a low voice. 'Watch,' he said.

The entire bed was covered with a gleaming red cloth,
spangled with quarter moons and shooting stars, and it
was these that caught the sunlight slanting through the
tiny window to throw glints on to the walls.

Barrington reached out with one hand, no other part of his
body appearing to move, and whipped off the scarlet cover.

There, on a dark, polished wooden board laid across
the bed, were packs of cards, sets of small containers,
square and round, a mound of brightly coloured silk handkerchiefs, an array of red and white balls and coloured
wooden cups, and so much more that Emma's amazed
gaze could not entirely take it all in.

'There's such a lot,' was all she could say.

'And more,' he said, his tone low and even, as if he
were already performing. 'But this will do to start with.'

'What am I suppose ter do?' It was a little alarming,
seeing all this. To think that all the while he'd played his
hurdy-gurdy, these had been sitting here in boxes. There
was no sign of the hurdy-gurdy. On the table where it had
once resided there was now a large leather Gladstone bag.
She would have liked to ask what he'd done with it but her
eyes were too taken by the wonders laid out before her.

'Simple tricks,' he said quietly. 'Come here tomorrow
evening when I will begin showing you what I require
of you.'

*

Emma walked back home past The Flying Swan, her mind in a daze. She hardly glanced at the groups of customers lounging outside the pub, taking advantage of the warm evening air after a hot, sunny day. The men with their collarless shirt necks open, caps on the back of their heads, jackets off to reveal well-worn, unbuttoned waistcoats, were enjoying their pints and ignoring the stinks a hot day in London could raise.

Women too, idled over a much needed drink, even though the beer would be lukewarm, chatting with each other with one eye on their kids, who raced about, ragged but eager, causing Emma to sidestep once as she passed so as to avoid a collision.

A barrel organ played where once the hurdy-gurdy man had stood. No one seemed to miss his presence as Emma passed and the children cavorted around the organ player as much as they had once cavorted around the other.

Those housewives of Mitre Street and Church Row, unable to afford a beer, had come to sit out of doors to gossip and find a bit of fresh air between the puffs of smoke from trains trundling past on the Blackwall railway above them. It was an hour or two to be enjoyed, but Emma's mind was more full of excited anticipation, fear and indecision.

Now it looked like happening, was she prepared? Did she want this? What was expected of her? He hadn't explained anything, had just said be there tomorrow. Maybe she would know more then. But she who could stand in a busy street trying to tempt people with her tiny bunches of paper flowers, who without a qualm put up with being ignored or having her offered wares rudely thrust aside, or being regarded with pity while only few stopped to buy; she who could put up with that, now trembled in her boots at being in the critical eye of the public in helping an entertainer.

Maud Beech's eyes lit up as they always did when presented with the empty tray. 'Yer got rid of 'em all then.'

'It's been such a lovely day,' Emma said, dropping the tray behind the door. 'I could of sold twice as many.'

'Looks like I'll 'ave ter start making a few more than usual then.'

Maud picked up a fork and turned the bit of meat she was cooking on a flat pan on the trivet before the fire. On top of the low flames, potatoes and carrots simmered in a saucepan. Here in this place summer brought as many problems as did winter. In cold weather a fire did at least warm the room as well as cook food but in summer it still had to be lit for cooking, turning the place into an oven. With cheap bits of meat needing to be cooked slowly to be anywhere near tender, there was no escaping the heat.

She'd opened the sash window as far as it would go, six inches, until the sash cord had stuck as it always did, and had sat near it as often as she could, trying to avail herself of what small draught came through, fanning herself with her apron or the cloth she used to handle the hot meat tray.

She envied those whose doors opened on to the street, allowing them to take out a chair and sit outside for a breath of air. From her window she could see neighbour chatting to neighbour while they peeled potatoes or shelled peas. Earlier this afternoon as the room became oppressive from the sunshine pouring through her window, even before she had lit the fire to cook, she'd gone downstairs to stand awhile by the open front door. The woman living in the room underneath her, Mrs Lovell, had joined her.

She was fat, slovenly, cuddling her little boy of some seven or eight months; her three-year-old daughter had died two months ago from some illness or other. She had been a weak child, never clean, suffering from impetigo and frequent bouts of vomiting. Maud had never asked what she'd died of and Mrs Lovell didn't seem to know, merely saying that the doctor who came had said it was a stomach thing, but she'd gone to the funeral, the child being put into a parish grave without a headstone, and the coffin a wooden box borne on a parish barrow. She'd made Mrs Lovell a little wreath of paper flowers, the best she could do for her. The trouble was that since then she couldn't move without Mrs Lovell trying to make up for her help by going out of her way to start up a conversation.

Maud had been glad to come back indoors, preferring to be stifled by heat rather than conversation. Besides that, the woman smelled of something unpleasant, a body odour that wasn't all to do with being unwashed. Her baby, a little boy whose name was George, smelled equally odd. How people ever paid her to take in washing for them was beyond Maud.

'I'd best get a few more bunches of flowers done after supper ready for yer to take out termorrer,' she said to Emma as she turned the sizzling bit of meat yet again. Ben had the lion's share, but even the tiniest portion for her and Emma made all the difference to a meal of vegetables.

'One thing about these light evenings,' she went on, 'yer can get a lot more done and yer don't 'ave ter strain yer eyes. I can sit by the window an' do 'em. Maybe you can 'elp me, luv.'

She didn't see her daughter's eyes widen uneasily at her reference to making a lot more flowers. In Emma's mind was the question of how was she going to combine selling flowers with helping Theodore Barrington.

'Up the West End, was yer?' Maud queried as Emma sat down on Ben's sofa.

Ben was at work, and Maud thanked the Lord for that. There was money coming in, hence decent meals for once, the rent paid on time, and even a bit over so Emma could take a bus or a tube all the way to the West End and back without having to walk part of it. Life was a lot easier lately.

'I only went as far as the Bank,' said Emma, taking off her straw boater. 'I stood outside the tube station and sold the lot.'

She said it with some pride, but Maud stopped probing the potatoes in their pot for softness to glare at her. 'Yer mean yer paid a full tuppence an' only went as far as the Bank? Gawd blimey, Em, yer can go all the way ter Shepherd's Bush fer that. It's why they call it the Tuppenny Tube.'

'I sold 'em all, didn't I?' came an exasperated sigh. 'Besides, it was stuffy and I needed to be up in the open air. They were gone in no time.'

Emma got up from the sofa and put the tin of coins on the table. Maud eyed them without as much satisfaction as she might have. 'Yer could of come 'ome and I could of given yer another lot.'

She saw the look of rebellion on Emma's face and quickly checked herself, turning back to lift the potatoes off the fire. No doubt Emma had spent the rest of her time looking round the shops. She was entitled to a bit of life. She worked hard, in all weathers, and who could begrudge her time to herself? She might even find herself a nice young lad. Though once a young man came along, would she still be willing to go out selling? And what when she finally got married? Maud only hoped that when that day came, the young man of Emma's choice would be in work and with prospects. She didn't want her suffering the life that had been forced on her.

On Thursday evening, weary from having worked hard to sell all the extra flowers Mum had made, confident that she could get rid of them too after having done so well previously, Emma stood in Theodore Barrington's room. He had on an evening suit, somewhat musty from storage, but his fair beard was now thick, and trimmed short and neat. It became him and did indeed give him the appearance of King Edward except that he was tall and upright, and the King was old with receding hair, and, she'd been told, much shorter.

'Tea?' Barrington enquired casually as he closed the door behind her.

Without waiting for her to reply, he began spooning a few leaves from a bag into the only mug he appeared to possess, pouring hot water from the kettle that had already been heated awaiting her arrival. He ladled in a single spoonful of condensed milk, stirring it for her before handing it over.

'There is no sugar, but the condensed milk is sweet.' His deep voice filled the empty room.

'Are you having some?' she asked, resorting to what she called her posh voice, taking it that this was what he would require of her.

He gave a sharp shake of his head, seeming not to have noticed her efforts, and taking down a small tumbler and a small bottle, quarter-full of amber liquid, from a shelf over the bed. 'I shall have this.'

With slow deliberation he poured a little of what she guessed was cheap whisky into the tumbler and as slowly, carefully, drained it as he stood. Putting bottle and glass back on to the shelf, he turned back to her.

'Now. Sit down, Amelia,' he said. 'Drink your tea, and watch.'

All the paraphernalia she'd seen yesterday was back in the boxes, and from one of them he brought out a pack of cards still in its wrapping. This he removed, and placing the pack on the table, swiftly spread the cards into two fans, and gathering them up, cut the deck and expertly riffled it.

'This illusion is performed before a large audience in a darkened theatre, five or six people each invited to draw a card, look at it and replace it back into the pack before my assistant passes on to the next person many rows and several seats away from the first. Now, you will take a card, look at it and place it face down in any part of the pack you wish. Do not let me see the card.'

Emma did as instructed and saw him hold the pack tightly, at the same time gazing deeply into her eyes as though seeing into her mind. 'You chose the ten of diamonds,' he announced.

Emma gasped. 'How did yer know?'

He remained gazing at her while she itched to know. If she were to be his assistant, would she be allowed into the secret? She noticed a frown on his brow and knew immediately what she had said.

'You,' she corrected and saw the brow slowly clear. 'How did you know?' she repeated.

'You have no idea at all?' he countered whimsically. 'Think.'

Emma thought, at a complete loss and shook her head.

'You cannot guess? Not at all?'

'No. Ain't you – I mean, aren't you going to tell me then?'

For reply he placed the whole pack, face up, into her hands. 'Look at them,' he commanded. Emma spread the cards a little tentatively and gave another gasp, this time one of accusation. Every card was a ten of diamonds, with the exception of the bottom one, which was two of clubs.

'It was just a trick!' she exclaimed, laughing at being duped.

'Of course it is a trick. But before a large audience and in a darkened theatre, who is going to know what the other saw?'

He did not laugh with her. To him, his career was no laughing matter. 'I merely ask those who take a card and then replace it at my assistant's bidding, to stand up.'

This time the smallest semblance of a smile touched Barrington's lips.

'As the lights come up I hold the pack aloft, tap it several times, stare at each person in turn and then announce the name of the card.'

'But they've all got the same card,' Emma cried. 'They'd know.'

'Who is going to consult with complete strangers, separated by several dozen seats from each other? I've already swapped the pack without their knowing. My tapping and staring and holding the pack aloft is called misdirection. In other words, I am taking an audience's attention from what I am really doing. By the time they recover themselves, I am on to another piece of magic. A simple pretence of mind-reading.'

Emma was stunned, longing to be part of this marvel. But he was asking her to watch again. Soon, cards, balls, kerchiefs, wands, were disappearing and reappearing before her eyes and from less than two feet away, all with such flourish that she couldn't believe what she saw. His fingers flew and rippled so fast that her eyes could not even follow, leaving her overawed.

'You're not going to tell me how you did that, are you?' she queried at one stage, to have him reply, 'No,' as he continued with hardly a pause.

The demonstrations coming to an end, he gazed intently at her. 'One day I shall thrust swords through your body, cause you to rise into the air with no sign of support, sever your head from your shoulders, cause you to vanish in flames and reappear in the wings. I shall present you to your audience, and you will smile to show yourself to be utterly unscathed.'

He touched her shoulder, the hand resting there. 'I will dress you in gowns such as you have never seen.

We will dine in the finest restaurants in the company of polite society and I will introduce you to the famous, the celebrated, the distinguished.' He was casting pearls before her radiant gaze.

'Oh, yes!' she whispered, her heart thumping like a steam engine. 'I can't 'ardly wait.' She broke off, meeting his sudden frown. 'Hardly,' she rectified hastily, then hurried on, this time trying hard to guard her speech. 'I just never knew you was ...'

'Were.'

'Were,' she said, sobering. '*Were* as clever as all that.'

Theodore allowed a smile. More at the effect his trifling demonstration of prestidigitation had had on her than being amused by her graceless effort to speak her tongue properly. Yet those eager attempts drew out something in his better self.

'You will do well, I can see that,' he said, his arm still resting on her shoulder. 'But you must not allow your excitement to take hold of you too soon, my dear. First I need to experiment on a street audience. Nothing too complicated to begin with. My movements are not yet as nimble as they should be.'

He stopped her as she made to protest. Obviously she had been in awe. 'Not to my satisfaction. I shall continue to practise, and you, my dear, must practise speaking in a manner to match your new life. As for myself, I admit I have some doubts as to whether I can do this after so long away.'

'I'll be with you though, won't I?' she said.

Her sincerity touched something within him and he drew her to him.

'My dear Amelia!' he whispered. 'You have given me hope where once I had none. Before meeting you,

I had fallen to such depths that I could see nothing but wretchedness ahead of me. That day we collided in the fog was the day I began to regain a purpose in life, and even now you give me reason to climb back to where I once was.' He knew it was drama, but he meant it.

His arms about her, he breathed in the natural perfume of her hair, finding it surprisingly pleasant. Pleasant too, the way she remained still.

Too surprised to extricate herself from this uncharacteristic embrace, she caught the taint of the whisky, the faint fragrance of tobacco and soap. Soap – this hovel with nowhere to wash properly; he probably went regularly to the public bath-house. Someone once used to cleanliness and order would surely seek cleanliness despite all else.

Even as he released her almost immediately with a muttered, 'Thank you for your trust, my dear,' her mind was made up. Her life would soon be changed, thanks to him, and there seemed no need at all for confirmation.

Ben slouched towards The Flying Swan. He hadn't been to that pub for ages even though it was his local. Afterwards he'd spend the rest of his Saturday night somewhere brighter.

He had a mauve-coloured, swollen area around his left eye, a cut and swollen lip and his solar plexus ached abominably, but he had money in his pocket. True, he hadn't correctly sized up the true weight of his opponent, and only climbing into the ring had he seen the error too late as the man dropped the robe he'd been wearing.

A real heavyweight, fourteen stone at least, a giant around the girth. Ben was around twelve even though he'd been leaner and younger and matched the man for height. Having to punch above his weight had taken it out of him, lasting nine rounds, by which time he'd been well tired, but so had his opponent. Yes, he'd taken a proper battering, but proving lighter on his feet and carrying the longer punch, he'd finally floored his man and come away with a purse of several quid. He intended to spend it all. The last time he'd been generous, Mum hadn't blinked an eye in gratitude, so this time it was all his. He'd earned it. Painfully.

Mum hadn't been pleased to see the state he was in. She thought he'd lost and he'd let her think that, incurring some of her anger, but what did it matter? He might drop a couple of bob on her table later, if there was any left. It all depended on how generous he felt or how broke he ended.

After a drink in The Flying Swan he'd look for a few of his mates in Commercial Road. Lively after dark, there were open-fronted shops with automatic sideshows, penny slot machines to play games on, others giving a peep into a domestic scene of girls undressing enough to get excited over; a penny in an automatic piano gave out lively popular tunes. There were sideshows and shooting galleries, and maybe in some alley they'd get in on a card game or pitch and toss, confident of the lookout on the corner, thumbs casually hooked in his belt, keeping an eye out for any copper nosing around. Tonight he felt lucky, might even make a killing.

Before finally going home he'd lounge around some bright and busy coffee stall past which girls would stroll, arm in arm. He'd gauge them like a crow spotting carrion, their way of looking at a bloke to show they were willing for a bit of fun. Some were obviously professional, demanding payment, but others were just silly little tarts ready to fall for any line. He was still seeing Clara on and off. After all these months going out with him from time to time, she was beginning to take it that they were courting. He'd have to put her right on that score, but she did come in handy when need be – very pretty and what was more, very willing. She obviously felt that he might not bother with her if she didn't give him what he wanted. She was small too. Small frames melted easily into a bloke's arms. It made him feel masterful.

He never saw her on Saturdays, preferring to be with his mates, and certainly never on Sunday, even though she'd asked. Sundays were for walking out with your intended on your arm and that would be just asking to commit himself. Clara was all right now and again, but for the rest of his life? He didn't think so. Not yet, anyway.

Halfway along Mitre Street he noticed two people passing the end of the turning into Three Colts Street, going towards the main road. The man was carrying a large Gladstone bag while the girl had a smaller one.

It was the girl who held his gaze. It was getting dark and he only had a glimpse of her but he was sure it was Emma. What was she doing with a man? It was a man – a lad would be lighter on his feet, even if with the hunched shoulders common to the thin, East End lad. This man held himself upright, his bearing full of confidence, his build definitely that of a man.

The need for a drink forgotten, Ben sprinted the short distance to the end of the street. If it was Em, he'd yank her back home as sure as God had made little apples. He'd teach a girl of hardly sixteen to keep company with strange men! In his mind were those girls he'd paid a tanner or two for a bit of relief up some alley. Was she at that lark too? His own sister? If she was, he'd give her a right wallop when he got her home.

On the corner of the main road there was a beer shop, liquor mainly served through a hatch. Racing up to it, he surveyed a sprinkling of drinkers outside on the pavement in the hope of apprehending those two, but there was no sign of them.

Sprinting here after what he'd been through earlier that evening made the beer shop appealing. He was aware of a desperate thirst, and maybe it hadn't been Em, but someone like her. He should have known, his sister wasn't that sort of girl.

Lounging against the brick wall of the beer shop with his pint and an evening paper bought from a newsboy still shouting his lungs out on the corner, he sipped his beer and read in complete contentment now. If the glow from the beer shop window revealed stark signs on his face of a fight, making those around him sidle away, he couldn't have cared less. He'd done his duty by his sister, realised it couldn't have been her, but at least he was keeping an eye on her, he told himself.

Chapter Ten

With her tray of unsold flowers dangling from its string around her neck, Emma stood a little way off from Theo – he had asked her to call him that – watching him display his conjuring skills to the queue waiting patiently to be allowed into the Apollo Music Hall in Bethnal Green.

'I merely require you to stand by and watch while you sell your own wares,' he'd instructed. 'That way you will learn and keep your mother appeased at one and the same time.'

Other than the few who bought a posy off her, her presence went unheeded, no one with any notion of a connection between her and him, and from her spot she could marvel how he made the playing cards, coins and kerchiefs disappear and reappear not three feet from the onlookers.

'I've chosen the Apollo to make my debut,' he'd said as he hailed a hackney cab in the Commercial Road. 'Nothing too ambitious to begin with.'

She had been surprised at him paying out good money for a cab. 'Can you afford it?' she'd asked and saw him smile.

'I've no intention of taking an omnibus attired as I am,' he said. In cape, opera hat and white gloves, he'd seemed full of confidence, although he must have felt some nervousness about this first performance after so long away from it. She knew she did, even if she was only standing by doing what she had always done while he captured the wonder of those watching.

It was a strange evening. Returning home, he saw her to her street like a gentleman, and like a gentleman came no further to put her at any disadvantage. He stayed until she was safely at her own door before leaving, in her hand five silver sixpences, half a crown in all, plus her own takings.

It still felt wrong accepting his money, she had done so little. 'This is your share,' he said severely. 'In time you will be required to do a good deal more than just stand watching, so do not be too eager with your scruples.'

He'd mentioned returning to the same pitch the following week, but with different tricks. 'One must not use the same routine too often, even though the queues change. They must always be kept guessing, never given too long to think about one trick before another is there before their eyes.'

As they parted, he'd said softly, 'I couldn't have done this without you, my dear. You gave me strength. I think it went well.'

'But I didn't do nothing,' she burst out.

There came the familiar disapproving frown. 'That is ungrammatical, Amelia, a double negative.' She had no idea what double negative was, but he'd taken her by the shoulders to stare deep into her eyes and explained, putting her right. 'If you did nothing, then that is what you say. If you *didn't do nothing,* it means you have done *something.* Think about it, Amelia.'

Left temporarily confused, she found herself sent on her way, vowing to please him and try harder to speak as he wished her to, to practise night and day if need be. The half-crown tightly clutched, she began practising immediately. *Hadn't done nothing* – no, *had done nothing.* There, she had mastered that one already! She would remember that for next time.

Pleased with herself, she let herself in and hurried up the stairs, the money comfortingly warm in her grasp. Quickly she put it in her skirt pocket before opening the door. Mum mustn't know. She'd ask questions and make life awkward. She'd tuck it away for the time being. When she had accrued more that would be the time to present Mum with it, and it would make awkward explanations about Theodore that much easier. Excitement gripped her.

It came to her that this was in fact her wages although he'd said nothing beforehand about that. But if she was to be paid, then she could look forward to having more money than she'd ever owned in her life. Who wouldn't be excited?

There was only one thing wrong – he'd spoken of playing the queues on both Friday and Saturday night. Friday was awkward – according to Mum's ritual, an evening for staying in and washing hair. Tight for money or not, she had maintained from the first that cleanliness was far more important than trying to make a living. 'We have our pride,' she'd say. 'We might live in squalid parts,' she'd say, 'but that don't mean we should let ourselves go filthy. I keep up me standards as best I can, and we wash our 'air regular as we've always done even if we can't always afford the public baths. Yer a self-respecting gel and I ain't seein' yer with dirty 'air.'

That meant a basin filled from laboriously heated pans over the fire, her dripping, waist-length auburn hair having to be rubbed for an hour or more until bone-dry, but never, it seemed, dry enough for her to dare go out into the night air and catch her death. Mum would wash hers for her, rinsing it from an old white jug of plain water, then with vinegar, if she had any, to bring out the natural auburn highlights. She in turn would do Mum's, the business of drying long hair taking up the whole evening.

She was going to have to tell Theo about Friday. As he requested, she went to see him on the Wednesday. 'I wish to make clear what will be required of you as time goes on,' he said, but her main purpose was to clear up this Friday business. After all, she'd hardly be needed, merely standing watching. He had proved he could do well enough without her for the time being, and of course, she wouldn't expect to get paid, not being there.

She had been wrong, and certainly hadn't anticipated the wrath her innocent words evoked, his voice rising, his face close to hers.

'Do you see this as some sort of game?' he thundered at her. 'I shall require you to be here whenever I need you. That was the agreement, I believe.' It was as if he owned her, and she wished she'd insisted on giving him back his money. She lifted her chin defiantly.

'I know what it looks like, but I ain't exactly promised to …'

'Ain't?' His roar made her jump. 'You know very well there is no such word.'

Emma drew in an angry breath. 'I don't care! You don't own me. I don't have to do what you say. So don't think you can tell me what I can do and what I can't.' She paused as his expression softened, the tight lips relaxing.

'You are right, my dear,' he said, lowering his tone. 'I didn't stop to think. You have a separate life, a duty to your family. I cannot force you.'

But she still felt defiant. 'I've got me mother to think of. If I don't go out selling what she works so hard at making, we won't get no money …'

She heard herself, stopped and began again. 'Or we won't get any money,' she corrected herself.

When Theo replied, he seemed to be a different person. 'If you stay with me,' he said quietly, 'there is no limit to what we can do. But you must be willing to work.'

'And Friday?' she reminded. 'I can't tell people about you yet. It may sound silly but I've got to be careful, and if I start talking about Fridays …'

He nodded slowly. 'We shall forget Friday. I made enough to keep me, modestly, until next Saturday, but I must keep going.'

'I know,' she said, contrite, until she remembered that he wasn't destitute, he did have resources, somewhere. But she didn't allude to it.

He became unexpectedly gentle. 'Come and sit here,' he said, drawing his one chair towards him and sitting himself on the edge of his bed. 'I shall explain what I want you to do from now on.'

It seemed quite normal to be sitting so close as he explained what her role would be from now on. 'For the time being,' he said. 'Once we make the theatre you will truly be helping me with *all* my illusions, as my assistant.'

'Do not disappoint me, Amelia,' he said, standing up as she finally made to leave after an exhilarating hour hearing what would be expected of her in the weeks to come. 'Never, *ever,* let me down, my dear.'

The caution sounded ominous, almost like a threat, and in the act of putting on her hat and jacket she turned to look at him. His expression had not altered but the tone had expressed all the disappointments that had come his way, the striving to reach what he'd finally attained, the setbacks, poor venues, unappreciative audiences, a wife who he felt had let him down, her death. But she felt that something more than that was buried deep, something she knew nothing about, and she remembered the vague warnings from Martin Page with a small shudder rippling through her.

Seconds later Theo touched her arm, leaning towards her to drop a light kiss on her cheek. The fair, now well-groomed beard felt surprisingly soft against her skin.

'I know I shall be able to trust you, Amelia,' he whispered, his words like those of a lover yet containing a demand for loyalty.

There was so much to learn – how to hand things to him as required, or take them from him, and do it beautifully; how to move among an audience, their eyes following and failing to see what he was doing – misdirection; how to deposit an object in a pocket without the owner being aware of it. This she found the hardest to do, and that was when she discovered Theo's strange, innate temper, his regard for her evidently counting for nothing as she fumbled something that seemed to him to be simple enough. He did not rant so much as contain displeasure with such control that his whole expression would change – his eyes narrow, their blue more intense, his voice deepening like the ominous, rumble of distant thunder, his mouth tightening without thinning, until she wanted only to run from the place and never come back.

'I'm doing my best!' she'd yell in despair.

'All I am asking of you is to hand me what I require,' would come the controlled reply. 'Doing that one simple thing without it resembling the movements of a carthorse!'

Moments later, on the verge of walking out, he'd apologise – he understood it was difficult for her, new to the business, he'd go more gently with her in future. She'd forgive him – until the next time and the whole process repeated. She knew she should walk away, yet there was ever the promised lure of the fame, the money and the fine clothes; it was hard to combat.

Every Saturday, with early autumn evenings closing in, Theo played the music hall queues, she was no longer required to stand by and watch, although in a way she still did. Prior to his arrival she'd take up a position outside the hall with her tray of paper flowers. He'd stroll up moments later and with a flourish open the large bag he carried and extract a folding table, don his opera hat and begin to set up the cups and ball trick. Everyone knew this game, as the three manipulated cups came to rest, betting a few pence on which one the ball was under. But this was different.

The first two hopefuls, their wives or sweethearts trying to dissuade them from temptation, would be allowed to win, then without warning, the ball would vanish to reveal a coloured handkerchief in its place, rolled into a tiny ball. With a flourish, he'd throw the ball of material into the air and from it would waft half a dozen variously coloured silks to the gasp of those in the queue.

There would begin half an hour of sheer magic – illusions so clever yet, Emma knew, they were so simple: the rabbit from the hat – a stuffed rabbit for street work – the disappearing salt, the glass of water poured into his opera hat yet never seeming to be empty and the hat not even damp – and so much else; money being tossed into the bag at the foot of the table until it was time for his audience to go in to see the entertainment they'd paid for.

The dexterity of his fingers, his skill at sleight of hand evoked even Emma's admiration as by October she realised just how much she had learned. When he'd told her she would take part in some of his illusions, she'd hardly been able to disguise her apprehension. Her admission had touched him. He told her there was no need to be afraid, speaking of audiences as a gullible lot whom he could make fools of every time. Although it didn't make her feel easier, she couldn't have backed out to save her life.

Her mother still had no idea that she was now part of his act as she stood selling her flowers a yard or two from where Theo was, contented that she sold the whole stock despite the deteriorating weather. Her job now was to gaze at him in wonder as he called for a volunteer from among the crowd to help with a particular trick. Tonight, before any could step forward, he glanced in her direction, and seeming to have an idea, called to her in his penetrating voice, and, with a compulsive gesture of his arm, to come over.

As rehearsed, Emma hesitated before moving shyly towards him as though bewildered by his summons. She felt his hand touch hers.

'You look quite lost there, my dear,' he said, his booming voice carrying over the heads of a growing crowd of the curious. 'I wonder, my child, how would you like to assist me in my work and put a little zest into your *obviously* dull little life?'

This brought sniggers from those watching. Emma even managed to hang her head as if with embarrassment, but her blushes were real enough, this first time as his secret accomplice, seen as a figure of fun if not pity. But one day these people would grin on the other side of their faces. She had a fleeting vision of herself a year from now, on a glittering stage, beautifully dressed, all eyes on her in wonder instead of mockery. The vision gave her heart to look up at Theo, her gaze trusting, that too not completely faked.

Taking her tray from her, he placed it on the pavement. It was an effort to control her rapid breathing. It was one thing rehearsing in the privacy of his room, quite another to stand in front of this sea of faces. She was more accustomed to being ignored as she sold her flowers, but no one would ignore her this evening. There wasn't a single nerve in her body that didn't quiver. What if some clumsiness revealed one of his tricks to them?

Theodore was explaining to them. 'Here I have an ordinary pack of cards,' he began. 'Whoever wishes can come and examine them.'

Several men stepped forward, their blunt faces eager yet suspicious. They found the pack all he said it was. He even took the arm of one man to make sure he actually touched the pack to prove to himself that they were, normal, everyday playing cards. Emma had to tighten her lips so as not to smile at this simple yet skilful move.

'Now, watch closely,' instructed Theo as the men moved back to the edge of the crowd. With a flourish he cut the pack, the movement followed by dozens of pairs of watchful eyes.

Placing one half on the table, he cut again, that portion also placed on the table, then twice more until all that was left were a bare half-dozen cards.

With these, his other hand motioning broadly to alert everyone as to what he was about to do, he executed a throwing movement so swift that the eye could not see where they had gone, but gone they were. A few spectators were even still gazing at the thin air into which they'd vanished.

'All gone,' Barrington announced in a deep and commanding tone. 'Ah, but see, my friends. Not all. What about this one?'

His hand made a plucking motion and to gasps from the crowd, a card appeared between his slim fingers as if from nowhere.

'And this one?' Another plucking movement, another card appeared. 'And this! And this!' As each new one appeared he threw it on to the table, continuing to pluck, faster and faster. Mesmerised by the speed, misdirected

137

by the continuing plucking motion that seemed to go on for ever, no one saw that the separated decks were no longer on the table, his free hand stacking these new cards as they appeared in his hand.

When all were retrieved, he held out the complete deck at arm's length for all to see. Eyes popped. Even if he'd had the whole pack up his sleeve, the fifty-two would have been hard to hang on to. It really was magic.

'Ah,' said Barrington as ragged applause rippled through the crowd. 'I need someone to make sure they are all here.'

Placing the deck on the small table, he fanned them a swift movement of his hand. Pointing to one of the men who'd earlier examined the deck, he said, 'Sir, might I ask you to check them?' Pleased at being picked out, the man stepped forward. 'Are you a card player, sir?' asked Barrington.

The man nodded. 'A bloody good one, mate!'

'Then you will soon know if this pack is incomplete.'

'On yer life, mate!' came the man's answer and deftly he collected all into their four separate suits. Suddenly he looked up, his eyes suspicious.

'The six of clubs ain't there, mate.'

Barrington's tone was incredulous. 'Are you sure?'

'As sure as I'm standin' in front of yer.'

For a moment Barrington appeared puzzled, then turning to Emma, who'd been standing mutely by, he said, 'Ah, young lady, now I shall need your help. I expect you were wondering why I asked for your assistance?'

Emma gave a small nod of her head, and, asked to dip her hand into the top pocket of the man's not too clean jacket, she gave a convincing gasp of surprise as she withdrew the missing card.

'Hold it aloft, my dear, for all to see.' Emma did as she was told, the card plucked from her by Theodore, who held it before the stunned man's face. 'Is this the missing card, sir?'

Dumbfounded, the man could only nod, then finding his voice, turned to the onlookers.

''E's right – it is the blooming six a'clubs what was missin'.'

To resounding applause, the man stepped back to converse in awe with the woman he was with. Barrington gave a flourishing bow and waved Emma away. 'You may go back to selling your flowers now, my dear, and thank you for your help.'

To her joy, as she retrieved her tray, several people stepped towards her and bought flowers, perhaps as souvenirs of what they had seen so close to their faces and no sign of trickery.

Others were dropping coins into the purple open-necked bag Theo had placed on the pavement in front of his little table. He acknowledged each with a small, dignified bow of his head as he put away the cards.

Two weeks later she was again standing a few feet from him with her tray, this time outside the Hippodrome in the busy West End. This time it was afternoon, broad daylight, a far cry from the humble, out-of-the-way Apollo Music Hall. Being fine weather, the Hippodrome would enjoy a full house for the matinée with circus acts as well as single performers. A considerable queue for the gods already lined a grubby side street off Leicester

Square, such queues inevitably tucked out of the sight of wealthier patrons.

Early arrivals had brought sandwiches in preparation for a long wait, even a folding stool or two to sit on. Those who came late were probably in for a fruitless wait, all seats filled before they got to the head of the queue and even standing room full.

Emma knew some of the type of acts the Hippodrome put on and as Theodore began setting up, she hissed to him in passing to take up her own pitch, 'So long as they've not got a magician on.'

'But they'll see me first,' Theodore whispered back with confidence.

She had to admire the flamboyance with which he began laying out his paraphernalia, with great flourish spreading the blue-checkered cloth corner-wise over the collapsible table as though that in itself were a trick, opening his bag and bringing out various items, holding each up for the 'audience' to see. Eyes were beginning to be turned by this arresting personage.

Emma took up her position as though she had nothing to do with him. Further along, a blind musician was treadling away at a portable piano-organ, his burly helper in ragged jacket and trousers, worn boots, grubby neck choker and stained cloth cap standing behind him. Towards the head of the queue she could see a man playing the spoons. A matinée queue, as she well knew, was the place to make a few pennies, provided there weren't too many street entertainers to take off the cream.

She cast a sideways glance at Barrington. He was ignoring her. They would do the trick with the card found in the pocket as they had done many times since

140

the Apollo. Then she would leave, no doubt rewarded by people noticing her enough to buy a paper flower to take home as a souvenir. No fear of her being seen as his associate. The rest of her flowers she'd sell elsewhere and meet him later for another show outside another theatre to another queue for the gods, this time an evening one. No fear of meeting the same audience.

The queue buzzing with chatter and mild vulgarity transferred its gaze from the blind musician to the posturing, self-assured figure in white gloves, opera hat and evening dress.

'Ladies and gentlemen, a well-known trick,' he was saying. 'As you know, many are fleeced of their money by this trick, but I am not asking anyone to put any money down at all as to where they think the ball is.'

He placed the ball under one cup, swirled all three around each other with deft movements, inviting several people to come and try their luck, adding, 'I will say that while I ask for none to place any money bet, I will give a penny to whoever finds the ball.'

There was an instant rush, forcing him to plead they behave soberly. Thus each in turn took their chance, Barrington revealing where the ball was and moving the cups about after each attempt.

Not one was successful, each man retiring in disappointment. Finally as the last disgruntled gambler moved away, Barrington lifted all the cups to show not a ball in sight. There now came a rumble of discontent. There had been no ball at all. They'd been diddled even though no one had laid down any money.

'I would not trick you,' Barrington said, interpreting the low murmur. 'Maybe a little magic has occurred.' He looked towards where Emma stood with her tray. 'My dear,' he called to her and as she looked uncertainly at him, added, 'Yes, you girl. May I prevail upon you to help me find this missing object?'

With a show of reluctance she came at his bidding, put her tray down by the table and stood with her shy, embarrassed smile while they all looked expectantly at her.

'Now, my dear, would you move among those who came up here to try their luck, and would you ask each one to feel in their trouser pockets?'

There was a buzz from everyone as Emma did as she was told. She glanced at Barrington. 'I never see who come up.'

He'd specifically told her not to speak nicely. 'That is reserved for the stage,' he'd said.

'No matter,' he said now. 'The first to try his luck was disappointed. He knows who he is. He will assist you, my child.'

And assist he did, as she was a young, pretty, shapely girl, smelling nicely of the lavender water Barrington had provided, her hazel eyes noticeably shy and apologetic; the man was glad to put her at ease, his masculine dominance secure. Feeling in his trouser pockets, unsure of what he was looking for, he gave a yell, his eyes widening as he brought out a red ball.

'It's 'ere! It was in me pocket!'

'Well done, sir!' Theo called to him. 'The young lady will bring it here so that I may examine it. Over here, my dear.' Taking it from her, he went on, 'This is indeed the one.'

A woman from the now substantial crowd, queuing forgotten for the moment, shouted, 'He must of pinched it!'

'Impossible, madam. But to prove my point, this young lady here will move among four other gentlemen at random. Go on, my dear, over there.'

He pointed her towards others in the queue. 'They did not come to this table. Would you be so kind as to go and ask one or two of those kind gentlemen to examine their pockets – four will be enough.'

This was the moment Emma had dreaded, though her move had been rehearsed during the week until perfected and Theo had been certain of feeling nothing as a ball was slipped into his pocket. Her heart racing, she did as she had been taught, praying not to be found out. In seconds, one of them, feeling in his pocket after she'd touched his arm before moving on, let out a coarse expletive. 'I got it! 'Ow in bleedin' 'ell did that get there?'

The other three were equally amazed, leaving Emma to retreat gratefully to pick up her tray.

Theo had one more thing to tempt appreciation from his audience as the queue began moving, the theatre door at last ready to admit them. He beckoned to the men who had unwittingly taken part in his illusion. He held up a coloured ball.

'Would those of you who found one of these in your pockets, would you all come here? It seems that by some magic or other you discovered where not one but several of these elusive balls disappeared to. Each of you is a winner and winners deserve a small prize – a whole penny in coloured tissue paper.'

A ripple of laughter ran through the queue and some appreciative applause. The winners took it all in good part as well as being as chuffed by an unearned penny as they would have been had they found it lying in the street. Theo's sprat to catch a mackerel had its effect, coins willingly tossed into the purple bag on the pavement as his audience slowly filed past. Even Emma, having gone back to her own pitch a little way down from him, found her flowers being readily bought, several remarking what a peach she was, and how brave she'd been to do what she had.

Theodore packed away his paraphernalia, folded his table and without a glance at her, walked off. As the queue dwindled, Emma too moved on down the now vacated side street into Leicester Square, making her way towards Haymarket, where she met Theo. They had something to eat before going on to the nearby Alhambra. Darkness falling, pickings from those waiting to go in to the second house of that theatre's revue were equally as good as they had been at the Hippodrome.

There was no fear of discovery by any in the previous audience, too busy wending their way home after the matinée.

Emma's success was twofold: her flowers all sold, and money in her pocket from helping Theo. Her little horde was mounting, and Mum still none the wiser. She told herself she wasn't being underhand. It wasn't as if she was squandering it, as Ben would have done. It was there to help if one day they should hit the depths of poverty. She told herself it was a life-saver. There was no wrong in that despite her being secretive about it.

One thing did bother her, though, as they came away to go home. 'I think I might have imagined it,' she remarked to Theo on his helping her into the four-wheeled cab. 'But I thought I saw someone watching us. Did you see anyone?'

She saw him smile. Theo had a nice smile when he cared to use it. 'I saw no one. Nor do I think it matters.'

But she had been so sure a couple of times of seeing someone lurking in the shadows not far from where Theo had been performing. He wouldn't have noticed but she'd had time while hovering to look around, and twice when she'd looked in a certain direction, a figure had flitted back into the shadows, the movement itself making it obvious someone was there. Only someone not wanting to be seen would act like that. So who was it? Or perhaps it had been just imagination.

With money in her pocket and the warm feeling of success that it brings, she shrugged off the slightly creepy feelings, and let her thoughts dream of the future. And what a future it could prove to be with Theo beside her.

Chapter Eleven

Barrington let himself into his lodgings after leaving Amelia, as he preferred to call her. Emma Beech was an ordinary girl from the East End. Amelia Beech, seventeen in three months, was an enchanting young woman of mystery, precisely as she should be for his purpose.

Things were going well for him, and for her. Soon he planned to be back in the spotlight. With Christmas virtually around the corner, he'd sent a telegram to that effect to his old theatrical agent, Jack Simmons, who had replied asking where the devil he had been and that all he had for him at this late stage in bookings was a fifteen-minute spot in some second-rate music hall. But it was a start. He'd begun small that first time and had climbed to the pinnacle of his career before the nightmare that had taken him out of the circuit altogether. He'd start again and reach that pinnacle even faster. He'd introduce his beautiful assistant, Amelia Beech, and have the audience sitting up in admiration in no time at all.

In a splendid gown he would choose for her – he planned to dress her in the finest costumes, the most alluring feathered hats, her hair beautifully styled in the latest fashions, her lovely face radiant with just a hint of stage make-up – she would stun them all, and he would be proud to show her off.

Theodore closed the door of the squalid room where he'd lived for nearly two years. Soon he'd be living again in luxury, and as Amelia began to attain a mature beauty, he'd propose to her and, young though she was, she was bound to leap at his offer of marriage. Money could do that. Their love would be tender, unlike the fiery traumas of his first marriage, for he was now older and wiser, more understanding and patient than he had once been. Being older, he felt oddly protective towards her, felt there would be a need to protect the young, innocent child in her for the rest of his life, even when she grew to mature womanhood.

But he must take things slowly. Nothing should be rushed. He would be kind and thoughtful, not an easy task, knowing his own shortcomings, and look upon her as a young and tender shoot. He would give that shoot time to blossom, fruit and ripen. He must curb this wave of love that persisted in flowing through him. He must give her time.

He should have trodden more carefully when he'd met Eleanor. He hadn't given himself time then to discover what an independent, spirited woman she'd been. Amelia too was spirited but in a quieter, more thoughtful way. She wasn't wilful, as Eleanor had been. With care and guidance she'd become more subdued to his wishes. He knew he was comparing his first marriage with what he hoped one day would be his second, but if it came about, it would be different.

They had met and married all in the space of six months, he with not a little desperation, being in his mid-thirties, a self-restrained man in fear of never finding himself a wife, he'd given himself no time to properly know her, her whims, her self-indulgence, her eye for the men and theirs for her. The fiery girl, a dancer when he'd met her, whose fire so enamoured him, had a mind of her own.

He'd still felt passion for her. It had probably been that which had led to jealousy, his eyes always watching for hers to stray. Making love was still full of passion, a flesh thing, but trust began slowly to crumble away, three years into marriage, when that first mad flush of passion had dulled, at least for her. He would not be caught again so easily.

Eleanor began to enjoy her social life with her old friends. While he drank brandy and smoked cigars with the high and mighty, she preferred champagne and the fashionable smoking of opium. Then into the last eighteen months of their marriage came Martin. He was eighteen and full of energy, with his laughing eyes and a carefree attitude; all she ever talked about was Martin. It was she who had persuaded him to team up with Martin as a second assistant to her; said it would invigorate the act. And so it did. But she was too invigorated and he was sure he knew why. Martin.

Still in love with her body, he hadn't wanted to lose her. Besides, it wouldn't have been good for his image. The tension made him drink more than was good for his act. Until that final evening in their dressing room when, feeling he had every right to lose his temper at her intention to go off to some party with Martin, she'd thrown the bottle of whisky at him, saying she wasn't going anywhere with some drunken sot, and had rushed from the theatre.

He couldn't have foreseen what had occurred. Only later did he begin to feel guilt that he didn't keep his head and reason with her instead of grabbing her arm and slapping her across the face.

One thing he knew, he'd never lose that temper with Amelia. She was too honest, vulnerable too, not hardened by the stage as Eleanor had been.

Emma was worried. Theo was talking about stepping up the number of evenings they were doing, playing to the queues at several different theatres on most days of the week from now on, evenings and matinées.

'Christmas is approaching,' he explained. 'People attend the theatre more often and they begin to feel more generous.'

Well, she knew that, from her own experience, but it would leave only the mornings for selling what Mum made.

Theo's temper reared itself, if only mildly, when she tried to explain.

'Dear God, girl!' he burst out. 'Get rid of the bloody stuff! In the damned gutter if you wish. Do I not give you money enough to match twice over what those ridiculous things make?'

She had to admit he did, even more if his takings were good. Even so, she did feel hurt at hearing her mother's hard work and skill being described as ridiculous. It was those ridiculous things that were her mother's only means of making a living; the silk work she still got from time to time when her employer thought fit to dole it out, which wasn't very often, brought in next to nothing – and then to have him sneer at her.

Theo hadn't seen it that way. 'If you are going to continue working for me,' he said, calming himself with an effort, 'it will be when I say.'

It came as a shock to realise that she was indeed working for him. Until now she had seen it as helping him, and he handing her a small gratuity at the end of it.

'Working for you?' she flared. 'Is that what I am to you, your worker? As if I was working in some factory?'

She wasn't having him intimidate her. He didn't own her. She could walk away whenever she pleased and he couldn't stop her. The thing was, she couldn't walk away, that money and the promise of wonderful things to come held her here. That thought sobered her.

'Mum will start wondering what I'm up to,' she said lamely.

'Tell her anything you please,' came the reply.

'I can't go on for ever lying about, well, what I'm up to.'

'Then *tell* her what you are ... up to.' The stress on those last words conveyed sarcasm, but Emma had an answer to that.

'She'll stop me from doing it.'

'Have you no will of your own?'

'Of course I have! But I've got some feeling for other people too. She'll be shocked when I tell her about you and me, and me only sixteen. She's bound to think I've been up to no good.'

He held her angry glare with his blue eyes now calm. 'Whether you lie or tell the truth is up to you, Amelia. But you either come with me or pull out altogether. It is no more complicated than that. Any complication will be with yourself – whether you want to be taken out of the gutter, be given fine clothes to wear, have yourself taken to move among genteel company, be the toast wherever you go, or prefer to stay as you are. For I am now resolved to aim for higher things and leave all *this* behind me.'

His arm swept out to encompass the filthy gutters, the dark buildings, the cracked pavements.

'I've decided to return to working on stage, and I want it to be with you beside me. Or are you content to stay here earning pennies? It is your decision. But I will not wait for you, Amelia.'

It was bluff, Emma was certain. But for her, he'd never have come this far. While Martin Page, who hadn't been seen since that evening he'd quietly left whilst she'd been talking to Theo, hadn't been able to persuade him, she had. Otherwise what had Theo been doing entertaining a theatre queue with magic instead of turning his miserable hurdy-gurdy? It was her persuasion that had got him started again.

But his resolution this evening had her worried. Hurrying home, she thought of all ways to tell Mum what had been going on. And really, it had been nothing to be ashamed of – a business alliance, nothing more.

Trouble was, Mum wouldn't see it that way, a middle-aged man consorting with a girl not yet seventeen. Nor could she go against Mum's decision though she'd do her best to argue, her ace being the money she'd saved from this secret alliance. She would go to its hiding place, so long as Ben wasn't there to see, and tip the lot out on to the table. Mum's eyes would pop. Then she'd tell her that this sort of money was this family's salvation. Without it Mum would be trapped here until the day she died. With it there'd be no need for her ever to work again. Nor would she ever have to worry about Ben. He could drink himself into the grave if he wished.

What Emma foresaw was a fortune just waiting in the wings for her to pick up. Surely Mum would see that and come round to her way of thinking.

'What yer mean, yer been 'elping some bloke do 'is magic?'

Emma knew immediately that it had been the wrong decision. So long as Mum had remained in ignorance, she could go on doing what she did. But the moment her mother forbade it, how could she go against her? And by the sound of Mum's tone, she was ready to forbid her. Now she was reaping the results of not having made a clean breast of it earlier. Her mother was looking shocked, and furious. Yet there was still a chance.

'Just a minute, Mum,' Emma broke in before she could get any steam up. 'Wait until you see what I've saved while I've been helping him.'

There was no need to revert to her old way of speaking now the truth was out. In good time she'd explain the reason for that too.

Hurrying into their bedroom, she bent down and fished under the gap beneath the flimsy chest of drawers that served them both, other clothes hung on pegs on the wall, and brought out an old and patched stocking of hers. Back in the other room she upended the stocking to pour a shining cascade of silver coins, threepenny pieces, sixpences, shillings, florins, even half-crowns, on to the table.

'I've not counted how much there is there, Mum, but there must be at least five or six pounds. I've saved every penny.'

She waited for her mother to register surprise, but the woman merely stood gazing down at it, silent.

'Well?' Emma prompted eagerly.

All this money, enough to feed them for weeks when things got tight, as they would come the freezing days of January and February. This surely would sway her.

Her mother's voice came quietly and very slowly. 'And what did yer 'ave ter do fer this?'

'What d'yer mean, what did I 'ave ter do for this?'

Her mother's gaze lifted itself to her face. 'I dare say only you'd know, of course.'

'Mum! If what you're thinking is right, then you're wrong. I've just been doing what I said I was doing, helping this man, this magician, with his tricks.'

'Hmm! Tricks, is it?'

'Illusions, the magic he does, I help him. People give him money, and he gives me a sort of wage out of it. And it's all here. And I can still sell me flowers ...'

She got no further. Mum's hand swept out and round, the palm catching her smartly on one cheek.

'Yer can go off an' 'elp 'im all yer like, miss, because I don't want yer selling me flowers for me. I can do it meself. An' I don't want yer money.'

She gave the coins a contemptuous shove with her hand. 'Yer can take it out of me sight. An' go off and live with this bloke yer've took up with. It's the one what Ben saw yer with, ain't it? That middle-aged bloke.'

As Emma gathered the coins into the stocking, she turned away and picked up the poker to prod the dying fire in a bout of furious energy. She still had her back to her as Emma, her cheek still smarting from the slap, came back from stashing away her well-meant hoard.

'Mum?' she ventured.

'Don't talk ter me! Ternight yer can sleep out 'ere, under the table. I'll get yer piller and a cover. I don't want yer in me bed.'

'But I ain't done nothing, Mum!'

'Who ain't done nothink?' Ben had come in unnoticed. 'What ain't yer done, Em?'

Before she could answer, her mother swung round on him. 'That man yer told me about, the one yer saw 'er with, the one yer said was twice 'er age, she's been going around with 'im be'ind me back.'

The poker was thrown down in the hearth with a dull crash.

'You knew what she was up to, and yer didn't even bother ter put a stop to it. Call yerself 'ead of the family? Well, *'ead of the family,* ain't yer supposed ter protect yer sister from men like that? Ain't yer supposed ter keep an eye on 'er? All you ever do is booze with yer mates. Look at yerself. Yer drunk now. You ain't no good ter man nor beast. Not ter me neither!'

'Don't bloody take it out on me!' Ben shouted, yanking off his cap and flinging it across the room in sudden rage. 'I can't be looking out for 'er every hour of the day. What did yer expect me ter do, drag 'er back 'ome by the scruff of 'er neck?'

Emma remembered the odd times she had glimpsed a figure hovering in the shadows. It had happened again tonight. As she turned towards it, the figure had moved hastily back into deep shadow as though not wanting to be seen. It had to be Ben, spying on her.

'I've not done anything wrong.' She wasn't going to say she'd seen him. What she needed was to justify the matter. 'It's someone I met ages ago. His name's Theodore Barrington and he suggested I'd be his assistant while he entertained theatre queues with magic tricks. He's a magician.'

She wanted to say more, but Mum's face was such a picture of anger and disbelief.

''Ow long's this been goin' on?'

'Since the beginning of summer,' she said, hating what lay behind her mother's insinuation. She hated Ben being here to hear this. Why did he have to come home now, poking his nose in?

'And you never said a word?'

'I didn't think you'd understand. All I've done is help him with his business. He's sort of employed me. There was no harm in it.'

'If there ain't no 'arm in it, then why did you 'ave ter keep it secret?'

'Because you'd have stopped me.' It was time to make a clean breast of things. Desperately she quickly related how she'd met Barrington, how she'd helped him regain confidence in himself; that he'd once been a famous magician on the stage, repeating his name to give it even more significance.

'Never heard of 'im!' The sneering remark from Ben was silenced with a look from Mum as Emma hurried on to say that he had in mind for her to be his assistant when he returned to doing theatre performances.

155

'And that money?' queried her mother.

'It's sort of wages. I earned it honestly.'

'What money?' queried Ben, his eyes widening with interest.

He was ignored. 'No man gives a gel that kind of money fer nothink.'

'What money?' Ben asked again, his eyes roaming the room.

'None of your business,' snapped his mother, but Ben wasn't done.

'Been giving 'er money, 'as he? Pay's fer it, do he? What is he? Some old goat what likes 'em 'ardly out of the cradle?'

His dirty chuckle went right through Emma. She pointed a vicious finger at him. 'You can talk. All them tarts you and yer mates pick up. Yer come home stinking of cheap scent, that and beer.'

Ben went over to his tankard, lifting it off the shelf to pour the dregs from an opened pint bottle of stout he'd taken from one frayed pocket of his jacket. His leering eye on her, he drained the tankard, a drop of brown liquid slopping down each side of his mouth on to his shirt. Holding the tankard away, he brushed his shirt with the back of his other hand then wiped his mouth, the movements loose and uncontrolled.

Her eyes lingering contemptuously on Ben, Emma addressed her mother, fine talk forgotten. 'He drinks away what little he does earn. He comes 'ome throwing 'is weight about and you never say a word. I work 'ard to bring in regular money, to 'elp keep us, and this is all you think of me?'

'But we know what yer doin' fer money,' Ben said, grinning slyly.

'You keep your dirty mind to yerself!' Emma flared at him.

She turned back to her mother. What she saw in those faded hazel eyes shocked her to her very soul. 'You can't believe I've been doing them sort of things.'

'I don't know *what* yer get up to.' That comment was the last straw.

'Then yer can think what yer like, Mum. I've kept meself decent. I've stood out in all weathers ter help keep us going. But if you think I've been doing other things, then I'd better leave. You and Ben can torment the life out of each other. He can drink away what 'e earns and you can go out and sell yer own flowers. But without me, Mum, yer'll end up in the workhouse before six months is up.'

Her outburst was met with silence and she turned on Ben. 'This is all your doing, spying on me, coming 'ome telling tales. I know, because I saw yer this evening, watching me.'

His grin was lazy. 'Why should I want ter spy on yer? I don't need to because yer've just condemned yerself.'

'I've done nothing of the sort!' She turned back to her mother in abject appeal. 'I told yer the truth, Mum.'

'I wish I could believe it,' came the saddened reply.

'All he's given me is from what he earns doing his magic and me helping.'

'Helping! Huh!' Ben sniggered, lifting his tankard to his lips though he'd drunk what was there. 'I just bet he enjoys every bit of yer *'elping* 'im!'

White rage surged up inside Emma. Without warning she leaped at him, her fist catching him on the side of the head. He let out a roar, his free hand trying to catch her flailing arms. She half saw the tankard raised above her head, and ducked. But her mother saw it and ran to part them.

It was she who took the downward swipe of his arm, its force throwing her to the floor. In that instant Emma left her assault on him in an effort to catch her and stop her fall. The next thing, a dull thud, like the heavy kick from a horse, caught her on the back of her head, making her brain whirl.

Chapter Twelve

Emma came to herself lying on the sofa with Mum bending over her. Ben was nowhere in sight.

Slowly recollection came back, she going for him, her mother intervening and being knocked sideways by a blow meant for herself, running to help Mum, swearing at Ben for the bully he was. She vaguely remembered yelling at him to see what he'd done and to apologise when something hit her head causing her to black out.

'What 'appened?' she managed. 'Where's Ben?'

'Sodded off out in a temper,' came the reply. 'And at this time of night. I don't suppose he'll come back 'ome till tomorrer now.'

She screwed up her face at the pain in her head. 'He hit me.'

'With that tankard. I don't think he meant ter knock you out. But yer did go for 'im. He was defending 'imself.'

With a tankard, against a girl. Emma's lip curled. And even now Mum was taking his side against hers. She sat up, wary of the thumping in her head.

'Are you orright, Em?'

'How can I be, with you and 'im going on at me for something I ain't done.'

Her mother stood up from her. 'Can yer blame me? Yer only sixteen.'

'Seventeen end of February,' Emma reminded. Her mother uttered an irritated huff.

'Still sixteen. Not old enough ter know what men 'ave got on their minds when they see some pretty girl.'

Of course she knew. Theo was different. 'He's not like that,' she said.

'How do you know he's not got yer on a bit of string, spinning yer a tale. All this rubbish about magic.'

Despite her thumping head, Emma gave a hard laugh, 'All concerned for me now, are we? A little while ago you said yer didn't want me sleeping next to yer. I was too disgusting.'

This was met with silence and she could sense just a touch of doubt. She went on in a kinder voice. 'Perhaps if he came to see you to explain what he does. He was a famous magician. He was in all the big theatres right across the country.' Speaking of him seemed to improve her diction as if he stood there right behind her. 'You must have heard of the Great Theodore?'

'No I ain't,' came the sharp reply. 'What time or money 'ave I ever 'ad, ter go off ter posh theatres, even when yer dad was alive, me bringing up the kids, and 'im working every hour he could get?'

'But if you just agreed to meet him. If I ask him to come and see you to explain what he has in mind, would you listen to him?'

'I don't want no truck with some dirty old man what's old enough ter be yer father.'

She'd been wrong, there had been no elements of doubt at all in her mother's mind, faint or otherwise.

'It's not like that.' She swung her legs to the floor, wincing at the pain it caused, and sat on the edge of the sofa. 'How can you condemn him when you've not even met him?'

Her mother interrupted her. 'And what's all this fancy talk?' She was regarding Emma as though she'd been mouthing a string of vile oaths. 'Yer sound like some fancy man's trollop, talking like that.'

Emma was on the verge of losing her temper. She fought to control it.

'He's planning a mind-reading act, and when I'm on the stage I have to speak nice ... nicely.'

'On the stage!' Mum was glaring down at her. 'No daughter of mine's going on the stage. Them sort ain't no better than they should be. No, me gel, you ain't goin' on no stage.'

Mum moved away from her as if to enforce her decision. 'I've never 'eard such stuff. I've brought you up ter be good an' clean, and I ain't 'aving yer showin' yer legs and things to a lot of gawping eyes what see yer as no better than a common tart.'

'What about the fine actresses we've got?' Emma struck back. 'Like Ethel Barrymore and Sarah Bernhardt? They're well respected. Everyone looks up to 'em.'

'I still ain't going ter let yer show me up by making yerself look cheap in front of people.'

'Do yer think standing in the kerb selling flowers ain't making meself look cheap?'

Her temper swinging out of control, all her nice accent fell about her in shreds. 'Do yer think it's all so special standing 'olding out a flower ter people passing by, begging 'em ter buy one and have meself ignored, or me 'and shoved aside, or if someone stops, do yer think I feel special when they drop a penny in me 'and with that look of pity and thank God my daughter don't 'ave ter do this, and me 'aving ter be grateful for their bloody pennies? I know what they're thinking. And I hate it. What I can get working for Mr Barrington will get me more than I get in one year selling paper flowers.'

She stopped and waited but her mother was silent.

'Don't yer see, Mum?' she went on. 'You saw what I've earned so far, just by helping Mr Barrington in his work, and it's not come from 'aving ter beg people to buy from me. It's real earnings, from proper entertaining.'

As she paused, running out of ideas, there came her mother's disparaging voice. 'Ill-gotten gains. And I can guess what else yer'll be expected ter do.'

The suggestion seared into her brain, rationality flung aside. 'I don't bloody care!' she burst out. 'If that's what you think, I *don't* bloody care.'

'Don't swear.' Her mother was holding on tightly to herself.

'Is that all yer can say?' Emma continued. 'Yer practically tell me I'm no better than a prostitute, then calmly tell me not ter swear?'

Her head was hurting. Dizzy, she felt a sudden need to sit down, so much anger coursing through her veins that she could hardly breathe. She stayed on her feet.

'Yer tell me yer don't want me next to yer in bed, and I can sleep under that table instead? Well, I ain't going to. If Ben comes 'ome tonight, me hearing 'im pissing in his pot and me not three feet away from him,

no thanks, Mum. I'd rather leave this place right now.'
But Mum was also in a temper.

'Where d'yer think yer'd go at this time of night? To
'im, I suppose.'

'Yes, if I have to! He's going back to his work and
taking me with 'im. I could be well off and get us all
out of this squalor. But you'd rather scrape along 'ere
because you think making yer flowers ter sell is more
respectable.' Her voice had risen to a shriek. 'Yer'd rather
work yerself ter death rather than me getting yer out of
this place. It suits yer ter play the bloody martyr. I think
you enjoy us living like we do in this stinking hole.'

'That's enough!' yelled her mother. 'I won't 'ave yer
talking like this.'

'Why not?' Emma yelled back. 'I've a right to my ...'

There came a mighty thumping on the floor above
them, their raised voices disturbing the couple living
up there. A man's muffled shout came faintly through
the floorboards.

'Shurrup down there! We're tryin' ter sleep. Yer know
what time it is?'

Mum's turned her thin face to the ceiling. 'You can
shut up too!'

'I'll come down there and tell yer who's ter shut up!'

'Go on then!' she yelled back. 'You don't pay the
rent fer the ole 'ouse. I can shout if I want in me own
rooms!' Her eyes were searching for the broom to bash
back at the ceiling with the handle end, no doubt merely
bringing down a piece of already flaking plaster on her
own head.

'We'll see about that,' returned the voice. 'I'm comin'
down and I'll bang on yer door, that's what I gonna do

if yer don't quieten down. Us bein' woke up not 'alf an hour ago by yer fighting, and now woken up again.'

Mum's mouth opened to scream a retort but Emma caught her arm. 'Mum, don't! We could get thrown out.'

Her mother closed her mouth and glared at her. 'Much you care,' she said, lowering her voice. The thumping stopped abruptly. They could hear the bedsprings creak above their head as they did every night.

For a while they stood without speaking. Mum shrugged off Emma's hand and went to her kitchen chair to sit down as though all her energy had deserted her. Emma regarded her for a moment, her own anger subsiding.

'Are yer going to let me sleep in our bed ternight then?'

'No.'

'I see.' Emma heard her own voice harden. 'Then I'll have to leave.'

'I suppose so.' Her mother's tone sounded full of defeat.

'If I go, Mum,' Emma said quietly, 'I'll never set foot in this house again.'

'What house?' murmured her mother, gazing slowly around herself at the shabby room. She said no more and Emma knew she was thinking of earlier times, better times, even though they too had been a struggle.

But she wasn't going to be persuaded by pity. She had been wronged. She'd tried to do her best by her mother, and what thanks had there been?

'I'll go then,' she said ineptly.

'Yes, go,' came the weary reply.

Theodore awoke from a deep and satisfied sleep to the sound of someone tapping on his door.

He had gone to bed at rights with the world. He hadn't yet told Amelia about Jack Simmons's telegram saying he'd got a spot for him, admittedly at the end of the bill, and admittedly in a seedy music hall, but it was a start. He was on his way.

She'd be surprised and excited when he told her. Any girl would be, taken from the gutter and put into the limelight, even if that limelight was mere coloured flame and not electric, the audience standing for the most part in ragged rows instead of sitting in plush seats, women in cheap boas and second-hand hats, men in scruffy jackets and shapeless trousers, collarless shirts and frayed caps.

He was starting again. Anyone starting again must put up with the rough before enjoying the smooth. But with her beside him he couldn't go wrong. Amelia Beech, far more satisfactory than Emma. Innocent and sweet, she had charmed the common street crowds. Now she would charm the common music hall rabble. Before long she would be enchanting the rich and elegant. Who would have thought that a child of the East End would possess such a remarkably retentive memory? With his mind-reading act, they'd reach the heights and once more he would be the Great Theodore.

When people asked where he'd been these past two years and a half, he would give a sly smile and leave them to continue to wonder. They would see it as mysterious, debate among themselves the reason for his sudden dis-appearance and just as sudden reappearance, like one of his famous tricks. Many would recall a similarly sudden disappearance – the mysterious and elusive man mostly known only by the name of Charlier who came on the scene around the 1870s and for thirteen years managed to astound audiences with his sleight of hand with the cards, only to disappear several years later without a trace. No one knew where Charlier came from or where he went. During the years, despite acclaim, he seemed to have lived in poverty, once discovered living in one room ten feet by eight.

Theo smiled to himself. Rather like this room; and on that thought he dozed off to be awoken by tapping on his door.

Shaking off sleep, he fumbled for matches, struck one, and turning the screw of the gas bracket on the wall, applied the match to the chalk fretwork of the mantle. In its sickly light, he opened the street door to find Amelia standing there, her face pale, her hazel eyes wide.

'I've left home,' she said, her voice trembling. She looked pale.

Startled, all he could find to say was, 'At this hour of the night?' Collecting his wits, he turned his back, saying, 'You had best come in.'

His first thought as she followed him in was to draw his one chair up close for her to sit while he sat on the edge of the bed.

Hands in her lap, her head bowed, she told him what had happened. Listening, he expected tears at some stage but though her eyes glistened when she lifted them to glance at him, there was no outburst of weeping. It prompted a depth of admiration in his heart. She looked far older than her sixteen years, more like eighteen. This was a girl who would not allow any sort of adversity to pull her down. He felt a surge of warmth for her that wasn't exactly fatherly love.

'You should have taken note of what your mother wanted,' he said to allay the sensation.

She looked at him, anger gleaming in her eyes. 'She's got no right to tell me what to do.'

'You are still very young, and whilst under her roof, she has.'

'Well, I'm not under her roof any more.' There was bitterness in her tone. 'Apparently I'm not too young to go standing in the gutter selling for her.'

'Children younger than you are hawking and begging,' he said. She remained silent, so he said, 'Where do you intend to stay?'

'I don't know,' she said in a small voice.

'You can't stay here. You must go back home. Tell your mother you are sorry.'

She shook her head, her expression set. He felt he had never seen such an unyielding look. This was a girl to be reckoned with. 'You might still be able to persuade her to allow you to follow your course.'

'That's not possible,' came the stiff reply. 'Me and Mum are alike. Neither of us has ever given way, and I have to go on, no matter what anyone says. Unless you tell me I can't.'

How could he go against such determination? But she couldn't stay the night in the same room as he, especially the way he'd felt about her a little while ago.

'I'm not going home,' she said emphatically as he sat looking at her, knowing she was adamant about that. Nor could he send her away. He couldn't allow her to walk the streets. He had a feeling that this was what she would do.

'I suppose you'd better stay here until the morning,' he said finally, apprehension driving out all the feelings he'd had a moment ago. 'Then we shall discuss what we must do. I shall find somewhere else to stay tonight and return in the morning.'

'You can't.' She was looking alarmed. 'Where will you go?'

Her concern made him smile. 'As a man I am quite safe and it is no bother to me. There are many who must seek doors or archways to sleep in and it is not that cold at night, despite being near to Christmas. I shall be in good company,' he ended wryly.

Mention of Christmas had made him remember Simmons's news. Two weeks from now, they would be entertaining in a warm, dry venue, albeit shoddy and run down.

'You're above that!' she burst out in a show of pride on his behalf, then compressed her lips. 'You must stay here. I can sit in the chair until daylight. I can doze.'

She was assuming herself quite safe with him. In one way he was flattered, in another afraid, afraid of his own feelings.

'No, my dear,' he said gently. 'It's not done.'

'Who's to know?'

It was late. He was tired after being awoken from a fine sleep. He needed to make a decision. 'If you are comfortable with that, so be it, child.' He uttered that word for his own comfort, not hers. 'But you can't sleep on a chair. You must have the bed, such as it is. I'll make it tidy enough for you.'

At least he'd cleaned the place a little since having known her. He had her to thank for that. He had her to thank for much of what had happened. He'd begun to see a future again, even to wonder why he'd needed to cast himself down into this pit of his own creating. In the morning he would tell her about Simmons.

'Where will you sleep?' she asked.

'I will be comfortable enough on the floor with my overcoat for a cover and I will fold one of my boxes to make a pillow.'

'It's your bed,' she protested. 'I don't mind the chair.'

'Good Lord, child!' Sudden annoyance caught him out. 'Allow me to be a gentleman. What gentleman would see a tender young girl sit up all night in a chair whilst he slumbers at his ease?'

'But ...'

'Enough, my dear. If you do not like the arrangement, then go home!'

For a moment she pondered, then seeing him smiling at her concern, she nodded, her own lips parting.

It did him good to see her smile, but already he was regretting allowing her to stay. She seemed to see no harm in it. Maybe there was no harm, not now, but did she realise how differently a man might feel in the quiet, dead of night with such a lovely young thing not a hand's reach away, and nothing but his own willpower to stop him giving way to such an urge as was in a man's nature, in some circumstances stronger even than willpower?

But he could hardly turn her out now. He knew she'd never go home, and to roam the dark streets was infinitely more dangerous than staying here, for he must control himself. Tonight this young and innocent girl must not only feel safe, she must be kept safe, no matter how affected he'd been by her nearness this night in this small room.

Chapter Thirteen

She must have fallen asleep the moment her head touched the pillow. He had made her a mug of tea, which she drank thirstily though she refused the bread and jam he'd offered. Since giving up the hurdy-gurdy, now lying unused under the table, he made sure of having provisions around.

While she drank her tea, he had gone to refill the kettle from the tap out back ready for tomorrow morning, and to visit the ramshackle hut that went under the name of water closet, used by every tenant in this building. When he returned, he found her fast asleep, still in her street jacket, her straw boater pushed to one side.

Gently he eased his overcoat from off the foot of the bed to draw out the blanket beneath it – another luxury he'd gained from entertaining with magic instead of the hurdy-gurdy – to lay over her.

He stood for a while gazing down on the slim form, the legs drawn up under her skirts, one cheek resting on her hands, the palms pressed together as if in prayer, the dark lashes lying softly on those cheeks, the full lips gently relaxed, and felt a depth of fondness, move him. Hastily he turned away. Putting the kettle down in the hearth, he settled himself on the floor beside the bed, the only space to be had, covering himself with his overcoat and using one of the cardboard boxes as a pillow. It was impossible to keep warm. The night air crept into the room through every crack and crevice, despite his having remarked on it not being all that cold for December.

Lying awake, the floor hard under his hip and shoulder, he listened intently to the gentle breathing just a foot above him. Now and again came a soft rustle as she turned in her sleep, her innocent sleep that sent his heart into turmoil. Fiercely he resisted the temptation to get up just to look at her. To do so could so easily be the preliminary to reaching out a careful hand to touch her arm or her cheek, and if she stirred, awoke, looked up at him with that lovely smile, to bend and kiss her.

What if she were to respond, reach up and touch his face? And if her fingers were to brush through his beard, would a kiss alarm her or would she draw him to her in her need for a little comfort? If he were to take advantage of it – man isn't made of wood – how easily it could develop into something else, something he dare not contemplate.

The thought brought a sensation surging through him that alarmed him and in desperation he turned his back, closing his eyes in an attempt to seek sleep and forget what had passed through his mind. When next he opened them, it was to feel his shoulder being gently shaken. Looking up, he saw her bending over him, and feeble sunlight being reflected into the room by the dingy walls of the houses opposite. Stiff and aching, he rose and sat on the edge of the bed she'd vacated so recently. It was

171

While the fire blazed, sending warmth through the room, he went to put the kettle on the scullery gas ring. They had risen so early that no one was about. While the water boiled he gazed through the dusty window. In the night there had been a sharp frost; everything was white and glistening, covering the filth of the East End. Just as well he hadn't been too gallant in his offer to spend the night elsewhere. He inhaled deeply, returning with hot water for the tea to find her making his bed. She glanced round at him and smiled.

'Thank you for letting me stay,' she said simply. Before turning back to her task she added, 'I don't know what I'd have done without you.'

'You could have found some friend,' he said. 'You do have friends?'

'Oh, yes. My best friend is Lizzie Wallis. She lives a few streets from me. I've not seen that much of her lately – too taken up doing what we've been doing and I've not said anything about it to her. I'd have to tell her why I've left home if I went there asking to be put up, wouldn't I? Anyway, at that time of night and her parents already with a house full, I don't think I could of asked them.'

'Could *have* asked,' he corrected automatically.

'Oh yes, sorry. Have! Could have asked.'

'I would feel happier if you at least attempted to make peace with your mother,' he ventured.

She shook her head and, folding his overcoat and jacket, placed them on the bed beside the tidied blanket. It came to him as a small shock that the whole room seemed to be glowing from the touch of a woman's hand.

'I'm never going to go back there,' she was saying. She'd taken the kettle from him and was dropping in a handful of tea ready to pour it into his one mug.

'You have the mug first,' she suggested brightly. She seemed suddenly so bright and cheerful almost as if some weight had been lifted from her shoulders by her decision. 'I can wait till you've finished. You must have been perished down there on that floor all night.'

He didn't argue as it was handed to him. There was more on his mind than who should have the mug first. 'Has it occurred to you, my dear, that your mother might be beside herself with worry as to where you might be?'

'She knows where I am,' she said, a bitter ring to the statement. 'She said I can go and live with my ... with you, for all she cared, and that I'm no better than a trollop. I'll never forgive 'er fer that.'

This time he didn't correct her. There was so much pain there that trivialities such as correct diction had no place. All he could think to say was, 'You know you cannot stay here, my dear. We must find you somewhere to live.'

Quickly he explained about theatrical lodging houses, hastening to convince her as she had left home without money, he would pay for her lodgings for the time being.

'Later on you will have to pay for yourself,' he said taking delight in seeing the concern that crept over her face. It was time to break the news Simmons had sent him, and with immense pleasure he saw the worried expression give way first to incredulity then an overt wave of excitement.

'In two weeks' time,' he said, grandly, 'we'll be on a music hall stage. It should take us up to Christmas.'

174

'Us,' she said, savouring the word. She moved forward until he could lay his arms about her waist, the intimate action feeling quite natural, and such a small, neat waist.

'Yes, my dear girl. Us. I intend to take you with me to the pinnacle of my profession. But for you, my dear Amelia, I would never have done this.'

He got hurriedly up from the bed, keenly aware of a sensation stirring inside him at the feel of that shapely waist beneath his hands. When he again spoke, it was to make his tone gruff and businesslike.

'Get your coat and hat. We will find a café for a quick and modest breakfast before seeking accommodation for you. After which we will begin work in earnest.'

He couldn't help his elation now at her having left home. In all truth it had been to his benefit. Without her family's yoke she was free to rehearse at any time, all day if necessary. His mind-reading act was now paramount.

Maud Beech could have sworn she hadn't slept a wink all night for thinking of Emma. Yet she hadn't heard Ben come home.

She came out of her room around half past seven, her old, faded blue bed shawl over her nightdress, to find him snoring on his sofa. He always complained long and bitterly about not having a proper bed, but it never kept him awake.

Creeping to the fireplace, she stirred the ashes. Not a spark. It would need re-laying and coaxing into life before she could get a kettle of water boiling for tea. First she must dress, go down and fill it from the yard tap and then she could begin her day.

Her day! What sort of day without Em? Maud felt lost. She tried to cheer herself up. No doubt Emma would come creeping back this morning, tail between her legs, apologising. Maud shuddered a little to think that that man must have taken her in. But what if he hadn't? What if she'd slept the night under some arches, at the mercy of the weather and God knows what else?

'No, he's taken 'er in,' she said aloud as much to give herself comfort as to come to any conclusion, although it gave little relief.

Ben snorted, stirred and turned over irascibly, raising himself on one elbow to focus his eyes on her with an effort, having had more than a drink or two last night.

'What you up for? What time is it?'

'Half past seven.'

'Gawdstruth!' He snorted again in disgust and sucked at his dry mouth. 'Can't yer let a bloke sleep? Raking that damned 'earth with the poker like you 'ated it.'

'What time did yer get in?'

'Do it matter?' he muttered. 'Where's Em?'

'Gorn.'

'What d'yer mean, gorn?'

Maud held herself in, her lips tight. 'Gorn. Left 'ome. Last night after you 'it her.'

'*I* hit 'er? Oh, yeah, we 'ad a row. Where's she gorn?'

'I don't know.' It was hard to keep the worry out of her voice. 'And I don't much care!'

This, said in summoned-up anger, failed to deaden the concern. Leaving him to sink back on the old cushion he used for a pillow, she went back into her room to dress.

It was hard trying to retain everything Theo was endeavouring to teach her. While they'd entertained queues outside a theatre, all she'd had to do was to use this simple trick he'd taught her of slipping some small object into an unsuspecting pocket, her hands so small and light that they were never felt. Now she'd be inside a theatre, lit up by footlights and spotlights, a hundred or more people just waiting to see through a trick. There was just this single week in which to be shown what to do and to do it well. Theo, she came to realise traumatically, was a perfectionist.

'No! I said *smoothly*! You're like a drunken cart horse.' How many more times was he going to tell her that? Yet when he wasn't rehearsing he'd say she was dainty, composed, had natural poise. 'You will be a fine lady a few years from now, my dear. I am so proud of you.'

At the moment he was reminding her that a week from now she would be in front of hundreds, which wasn't helping her composure one bit.

But there were wonders to help alleviate her doubts. From those cardboard boxes she'd never before seen opened, he brought out other boxes whose false backs and sides she could not detect even a few feet away.

'This,' he said, grandly, bringing from one box a plain straight-sided cooking pan with a lid, silvery and shining, which had never seen a cooking fire, 'this is a dove pan. But it can accommodate more or less anything.'

He took off the lid. The base was quite empty. 'I have not used this for street entertainment,' he said. 'This is for stage work.'

Emma watched as he put the lid on the pan, not knowing what to expect, if there was anything at all to expect. A second later he'd whipped off the lid, and there in the previously empty space was a mass of coloured, soft balls.

'Where did they come from?' she gasped in pleasure. 'Do that again!'

177

'Not at the moment.'

'Why not?

'Surprise, my dear. Magic needs the element of surprise. Hesitate, or repeat the same trick immediately on request, and the chances are that a previously mystified onlooker will deduce how it is done. For an illusionist, surprise and misdirection are everything.'

'But I'm your assistant.' As she pouted, he laughed. A deep laugh, faintly sinister, but which she found fascinating. 'Won't I have to know if I'm to be helping you on stage?' They sounded wonderful, those words, 'on stage'. She could hardly believe she was saying it with such conviction.

'Of course, my dear,' he said, relenting. 'Now come and look.' She came nearer. 'This is the basis of most illusions: boxes, cages, all illusion, this and the swiftness of the hand deceiving the eye. People are so easily deluded.'

He waited until she briefly inspected the object. 'Did you not notice?' he asked as she looked up. 'It has not two parts, a lid and a base, but three – a lid, a base and a "fake". The first thing one does is to show the empty pan to the audience. There are springs attached to the inner wall of the lid. They project slightly inwards. When the fake holding your doves, or balls, is pushed up into the lid, the projecting rim of the base will push back the springs so that when the lid is removed from the pan the fake is left behind, revealing the doves or whatever else you have there.'

For her benefit, he demonstrated several times. Her face close to his in order to see what was happening, she could feel the warmth emanating from it. She heard him draw a deep breath, letting it out slowly.

'Once more.' His voice shook. 'Place the lid on the base. The base pushes back the springs, when the lid is lifted the fake is left behind in the pan with its contents for the audience to see. Using live birds is made quite dramatic by placing a sheet of paper in the pan and setting it alight for all to see. Replacing the lid extinguishes the flame, but immediately removed, reveals the doves, unhurt, like a phoenix rising from the fire. Very effective.'

As Emma nodded, she felt his lips brush her cheek as if in triumph. It felt nice, made her feel part of it all.

'In time,' he said, moving quickly away, 'I shall buy live doves and rabbits. By their very nature they crouch, very still, when in dark spaces. Only on release will they move. It makes matters simple for an illusionist.'

The morning was taken up with various clever demonstrations: a cage lined with black velvet, a hinged lid situated so as to conceal its contents from the view of the audience, who would see only empty bars, a silk handkerchief held in front of the cage for only a second or two, to be removed with a flourish, and then a shoe where once had been empty space. 'It is meant to be the rabbit, of course,' he laughed, and she laughed with him.

There were endless other tricks, unfathomable, yet when shown, so simple. It was a wonderful morning, if marred at intervals by his sudden fit of anger at something she had not done quite to his liking which made her wonder if selling flowers wasn't preferable. She refused to let it upset her, knowing she could no longer go home, not after what had passed between her and Mum, having to face the accusations and having Ben sneer at her and being called names that weren't true. It was at these moments of Theo's temper that she longed to see her mother, find out how she was, and let her know that she was all right, but it would only start up friction all over again.

She came to hate Theo's rages, brief though they were. In defiance she would revert to her old way of speaking, which made him all the more angry, accusing her of speaking like a guttersnipe and saying it would be better to forget all this and send her away. It was the one thing that frightened her into behaving herself, the prospect of her bright future fading, and wealth along with it.

The accommodation he'd found her was plain but clean. It was warm, too. Fires in the dining room and kitchen always blazing, the heat drifted through the hall and up the stairs, warming the walls so that there was little need to feed pennies into the gas meter in her room. It seemed that the theatre folk whom the landlady, Mrs Tankerton, mainly catered for, lived quite cosily, a far cry from the cold impoverishment where she had lived.

Meals were simple but wholesome. The lodgers seemed to be a friendly lot. The meal table accommodated around ten, all in exuberant discussion as to who was working, where and what at, rude audiences, unbearable stage managers, dreadful dressing areas, their hopes for their next engagement or downcast complaints of there being nothing on the horizon as yet. All this Emma devoured as eagerly as she devoured her meals.

Mrs Tankerton was something of a fierce soul, brooking no nonsense from her guests while sympathetic to their problems, except financial ones if room rent was not continuously forthcoming. Here Emma felt safe. Yet for all the comfort, with Christmas two weeks away, she was missing Mum.

She'd written with her address and describing her lodgings, prudently leaving out any mention of the night she'd spent with Theo for all it had been harmless. Mum did not reply; she was very poor with a pen, Emma recalled, excusing her.

She missed her friend Lizzie, too, who was probably thinking she no longer had time for her. The first chance she got she'd go and see Lizzie, tell her all that had happened to her. But there never seemed to be a chance.

Theo had suddenly rented the room that had recently fallen vacant next to hers. 'Easier to rehearse,' he said, so there was now even less time to herself with him in and out of her room, pressing her to learn even more, or sometimes merely coming in to sit and relate his plans and the luxuries she would eventually come to enjoy, the luxuries they would both enjoy.

With him at her elbow all the time, making sure she learned and memorised all the codes necessary for this flamboyant mind-reading act he had in mind, she hardly had space to breathe much less visit her mother or old friends.

'My mind-reading routine was always my pièce de résistance, all else mere prelude,' he told her with magnificent self-confidence, and she was coming to realise that he did indeed possess enormous self-confidence, the humble days of the hurdy-gurdy put behind him as if they'd never been.

So now she was being required to become unfailingly familiar with certain voice inflections, special words dropped, hand and body movements, all to convey to her what he required of her in response. Over those two weeks it became a crushing responsibility for her, and there was no time for Lizzie.

181

Chapter Fourteen

'Are you ready?' Theo had taken her hand and was now smoothing the bare flesh of her forearm.

'I think so.' It was as much as she could concede.

She felt far from ready. Standing backstage in the Cambridge Music Hall, Shoreditch, her heart pumping almost up into her throat, great, deep, suffocating thumps, all the complicated information he'd drummed into her head these past two weeks seemed to have fled. Terrifying enough soon to be on stage for the first time in her life, but being jostled by throngs of other entertainers, surrounded by chatter and the smell of sweat and greasepaint, made her feel slightly sick. She'd never imagined this went on backstage and she felt completely confused.

The corridors, already cluttered with old props, bustled with turns waiting to go on, others coming off to rush away somewhere else to do their turn all over again. It was usual to do three or four different venues in an evening so as to make a decent living, and everyone was in a hurry. No time for a chat or the niceties of recognition other than a passing hello, they mostly ignored each other, and especially the tall man clad in cape and evening suit with a slim, breathless girl hurrying behind him.

Carrying a case, Theo had threaded his way to a less noisy corner to sort out his props, closely followed by Emma, carrying his other case. He'd wisely suggested that they dress at home ready to go on, knowing the drill of old in many places like this. Most changed at home or en route, coming by brougham, as he had, or if a troupe, in a privately hired omnibus. It was the quickest way to get to the next venue on time.

Theo had seen her dismay at the state and confusion of backstage in this music hall. 'We'll not have to suffer this for ever,' he said, having asked her if she was ready. 'In time I will have my own dressing room.'

They'd finally made their way to the wings to await their cue to go on stage. He looked at her with that deep, penetrating stare of his. 'You are *sure* you are ready?' It seemed couched in reproof rather than concern.

'I feel nervous,' she admitted.

'That is how it should be. The day you do not feel nervous is the day you should leave the business.'

Emma nodded. 'I can't remember nothing.'

'You cannot, *what*?'

Surely not at a time like this? 'Sorry,' was all she could say, terse and huffy, like a chastised schoolgirl. 'I can't remember anything.'

In the midst of all this, this new life she was being thrust into, he could pick up on some triviality? Incredulity gave way to ill will, yet it was that moment of rancour that instantly brought all she'd learned flowing back into her head, every last command of it.

The previous turn was coming off. A ragged, grudging applause staggered through the wings in the wake of a relieved, sweating comedian who seemed not to have gone down all that well. He gave the next pair a wry grin. 'Right tough lot ternight.'

Theo glanced at Emma. 'You remember all I've taught you?'

She wasn't going to let him see her fear. 'Of course I do,' she said sharply, and he nodded, satisfied.

'Fine!' he said.

It was a different Theodore Barrington who stood on that large empty stage. There was a commanding presence about him that hushed the audience the second the curtains were drawn back.

Emma saw him stand for a second or two that seemed to her to take far too long, minutes, it seemed. Any moment now the audience would lose patience, begin to boo. He seemed not at all perturbed by that possibility as he surveyed the sea of shadowy faces below him, turning his head slowly to take stock of each individual face.

Peeping from the wings, Emma could see those faces nearest the stage gaping back, instantly mesmerised. Then very slowly, he took off his black, flowing cape and dramatically draped it over the table hurriedly brought in and unfolded by a stagehand before the curtains parted, the man having already run on with the two heavy boxes to place beside the table.

Once he had gained the audience's attention, Theo's sonorous voice resounded around the auditorium, bringing to a sudden halt the usual movements of those traditionally accustomed to coming in or going out as they pleased throughout any of the many palaces of variety's continuous performances. The atmosphere had become instantly electric, as they sat down as though commanded.

In the wings, awaiting her cue, Emma felt awe run through her own veins like a chill river. What a man she had teamed up with. At that moment she knew she was going to experience such a life and luxury as she could never have dreamed of. In that instant all else was forgotten but what would be required of her in these next ten minutes, the duration of this debut of Theo's after so long away. She was not going to let him down.

It had been exacting. Emma was exhausted. Both the afternoon and the evening performances had gone without a hitch, worth all that hard work.

'But it doesn't mean taking things easy,' Theo warned her as he poured champagne for them as a small celebration. 'Rehearsing never stops. All must be perfect, perfectly timed, perfectly executed. The smallest lapse of concentration will seek me out unmercifully, as it did once before. But I will not speak of that.'

He took another sip and grimaced, surveying the liquid in the wide glass. 'One day we will drink only the best. This is just a beginning, my dear. I promise you, Amelia, that you will drink only the best champagne and nibble the finest caviar.'

At this moment she couldn't have cared less. Animated and beside himself with his triumph, he'd done nothing but talk since coming back to her room. She didn't think she'd ever heard him talk so much, telling her about all the wonders she'd one day experience, reminiscing excitedly on past triumphs and the great names he'd rubbed shoulders with, the magnificent parties he'd attended. 'And it will all be the same for you, my dear. I shall make sure of that. Together we will hit the height of fame.'

He had kissed her cheek more than once, refilling her glass until she felt quite tipsy. 'You are quite, quite beautiful,' he said time and time again, 'quite stunning,' and she knew that he also had enjoyed too much to drink. She was glad when he finally returned to his own room leaving her to lie in her bed, stare up at the ceiling and go over this marvellous day.

To think she'd been so afraid, had felt so unsure of her abilities as she came on stage to have him take her by the hand in an elaborate gesture for the audience to see. Applause broke out at the sight of her in the green gown he'd found for her, which she suspected might have belonged to his late wife but which showed off her own auburn hair, piled up and puffed out in bouffant style, making her look at least eighteen. Her throat bereft of jewellery had caused the heady, dangling earrings to look far more expensive than they really were.

The gown, boned breathlessly tight at the waist, flowing over her rounded hips to fall softly to the ground in a small flare, had a low square neckline that revealed her throat as Theo theatrically removed the flimsy decency frill from her shoulders, as if she'd been a manikin on display.

'May I introduce to you,' he had boomed, 'my assistant, Amelia Beech. During my mind-reading act, she will come among you, but do not be afraid – she will be gentle with you!'

This had led to a gale of laughter and more clapping, Theo triumphing hardly before he had begun. The angel sleeves falling away as he lifted her hand to his lips in response to the clapping had revealed how slim and shapely was that arm, bringing even louder applause. It had indeed made her feel beautiful.

Moving smoothly and daintily, she had brought him whatever he asked for, faultlessly responding to every command as he went through a flawless routine and finally making not one mistake as he enthralled his audience with a mind-reading act that had them all gasping. As he came off stage, he had taken her in his arms and had kissed her on both her cheeks and her forehead. That evening in her room he'd been like an excited schoolboy. The Theodore who'd been on stage, and the perfectionist who'd rehearsed her quite savagely at times, seemed left behind. He'd kissed her cheek once more before bidding her goodnight.

Reminiscing, she washed, combing her hair down, and she gazed at her reflection in the mirror. The face gazing back at her was radiant. 'I can't believe you're me,' she said to it, and it smiled back at her. Dreamily she got out of her theatrical clothes and donned her nightdress.

Turning off the light – electric light, even in a mediocre boarding house, such luxury – she slipped into bed, sighing with happiness. A million lovely thoughts of the future parading through her head, she closed her eyes to savour them in the most blissful contentment she had ever known.

In this mood, she thought quite suddenly of her mother and for a moment the euphoria fled. What sort of Christmas would Mum have? She would have to go and see her. She might risk Mum shutting the door in her face, but she'd have to face that. By the end of the week Theo would have money, far more than when they'd played to the theatre queues. Some of what he'd give her could be sent to Mum to make possible for her a better Christmas than she expected. Mum could hardly say no to that.

This resolved, Emma returned to happier thoughts. This time next Christmas she and Theo would be in the money. It seemed unbelievable. If he was right about them going places, then …

She broke off as she heard a light tapping on her door. She sat upright. What did he want now? It was late and she was exhausted, and in her nightdress too. Giving a mighty sigh, Emma got up, reached for her wrap and hurried over to switch on the light. It was cold, the fires downstairs extinguished for the night. She hadn't fed a coin into the meter for the gas fire, thinking it not worth it, as it was so late. She was going to remind Theo in no uncertain terms just how late it was. Going to the door, she opened it a fraction. The face she saw made her gasp.

'You! What d'you want?'

Already she was peering beyond Martin Page to see where Theo was, but there was no sign of him. Sounds came from other rooms opposite and above her own: someone rehearsing lines, the muffled sound of a violin being tentatively tuned at this late hour, someone talking.

As he continued to regard her she became aware of being in her night attire, no petticoat, no corset, no drawers. Clutching her wrap securely to her throat, she made to close the door on him, but he put the flat of his hand against the wood, preventing it, firmly though not aggressively.

'I just need to have a word with you,' he said. 'Please?'

She held on to the door. 'You can speak to Theo. His room's there.' She pointed quickly to the one next to hers.'

'No, he isn't.'

Had he already knocked on that door? 'He's probably fast asleep,' she said.

'No, he isn't. He's not there. Anyway, it's you I need to see. I'll get nothing out of him. But you might be able to tell me what's going on.'

Emma let the door go. 'What d'you mean, what's going on?'

Page gave an apologetic smile and glanced along the empty passage. 'Look, it doesn't seem right, me standing at a young lady's door at this time of night. Would you mind if I came inside? I mean you no disrespect.'

'No, you can't!'

'It is important. You can keep the door open if you wish. I just need a minute of your time.'

He was right. She couldn't have him stand here. And she had become far too intrigued to tell him to go away.

Wondering why she should do so, Emma stood back for him. 'It's late,' she said inadequately.

She was glad to see that he merely closed the door a fraction so that anyone passing would not see in. Even so, feeling it prudent to keep distance between them, she went over to the washbasin, there to turn to look at him, feeling safer there. He hadn't moved from the spot.

His dark eyes were trained on her, his narrow, handsome face deeply serious.

'I do apologise for the intrusion at this late hour, but when I saw Theo leaving, I thought I ought to seize the opportunity while it presented itself. Theo would only fob me off with lies and show that anger he feels for me.'

'Leaving?' she echoed. 'When?'

'Some time ago,' came the reply.

'Where was he going? Why should he want to go out at this time of night?' She glanced at the tiny clock on the shelf over the gas fire. It was registering almost midnight. He'd said nothing to her about going out again.

'I didn't ask him.' A wry grin played around his lips. 'He wouldn't have thanked me. He was in a devil of a hurry so I thought I'd ask you if you knew what he was up to.'

He was gazing about the small room with its flowered wallpaper, flowered central lampshade, flowered bedspread and curtains, all of which made it seem even smaller, yet cosy.

'It looks as if the pair of you are beginning to do well for yourselves. I take it he's paying the rent. He must have forked out his own money on this. First night on stage, even if in some second-rate music hall, he couldn't have made much from it yet.'

How did he know what they were doing unless he'd been spying on them? He could have seen Theo's name on the billboard, of course. It was still well down the list of turns but even so, worded 'Return of the famous Great Theodore, magician extraordinaire!' was there for all to see. Perhaps he'd even been in the audience, but why so furtive? What was Martin Page up to?

'Is it you who's been watching us?' she hazarded a guess. 'When we were playing to the queues outside the theatres?'

Page nodded. 'I'm sorry. I had to know.'

'Why?' So it hadn't been Ben after all.

'I needed to know what he was up to,' Page said. 'I kept thinking, is he content just to go on entertaining in the gutter or does he have higher aims? If so, I need to have things out with him. I can't have him continuing to think I was carrying on with his wife. I wasn't. Yes, she was flirtatious and she did try it on with me, but she was so much older than I was and I had no feelings for her beyond friendship. I wanted to be loyal to Theo. But for all my efforts, he rewarded me with suspicion. Ridiculous, I know, but it still plagues me.'

He looked down at the bowler he held in his hands. He was turning the brim round and round between his fingers, and watching him, Emma felt suddenly sad.

'Tonight,' he said, 'I followed you two back here. I wondered if you and he had struck up something more than a mere business relationship.'

He didn't look up to meet her gaze, so she couldn't see his expression. 'I hung about outside for a while,' he went on. 'Then I saw him come out. I followed. I don't know why. All I could think was he's had what he wants from her, now he's going back to that hovel of his.'

Emma's eyes blazed. She came forwards a fraction. 'Is that what you think? Me and him is having an affair?' For a second good diction was forgotten. 'I think you ought ter leave. He's living in the same lodging house as me, not the same room! He's here because it's more convenient for his work, nothing more than that!'

Mollified by Page nodding in agreement, she calmed down. 'You said you followed him. Where to?'

'I'll leave him to tell you that. But it seems he's regained his self-confidence enough to tread the boards again and to get back to his former glory, no doubt ruling someone else's life.' It was an odd statement, a bitter one. 'If he does intend to climb back to the top,' he went on, 'I need to be there too.'

His eyes were taking her in to such an extent that she drew her wrap even tighter about her neck, feeling suddenly very aware of her body beneath the lightweight material.

'Why?' she asked, squirming beneath his far too candid scrutiny. 'You and he have parted company. He doesn't want you back.'

'I need to be around, that's all,' he said. He shook his head. 'My God, you're a beauty. I don't wonder he chose you.' The brown eyes became suddenly serious and intense. 'Be wary of him, Emily.'

It startled her to hear her own name spoken after being constantly referred to as Amelia. But she wasn't happy with such open admiration.

'What d'you mean, be wary of him?' she asked sharply. Page levelled a warning finger at her.

'All I'm saying is, Theo's an odd sort of chap. He can become insanely jealous, even dangerously jealous. When he confronted me over Eleanor, his wife, he said he'd kill me, and he meant it. I have to admit that the look he gave was quite frightening. But with her sidling up to me at odd times, the imprudent way she would lay an arm over my shoulders, it was getting dangerous. I told him I was thinking of leaving, although I hadn't wanted to. It was the only way I could convince him of my loyalty to him as Eleanor's husband. It was to remind him that I had no intentions towards his wife. After that, with no proof, he accused her of having an affair with me – trying it on, and ... well, you know what happened.'

As she stared at him in bewildered silence he seemed to pull himself up sharply. 'All I'm saying is that while he can be very jolly, very sociable, enjoyable company, he can suddenly turn. He is very possessive, you know. You need to be strong. Be careful of him. Once, by accident, he let slip that he'd practised hypnotism as a young man. I asked why he no longer practised it. He got angry and said it could have strange, even fatal results. The way he said it sent shivers down my spine. I think something must have gone terribly wrong at one time. It may be foolish, but I think it would be wise never to let him hypnotise you or cause you to do anything you don't feel is right. Just be careful.'

She was still vaguely annoyed, feeling herself being dictated to. 'Why should my safety be of any concern to you?' she challenged. 'I hardly know you. Are you just trying to frighten me off so you can take my place?'

'I am concerned for you,' he said solemnly. 'If I were around I could be there to prevent you coming to harm. That's why I want you to suggest he takes on a second assistant once he's on his way up. Some magicians have more than one, and he once had me and Eleanor. He would be able to use me because I've worked with him. I know him and he knows what I can do. All I want to do is to keep an eye on you, see you come to no harm.'

'Why should that concern you?'

Emma took another step forward. How dare he presume her innocent of danger? Brought up in the East End, she'd seen too many disreputables to be worried by Theo. She'd seen fights, even women against women, wives being knocked about in the street, giving the husband as good as he got, and woe betide a bystander stepping

193

in to take her part, finding himself treated to a free wallop from the abused woman herself for his interference. She'd seen more than this gently brought-up young man could imagine. So why fear Theo?

'I think I can look after myself,' she said firmly. 'Now, it's late. So if you don't mind ...'

'Just so that you might give a thought to suggesting me to him,' he persisted. 'Not right away, but at some time.'

'Yes, all right,' she said, needing him to leave.

She was glad to see him give her a nod of the head as though he had accomplished something, and opening the door wider, let himself out. He had made no apology for disturbing her, which she thought was very rude. Yet he seemed genuinely to have had her wellbeing at heart, though why she had no idea.

Yet what he'd said about Theo affected her as she lay in her bed trying to seek sleep. What did she really know of Theodore Barrington? Awed and excited by the change in her life, preoccupied with all he had been teaching her, she hadn't delved all that much into his past life since those first speculations she'd had about him. He had spoken about his wife's death and a bit about what had led up to it but of nothing of his life before that. Now, after what Martin Page had said about hypnotism, she found herself lying awake wondering what it was about Theo's past that prompted him to issue such veiled warnings.

Chapter Fifteen

It seemed to Emma that she lay awake for hours thinking of hypnotism. Mesmerism, as it was more commonly known among those with money for this sort of treatment to alleviate high-strung nerves, was lately attracting a great deal of interest. It was even said to be practised by surgeons for some operations. Though how anyone would willingly brave the surgeon's knife fully conscious, relying only on mesmerism to kill the pain, didn't bear thinking about. But why Theo would wish to do her harm with it was beyond her.

Taking ages to get to sleep, being so upset by Martin Page's stupid cautions, she was annoyed to be awakened by excitable knocking on her door. She snapped awake with daylight just emerging at eight o'clock, to realise it was Sunday morning.

For a moment she thought Page had returned. With angry words ready on her lips, she rose, fumbling for her wrap, and staggered to the door. Yanking it open, she found Theo standing there, washed and dressed in a good suit of clothes, his beard trimmed, his hair neat.

He was looking utterly pleased, his expression of triumph evoking enough curiosity to sweep away all thought of Martin Page.

'Get dressed!' he burst out. 'I've wonderful news!'

Barging unceremoniously past her into her room, he turned to look at her as she half closed the door. 'I have done it, my dear! We are on our way, you and I. Goodbye to flea-bitten music halls.'

She stared uncomprehendingly at him. They'd played just one night of the two-week booking. She'd seen him gaze about in disdain as they went in, speaking slightingly of those rushing from one place to another to make their money. 'I will not demean myself by haring around looking for ten minutes here, ten minutes there,' he'd remarked haughtily. 'I am above that.'

She'd thought, he might think himself above that, but this was virtually a hand-out for the Christmas season where otherwise he'd have been still entertaining theatre queues for pennies. Beggars could never be choosers and he should have been appreciative of what the theatrical agent had found for him, at least for the time being. That was her opinion anyway, but she hadn't made any comment. 'On our way?' she echoed now.

'Get yourself dressed and ready. We are going out.'

'Where?'

'I will tell you as we go. Hurry now. Put on your Sunday best.'

He was looking every inch a successful man. He looked swell enough in his stage clothes, but here he appeared a real gent in homburg and good overcoat.

As she came downstairs, dressed in a dark blue walking costume and a matching toque that he'd bought for

196

her only last week, aware that he'd be working in the legitimate theatre from now on, he had already hailed a brougham. It was still early, the streets quiet. The clip-clop of the horse's hooves echoed on the cobbles, its rump steaming in the cold morning air.

'Where are we off to?' she asked

'To my theatrical agent,' he answered. Saying no more, he lit a cigarette, taking short, tense lungfuls of smoke.

'It's Sunday,' Emma persisted. 'Does he work on Sundays, then?'

He did not reply, and made uneasy by his silence, she mentioned Martin Page's visit last night. She should have known better. Theo turned to her abruptly, his face fierce and dark.

'You say that wretch had the audacity to harass you?'

'He didn't harass me. He meant no harm.'

'Why did you open the door to him?'

'I thought it was you.'

'Why should you have thought that? We'd already said goodnight.'

'I thought you was coming back for something you forgot to say.'

He did not correct her grammar. 'So the man now knows where we are living. He has to have been watching us, following us, the scoundrel, spying on me.'

'I thought it was my brother spying on *me*,' she said. 'I had no idea it was Martin Page.'

Theodore dropped the half-smoked cigarette on to the floor, stubbing it out with an angry foot. 'Why didn't you tell me this earlier?'

He was making her nervous and angry. 'Because you was out and I didn't hear you come back and this morning you didn't give me no chance to tell you. That's why I'm telling you now.'

Theo rounded on her, his voice sharp. 'For God's sake, girl, speak properly! I will not have you letting me down at this crucial time. This is important to me, do you understand?'

'Yes!' she shot at him, sharp and tight-lipped. No more was said.

After fifteen minutes the brougham entered a mews, not too clean, with bits of waste paper blowing about the cobbles and narrow pavement before a wind that had sprung up that morning. The door they pulled up at was in need of a coat of paint, the green faded by sunlight. Helped down from the brougham, she waited as Theo paid the driver, then, taking her arm, he led her up the three shallow steps between the railings to the front door.

His anger had melted slightly. 'I should have told you where I was last night. I tapped on your door but you were asleep and I didn't want to wake you.' Theo rapped on the brass doorknocker. 'I was here last night. I telephoned on a mere whim and was told there had occurred a splendid opening if I wanted it. Just for the one evening but for as much money as the two whole weeks in that place we are currently appearing, and infinitely more prestige. Late though it was, I was invited here last night for a chat about it. But he wants to see you, my dear.'

He said no more as a maid opened the door to them. Theo stated his errand, and she gave a small curtsey for them to enter. Emma found herself in a wide hall that belied the scruffy front door. It was like walking into a palace.

'If you'd wait here, please,' said the girl, 'I'll tell Mr Simmons you're here.'

Seconds after she had knocked on one of the three doors leading off the hall, and was bidden to enter, Simmons appeared, hand extended to Theodore as he approached, his welcome loud and bluff.

'And how are you this morning, Barrington, old chap, after all my whisky you put away last night, hey?'

Theo's hand was pumped vigorously; Simmons's smile was as broad and plump as his face and body. Short in height, in a check suit that caused him to appear even shorter and broader, he beamed up at Emma.

'So this is the young lady. You're right, old chap – she is pretty, lovely, in fact. You made a damned fine choice, Barrington. Well, come in. I don't suppose you've break-fasted – here so early after a late night mulling over old times?' He led them into the room he'd come from. Now he turned to the hovering maid. 'Tilly, tea and crumpets for my visitors, quick as you can.'

The girl bobbed and hurried off and Simmons indicated for them to find somewhere to sit; the brown leather sofa and armchairs, as with many of the matching upright chairs, were all littered with stacks of paper.

'Push something aside, old chap. I know where every-thing is.'

He rubbed his podgy hands together as they found room to sit, he himself sinking into a brown leather swivel chair beside a heavy oak desk similarly littered.

'Right, now.' He leaned forward, the chair creaking. 'Let's get down to brass tacks while we're waiting for breakfast. Barrington, if you really are serious about getting back into the theatre, it'll cause quite a bit of a stir, I can tell you. It'll be different, I can say that!'

He relaxed, lounging back in his chair. 'Not much has changed since you did your disappearing act. Plenty of talk, of course. Some said you were doing a Charlier, as they say. No one ever knew where that mysterious old codger went to. Some said you were trying the same sort of thing, just for effect, but while old Charlier completely vanished off the face of the earth like one of his crafty card tricks and not a word heard of him from that day to this, you've returned to the scene, as it were.'

He paused as the door opened and the maid came in with a trolley bearing cups, saucers, teapot, milk jug and sugar bowl, plates, knives and a large dish of hot crumpets, a butter dish beside it.

Left to it, Simmons began doing the honours and Emma, sitting quietly by, on the edge of the sofa, self-conscious for once, was glad not to be asked to do them as the only female in the room. In fact, after his initial appraisal of her, Simmons had behaved as though she wasn't here. Now he got up and handed her the cup of tea he'd poured for her.

'Milk?' She nodded and he poured it for her. 'Sugar?' Again she nodded. 'One lump or two?'

'One,' she said softly. He looked at her.

'Nice attractive voice. Should go down well. Help yourself to crumpets. The butter is there. Have as many as you like. Enjoy yourself while me and Barrington have a little chat.'

Tea served, crumpets being scoffed, he began to explain what he had on offer.

'There's a rather splendid, rather special Christmas party to be held at a rather good address in Chelsea. Some rather important guests, I've been informed. I'll tell you about that later. Don't want to frighten the young lady here. They're looking for top-quality entertainers. I told them you were back in business ...'

He had drawn his swivel chair close to Theodore, leaning towards him, halfway through the information, his voice having sunk low, leaving Emma unable to catch what he was saying. Now his voice rose again.

'So, it's a deal?' he concluded, sitting upright.

'Most definitely,' said Theodore, but then leaned towards him. 'Has Martin Page been in touch with you?' he asked.

'Not that I know of,' came the reply.

'He's been following me around, you know.'

'Has he indeed?'

'How did he discover where I was living?'

Simmons gave a small laugh. 'Well, when I said, not that I know of, I meant not lately that I know of. He did come here ... when was it? Must be a year ago. I had an address of sorts and he seemed very keen to find you.'

'You didn't *have* my address,' Theo barked. Simmons smiled.

'Not exactly. I didn't know where you were. But someone, I don't know who, said he thought he'd seen you around the East End, somewhere in the West India Dock Road area. That's all I knew. That's all I told Page. It must have been how he traced you. He seemed pretty well keen to find you. God knows why! You can be a bit of a bastard!'

Simmons chuckled at his own joke. Theo didn't even smile.

'So what did he imagine was in it for him?'

'I've no idea. He must have some motive. Don't ask me.'

'Well, he found me, visited me, but I wanted nothing to do with him.'

'I heard something about that,' Simmons said quietly, more or less to himself. The remark was ignored.

'And he has been lurking around watching me ever since. I've noticed him on several occasions, and he has now made himself known to Amelia, harassing her, I might add. All I can say is that he must be desperate.'

'He *was* a damned good magician's assistant, despite … well …' Simmons gave a dismissive shrug. 'Had one of the best retentive memories in the business.'

Listening to them, Emma was shocked. Theo had known all along that it was Martin Page sneaking about after them. Why hadn't he mentioned it to her, leaving her to believe it was her brother?

'Maybe he hopes you'll take him back on to the payroll,' Simmons was saying, between mouthfuls of crumpet, devouring it without once taking it from his lips, entire thing disappearing the way a small creature would into a snake's mouth. She'd once seen it happen at Regent's Park Zoological Gardens when she'd been there as a child with her father. The sight had made her feel ill.

'After all,' Simmons was saying, munching on the last of the crumpet, 'the lad plainly feels done down. He told me he was innocent of … Well, no matter, I know he could find something in the theatre business himself, but he sounded quite embittered. Maybe you had reason but you must beware of riding roughshod over people, old chap. It can come back at you, y'know. I think he was more hoping you'd let bygones be bygones and take him on again. This is only from someone who knows the business, you understand.'

'What would I want with two assistants?' asked Barrington, who seemed completely unruffled by all this information.

Simmons reached for another crumpet, began buttering it, his actions casual. 'I dunno. You might work up an act that needed two. There are some doing it these days – usually a couple of young ladies, but male and female, both young, good-looking, attractive to an audience, you know. Could work up a fine act that way.'

'I already have a fine act.' Theo smiled and glanced across at Emma.

'Well,' said Simmons, 'think about it for some time in the future.'

Far from being irritated, Theo was nodding thoughtfully. 'We will see,' he said, then leaned forward. 'Now this opening you have.'

Emma, staring at the heavily laced curtained window through which weak, wintry sunlight was filtering, having finally broken through the heavy layer of morning cloud, listened to details of this one evening's engagement.

Simmons was stressing what a real start it was. 'Better than where you are now, working for a mere crust. And this'll bring you much more than money, old man. With the names I've mentioned your future's assured.'

By the way Theo's face brightened, he certainly appeared to agree as Simmons stood up to shake hands. Simmons nodded appreciatively at Emma.

'Very nice. Good choice.' He paused. 'I'll keep an eye out for any more interesting stuff coming along.' He gave another of his big laughs. 'After all, it behoves me to – to get my ten per cent out of you and all that.'

He saw them to the door, saying that he would relish his ten per cent of this present booking, still in a jovial mood, and giving Theo some paper work bearing the address and the amount that had been agreed, and as Emma moved past him, he gave her rump a far too familiar tap which made itself uncomfortably felt through the entire thickness of skirt and undergarments.

In view of Martin Page's warning of Theo's notorious jealous streak, she thought it better not to say anything to him about his agent's gesture of familiarity in case he got angry and spoiled this apparently wonderful offer. It had been only a passing thing, playful, and maybe what she must come to expect, being on the stage now. Her mother had said as much.

Theo was quiet on the way home, but she could see he was happy with all that had occurred.

'What about the two weeks we've still got to do at the Cambridge? Do we forget them?'

He looked at her as though she'd uttered a profanity. 'An entertainer never lets down the manager who hires him. For the rest of your life, Amelia, you will remember that. Do you understand?'

Chastened, Emma nodded and said no more the rest of the way home.

*

204

Three days to go to their one-night engagement in Chelsea. It would be on Christmas Eve. Theo had drilled her until Emma felt she could hardly store another item in her head; it was so full of numbers and gestures that they went round and round in her brain as she sought sleep. It would be a relief when it was all over and this engagement behind them.

But Christmas Eve! She'd hoped to go and see her mother on that day, but now that had to be put aside. And with all this rehearsing, it looked as though she wouldn't see her until after Christmas. She was able, though, to send her a postal order for two pounds with a promise to see her as soon as she had a moment to herself.

She could well afford the money. In fact she was richer than she'd ever been in her life, and stood to be even richer as time went on.

At the Cambridge, Theo had come away with twenty pounds for the two weeks. Out of that Simmons had claimed his ten per cent, of course. But Theo had generously given her five pounds as her share. She was now being required to pay for the rent of her own room, but that came to seven shillings a week, bed and board, which had left four pounds thirteen shillings. Even after sending Mum the postal order she'd been left with two pounds thirteen shillings all to herself. Wealth indeed for one who up to a few months ago had never had more than a shilling in her pocket, and that on only a very rare occasion.

Now Theo was being promised thirty guineas for one performance. Thirty guineas in one night! It sounded incredible. She'd caught a faint mention of the amount just before Simmons had given her rump that pat. How much would Theo give her out of it? Whatever it was, she'd be more than happy, but that was still to come.

She wrote to her mother about all that had happened to her these last weeks, again saying where she was living, and she waited for a reply. Mum wasn't much of a writer, actually she was partially illiterate, but had made sure her children had stayed at school. But surely, on receiving the money, she would put together a few words if only thank you. Ben might help her word a reply. That was if she told him about the money. But forty shillings arriving out of the blue wasn't to be sneezed at.

No letter came, not even a badly scribbled one. Perhaps it was just as well she hadn't gone in person. Having the door slammed in her face would have been more than she could have borne, and the lack of a reply made it all too likely that it was indeed what would have happened.

Cloaking her bitterness, Emma threw herself into her work, earning a good deal of delight from Theo for her dedication. He didn't know the truth behind it, but it did get her more prepared for what was in store, though as the day drew nearer she found her nerves getting the better of her. No time to worry about Mum.

He too seemed on edge, making it seem all the more intimidating. She hadn't caught the names of those to whom he'd be performing, but they had to be quite important to make a self-assured man like Theo nervous.

'It is never good to be complacent beforehand,' he told her when she asked how he felt. 'It is so with the very best. Nerves are designed to keep a performer on his toes. Once you are out there in front of your audience, you will be fine, my dear.'

He was always telling her she would be fine. She just hoped so. Such had been proved these last two weeks. The Cambridge held around fifteen hundred, small compared to some West End palaces of variety, and the first time on stage had dried her mouth as though flour had been poured into it. She'd got used to it, although having to move amongst so many at Theo's command had been somewhat alarming. Theo said there'd be around a hundred at this Christmas Eve party, so perhaps it wouldn't be too bad.

Chapter Sixteen

'How are you feeling?' Theo whispered as he handed her down from the four-wheeler where it had drawn up at the servants' entrance.

'Just the usual butterflies,' she said, hoping her reply didn't betray how scared she really felt.

After having got used to two weeks on stage in a music hall, this was something quite different. They'd passed the wide forecourt with its bevy of landaulettes and hackney carriages, even a couple of motor carriages, guests making their way up shallow steps to a marble portico to the front entrance while attendants ran back and forth helping others from their conveyances, all in the golden glow from a dozen lighted windows of the Chelsea mansion where Theo would perform his magic.

She stood now beside the four-wheeler while he took charge of unloading the equipment, the sharpness of his commands to the driver telling her that he too was edgy.

The man's reaction, typical of the nickname, growlers, for these four-wheelers, was making his grievances known by growling and grumbling as he dumped box after box inside the side entrance that he was a bloody cabby, not a bloody carter. But offered a sizeable tip, his churlishness ceased and he tipped his cap. 'Thanks, guv,' he muttered hoarsely.

Emma was glad to be out of the vehicle that smelled of damp leather after a day of sleet. The clouds, thankfully, had parted and a full, cold moon lit up the gravel driveway as Theo led the way. A short, broad-chested man carrying a portmanteau was being admitted by a manservant in a black apron, grandly stating his name and what he did before proceeding inside.

Theo sounded equally grandiose as he too announced himself, his voice deep compared to the other, apparently some well-known operatic tenor, though Emma had never heard of him. But what would she know of opera, having never been?

The footman moved back to the announcement, 'The Great Theodore!'

'Oh, yes, the magician. Right.' He glanced down at the array of boxes. 'I'll get them taken in for you, sir.'

Theo nodded curtly. The man continued, 'Right, this way then, Mr Theodore. We've a room set aside just along here for all the entertainers.'

'How many of us?' enquired Theo. The man looked back over his shoulder as he led the way.

'There's you, there's that opera singer, the one following you in is a violinist. There's a minstrel group and a Shakespearean chap that's going to recite, and when it's all over there's a quartet that's going to play for Lady G's cotillion. That's dancing, y'know.'

'I know what a cotillion is,' said Theo. Emma said nothing, following close behind.

'Well, it's a dance all right,' said the man, 'but these days they call the whole evening of dancing after it now.'

'I am aware of that. Are these the only entertainers?'

'Yes. You're the last to go on before the dancing starts. She your assistant, the young lady?'

Theodore deigned not to reply as they were shown into a large room sparsely furnished with dark wood cupboards and chests. It had several tables with mirrors on them, chairs, some screens for the privacy of performers who needed to change; it was probably used as a storeroom between times.

Nodding in response to a reminder that refreshments would arrive shortly, to be partaken whilst Lady G's guests were at dinner, Theodore sought out a corner for himself and Emma, arranging the screen supplied for privacy to form a small room, and ignoring the other performers as if they were below him.

'This will have to do,' he said, sitting at the table provided and gazing around for room to put the equipment. There was time to set things up and to dress in what they would wear.

Theo's evening clothes had secret compartments for items that would appear magically before his audience. She would have a gown of pale green chiffon, a colour he insisted on to bring out her auburn hair, flouting the old superstition of green being unlucky. He had chosen everything for her, paying for it himself – the gown, the elbow-length cream gloves, the sparkling choker and tiara of emeralds, glass of course not real – 'They'll be real one day, my dear,' he promised in soft tones – enhancing her so that she seemed at least two years older than a girl just two months off seventeen. She wished she felt

210

like that. While he went off to organise the setting-up of his equipment, she dressed, unable to touch any of the sumptuous refreshment for nerves, but when he returned she saw admiration in his eyes as he regarded her.

'Yes,' he said slowly. 'You will enchant them. There are among the audience tonight some who themselves have to do with the legitimate stage, as well as several titled personages and eminent business people.'

It did little to eradicate her already nervous state. 'I'm starting to feel awfully jittery,' she admitted, risking his irritation, but he took one of her hands in his own and raised it to his lips, his beard soft against her skin.

'Don't be,' he murmured, turning her to hook her back fastenings for her. 'They are only people. The time to be jittery is if you let me down.'

It had been said gently enough, but it carried the faintest of threats for her to do well. 'When you go on, you leave your nerves behind you. If you let them take hold while performing, you'll be incapable of doing your job.' To her mind, as much to say, don't make a fool of him. Thereafter she withheld her feelings from him.

Now they were dressed and waiting, time seemed to creep when all she wanted was for it to be over and to be on their way home. Just fifteen minutes, she kept telling herself, that's all it is, just fifteen minutes of your life, fifteen minutes you'd hardly notice go by, normally. It didn't help at all.

She tried to distract her mind from what lay ahead by listening to the sounds of preparations beyond their screen: the tentative tuning of violin, cello, flute and viola by the quartet; the recitalist chatting in sonorous tones to the opera singer from whom wafted waves of perfume; the minstrels were going through their song parts in small snatches of harmony. All of them waiting their turn to appear before this illustrious gathering; were they as terrified as she?

Apart from a certain amount of tension in making sure his equipment was in its correct order, Theodore alone seemed composed, though he had spoken to no one other than her.

'Watch me well when we are on,' he said as he surveyed her to make certain her appearance was impeccable. 'I want no hesitation in replying to my questions except where rehearsed, no fumbling when you hand me what I require, all must be done gracefully, smoothly, efficiently.'

'I know what to do,' she hissed back, adjusting her shoulder straps. 'We've rehearsed it enough times.'

'One can never rehearse *enough*,' came the sharp reply.

Knowing it unwise to make another retort, Emma occupied herself by tweaking at her décolletage. It was far too low, far too revealing. How would they see her out there on stage or whatever other arrangements had been made for a stage in this private house – an alluring young woman or just a showgirl? A footman was requesting the first performer to follow him. Emma peeped through a gap in the screen to see the Shakespearean actor tug at the jacket of his evening dress and smooth a hand over his thin, dark hair before following the man. She looked at Theodore, adjusting the hidden pockets of his own evening dress.

'We're last,' she said unnecessarily.

'All the better,' he returned evenly. 'No one to see you going through your final paces, except those returning to depart after their performance. Then it will not matter. You must be nothing less than perfect. The whole of my future career depends on tonight. I am putting my head on the block, trusting that you will not let me down. You understand me, my dear?'

She nodded. He should have had Martin Page for this, not Emma, who had no experience beyond a few months having her role drummed into her and playing to street audiences, and two weeks on a stage before a gaping, toffee-munching, beer-swilling crowd. But she dared not voice it. Not now.

'Then see you do,' he said. 'Already I have misgivings.'

It was as if he read her thoughts. As if his mind-reading act was far more real than she imagined. Emma stemmed a small shiver and turned her thoughts to the mind-reading, concentrating on all those tiny nuances that called for her response to the slightest variation of movement from him, the faintest inflection of tone and sequence of words that would bring from her the reply he was asking for – all to lodge in her brain as though a part of it.

Yet still Theo wasn't satisfied. 'What am I asking you to say when I hold my hand thus? What am I asking you to tell me when I turn my head thus on speaking the words, "What do I have here?" What, when I look up at the ceiling as though in thought? What, when I turn my head to the right?'

Thought transference and mental telepathy worried the life out of her, afraid that she'd forget a certain sound or move.

'You remember the sequence of the numbers, the letters, the moves we have rehearsed?' He was torturing her with his badgering.

213

'Yes. Yes,' she said, her head already reeling, but still he drilled her.

It was imperative, of course, that she make no errors. It still surprised her that she'd learned to retain so much in such a short time, how retentive was her memory.

She'd left school at such a young age that she'd never realised how good a brain she had, regarding herself as dim and not worthy of learning, but her schoolteachers had not been the dedicated type. Had her father been well off she now felt sure she might have gone on to one of those universities for young women that in this still young century were beginning to spring up for those who could afford it. She'd had lots of confidence in herself but of the street sort, a natural gift for survival. But she had Theo to thank for opening her eyes to what she really could attain.

The Shakespearean actor had returned. He saw her standing by the now half-drawn-back screen. He smiled at her, winked encouragingly, but as Theo glared at him and pulled her slightly back, he went on without saying a word. Going to his corner, he began packing ready to depart. An office near to the servants' side door would have his fee waiting for him.

The opera singer was being summoned, stalking by without looking right or left. He returned after twenty minutes, still looking imperiously ahead.

The minstrels, probably hired to add a little lightness to the evening, were a lively group, chatting and laughing loud enough for a footman to come and shush them. All young men, one winked at Emma, another saucily eyed her up and down. Thankfully Theo didn't see them, being busy with his preparations.

As they left in their street clothes, one said cheerily, 'You're in for a bit of a nice surprise, old matey, when you get out there and see who they've got as one of their guests.' Theo didn't reply.

Then came the turn of the violinist, a small and wiry, pale-faced man, with black hair that seemed in need of a trim. He glanced sideways at the magician as he hurried after the footman. The quartet, of course, would be needed for the dancing.

The violinist approaching his finale, Emma and Theo were conducted up a flight of stairs and along a carpeted corridor with wide, double doors at the end. They were open and Emma could see that a low stage had been set up in the room beyond, with curtains on one side of the double doors to serve as the wings. There were heavy, drawn curtains before the windows, behind which Theo had set up his special equipment while the guests were at dinner in another room.

Out of sight behind the side curtains as they waited their turn to go on, Emma felt a sickness in her stomach at the sight of the great room. It was all a-glitter with huge chandeliers. Rosewood chairs had been set in rows on a highly polished floor. There were deep sofas all around the room's perimeter, the furnishings and drapes in rich fawn velvet. There were beautiful vases everywhere, and gilt statuettes, and huge paintings. At one end of the room was another pair of tall, wide, double doors like those at this end. The walls were covered in pale blue, in a fabric that looked like silk, and the ceiling was a sight to behold with gilt and plaster cherubs smiling down from the frieze.

It was the audience, sitting very stiff and upright on their chairs, that threw her into a flurry. Such dresses, such evening clothes. Perfume wafted towards her, as did the well-bred chatter and occasional genteel laugh. She had never seen such people, even those coming out of a theatre in their outdoor finery who had usually hurried by with hardly a glance at her, hardly seeing her. Now, they would all see her.

What if she were to make a mistake? What she had to do had been drilled into her, yet what if … ? How could she face the titter that would ripple around the audience, the sighs, the fidgeting, polite coughing?

It had once happened to Theodore Barrington, not polite coughing but hoots and jeers. It had taken him more than a year to recover, using the death of his wife as an excuse for the loss of his reputation rather than blaming himself. He'd told her that she had been his salvation, and she liked to think that it was she who'd helped fish him out of that mire of dejection. But who would fish her out? He had as good as warned her that she was only as good as her act, that he'd not want her if she let him down.

All she could do was pray. No backing out now, at the very point of going on as a polite clapping followed the quiet announcement of the renowned, Great Theodore, 'restored to us from the darkness into which he vanished so long ago.' After such an announcement she wasn't about to let him see the terror that was washing over her.

He looked tall and imposing and most regal in his opera hat, evening suit and cape, his fair beard groomed and pointed, his fair hair plastered neatly back from his high forehead, prepared to entertain, to awe, perhaps even to frighten. He was ready. She felt she surely would never be.

Switching her eyes from him, Emma gazed again at the audience. It was then that her heart almost stopped.

Sitting right in front beside a beautiful, elegant and dignified woman on whose head was the most splendid diamond tiara, was a portly figure, similarly bearded to Theo except that his beard was grey and his head was balding.

She knew instantly who he was, from pictures of him. King Edward himself! Her heart having missed its beat, thudded on against her ribs hard enough to stifle her. She felt herself trembling and she was sure she was about to faint.

Theo's whispered words as they'd made their way along a corridor to this room, were ringing in her ears: 'Let me down just once and I will have done with you. You can return to where you came from.'

It had hit her as unfair after all the trust she'd put in him, after all the times she had urged him to find himself again.

His voice though low had been fierce, had hissed as though she were his sworn enemy instead of his confederate, his confidante. For the first time ever she felt what it could really be like to be on the wrong side of him.

Making her way down that corridor with Theo beside her and the enigmatic footman walking with measured steps ahead of them, she had shuddered despite herself. But it was nothing compared to what swept over her at the sight of that eminent figure of the King.

Theo must have known. She recalled his theatrical agent whispering names of those who'd be here, names she couldn't catch. Why hadn't he warned her? She would have been prepared. Surely he hadn't intended to allow her to be shocked rigid and perhaps ruin his performance by it.

He glanced at her and smiled. 'Hold yourself upright, my dear.' It was said kindly. She must have been slumping and she must have gone white. It was his next words that made her come to her senses. 'Remember, no matter who is out there, they are only people, with the same functions as you and I. We all need to visit once a day!'

Despite herself, Emma burst into silent laughter and suddenly all fear left her. When she followed him on out from the wings, everything she'd been taught came flooding back. As he bowed, she curtseyed as taught, and taking her cue from him directed her obeisance at Their Majesties in a curtsey deeper and more studied than even Theo had shown her.

Her head was lowered, but when she looked up, the royal eyes, pale blue yet glinting, were smiling directly at her, the royal head nodding approval of her. Her nerves unexpectedly vanished. She smiled shyly back and with sparkling eyes surveyed the audience. It was as Theo had said. She was here and the audience was there. She could do what they couldn't, and by that token held them in the palm of her hand, even a king.

It was almost tangible, this knowledge, and now she knew what Theo had meant when he'd spoken nostalgically of the romance of the stage, the pull of it and how he had grieved leaving it behind even while using his departure as self-punishment.

The act was over so quickly. It couldn't have gone better. Theo's hands were fast, the audience gasping at the wonders performed before them, applauding as a whole deck of cards appeared one by one between his fingers, the empty box erected piece by piece before their eyes and opened to reveal herself, he having drilled her into becoming quick and supple; the empty canister in which he set fire to a piece of gauze, revealing an unruffled dove as the lid extinguishing the flame was lifted once more; the laughter at the trick of Mama and Papa Rabbit made of soft sponge rubber placed in the hand of someone in the audience, to suddenly produce a whole litter of baby rabbits as the hand was opened. Trickery, yet by their gasps they appeared to believe everything they saw as pure magic.

Then the room was dimmed for the mind-reading act, the thing she had dreaded. Yet it all fell so precisely into place, her interpreting the codes so perfectly that the dim room filled with awed gasps and even polite cries of alarm from the ladies every now and again.

Theo was awe-inspiring, as if possessing powers beyond comprehension. He held his audience in his grip. Even Their Majesties, who'd been smiling throughout more light-hearted illusions, became stern-faced and watchful.

When the lights were brought up again the applause was tremendous, yet more tremendous still as the Great Theodore ended with a flourish that astonished them all.

Producing several sheets of coloured tissue to tear the shapes of small butterflies from them, he dropped the pieces into a shallow bowl of water. He stirred them into a sodden mass with a chopstick and held up the remains of the tissue paper for them all to see the holes that were left.

Producing a square Chinese fan, red, with a large black circle at the centre, with his other hand he scooped the pulped mass from the water, squeezed it in his palm until every drop of water was gone, then bounced the wet pellet on the fan, catching and bouncing. Then before an audience wondering what this was all about, he waved the fan at the fist he'd made, causing a few paper butterflies to fly up from the still closed fingers.

Again and again they flew, thicker and thicker, faster and faster as the applause grew, he slowly backing towards the curtained window, and as he disappeared from view, a veritable cloud of coloured paper butterflies fluttered outwards all over the small stage.

It was a graceful, wondrous sight, and the elegant audience was loud with its approval as he reappeared to take his bow, bringing Emma forward to take her encore. The King rose to his feet, still applauding. Dutifully, the audience did the same as the amazing performer with his beautiful assistant departed through the side curtains, leaving his equipment to be removed by footmen.

The last she saw on leaving the stage was the King beaming. In all her life she felt that never again would she experience such pride and joy. It was over. She'd done well. The King of England had hardly taken his eyes off her. For the first time ever she became vividly aware that she actually possessed real beauty.

Chapter Seventeen

'Mr Barrington?'

'Yes?' Theo and Emma looked up in surprise from packing away the equipment to see a royal equerry standing at the door of the deserted dressing room.

'His Majesty the King.'

The man stepped smartly aside for the portly, royal figure to move into the room, alone but for his equerry.

Theodore instantly came to attention and bowed low, Emma dropping into a deep curtsey at His Majesty's approach.

'Wonderful entertainment!' came an exuberant exclamation as both straightened up in readiness to be met. 'I've been eager to see how you'd perform after so long an absence, having heard so much about your abilities, and many times found myself wondering where you went. But no matter, you are with us again, performing splendidly, fulfilling our every expectation, thoroughly mystifying us all. I simply had to leave the dancing to the others for a while and sneak off down here and offer my personal congratulations to you.'

Emma could hear faint music emanating from the rooms above as the King continued: 'I can see why you were so popular, that is before you vanished, like one of your tricks, eh?'

He gave a wicked chuckle, adding, 'And now back again and with a charming young lady to assist you. My dear man, where did you find her?'

Not waiting for a reply he turned to Emma. 'How pretty you are, my dear. What is your name?'

Curtseying once more, the deepest she could muster, her heart pounding, hardly able to find her voice, she managed to squeak her reply, using the name of Amelia Beech as Theo would have wanted, as this from now on was to be the name she was to be known by.

Her mouth had gone dry, but at least in this low posture she felt safer, and who knows, the ground might even open up and swallow her to take her from this unnerving royal presence.

It had been bad enough finding him sitting out there in front, though with all that concentrating on what Theo was asking of her she'd almost forgotten His Majesty was there. But to have him come in person to where they were changing terrified the life out of her all over again.

Managing to recover her normal voice, she added, 'Your Majesty,' her curtsey still keeping her below the royal gaze. Without looking up she saw him bend towards her and next moment he was lifting her upright.

'One curtsey is quite enough, my dear.'

Taking her hand he lifted it to his lips and she was conscious of the soft pressure of his beard even with the long cream gloves she still wore with the lovely pale green chiffon dress.

Still bending over her hand, he glanced up at her. 'May I say how beautiful your eyes are, my dear, as is the rest of you? Indeed, I cannot help thinking how truly pleasant it would be to have the company of such a pretty young lady at supper one evening. Not this evening, I regret. My time is being taken up by others ...'

He offered her a wry smile and tilted his pale eyes ceiling-wards above which music could still be heard. 'Such a bore, when I am far more content with things here. But there it is.'

He gave a resigned shrug, then as though on a whim reached into the inner breast pocket of his dinner jacket and produced a plain white card and handed it to her. 'Telephone number to my private apartments. Given only to a few chosen friends, if you know what I mean, my dear?'

She knew what he meant, if only by his look of caution. Not to be passed on. And of course it would not be. She felt utterly flattered. Lost for words, not in her wildest dreams did she imagine this could happen to her.

'All you will need, my dear,' he continued, 'is to give your name to my secretary, who will have instructions to put you through to me personally should you wish to avail yourself of my offer. I eagerly await your call some time.'

Turning slowly from her to Theo, he said, 'The most exquisite creature I have ever seen. You are a lucky man, Mr Barrington, if indeed she is more than just your assistant.' He squinted sagely at him. 'Though I now perceive that she is not. Am I correct?' He smiled as Theodore half tilted his head in grudging confirmation.

'Yes, my dear man, I see that I am.' He gave a small sigh. 'Dear, dear, such beauty shouldn't be wasted. But now, duty calls. I must devote myself to my gracious hostess, Lady Gingham. Goodbye, and thank you for a very pleasant and intriguing finish to our evening's entertainment.'

Giving Theo a small, courteous but brief nod of the head and receiving Theo's deep response, he turned back to Emma, once more taking her hand to bend over it before departing with the equerry, who was now anxious to have him return to the dancing.

As he left, Emma heard him say to the equerry, 'Pretty little thing, Harry, don't you think? Quite exquisite. I really must meet her again.' To which the man inclined his head, throwing Emma a sly look as he did so.

Her cheeks flushed and, virtually beside herself with delight, she turned to Theo with excited incredulity. 'I can't believe ...'

She was surprised to see his expression dark and brooding. All she was about to say died on her lips, her joy replaced by concern.

'What's the matter?' she asked. 'What's wrong?'

His expression hadn't altered. 'Should something be wrong?'

'I don't know,' she replied, worried. 'But something is. Didn't I do as well as you'd hoped?'

'You did well enough,' he said slowly. 'In fact I suppose I really should congratulate you.'

'Then what is it?'

He began concentrating on unbuttoning the jacket and waistcoat of his stage clothes. 'We shall celebrate your debut, Amelia. We will have supper and drink champagne.'

'Champagne?'

'I am being given a good fee for this one performance, and so I should, with *His Majesty* being present.' The

224

stress he put on the royal title made Emma frown as he moved behind the screen to change. 'If you intend to change, you had best hurry,' came his voice. 'Going out as you are, you could be mistaken for a woman of easy virtue I've picked up.'

It was a cruel remark, cruel and unnecessary. It hurt and confused. He'd said she'd done well this evening. So why talk as if he'd taken an intense dislike to her? She'd never seen him behave like this before.

Bewildered, she slid behind a vacant screen to change. 'Please, Theo, is it me? Have I done something to upset you?'

His only response was, 'Hurry up. The sooner we leave the better.'

It was best not to pursue it. Perhaps later, when he felt better, he'd tell her what had so annoyed him.

The supper wasn't terribly expensive but the restaurant was quite exclusive, with a table in an alcove which made her wonder if he had booked it especially for them when he'd been in a more receptive mood before going to do his act.

They ate in silence and she gave up trying to draw him out. But after a glass or two of the champagne she felt more emboldened to ask again what had upset him so. Mellowed by champagne and brandy, he became suddenly more forthcoming.

'Drooling over you, and you not yet seventeen. It disgusted me. He might be our sovereign but he's a woman-chasing old goat and that's no secret. Didn't it occur to you that he was flirting with you, and you blushing and simpering and casting down your eyes for him? It sickened me.'

So that was it. Theo's attitude had changed moments after the royal visit. Too much attention had been paid to her and Theo had felt slighted.

She watched him moodily replenishing his brandy glass. He'd already had too much, on top of the champagne as well. She too was feeling the effects of the lovely, pale, fizzy stuff. After supper he tried to tempt her to sip the brandy but she didn't like its taste. It also caught in her throat so that she could hardly swallow any more, leaving him to consume the rest.

Longing only to be safely back in her bed, to fall asleep and forget this evening, which had started so well if nerve-rackingly, and ended so miserably, she watched him slowly drift into a world of his own, ignoring her. By the time a handsome cab was ordered, he was certainly far from sober.

On the short ride back he held her hand between his. The palms felt hot against her skin as he told her over and over how well she had followed his every instruction during their act, his jealousy apparently forgotten. It didn't seem proper for a person such as Theodore to grow maudlin.

'You've accomplished a miracle,' he slurred, breathing in her face. 'I've made a wise choice. You're better than he ever was, Martin Page. He was good, yes, very good, and young. It's what the audience likes – beauty and youth.'

How could a man refer to another as being beautiful? He was peering at her in the dimness of the hansom cab. 'You are bewildered by my reference to beauty. But youth is beautiful. He was young. You are young. I derive pleasure from youth – unblemished, untainted, vital – innocent as yet of ... of how life can bear down on one – age one. Oh, the boundless … the boundless energy of the young.' He was having trouble pronouncing his words.

'Shameful, the waste of my youth,' he slurred on as though speaking to himself. 'Lonely. Could've been so easily remedied. We take our youth for granted. The young expect it to go on for ever. But it doesn't. It can't be recaptured. All I do now is admire it, try to catch and hold it in my hands awhile. He took that from me when he and she … Then deserted me …'

Emma was aware that he was still talking about Martin Page. 'You told him to leave,' she ventured. 'I was there when he came begging you to return to the stage, but you sent him away.'

'Had he persisted, I might have …'

'But he came back the other night and you were angry over that too.'

'For spying on me. I have you now, my dear. All that went before – all over and done with. Now I have you. You have given me a reason to feel young once more.'

Turning, he lifted his hands towards her, one moving up to touch her cheek, but one came to rest on the curve of her breast. With a gasp of alarm, Emma shrank back. Instantly he withdrew both hands.

'My dear, forgive me. I humbly apologise.' He seemed shocked at his own conduct.

'It's all right,' she said, recovering. But the pressure on her bosom had awakened a strange sensation she hadn't known before. Five minutes later, with gentlemanly courtesy and surprisingly steady on his feet, he was helping her down from the hansom. With stiff formality he saw her to the door of her room. It was as though the episode in the cab hadn't occurred. Maybe the touch had been purely accidental after all. Even if it hadn't been, he'd been putting away a little too much brandy and champagne and had probably been a little carried away for a moment. She sought to excuse him.

'I'm sorry about being so silly. I was taken by surprise.'

She was gratified to see him relax a little. Beneath that stiff, awesome composure of his, he was probably lonely, pining for the wife he'd lost, his life loveless. He had spoken of loneliness and her heart went out to him.

'Would you like to come in for a while so we can talk?'

She needed to find out more about him and be sure of that sensation she'd experienced. If she knew more of his background, his marriage, his earlier life, it would make him seem in a way more human.

'I've got a little sherry in my room.' She'd bought it when continuous rehearsals had got on top of her, hoping it might help quell the confusion in her head. It had worked and after the first glass or two she hadn't needed it again. It remained on her bedside commode, but now was a time to share it with him and settle her own mind on how she really felt about him.

He regarded her with that steady, penetrating stare that could unnerve, as if reading her thoughts, his mind-reading actually becoming real. Then he nodded and she turned to lead the way.

There was only one chair in the room. She thought he would take it while she sat on the edge of her bed, but to her surprise he ignored it, sitting beside her instead. She wanted to spring up.

'The sherry,' she reminded, but before she could move, his hand came over hers.

Emma stiffened. Had he mistaken her invitation to enter her room as an entirely different sort of offer? Alarm increased as he leaned towards her, but it wasn't for what she had expected.

'Will you take advantage of that proposal?'

'What proposal?'

'The King's proposal to have supper with him at some time.'

Emma gave a small giggle of relief. 'Of course not! The likes of me?'

Theodore didn't laugh. 'It is the likes of you, as you put it, whom he finds intriguing. Everyone knows of Edward's fondness for the fairer sex, whereas I speak nothing but truth when I say you are the loveliest creature I have ever known.'

Emma looked down at the hand covering hers to hide her blush that stemmed not just from self-consciousness. The hand was large. It felt warm. There was a hint of pressure in its grip, and suddenly she knew what had so upset him. He'd been jealous of the King's attention to her. One had to be in love to be jealous. A warm happiness spread through her. All else forgotten, she still couldn't believe what had happened to her, an ordinary girl like her, first receiving attention from the King of England who had suggested she have supper with him – whether said light-heartedly or not, she was still dazzled – and now Theo, the Great Theodore, with promise of wonderful things to come from this one appearance before royalty, behaving as though he adored her.

Looking up at him, her eyes bright, she saw his face very close to hers so that his breath caressed her cheek.

'I am in love with you, Amelia,' she heard him whisper.

His lips were on hers, his moustache and beard soft against her skin. Too dazed to pull away, whether she had wanted to or not, she felt her body being slowly eased downward until her head and shoulders were on the pillow.

'I could not have borne to have you to accept that man's offer,' he whispered between kisses moving over her cheeks, her eyelids, and back to her mouth. 'Tell me, my dearest, do you return my love? Or are your sights set on a king?'

Theatrical enough to draw a laugh in any other circumstances, but she could only nod to the first question and shake her head to the second, unable to speak under the increasing pressure of his lips on hers.

Not quite sure what to do, she lay still. He was undoing the buttons of her outdoor jacket, undoing those of her blouse. Warm fingers were between her bare flesh and the camisole and corset. The touch brought a wonderful sensation that seemed to climb all over her as the groping hand eased her breast free of its prison. His lips moving downward to the exposed flesh brought a whimper of joy to her lips.

Instantly the hand was pulled away. 'Dear God!' The exclamation wasn't directed at her, but himself. 'In God's name what am I doing?'

His weight lifted off her. His eyes seemed to bore into hers, holding her questioning stare. Then he turned away to sit up, his back to her.

'Why didn't you stop me? Why didn't you protest?' It was as though he was blaming her, almost accusing her of enticing him. Maybe he thought she had, inviting him into her room. But it had been in all innocence. Yet had it been so innocent? Had she known all along, deep down, that she was asking for something like this to happen? Maybe it was her fault.

'I'm sorry,' was all she could say.

As if her words were a searing iron, he leaped up from the bed, making for the door. There he paused, still with his back to her. 'Never,' she heard him say, 'never, ever try to tempt me again,' leaving her in a daze.

Jack Simmons leaned back in his creaking swivel chair, fiddling with a pencil between the fingers and thumbs of both hands while he regarded Theodore Barrington. 'I take it, it went well.'

Behind Theodore, Emma stood in silence, subdued by all that had happened on Saturday evening. The traumatic experience of finding herself on stage before royalty, then King Edward himself attempting to proposition her, she'd been delighted and flattered. Then she had experienced Theo's unreasonably jealous behaivour. Then to welcome his advances only to have him blame her for something that had been of his doing. Then as if he was punishing her still more, he had stayed in his room throughout Sunday.

He hadn't appeared for any meals. Mrs Tankerton was asked politely if she would kindly take a snack and a pot of tea up to him some time during the day, something she was quite willing to do, as by Sunday lunch she had become a little concerned for him.

'Is he feeling unwell, your Mr Barrington?' she had asked Emma when he didn't appear at breakfast. Emma said she wasn't sure, that she'd knocked on his door and been told to please go and leave him be. 'He's likely a bit under the weather, then,' Mrs Tankerton had concluded.

'A cold night and having a little too much to drink.' Her eyes never missed a thing. She even perhaps knew what had gone on in Emma's room. No doubt she saw it her job to know what her guests were up to, and so get rid of undesirables.

In Jack Simmons's office this Monday morning, Emma kept discreetly in the background, hoping not to be noticed, leaving the two men to get on with their business.

'It went very well,' Theo was saying to Simmons's question. 'But why didn't you tell me the King and Queen would be there? Or didn't you know that?' Listening, Emma silently forgave Theo – he hadn't known after all.

Simmons leaned further back in his chair, making it creak even more, his broad face wreathed in a grin. 'If I'd told you, old boy, you'd have got cold feet and backed out with stage fright.'

'I never have stage fright.'

Simmons's eyes widened with mock surprise. 'So what were these last eighteen months in the wilderness all about?'

'My reasons are my own, Jack, my agent or not.' Having given a curt answer, he went on more amiably, 'So now, what else do you have for me?'

Simmons pursed thick lips, as sanguine as his cheeks, and creaked forward in the chair to begin thumbing through an untidy sheath of papers on his desk.

'There's an opening at the Pavilion, Whitechapel, variety show, this Saturday coming until the twenty-fourth. Not top billing, of course.'

'It should be,' interrupted Theodore. 'I have just played before the King, and you offer me a flea-pit?'

'Not the grandest of places I admit, but give it time. The word of you playing before the King won't have got around yet. When it does, you'll be in demand right enough. You couldn't have a better start than you did on Saturday. I leaned over backwards there for you. You should be grateful, old boy. So thank me!'

His client said nothing.

'Look,' Simmons went on. 'Take this for now. Pantomime season, y'know. Most places are busy with that. I only got this opening this morning – singer they booked gone down with laryngitis, left them in a spot. It'll keep you going until word gets around of your tremendous success after eighteen months' silence.'

He let the papers rest on his deck while he looked earnestly across it at Theo. 'I telephoned the hostess yesterday, even though it was Christmas Day. She was singing your praises. Her little soirée was a roaring success, and apparently the King was well taken by your little assistant there. Couldn't stop talking about her. Queen wasn't too happy, but that's too bad.'

He nodded towards Emma without looking at her. 'You'll go far with someone as pretty as that. Hang on to her. She's a splendid draw to the male audience. While you're about it, Barrington, how about thinking again about taking on that second assistant I spoke about a while ago. Dare I mention that young man Martin Page? He's a handsome young man. He'd take the wives' eyes off their ogling husbands.'

He threw Emma a significant glance. 'Know what I mean?'

Theodore ignored it. Simmons shrugged. 'Well, think about it. But I can assure you, Theodore, after Saturday, theatre managers will be lining up to book you. As I said, you couldn't have had a better start. Count yourself lucky. I heard that a bonus was arranged on top of your fee. Apparently it was King Edward's personal wish.' Simmons was looking at her at last. 'You did all right, young lady?'

Emma coloured as Theo also turned to regard her, his eyes, though cold, taking her in a little too fully, she felt.

'She did well,' he said coolly. 'She is exceptionally bright, though you wouldn't have thought it had you seen her some months back.'

'So, what d'you think about taking Page back?'

'Why change horses mid-stream?' queried Theodore, making Emma's hackles rise at the remark about horses. Without her the mind-reading act, the best bit of it apart from the final butterflies trick, wouldn't have gone on.

'Why indeed?' echoed Simmons. 'But why change them at all? Why not have both, as I keep saying? Think of the draw. Think of the attention. Think of her and him standing there together, each attracting the gaze of the opposite sex. It would certainly be different.'

He ended by sitting back, well pleased with the vision he hoped he had created in Theo's mind, while Emma seethed.

It was humiliating being discussed in this fashion, as if she were some creature in a cage, or not here at all. To her surprise Theo drew in a deep, thoughtful breath.

'We will see. I don't wish to count my chickens too soon. I would be insane to consider two salaries before I know if it is worth it.'

Salary? This morning Theo had given her a full quarter of his fee, eight pounds. After what had happened last night, she had let it lie where he'd left it, on her dressing table, seeing it as some sort of conscience money. But here he was talking about *salary*, and twenty-five per cent of his fees at that! It was generous beyond measure. Emma felt forgiveness begin to flood through her veins.

Theodore was regarding his agent. 'Tell me, Simmons, what made you mention Page's name?'

Simmons gave a defeated grin. 'He came here on Saturday evening, wanting to see me, hoping you might consider him now that you're back in business.'

'Damn his impudence!'

Simmons let out a guffaw. 'Impudent or not, he's got plenty of spirit. Well, think about it, Barrington. So you'll do the Pavilion then?'

Theo's outgoing breath conveyed resignation. 'If you can guarantee work from now on.'

Simmons gave a hearty nod. 'Oh, I can guarantee that all right.'

'And if something good comes up in the meantime, you'll get in touch immediately.'

'Without fail, old man.' Simmons knew this was not a request but an order and if he didn't agree he could lose a valuable client. Theodore and his beautiful young assistant were destined for great things. Very soon every theatrical agent in London would be slavering to have the Great Theodore on his books. But he wasn't prepared to let go now.

Chapter Eighteen

By the end of January Emma had money enough to open a small bank account and see her mother all right – as soon as she found time to visit. She'd sent money by postal order, but it wasn't the same as going in person.

It wasn't easy finding the time, she and Theo appearing every night at the Pavilion, and then on to the Cambridge straight after, two venues each night – something he said he'd never do – plus the endless rehearsing that he maintained was essential. He was right of course – no magician dare let his work slip – besides which he was forever devising new illusions in which she was required to take part.

So far, they'd done ten nights at the Pavilion and the Cambridge, with Jack Simmons's promise of greater things to come from Theo's appearance before royalty not having materialised as yet.

'Be patient, he tells me,' Theo complained. 'How long is one expected to be patient? If he doesn't look out I shall find myself another theatrical agent. He needs to keep in mind that I have performed before royalty, no less, and if he cannot take up on that ...'

The obvious threat drifting off into silence, Emma allowed him a smile of mild agreement. She'd come to know Theo's mercurial nature, one minute filled with ego, the next morose and easily ruffled. That was when he'd take to his room and not come out, and she knew he'd be having himself more than one drink, for he'd become maudlin and benevolent.

One thing though, he hadn't touched her since that night after the King's proposal. She wasn't sure whether to be glad or sorry. It had been a strange, wonderful experience, leaving her uncertain of herself.

As for His Majesty's proposal, far from being flattered, she now saw it as outrageous. Had she taken up the offer, she could have discovered herself entirely forgotten; and how embarrassed she'd have been, faced by his equerry's cold reception. She wasn't sure about Theo's jealousy, but he was right to have been annoyed. He was always right.

This morning Theo was with his agent, no doubt reminding him yet again of that royal performance and hopefully negotiating some deal or other. He would not tell her what it was until settled, reluctant to lose face by saying too much too soon. She'd have to be patient.

Today, left alone for once, she would take advantage of Theo's rare absence and summon up courage to go and see her mother if only to wish her a belated happy 1904. She found it difficult after two months without setting eyes on her. There had never been a single response to any of the money she'd sent in the past, much less a thank you. It proved just how deep the hurt of her leaving home had gone. Turning up this morning might even make things worse, but she had to try. There had been so many times when she had longed to put things right and now was the time.

As she entered the tenement block with its familiar musty odour, she wondered how she had ever got so used to it that she had no longer been aware of it, as she tried now not to breathe too deeply. Mrs Lovell was still living here. She came to her door to watch Emma's progress up the bare wooden stairs. Her boy, now toddling, hung on her stained skirts, and as Emma turned to smile amiably at her, she took up the child and pulled him back inside, closing the door after her, leaving Emma with the feeling that Mum must have mentioned her leaving and she had surmised the rest.

Smiling grimly, Emma continued up the stairs. Mum answered her knock, holding a few strands of brown silk in her hand and a hostile look on her face for the caller who dared interrupt her intricate work. The many-coloured silks were pinned out on a board, the difficult pattern in her head; woe betide anyone breaking that concentration. At least, Emma deduced, she had proper work instead of making paper flowers to sell at the kerbside.

'Hullo, Mum,' she said tentatively, trying to be bright. 'It's me.'

'I can see that.' At least she hadn't shut the door in her face, or told her to go away.

'I thought I'd come to see how you are,' Emma hurried on. 'Just to say I think of you a lot and to wish you a happy new year. I hope you didn't mind me coming.'

Words poured from her as though to pause for breath would have had the door close in her face. Instead, her mother opened it wider.

'Yer'd best come in,' she said curtly. 'On the doorstep, letting the whole neighbour'ood know our business. The only thing this 'ouse is good for is ears, hers downstairs and theirs upstairs. I bet her door's ajar, with her ear-wigging everything yer've said.'

'She looked out as I came past,' said Emma, grateful to step inside. To her relief Mum was being quite cordial. 'As scruffy as ever,' she added, attempting a feeble joke. Mum didn't smile, but at least she was talking.

'The whole place is dirty,' she said, leading the way into the room. 'Stinks. If I 'ad enough brass ter get out of it, I would. But yer brother's lazy as ever. It's left ter me ter keep us both.' She went to the fire and stood the kettle on the trivet to boil, which it began to do immediately, most likely not long boiled for her morning mug of tea.

'Is Ben at work?' Emma asked, standing in the middle of the room, not wanting to take it upon herself to sit down.

Her mother remained gazing into the low fire. 'Work? It's a filthy word with 'im. He says he's lookin' fer work, but more like he's with 'is mates, or some trollop or other. Sees a lot of some tart called Clara. Always seems to 'ave a bit of cash about 'im, and I reckon he's up ter no good most of the time. I wouldn't put 'im past doing a bit of tealeafing. Pity he ain't clever enough ter really make a decent haul if that's what he's up to. Maybe we'd eat better.'

That was a signal for Emma to ask, 'Did you get the money I sent at Christmas?'

She glanced around the room. This had once been home to her and, poverty-stricken though it was, there came a brief wave of nostalgia, passing as quickly as it had come. It seemed incredible that she had once accepted all this. In time she'd find Mum somewhere far more pleasant to live. At the moment it would take up every penny she was earning, but soon Theo would be getting better work and she'd make sure Mum benefited by it. She had Theo to look out for her, Mum had no one. Certainly Ben was no use. She'd struggled so hard to keep them all out of the workhouse, she deserved to be looked after, for all their differences.

Mum was putting another coal on the fire. 'Yes, I got it.'

Not a thank you. Just that she'd got it. Almost like a condemnation. Emma bit back a ready retort and found herself stuck with a problem of how to hand over the three guineas she'd brought along for her. It was a lot of money to Mum and would probably raise the question of how she came by such wealth, her mother looking on it as money for favours, as she'd once called it.

'Mum, how are you off for money?' she ventured cautiously. 'Only I have ...' The question was interrupted.

'Talk posh nowadays, don't we? Did 'e teach yer ter talk like that? Too good ter talk the way yer was brought up?'

'Mum!'

'Don't s'pose any of us are good enough for yer now. Must've 'ad ter work hard ter talk like that. So 'igh an' mighty now, I wonder you even bothered ter come 'ere at all.'

'I come because I wanted to see you.'

It didn't seem to matter now how she spoke. Clearly Mum was giving vent to pent-up anger remaining from when she'd gone off into the blue. She'd often told herself that it had been as much Mum's fault, virtually telling her to go, as it had been hers in going. She used it as a shield against her own conscience and it had never occurred to her that Mum too was blaming herself and in taking it out on her was hiding behind her own shield.

So many times, suffering the pangs of that fight, Emma had wanted to make reparation yet feared repulsion, the things said to each other too harsh to put away as easily as all that. So many times she had wanted to ask face to face how Mum was, rather than by letter, letters never answered, in their way confirming the reception she'd get. Again as a shield, she had brushed aside the thought that Mum too must have been hurt, must have wondered about her daughter, unable to forgive yet missing her. Now she was finding out, and it was proving painful.

'I just want to know how you are, that's all. If you need anything.'

That too was dangerous, a reminder of the silence that had grown between them since her leaving home.

'If yer was asking 'ow I've been all the time I 'aven't seen yer, I was down with a rotten cold over Christmas. But of course, yer wouldn't know about that, would yer, never coming ter find out.'

'I was so busy.' God, how must that sound?

Her mother went on as if she hadn't heard. 'I got a bit of goose grease for me chest what the butcher was kind enough ter give me fer a penny, which was good of 'im.'

Was Mum really trying to put on the poverty-stricken bit? What had happened to the money she'd sent? It would have covered a doctor's bill, and more.

'I dosed meself with some cough mixture Mrs Abrahams upstairs had left over and give ter me. I was in bed fer two days. Ben was no 'elp. All 'e did was go on about 'aving no dinner cooked for 'im.'

'Why didn't you tell me?' demanded Emma. 'You know where I'm living. You've got me address on the letters I've written to you. I could easily have bought some cough medicine and whatever else you needed.'

'Didn't think ter bother yer, you bein' so busy.' Emma looked at her mother's back as she bent to lift the now boiling kettle off the trivet with a piece of cloth shielding her hands from its hot handle.

'I don't s'pose yer want a cuppa before yer go?' She turned to glance at Emma, her expression blank, but the question broadly loaded with a hint that pierced right through Emma.

Her question about money and help had been totally ignored, but Emma wasn't prepared to let it go as easily as that.

'Look, Mum.' She knew she was about to say all the wrong things but she was rankled. 'I know you don't approve of what I do, but despite what you think, I've kept respectable. Whether it offends you or not, Mum, I'm leaving some money on the table for you. You can do what you like with it. Throw it in the gutter or give it all to Ben if you want.'

The money she'd sent her at Christmas had probably been given to him, which was why Mum was pleading poverty now. 'I'm trying to do something for you. I want to see you better off,' she added, but her mother dismissed it with a flick of her work-worn hand.

'I don't need yer money.'

The kettle held firmly in Mum's hands, prevented the three glittering guineas being picked up and thrown back at her, but she might as well have done, the way she completely ignored them. It was the last straw to Emma's efforts to appease. 'Well, it's up to you,' she said abruptly. 'I've got ter go. I'll have yer tea another time.'

Halfway down the short flight of bare stairs she saw the door below begin to close, the woman caught on the hop, and as she passed, Emma called out pointedly, 'Nice ter see yer again, Mrs Lovell!'

It was February and she could hardly wait to be seventeen. That evening, Theo's agent having at last got him an engagement at the prestigious Alhambra in Leicester Square, Theo was introducing her to people she had never even dreamed she would ever come close to, much less meet. An impresario, a wealthy financial backer was giving the party in honour of his wife's birthday. Theo had been invited, was being greeted like a lost friend by those he'd not seen for two years and in whose circles he'd once moved.

Knowing no one there and feeling rather like a fish out of water, Emma stayed close. She had never been one to lose out on conversation, but amid these milling groups of people, all talking furiously and no one apparently listening, little notice was being taken of her. To become separated from Theo would be to end up standing by herself, lost, everyone drifting by, their interest centred on each other. It didn't matter that she was beautifully dressed in a cream-coloured, low-cut gown of soft *soie-de-chine* that Theo had chosen for her; she was no better dressed than any of the ladies here, and in fact most were far more richly attired than her.

Her glass of champagne in her hand untouched, she clung to his arm as a rotund, middle-aged man touched him heartily on the shoulder, taking his attention away from her.

'Hullo, Barrington, old man, I saw you at the Alhambra. I heard all about your appearance before His Majesty, no less! I must say, what a splendid reintroduction. You've always gone in with both feet, and with a new assistant too.'

The small eyes focused beadily on her for a second and she lifted her chin in response, refusing to blush, but already he had turned back to Theo.

'Saw her go through her paces. She's good. She's certainly got the makings. You have her well trained, old man, no doubt about that!'

Theo, holding a large glass of brandy, barely glanced at her. 'She's a damned sight brighter than first I imagined her to be.'

In pique, Emma withdrew her arm from his, telling herself she might as well not be there at all, as Theo's companion went on heartily, 'So, what happened to the young man, the assistant you had? I remember him – he used to be good.'

Theo's reply was swamped by the invasion of a tall female in a rose silk evening gown, shoulders exposed by a low décolletage with a fichu of lace, a painfully pinched waist necessitating her to wave her cream silk fan at her cheeks with frantic energy. 'Oh, here you are, Claud!' She bore down on the man, probably her husband by his look of resignation, to drag him away to another group in some other part of the crowded, stuffy room.

Emma was glad to see the back of him and perhaps have Theo to herself. It wasn't to be. A rakish-looking, fair-haired man with a pale, upright moustache, immediately took his place, but was a little more considerate in his admiration of her.

'Lovely girl, Theo. Aren't you going to introduce me then?'

Formally introduced, Mr Bertram Calforth gave her a gentlemanly bow. 'Amelia Beech – nice name. Is it your own or your stage name?'

'It's really Emma,' she answered readily. 'Short for Emily. Theodore calls me Amelia and I suppose it is my stage name.'

She saw Theo look at her with a dark frown and said no more.

'I expect you're an asset to him, my dear,' said Calforth. 'You are quite adorable.'

She found herself quickly propelled away from her admirer, Theo's attitude grown suddenly strained.

'Watch people like him,' came the harsh warning. 'Go off and mingle with a few of the women and don't let your eyes roam too much or his sort could get the wrong impression of you.'

But she didn't know any of the women and wasn't about to barge in on their conversations. Besides, though she spoke well enough now, they'd been speaking well all their lives and she would just show herself up.

Theo had moved off to join a group where he'd espied a couple of old friends, leaving her on her own. She felt sure it had been deliberate. He had turned odd from the very moment Calforth had taken notice of her. Upset and frustrated and without him next to her, she was lost. He had been most unfair to her, and it wasn't as if she had batted her eyes at the man, though she might have simpered a little at being called adorable in such a nice way.

She sipped her champagne for something to occupy her other than just staring vacantly at glittering chandeliers. She also managed to avoid a chance glance from any of the flushed-faced men in tight, starched collars and formal dinner jackets, and being ignored by ladies upright in their restrictive corsets, as hers was restricting her, the new S-bend shape purported to be safe and comfortable but seeming to be neither.

She thought of her mother. Her heart began to ache with longing to know again the normality of the place she'd once called home. Nothing here seemed normal, everyone putting on airs and graces, the women talking in high-pitched voices, fans fluttering, men's voices booming, an orchestra playing medleys no one was listening to, the chink of drinking glasses and the aroma of an excellent buffet mixing with the delicate perfumes of the ladies and the brilliantine pomade of men's hair, and over it all the blinding glitter of the chandeliers. Suddenly she wanted none of it. Who did she think she was, mixing with these people, looking to be as famous as Theo expected to be again one day? Suddenly she wanted to run away from it all.

Standing by a high, narrow window with its deep blue velvet curtains, she felt her eyes mist with longing for home.

'Emily?' A familiar voice swept away threatening tears, replacing them with surprise and guarded suspicion.

'What're you doing here?'

246

There was an easy though not unkindly smile on Martin Page's lips. 'I was invited, like you.'

'Why?' she queried stupidly.

'I still have friends in the business.' He leaned against the frame of the window, disarraying the curtains. 'And my family is quite well connected, if not in theatrical circles, but it helps. I guessed Theo would be invited now that he's becoming known once more. Amazing how easily you can get back into the swim of things once you've played before royalty. That goes for you too, Emily.'

He'd spoken the name in all seriousness. It sounded rather nice on his lips. 'You knew about that?' she asked.

'Everyone knows about it,' he replied flippantly. 'I also gathered he was at the Whitechapel Pavilion after that. Bit of a comedown, I thought at the time, but big oaks from little acorns ... that sort of thing. But now you and he are at the Alhambra. Wish it was me, but good luck to you both.'

Emma nodded her acceptance. 'And what are you doing now?' she asked, savouring the relief of having someone to talk to whom she knew. She could have heaped blessings on Martin Page's head for this unwitting and timely arrival. Suddenly she noticed how attractive his smile was.

'In the theatre you mean?' he queried, gazing around. 'Nothing. I'm back in the family business at the moment – coffee importers, pretty big. But sitting in an office can't compare to playing before an audience, hearing that applause, even if you are just a conjuror's assistant. *That's* the magic! As you have probably found out. There's nothing like it.'

He looked momentarily so sad that she felt it flow over her too.

They fell silent. She wanted so much to probe deeper into the whys and wherefores of the rift between him and Theo, to ask if there was any truth in his denial of guilt regarding Theo's wife, but that was out of the question and somehow she knew Page was innocent. Finally she said, 'Do you think you two might get back together?'

He shrugged, still gazing around the crowded room. 'You probably know by now what a strange person he can be – not the easiest man to get along with. He might be different with you.'

She wondered. He was a strange man. The way he had suddenly forsaken her here this evening, merely because a man had admired her. Yet did he not want her to be admired? Wasn't that his aim? And the odd way he'd kept her at arm's length after being on the point of making love to her that night of the King's empty proposition. To be jealous of a king! He could not know what he had awakened in her that night. And now, it seemed, he didn't care. It was as if that evening hadn't happened.

'You don't appear to be enjoying yourself all that much,' Page was saying. Emma came to herself with a start and sighed.

'All these rich people, the way they seem so at ease with each other.'

He gave a short laugh. 'Don't you believe it. Every one trying to outdo the other, everyone on edge in case they lose out to someone else. I've seen this charade acted out so often in my father's walk of life. You can get sick of seeing it. There's none of this parrying among the poor. I almost envy them.'

It was Emma's turn to scoff. 'You don't know half of it. You only see us from a distance, too far off to see that we've got the same needs, only ours is to survive, physically not socially. Grab that job before someone else grabs it.' She heard her tone becoming heated. 'My Mum scrabbling under market stalls for bits enough to make a meal before some other woman can get her hands on them, and scratch her eyes out to get to them if need be. Oh, there's enough parrying goes on all right in my world!'

It was her world, in spite of having moved on. It was in her blood and at this moment she didn't care who knew it, even him.

Martin was nodding apologetically. 'I'm sorry. People like me can talk a lot of bunk sometimes.' He brightened. 'Look, can I get you another drink?'

Emma realised that she had an empty glass though she couldn't remember having sipped until it was all gone. She smiled her acceptance, and as he hurried off to get her another drink, all at once she found this party a wonderful place to be.

Chapter Nineteen

Hardly had Martin left than she saw Theo moving towards her through the throng. He was a good head taller than most and Emma could see a set expression on his face.

'There is someone I wish you to meet,' he stated as he reached her. He took hold of her upper arm in a strong grip that refused any protest, but protest she did, mildly, but at the same time puzzled by his purposefulness.

'I was just waiting for ...' she began, but he cut her short.

'It doesn't matter. This won't take long.' Before she could protest further, she was being escorted rather than guided between the chattering guests, who moved aside in some surprise before the urgent progress, like sea spume before the bows of a great ship, coming together again as they passed.

Reaching two couples in deep conversation, total strangers to her, Emma found herself brusquely introduced, confused, unable to catch their names, and then left with them, they looking as stunned as she was. One of the women smiled at her and made a kindly attempt to acquaint her with the conversation they were having, but Emma's eyes were following Theo's progress back to where he'd found her.

Through a gap in the crowd she could see Martin taking two glasses from a waiter's tray, turning as Theo reached him. Her attention taken for a moment by the lady who had first spoken to her, the next time Emma looked, Theo and Martin were in animated conversation. She wondered what about, but when she looked again moments later, there was no sign of Martin, and Theo was shouldering his way back.

It was now seven months since that evening and she hadn't seen Martin since, though she often wondered about him, what their conversation had been about and why he'd left without saying goodbye. No doubt he was back in a stuffy office on his family's importing business, but in a way she felt vaguely indebted to him for having momentarily brightened her evening. But with 1904 proving to be the finest year of her life, her mind was often distracted elsewhere. Theo was in great demand. Throughout spring and summer they'd done a lot of travelling, long weary train journeys from one city to another, Manchester, Edinburgh, Brighton, Leeds, back to London, then off again, different places, different hotels, the humble days of boarding houses left well behind. When in London, Emma made a point of going to see her mother, but there was no pleasure in it and it felt as though she was putting her head in a noose; she felt foreboding, reluctance, misgivings, and was hardly able to wait to get away.

Mum hadn't changed. No longer were there arguments and she seemed to have accepted her idea of what her daughter had become, just as she accepted the money Emma sent her, these days with grudging gratitude. The place looked spick and span as always but now embellished with all those little bits and bobs that went to make two rented rooms into a home. There were now good meals on the table and money enough for gas and other little luxuries.

Her brother was still the same as ever, making sure of his share of what Emma sent to her mother. He boxed, gambled, lived on the seamy side of life, dock work put behind him.

'Bloody peanuts!' he spat when Emma tried to remind him that honest work shouldn't be sneezed at, to which Mum shrugged, somewhat pointedly, as though she thought Emma could talk.

Promising that soon she'd be able to find Mum somewhere better to live brought another shrug and the response that she was all right here and wouldn't feel easy living elsewhere on another's money. Emma shrugged too and let it go.

Once or twice she'd looked up one or two old friends, like Lizzie, and they were friendly enough, but there was now a strained atmosphere that made her realise that she'd moved on, and though she would still see Mum, as was her duty to, she had left her old friends behind. It was sad but life had to go on, and her life was different now.

As for Mum, it no longer mattered what Mum thought of what she did, she would always do her best by her, and she could do that now. She was at last reaping the harvest of all the hard work that being the assistant to a brilliant illusionist entailed. Theo *was* brilliant, and acclaimed, and she was proud to be at his side. At seventeen she was a capable young woman, as much part of his act as his right arm. She had more money than she'd ever dreamed as he commanded larger and larger fees for each appearance, of which there were plenty. She had lovely clothes, jewellery, and that gorgeous sapphire dress ring he'd given her for her seventeenth birthday. She was being noticed, and now had the elegance Theo's work expected from her, in fact demanded. Sometimes it did get on top of her. The life of ease she'd imagined went with the luxury of success was a myth. In fact, the higher Theo climbed, the more exacting were his expectations of her.

'One more slip like that,' he reprimanded her after a trifling little lapse of concentration on her part this Sunday afternoon, using her hotel room as a rehearsal area, 'and the whole thing will be ruined, myself demeaned.'

She was livid, as often she was at such times, and there had been many of these over the past seven months.

'We've been at this one illusion for four hours,' she raged. 'And I'm tired. My brain isn't working any more.'

He'd been pacing the room in his own tantrum. He now stopped and swung round to face her. 'What if this happened on stage?'

'It won't! On stage I'll be fresh. We're only on for fifteen minutes at a time. Of course I won't make any slip-up. But we're not on stage and you've been working me all morning. I'm exhausted. I'm bound to make mistakes.'

'Not with me you don't, Amelia.'

He had adopted that ominous tone that, while carrying no threat of violence of any sort, had the power to silence her. Her only defence was to appeal to his gentler nature, tears very near the surface, from weariness rather than female weakness.

'I feel as if I'm being pounded into the ground, Theo. And you're always changing the routine.'

'I need to if I intend to stay at the top.'

'Are we at the top?' she challenged, eyes moist and glistening.

'A year from now we will be, I guarantee you that, my dear. And *don't* start crying! I need you to get on top of this and apply yourself. Tears will make you useless to me.'

She stifled her emotions. She never cried, not in his presence anyway, no matter how hard he worked her, and he wasn't going to see her do that now.

'A lapse of concentration during a mind-reading will spoil the mystery at which I am aiming,' he was saying, 'but a mistake during one of my illusions could be dangerous, to you, Amelia, do you understand? You could be injured.'

'Yes,' she snapped, hating to give in. But she knew what he meant.

He had developed some startling illusions of late. What had once been simple now called for dexterity from her, agility which she practised every waking hour: how to contort herself into tiny spaces, how to move fast so as to reappear seconds after a concealing sheet was whisked away from where she had been a moment before. He was now using swords in his act, apparently piercing her with them. It was exacting and if she didn't draw up her body sufficiently, one could draw blood and it would never do for an audience to see that. Never mind her being hurt!

So work went on, seven days a week without respite. Theo's stamina was inexhaustible. Other than considering timetables, he never seemed to recognise weekdays from weekends.

'If I worked in a shop,' she said as he bent to take apart a trick box with its false back, 'at least I'd have Sunday off.'

'You don't work in a shop,' he said. 'And you make as much money in one week as a shop girl could make in a year.'

'I know, but I feel trapped. I feel as though I'm in a prison.'

Standing by the window, she could see over Kensington Gardens. Here, as in all the London parks on this beautiful, sundrenched September Sunday afternoon, people were taking life easy after their working week. How nice it would be to laze under a parasol, the light material of a summer dress spread out around her legs. She had a sudden image of Theo sitting beside her, tenderly holding her hand. Beside them a small picnic would be laid out, or maybe they would be gliding in a boat on the Serpentine in Hyde Park. Instead they were in this stuffy hotel room.

'You have to let me rest sometimes,' she pleaded. 'If you don't, I'll end up going mad!' Perhaps it was the way she glowered at him as he returned her look, but his own glare faded and when he spoke his voice had become gentle.

'Come here,' he said quietly. Her frustration melting away, she did as he asked and felt his arms encircle her. His breath was warm on her cheek. It had the usual immediate soothing effect and she found herself relaxing in one way, and in another tensing to the feelings the touch of his breath evoked. Many times over the months he'd held her like this, but never more than this. She was fully aware that he would go no further. It was as if he feared to allow himself that chance but she could almost sense the tension building inside him.

'Perhaps I *am* working you too hard, my dear,' he murmured. 'Of course you need to rest.'

She didn't believe him. His idea of resting was hardly ten or fifteen minutes before he was again chafing at the bit. Emma lifted her face to tell him so and without warning his lips closed upon hers, surprising her, his embrace tightening. Through the kiss, came his whisper: 'You are so young, so innocent.' There was a pause, and then, 'so adorable'. The pressure of his lips again bore down on hers, this time even harder.

Since the interrupted moment of love that evening last Christmas, he had never attempted to hold her in this way, but she hadn't forgotten the feelings it aroused. This time he didn't pull away sharply as he had that last time. She felt him lift her. She was being carried to her bed and a wave of fear swept through her, not quite knowing why.

'Theo, no!' She could hear the fear in her voice. He must have detected it too. He paused, looked down at her for a second, but continued to bear her to her bed. There he laid her down gently while she steeled herself to accept this inevitable culmination of his need, aware that her reluctance came only from an instinctive fear of the unknown.

He had straightened up, to prepare himself, came the thought, and she shut her eyes tight. How would he react should she refuse him? Yet she felt her lips forming silent words: 'Please, Theo, I don't feel ready.'

His voice broke through her silent plea, deep, hollow and abrupt. 'As you wish.'

There was a movement. When she opened her eyes it was to see her door closing behind him, leaving her alone to wonder how much offence he may have taken at her petty show of weakness, but more, why she had felt the need to push him away, miserable now because of a deep sense of a moment unfulfilled, even as she felt relieved that he hadn't pursued his intentions.

October saw preparations already stepping up in the approach of the Christmas season, major artistes being sought, less important ones growing a little frantic. Jack Simmons was having no trouble finding work for Theo.

They sat in his office, Emma sitting a little to one side as usual while he and Theo discussed some likely opening out of the several on his file. At one point, Simmons let his gaze drift towards her. 'Does she need to be here, Barrington? She's getting to be like your shadow these days. Can't move an inch without her.'

Theo didn't even follow his gaze. 'I prefer her with me.'

Simmons chuckled. 'Don't like letting her out of your sight, eh? Worried in case she strays, is that it?'

Emma had become accustomed to being discussed by these two as though she wasn't there, yet it still irked as Simmons continued in a joking vein, 'Why don't you marry her, Barrington? With her looks it strikes me it's the only way you're going to hang on to her. Otherwise, one day you'll find her off with someone else. Then where will you be?'

Theodore scowled at him, evading the quip about marriage. 'Are you implying that my act relies solely on her?'

'I'm saying she's so much part of it now and that without her it just wouldn't quite be the same. My advice? Marry her.'

Annoyed by the flippant exchange, Emma wanted to tell them that it was up to her who she married, though for a while now, half her mind had been toying with the fine sound of being called Mrs Theodore Barrington. So far Theo had never made any mention of marriage, nor had she ever brought the matter up, aware that in everything he judged himself the one to make decisions.

By the time she'd thought about her answer, the conversation had moved on to the run-up to Christmas and the demand for top-quality turns by all the better-class variety theatres, Theo's mystifying illusions and mind-reading act now topping the bill with other famous names.

Emma gloried in seeing queues outside the theatres they played, ones she and Theo had once played for pennies – less than a year ago. Hard to believe how far they'd come. It was she on whom Theo's mind-reading act depended, which was worth the hard work, the pounding headaches trying to remember so much, the tears, the arguments, the sleepless nights with numbers and signs marching across her brain. Worth it when the lights dimmed, and in a darkened theatre with haunting music from the orchestra in the pit, Theo moved among the hushed audience, she motionless on the stage, her figure lit by a dim light that turned her green gown – always a green gown – virtually colourless, her auburn hair mysteriously dark so that she looked like a statue, completely still. Eyes turned upward, though like a hawk she was watching his every move, she waited for signals, ears keened to every nuance in tone, where and how certain words were placed, the slightest alteration to voice or body movement. She loved the gasp of the audience, or a woman's startled, often alarmed cry as she correctly described the colour of the embroidery on the woman's handkerchief and the design, or repeated the inscription on a ring; a man's stunned exclamation as the contents of his pocket book were told him from an incredible distance away. Yes, worth it all.

Theo moving among the audience was awesome, but without her apparently ethereal presence up there on the stage, Emma was certain that his act wouldn't be what it now was. Theatrical pamphlets spoke highly of his act, as well as the lasting impression her beauty left on people who saw her. The latter didn't please Theo as much as she would have thought – almost as if he was jealous of any praise she might receive. But perhaps she was wrong. She was after all merely his assistant, his employee, and was perhaps in a way stealing his thunder.

With these thoughts in her mind, she sat to one side in Simmons's office and tried not to feel too annoyed at being discussed by them.

'We will dine out this evening,' Theo declared as they returned to the hotel where they were staying. 'Just the two of us for once. Somewhere special, I think.' He was being very emphatic. She wondered why.

259

Mostly they dined out with others, theatre people, a few quite eminent people loosely connected with the theatre, some with real money, and friends, as that host of hangers-on preferred to call themselves, as he had again become an important person to be seen with. He would unwind with them, allowing Emma to see a totally different side of him – talkative, jovial, entertaining, with a laugh that, deep and sudden, exploded and ended before others could begin to join in.

There was always lots of sparkling conversation, a great deal of merriment and easy camaraderie, and high-pitched laughter would ripple around the table if Emma after a drink or two said a wrong thing or her speech slipped. The men with eyes feasting upon her would slap the table while women remarked how delightfully droll had been her misusage of the King's English, making note of it to repeat to others as their own idea. On the strength of too much wine she even dared to think that some of what she said in error might creep into fashionable idiom. On these occasions Theo either didn't seem to mind her odd slip of the tongue or was too mellowed by brandy to have noticed.

This evening, however, for just the two of them, Theo had chosen the Criterion in which to dine, in a secluded alcove away from the general hubbub of evening diners, but he was not merry. In fact he seemed in a strange mood. Most of the time he merely picked at his food, was brusque with the waiters whose subtleness could make an evening as pleasant or as difficult as they wished, and seemed to be in a world of his own, consuming far too much brandy for her liking. All she could do was resort either to a trivial, one-sided conversation or like him, eat in silence. It was a relief when he eventually called for the bill and ushered her out into a breezy night.

'You're very quiet,' she remarked as they returned to their hotel by one of those noisy motor cabs that had begun to appear on the streets. Not half as comfortable as hansom cabs, but they got a passenger to his destination much quicker, though the fumes from the engine assaulted the nostrils as never did the warm odour of horse-flesh.

'I have reason to be, I think,' Theo replied. As she wondered how she had upset him, he turned abruptly to her. 'I would like your opinion of the suggestion Simmons made when we were in his office.'

She remembered reference to the several excellent engagements the man had got for him, top billing at the Strand, the first of several fine spots taking him up to Christmas and beyond, one being the Oxford in Oxford Street, another the Alhambra in Leicester Square, and after that the most prestigious one of all, the Coliseum in St Martin's Lane, set to open for the first time on Christmas Eve, a huge variety house built and decorated in the style of an ancient Roman coliseum, but with a revolving stage, the first one in London, a foyer of granite columns and statues of chariots, and lifts as well as stairways.

'What suggestion?' she asked absently.

'That I marry you.'

Taken aback, Emma's instant response came in a bubble of laughter. 'He suggested ...' It was an effort to control the giggle except that it was tinged with indignation. 'He suggested that you marry *me?* I always thought that a gentleman asks a girl if she would marry *him*.'

'Your opinion of his suggestion is all I have asked for,' he returned stiffly.

Emma said nothing, but stared ahead, all laughter erased as she fumed at Simmons's audacity, aware all the time of Theo's gaze boring into her temples.

When he spoke, his voice was low. 'I'm sorry if I have offended you, Amelia,' he said, so sadly that she suddenly realised how deeply her flippant reaction had wounded him.

The remaining few minutes of their journey was spent in silence. He only spoke again to say goodnight on proceeding on to his own bedroom, not even pausing to drop a kiss on her cheek as he usually did.

The withheld kiss bothered her more than she imagined as she lay alone in bed that night. After what she assumed she had been to him this last few weeks, for him to behave this way. She'd been so sure of herself with him, and now this. Suddenly she didn't feel sure any more. She should have stopped to think before giggling at his awkward proposal; it had been meant as a proposal, and it was never easy for a man to commit himself to a woman. Even at her tender age she instinctively knew that. She had hurt him deeply, and no man can take ridicule, especially a man like Theo, his pride a flaming staff no less. Had she waited a moment longer, suppressed that tipsy giggle, which mistakenly had been made to cover her own ruffled feathers, he might now be lying here beside her, her place beside him assured, her whole future assured. She'd made a stupid mess of it.

*

Theo had hardly spoken to her for over two weeks. Rehearsals continued as normal, except that he was being almost too careful not to overwork her. It wasn't like him, and sometimes it felt as though she was working with a virtual stranger. This Friday, November the fourth, the day before Guy Fawkes' Night, when she had mentioned a wish to see how her mother was, he offered no protest that she was needed here, not even a frown.

'As you wish, my dear,' he said, frigidly, not even looking up from his morning paper. 'As long as you are back here in time to be ready for tonight's appearance.'

'Of course,' she agreed, her reply equally as frigid, and for good measure, added huffily, 'I've always been on time for the theatre. I don't mean to change that now.'

He hadn't answered, going back to his paper, and she had left without kissing his cheek. So now she was alighting from the motor cab outside St Anne's Church, around eleven-thirty, her face turned towards her mother's, her mood far from matching the late autumn sunshine that tried to brighten the squalor of Church Row with its tenements permanently smoke-blackened from the Blackwall Railway.

She hadn't let the cab proceed into Church Row itself. People around here would gawp and Mum wouldn't have been happy at her advertising her coming to all and sundry.

She hated coming here. It was only filial duty and guilty conscience that brought her, weekly postal orders and notes asking after her mother and always unanswered were not enough. Her visits, few and far between as they were, at least eased her conscience even though Mum would never be reconciled to her work on the stage. Sometimes she'd bring a handbill from the theatre in which the Great Theodore was appearing to show her how respectable and respected he was, but it made little difference. To Mum she was still a girl showing off her legs on the stage. Today would be the same and Emma already knew the reception she would get from Mum. Yet she had to come.

A group of ragged urchins passed her, battling with a squeaking wheelbarrow full of old wood, newspaper, broken bits of furniture, calling out continuously as they went: 'Throw out yer rubbish!'

Whatever they collected would be added to the bonfire they'd been building for more than a week in readiness for the fifth of November, when a badly made effigy of Guy Fawkes – one they'd taken around propped up on an old chair beside which they'd probably taken up residence outside a butcher's shop or some other place that saw regular customers, pleading them to give a 'Penny fer the Guy, missus! Don't fergit the Guy, sir!' although even farthings were accepted – would be placed on top of the bonfire, the lot set ablaze to the bangs and shrieks of ha'penny squibs, proceeds of their particular form of begging. Tomorrow night, every neighbourhood would be full of stinking smoke from the burning of mounds of dubious rubbish and saltpetre from the exploding fireworks.

As she passed, their chanting paused while they gawped at the fine-dressed lady with her fine hat, until their attention became distracted by an upper window across the road opening and a wooden box aimed down into the narrow street. It landed on the cobbles at Emma's feet with an almighty crash that made her leap aside in a most unladylike fashion.

'Don't worrit, me lidy,' quipped one young wag, his mind on gathering up the splintered box. 'It wouldn't of 'it yer and spoilt yer nice cloves.'

Half smiling she moved on, heard behind her the sounds of, 'la-de-da!' and 'what me eye!' and guessed that they were mimicking her progress with exaggerated steps and swaying shoulders.

There'd been a time when she'd have done the same, half admiring, half envious, she in her old skirt, blouse and jacket, her boots and her straw boater with its frayed ribbon.

Elsewhere could be heard other, fainter chants: 'Guy! Guy! Guy! Stick 'im up on 'igh! Gunpowder, treason an' plot!' Again Emma smiled.

Reaching where Mum lived, she pushed open the main door, still as warped and ill-fitting as ever. She started up the stairs, already aware of Mrs Lovell peeping out to watch her progress. If this area could afford burglars, none would have ever been able to slip by Mrs Lovell. Emma could feel her eyes on her through the barely open crack of the door, but couldn't escape the overpowering odour of squalor that wafted through it as well as she hurried on up the stained and echoing stairs.

Chapter Twenty

As ever, her mother stood for a moment staring at her as though looking at an apparition or someone she didn't recognise, then she gave the welcome Emma had come to expect.

'Oh, it's you. Well, yer best come in then.'

Once inside, stiff formality took over. 'Yer'd best sit down, d'yer want a cuppa tea?'

It couldn't have been more grudgingly said had she prefixed it with the words, 'I suppose you want.'

No continuing conversation presenting itself, Emma sat and watched in silence the two spoons of tea being ladled into a pot to be filled from the kettle simmering on the trivet in front of the fire – a fire now bright and cheery where once it would have been parsimoniously fed one grudgingly spared piece of coal or bit of wood at a time as it threatened to die.

The money she sent Mum was helping to make life more comfortable, the decent fire, a new blouse and skirt by the look of it, maybe still off a cheap market stall but certainly an improvement to second-hand bits scrounged from a woman on some corner also hardly able to keep her head above water. When Dad had been alive, Mum had always dressed decently. It had been heartbreaking to witness and share in that downhill trend after losing him. All different now: Mum was looking a treat.

The cup filled and sweetened with condensed milk was no longer a chipped one. Emma sipped it, gratified to know her money was achieving something at least.

'How are you, Mum?' she asked.

'All right.'

The reply was brief. Her mother came and sat opposite her at the table, lifting her own cup to her lips, leaving Emma to rack her brains for something else to say. There was no common ground any more on which to base conversation. To even mention her life would be to provoke the usual disapproving reaction from her. This visit was as always a duty, nothing more. She was almost relieved to see the door open and Ben slouch in.

Emma had never seen him look so presentable, if that was the word, the ragged jacket, shapeless trousers tied at the knee, the frayed cap and greasy rag neckerchief, gone, in their place a loud and flashy check jacket, trousers, waistcoat, and though he still wore a choker it was new.

He took off the brown bowler and tossed it on to the sofa where he no doubt still slept, but his eyes were on Emma.

'So what you doin' 'ere? Come ter give us anuvver little 'and-out?'

His big frame followed the bowler to lounge back on the sofa's two cushions, new, Emma noted, another bit of luxury that her hand-outs as he called it had provided.

'All togged up, I see,' he commented from the sofa. 'Look as if yer doin' well fer yerself.'

Emma forced her lips into a smile. 'You don't look so poor yourself.' In truth he looked as if he'd been drinking, which wasn't impossible for him. 'Are you working?'

'Huh!' he said. She knew by that response that he wasn't.

'When did you last have a job?' It was more challenge than question, but if he were living off what she was sending Mum, and that suit, as cheap as it looked, could be proof enough, she'd have something to say.

Ben shrugged, grinned and lounged even further back, giving her a look that said what's it to do with you? But his reply was unruffled. There was even a tinge of pride in it.

'I makes me way, one way or anuvver, usually anuvver.'

Mum was looking uneasy. 'So what do you do?' Emma persisted.

'All sorts of fings.' The grin became cunning, broadening to spread across his face, a face that as he approached twenty-one was becoming more heavy, more solid, the hazel eyes in the handsome features full of egotism and self-assured belligerence. There was a lump over one eyebrow with a small half-healed cut at its centre. From boxing or some street fight, she wasn't prepared to guess.

'What sort of things?' Emma asked.

He gave another self-opinionated shrug. 'Bit o' this, bit o' that. Spot of boxin', as yer can see.' He touched the lump over his eye with a casual finger. 'Bit of gambling.'

'And you make money?'

'What's the point if yer don't?' he countered.

Mum reached out and lifted the teapot to replenish her cup, spooning in condensed milk and stirring energetically.

'So yer do all right for yerself?' Emma concluded.

'Not bad.' The easy expression clouded over, the eyes grew shrewd. 'Anyway, what's it got ter do with you? What's all the questions for?'

'Just interested.'

'Well, don't! What I do's me own business.' He scowled. 'You ain't got much ter brag about, in yer fancy clothes and yer bloody big expensive 'at.' She was still wearing the hat, the long pins keeping it in place being hard to reinsert.

'And yer wearing powder on yer face,' he went on. 'Yer smell like some of the women I know.' That was obviously not meant as a compliment. 'I take it yer still with that fancy bloke yer went orf with. Done orright fer yerself there, ain't yer?'

It was hard not to retaliate. She tried to bury her feelings in her cup, sipping the last dregs furiously, but it wasn't working. 'At least my income is above board. I'm not crooked!'

Ben came upright, glaring at her. 'You saying I am?'

She was ready for him, slowly taking in what he was wearing. 'In that clobber? Unless you've been helping yourself to what I send Mum, and I sent it for her, not you, and you say you ain't working, then yer must be making yer money somewhere else.' Her refined accent had fled. 'Them kind of clothes on a bloke like you don't come from honest work. You ain't that good a boxer – still the old sideshow booths, still gambling for a few bob on street corners. I reckon clothes like that come more from a bit of tealeafing, a bit of breaking and entering.'

Ben shot to his feet. So did Mum, getting herself between him and Emma, who still sat holding her empty teacup. Her eyes were on Emma. 'Look, if you've just come 'ere ter start a row, then yer'd better go.'

Emma stared up at her in disbelief. 'I came ter see you, to find out if you were all right, see if you've got enough money.'

'Well, yer've seen!' came the reply. 'And I can do without yer ill-gotten money.'

'It ain't ill-gotten enough for yer to 'ave bought all this.' She thumped the cup down on the table, taking her temper out on it, and stood up, one arm gesturing to embrace the room with all the new things being accrued on her money. Her face close to her mother's, she added. 'I don't see you throwing all this back in me face, the extra coal on the fire, the better food you're eating, that new blouse. And I bet Ben does all right out of ...'

She broke off to step back as her mother moved sharply towards her. 'Is that me thanks, Mum, you ready to lash out?'

Her mother drew herself up, controlling her fury but not her indignation. 'I think you'd better go, Em.'

'I think I'd better. But what I send you is earned honestly. And don't forget that, Mum. No matter what you think, I work for my money.' She cast a pointed glance at Ben, who smirked.

'Prostitutes say the same thing,' he said calmly. 'Call it work!'

Emma swung round on him. 'Keep your dirty mouth to yerself.' The way she looked at him made him frown suddenly.

'He don't make yer, does 'e? If this geezer's livin' off yer, I'll kill 'im, an' it don't matter 'ow famous 'e is, he ain't using my sister.'

He shrugged his mother away as she made to stop him going on any more. 'Don't tell me yer money's all comin' from workin' on the stage.'

Emma drew herself up, refusing to lower herself to deny what he was surmising or even throw his show of sudden protectiveness back in his face and say she didn't need his protection.

'I think I'd better go,' she said slowly.

She was surprised by Mum saying, 'No, don't go, Emma.'

She saw her turn on Ben, 'Now see what yer've done?'

Turning back to Emma, she repeated her plea. 'Stay a bit longer, Em, please. Ben's a silly sod, that's what he is!'

Emma hesitated. A cruel little voice inside her head was saying that Mum's fear was that were she to go, there'd be no more money forthcoming. As if she'd see Mum return to the terrible conditions she'd once had to battle with.

'I won't stop sending you money, Mum,' she said, and it wasn't a knock at her, she meant it. 'But I must get back. We're at the Oxford this evening and I must get ready. Theodore will be waiting for me.' Her carefully nurtured accents had returned on mentioning Theo's name. 'He'll be furious if I'm late. We can't let the show …'

271

The look on her mother's face, alarmed – a mother shielding her chick – made her break off. 'He wouldn't hit yer, would 'e?'

Emma wanted to laugh except that the look stopped her. 'He wouldn't dare!' she said, but there was no way to explain that a single look from him could be as hard to deal with as any blow. Over the months she'd discovered that Theo possessed the power to diminish a person with a single glance.

At the door she turned to look at Ben to see him glowering into space, muttering, 'I'll kill 'im, the bleeder!' being directed at what he imagined this bloke of hers might be making her do. She smirked. Ben was all bombast.

'I'll always see you all right for money, Mum, no matter what,' she repeated as she stepped out on to the landing. One thing she wouldn't do was to come here too often. It caused too many upsets.

'Don't make yerself short, luv,' Mum said anxiously.

This time she did laugh, mostly at this rapid change of heart but to Mum it probably sounded friendly. There was relief on Mum's face that the argument they'd had was now patched up. It would not even have begun at all if Ben hadn't come in.

'Don't worry, Mum,' she said easily, 'I can afford it.'

Mum had no idea how much Theo gave her. His fame going ahead of him, gone was the time of running from one hall to another, and he was now guaranteed at least ninety pounds a week for an exclusive appearance at one hall, even a hundred, demonstrating how popular was his act; and she was part of it.

Each week he handed her twenty pounds. Some would say she was worth more, and perhaps she was. But Theo bought all her clothes for her, her stage make-up, paid for her hair to be professionally styled, and paid all the hotel bills as well as taking her out to lunches, dinners and suppers. Simmons had to have his ten per cent, and there were other bills too. She was happy enough with her twenty pounds, with the opportunity of even putting some of it into savings – for that rainy day, she told herself.

She was well aware that, faced with unexpected wealth, most poor people would spend it like a starving man devouring a feast, or save it in fear of such a fortune coming to a sudden end. Emma was the saving kind. She knew too well how easily money slips through careless fingers, and once having had it, the lack of it would be all the worse.

She hoped she wasn't a selfish saver and there was one thing she would always make certain of: Mum would never go short of cash again. And if all this good fortune did come to an end, then a bit of savings would be there for lean times; God forbid they should ever come again. Emma could bet her life that Mum would also save. She'd always been like that – if she had sixpence she would try to put a penny of it aside. Emma only hoped she was keeping what she had now well hidden from Ben's prying eyes.

As Emma passed the downstairs door, it was opened and Mrs Lovell appeared in a man's flat cap, prepared now to chat, to probe, no doubt.

'It's young Emma Beech, ain't it? My, yer look swell. I 'ardly recognise yer. In a bit of an 'urry, are yer, then?'

Emma wanted to move on but politeness forced her to pause. 'I am, in fact. Hope you're well, Mrs Lovell.'

A grin revealed the missing front tooth. 'Oh, I'm fine. Got meself a man, I 'ave. As yer can see.'

Obviously she'd come to her door eager to convey the news. Emma could see a big, burly, unshaven individual standing behind her. Scruffily dressed, his grubby brown waistcoat undone to reveal a sweaty, striped, collarless shirt, he removed a tobacco-stained, hand-rolled cigarette from his lips and grinned. Having made her acquaintance he lifted a chipped pint glass by its handle and took a swig of the beer, leaving a frothy rime on his heavy, yellow-tinged moustache, and replaced the cigarette.

'This is 'Erbert,' Mrs Lovell went on. 'Looks after me a treat, 'e do. Next month I'll be Mrs 'Erbert Arfer Skipman.'

Her little boy had come to cling to the sackcloth covering his mother's skirt. Thumb in mouth, the grooves below his nose revealed twin smears of mucus while the remains of whatever he'd been eating clung to the corners of his lips. Emma hastily removed her glance.

'Congratulations,' she managed, looking to escape, but the woman had more to say.

'This one'll 'ave a dad at last.' She looked down at her offspring, patting the grubby cheek. 'Gawd knows where his own dad went. Me ready ter marry 'im an' orf 'e goes, never seen again and me wiv this one just born. But we're lookin' forward ter termorrer. Guy Fawkes Night, y'know. This one can't remember last year's one.'

She gave the child another pat on the cheek and the boy snuggled close with his face, leaving a trail of mucus on the sackcloth. 'My 'Erbert's got us a big bag of squibs an' bangers an' coloured ones,' she went on. 'More fireworks than we've ever seen. They're in a box on the floor, all ready ter let orf. This one,' again she patted her boy, 'keeps playin' wiv 'em. Wait till 'e sees what they can do.'

'Very nice, but I must be away,' said Emma, wondering how someone as unsavoury as Mrs Lovell with her awful little child could persuade any man to marry her. But one look at Herbert Arthur Skipman was enough to see an example of like attracting like.

Time was getting on. Glad to be in relatively open air, Emma turned her face towards Commercial Road, starting to walk briskly, her skirt swaying about her ankles with each step. There would be a motor cab in Commercial Road.

She had hardly gone a dozen yards when what sounded like a muffled, deep-throated thump, followed by a woman's shriek, made her turn. The next second came a series of equally muffled cracks and bangs, growing suddenly sharper as Mrs Lovell burst out of her street door, screaming for help.

Emma ran back to her. 'What is it?'

'Me baby! Me baby! The fireworks caught fire!'

Before Emma could stop her, she had run back inside. Following her, Emma could see low flames licking almost lazily across part of the room's floor, years of cooking grease absorbed by floorboards having ignited. The man was frantically pounding at them with a piece of towel, causing more draught to feed them. He would soon be fighting a losing battle.

Emma could just see a now blazing box of fireworks by the fireplace. A piece of wood must have tumbled from the fire grate and into the box. Even as she looked, the flames were being fanned by the man's efforts into an inferno. In a panic, Emma moved back. But Mrs Lovell, for all her bulk, seemed to take wings, flying past her and into the flames, screaming for her baby, dimly seen through the now coiling, black and oily smoke, standing in the far corner.

The man was cursing – high-pitched words of terror and anger. 'Come out, yer silly cow! Yer can't get to 'im, yer silly bitch! Come away!'

The fire was already running up the table's greasy legs and across its greasy surface. Skipman was backing out before the heat. Emma couldn't see Mrs Lovell for flames and smoke, but she could hear her choking and shrieking, 'Me baby!' from the far corner.

Once Emma caught a glimpse of her, the boy in her arms, before the rolling, black smoke enveloped them again. She could hear them coughing, could see flickering tongues of orange within the pall of smoke, the terrified woman with her child now completely hidden from view.

'Mrs Lovell!' Emma was yelling. 'Come on out – quick! This way!'

It was the smoke beginning to pour out through the door that brought Emma to her senses. Mum was upstairs.

Automatically she turned and stumbled up them to hammer on the door.

'Mum! The place is on fire! Yer've got ter get out.'

The door opened and her mother's alarmed eyes glanced first at her, then down the stairs. She turned, her voice high. 'Oh, Gawd! Ben – the 'ouse is alight.'

Seconds later they were stumbling downstairs. Behind them clattered the couple from upstairs, alerted by Emma's cries and screams coming from somewhere below.

Shuffling behind, step by painful step, both hands on the rickety banisters to help him, came a frail, elderly man who lived alone in the room across the landing to them, someone Emma had never seen.

The heat in the hall was already almost too much to bear, the flames now flickering around the downstairs room door. Emma, only half hearing short bursts of high-pitched, choking shrieks, ran with the rest out into the street, tugging along the elderly man, who was tottering, ready to fall. All she knew was the welcome impact of the cold, November afternoon air on her face. It was then that she saw that Skipman had followed them out. He was alone.

She turned to him. 'Where's Mrs Lovell and her little boy?'

He was panting. They all were. But his face, where not streaked with black, was ashen, his pale eyes were wide with horror,

'I couldn't get to 'em. I yelled fer 'er not ter be a bloody fool but she didn't come. I begged ...'

Not for long, the thought crossed Emma's mind to be doused in the very same instant. She felt too sick and exhausted to condemn, trembling with sickness and a strange sort of exhaustion, bringing her to the verge of weeping with tiredness. Her legs seemed ready to give way under her as though she'd been in a battle as the horror of a woman and a child burned to death assailed her like some living, evil thing.

People were coming from other houses, mothers holding wide-eyed children protectively to their skirts in the knowledge that this tragedy could easily have been theirs in these filthy, decaying, cinder-dry tenements.

The flames were already licking at the downstairs window. A pall of smoke would by now be rising up the stairs to suffocate them had they not got out in time. Soon the blaze would follow, would burst out of the windows and out through the roof. All that Mum owned would be consumed. Nothing left. But she and Ben still had their lives.

Men had run across with the vain intention of tackling the blaze, only to stand in despair at the way it had got hold of the old timbers. There were plenty of men, out of work, killing time with hopes of one day finding a job and security.

Several had raced at top speed to alert the fire station in Commercial Road while the women hurried to give comfort to the stunned, bedraggled little group, ushering them away from the fire, coming out with cups of tea, an ever-present soothing balm for any situation.

Soon there came the jangle of fire bells. The red vehicle heaved into sight, its gleaming brass funnel belching smoke to add to that already filling the narrow, cobbled street. Flaring-eyed horses, manes flying, heads tossing, snorted to a halt, as men in gold-braided uniforms and brass helmets leaped down to begin frantically unrolling the hoses.

Cup of tea in hand, Emma watched from the far side of the narrow street as ladders were lifted down, the hoses filled to spurt water through windows and the door at the relentless flames, the steam pump adding its racket to the crackle of fire. Even so, they'd bring it under control only when there was nothing left to burn. All they could do was try to keep it from spreading to the adjoining houses, all mere tinderboxes, while the occupants gathered in groups, some in fear that their own homes might catch fire, others in dismay at seeing their possessions already going up in flames.

Bleakly watching, the only thing Emma kept thinking was not that her mother's life had been saved or even that the life of a woman and child hadn't, but that the few well-loved treasures Mum had desperately clung to in remembrance of a better life and the husband she had lost, were all gone. She and Ben had nothing but what they stood up in. There hadn't been time to grab a single thing.

'Come inside, luv,' offered the woman who'd given her and Mum the cup of tea. 'Don't want ter stand out 'ere watchin' it. I expect yer need ter sit down an' recover a bit.'

Emma was grateful. Her heart was still beating with sickening thuds, her mind a whirl about what she must do. Her mother needed somewhere to stay. Ben, still outside watching the firemen, could fend for himself.

'What yer goin' ter do now, Mum?' she asked falling easily into her old way of speaking. No reason to put on airs.

The blankness in her mother's eyes shook her to her very soul. In that instant she brought her mind to focus on the problem.

'We need ter find you somewhere. Somewhere really nice.'

Odd how this terrible business had offered an adequate way to get Mum out of that awful place without her feeling she was being patronised. Emma had hoped to see the bit of money she'd put by grow, but for now that must be sacrificed. Mum needed somewhere permanent and decent to live. This was her opportunity.

'She could stay 'ere fer a bit if she wants,' offered the woman who'd asked them in. 'She could bunk in wiv me daughter.'

Emma turned and smiled at her. 'There's me brother too. He ain't got nowhere either. But thanks anyway,' she added as the woman's expression changed. Ben's reputation for belligerent behaviour clung to him like a dirty odour to a drainpipe. 'I'll be able to sort me mum out. Probably me brother too.'

There was a look of instant relief.

The fire finally overcome with just a little singeing to the adjacent tenements, Skipman was assisting in picking over the smouldering wood of the downstairs room, the stairs completely gone, the contents of the second floor also gone. They'd found the two bodies, and a covered ambulance took them away.

It was a sad little sight. Emma, with tears in her eyes, was surprised to see her mother weeping openly, she who seldom showed emotion. Emma knew with a pang of affection for her mother that it wasn't lost possessions she was grieving over but a neighbour and her little boy.

Chapter Twenty-One

It was four o'clock and getting dark before Emma and her mother finally turned their backs on what had once been her home.

'Where am I supposed ter go?' Ben queried.

'You're a man,' she told him. 'You can fend for yourself. There are lots of men's lodging houses about. Once Mum's settled perhaps you can both come to some arrangement, but for now I need to worry about her.'

She had enough to do sorting Mum out without him expecting to be propped up. And especially after the way he'd acted. Maybe he had spoken about protecting his sister against what he saw as Theo living off her, but he had only been making sure his authority was being asserted, not from any kindness of heart.

She would let him know where Mum was. But it was Mum she was thinking of. She shouldn't be left all alone after what had happened, and even Ben was company, and he might not be so bullying and bossy in a nicer place.

'I'll try to find something to suit you both,' she'd promised.

It had taken time to find somewhere decent. She took Mum back to her hotel to pick up the money she'd been saving, enough to pay a month's rent in advance that would most certainly be asked for.

There'd been no sign of Theo; he was probably in his room wondering where she was. There was only about an hour and a half to find her mother a place to live and settle her in before rushing off to the theatre, and she'd be compelled to stay with her for a short while after her traumatic experience. It left hardly time to gather up her things and compose her jangled nerves.

Jangled was right. By the time she found two nice rooms with a small kitchen suitable for a decent woman, Mum was shaking a little from delayed shock.

'I'll be orright,' she told Emma, though she didn't sound so as they stood in the rooms the landlady had shown them into. Her lips were firm, battening down any show of weakness as the woman stood back after showing them around. 'Yer can't afford this, luv,' she said to Emma

'I can.'

'I ain't takin' yer money.'

'Then what *are* you going to do, Mum? Roam the streets? Sleep under some arches with a bit of newspaper for a cover?'

It wasn't large but it was neat and tidy and furnished. Emma had found it among the evening newspaper adverts, the top floor of a three-storyed house just off Whitechapel Road, not an especially smart area of London but far better than the slum she'd just left. Anything would have been better than that! Mum could hold up her head here. The rent of six shillings a week was a bit steep but she was earning.

As for Ben, she'd contact him through Mum's old neighbours and let him know where Mum was. She would speak to the landlady, who name was Mrs Blacker, about it.

But now she must be off. 'You'll be all right here,' Emma reassured her mother after having told Mrs Blacker that they'd take it. 'Try and get a good night's sleep. I'll pop over tomorrow morning,' she promised. 'You can make yourself a cup of tea and something to eat. There's a proper kitchen with a sink. There's a teapot and kettle, cutlery, cups and plates, even a gas stove.' It was a black, skeletal, two gas-ringed thing with the tiniest oven, but Mum would no longer have to cook on an open fire.

She and Mum were still exploring all this luxury, when Mrs Blacker came back upstairs with a drop of milk, a little tea and sugar, a few slices of bread and some jam, even a slice of cake.

'Such a terrible time you've been through,' she said in a husky voice, having been told of the catastrophe. 'Blessings be to God you wasn't injured. But now here's this to keep you going till morning.'

From Emma's own experience of Jewish people they'd always struck her as kind to those in distress no matter who they were; they looked after their own and drove a hard bargain but were generous and helpful when need be, as Mum's case proved. Mrs Blacker did not have to have brought up provisions.

'You feel a bit out of sorts,' she said to Mum, 'come down for a bit of company,' which made Emma sure she'd found the right place.

But whether Mrs Blacker would stomach Ben was another matter. Though knowing where her bread was buttered she'd probably ask a few shillings more on the rent. And who could blame her?

Quarter past seven – Emma, mentally urging the motor taxi to go even faster towards her hotel, fretted at the slightest hold-up by every slow hansom cab, hackney, trundling 'growler', omnibus and tradesmen's cart that seemed to be waging a personal vendetta against her and stopping her reaching her destination. She still had to gather up her stage clothes and stage make-up, and settle her jangled nerves enough to follow Theo's commands without any mistakes.

The way she felt, she was going to make every blunder possible. Fear of Theo's anger ran through her like hot steel rods, or as if those razor sharp swords he used in his newest illusion were piercing her. He'd drilled her on doubling herself up small to avoid them as they drove through the wooden box in which she was concealed.

It had taken months to perfect, she was constantly exercising so as to manipulate her slim body into the tiny space the way he wanted, indeed the way she must if she wasn't to be harmed. When she'd told him she couldn't possibly contort herself to such extremes he'd said that she was young and supple enough to be able to master it.

On stage she would slip out of the flowing gown and stand in spangled tights; a dress would have got in the way.

That first time, she had felt so exposed as to feel almost naked before the gaping of the audience, and she forgot to be frightened of making any disastrous errors, glad only to disappear into the box and away from all those eyes.

The lid closed, she'd contorted her body so much that it seemed her sinews would snap, but the illusion had been a huge success that night, and still was.

Theo was now working on having her escape from the box without being seen so that when it was opened with the knives still in place, she would have disappeared.

The skill was to move fast enough through the false opening at the rear and slither, flat as a pancake, under a striped cloth laid behind and around the box, the stripes helping to disguise any movement, and to appear from the wings the second the audience was shown the box, empty but for the crisscross of swords, quite unharmed.

Hurrying to Theo's room, she knocked. There was no reply. Going to her own room she found a pencilled note jammed under the room number:

'SEVEN-FORTY. WHERE ARE YOU? GONE ON ALONE. BE QUICK!'

He'd waited until the last minute, the curtain going up at eight. True, they had the main spot that wasn't until later, but there were preparations to be gone through, a last-minute adjustment requiring her to be there. She could imagine him pacing about backstage, irritable. She found herself preparing for his fury. By the time she'd gathered what she needed there were barely fifteen minutes left to get there. What state would she be in after all this rush she dared not think. This had never happened before, and she felt guilty about it even though she had a good reason.

The hotel doorman swiftly got her a cab. Even that short journey to the theatre seemed to go on for ever. She arrived to see the queues outside had all gone. She almost fell through the stage door. As she got to the tiny dressing room she and Theo shared, he was standing outside the door, his expression dark.

Seeing her, he turned and went inside without saying a word. Out of breath, she followed him in, ready with her explanation. But before she could say a word he swung round on her.

'I've had to cancel.'

'Why?' An apology died on her lips.

'I wasn't to know when or even if you'd arrive.'

Emma was breathing hard, not just from hurrying but from all that had happened – the trauma of the fire, people killed, her mother losing everything, the anxiety of finding her somewhere to stay, having to leave her on her own after all she'd been through; now Theo, who must have seen that she wasn't herself and that something very unusual must have occurred to make her so late, had the audacity to think only of the show. Damn the show! Her mother was far more important.

Perhaps it was the abrupt manner in which she started telling him what had happened that made him interrupt her when she had hardly begun.

'This is where you are needed. Here. Not somewhere else.'

'You know I went to visit my mother,' she flared.

'What possessed you to stay out so long?'

'I made sure I had plenty of time to get back. But what happened was that there was a fire, and ...'

'It doesn't matter what happened. I was here on time. You thought not to be.'

Outrage at his attitude began to take hold. 'I told you, there was a fire. My mother's home has gone up in flames! It was important to …'

'Nothing is more important than honouring one's contract.'

How could he be so callous? 'Don't you understand?' she tried again. 'My mother's home burned down. She's homeless. Everything she has is gone. She could have been burned to death. A neighbour and her son were.'

Her voice rose as he regarded her with not the slightest change of expression. 'What did you expect me to do?' she raged. 'Leave her? Tell her I had to be somewhere else, playing the fool to a lot of other fools?'

Anger in Theo seemed to be frozen, his tone low and steady and threatening. 'Is that how you feel about what I do?'

That deep-toned accusation shook her, her voice high-pitched and emotional. 'But when it comes to someone of your own in dire trouble with nowhere to turn, then it has to take second place.' How could he hold his temper in such check when she was seething and she knew he was too?

'You do recognise the words, "the show must go on"?' he said slowly. How many times had that been drummed into her?

'We have to draw a line somewhere!'

'I have seen an actor force himself on to the stage for the sake of those words while his father lay dying.'

'Then that's just stupid!' Emma snapped, throwing down her case with its stage clothes and make-up. 'And

287

selfish. An understudy could have gone on in his place. His father, it seemed, had no one to ease him.'

Theo's voice had grown even deeper. 'After my wife's death I was on stage for the next performance. Those who have paid good money to see a show must not be let down.'

'What if you'd been the only one there to save her life?' Emma burst out. She was sick of being treated like a recalcitrant child.

'Would you have gone and left her just so as *not to disappoint your audience*?'

She couldn't help it, the sarcasm that had crept into her tone. In pent-up anger she began feverishly unpacking the case though she knew it was futile – they wouldn't be appearing tonight. He'd said so.

'I did not have the choice,' came the quiet reply. 'She was already dead, and there was nothing I could do.'

The quiet way it was said stopped her frantic activity.

With those few words she saw a man who was still living with the knowledge that he had driven the woman he loved to her death by a once uncontrollable temper, perhaps from a drinking habit that had started long before the tragedy.

She knew about that. Was this why he was holding his temper so firmly in check now?

She fell silent, and the silence drew itself out, leaving distant laughter and applause to trickle into the room as a comedy artiste took his bow before leaving the stage. Emma saw Theo's lips tighten at the joyous sounds, knowing that he wouldn't be on stage tonight. He was interested only in what concerned him, came the smouldering thought. Had he been concerned only with himself when he drove his wife to such a point that she had rushed blindly from their dressing room and out into the street to her death?

There came a light rap on the door.

'Enter!' Theo's full tone made her jump. The door opened and the stage manager stood there looking from him to her, his look hostile, seeing her there.

'So what went wrong?' he enquired brusquely.

Before Theo could address him, Emma spoke, her explanation tumbling out in a torrent: the fire, the death of a neighbour, her mother homeless, her possessions gone and nowhere to go but the streets and having to find her somewhere to stay, as well as the need to comfort her after the shock of it all. The recollection made her voice waver and break, her lips tremble and her eyes mist over. When she had done, the man cleared his throat, hostility fading.

'Well, indeed, I'm sorry,' he said awkwardly. 'Still, we managed. Had a chap step in at the last moment, damned good turn, pretty well liked. I gave an excuse of some accident on your way here. Seems in a way I was right. Accidents can happen. Pretty well unavoidable, I suppose.'

He gave Emma a glance that wasn't unkind, and she felt that he was talking for her benefit where otherwise he might have been curt and offhand with Theo on his own.

'Too late, you going on now. Can't overrun, not to that extent. If I'd known earlier, but having already made the announcement ... You being top of the bill, there's deep disappointment. All I could do is honour their tickets for any time in the coming week provided they're happy to accept whatever empty seats we have, so long as you can guarantee no more little unforeseen problems, Mr Barrington. This sort of thing doesn't go down well.'

He was being nicer, Emma suspected, for her sake, but was still put out. Those performing in theatres like the Oxford didn't let the management down.

After he'd gone, silence again descended. Theo's equipment was to be left, and he put personal things back into a valise without giving her so much as a glance, but the tension was beginning to undermine her. She felt indignation too. He could have waited a little longer, trusting her to turn up.

She hadn't the courage to say he'd been over-hasty, or even that her being a little late wouldn't have mattered. They still could have made it.

'I didn't plan it,' she said at last. 'My mother was in such a state and I couldn't leave her. I had to find her somewhere to stay. She don't have no one else but me.'

'*Doesn't*,' he corrected, 'have *anyone* else,' leaving her staring at him in disbelief. How could he worry about something so trivial? And his voice sound so level and calm? Yet she knew he was not calm. Correcting her was proof. When would the storm break? When it did she must be ready for it. She would not be cowed when what she had done had not been possible to avoid. She was in the right.

Neither spoke on the way back to their hotel. She'd said her say and if he wasn't prepared to accept that or even forgive, so be it.

She went to her room, still with neither of them saying a word to the other, not even goodnight. Granted, he had cause to be angry, but there was no need to have made such a fuss, cancelling as he did and upsetting the management. If he had waited a little longer, had trusted her to turn up in time, everything would have been all right. He was at fault, not her.

His silence was worse to bear than the reaction of the theatre manager. She'd have felt better if he'd stormed at her. It would have given her a chance to answer back. But he just stuck to this unnerving silence.

Slowly she undressed, washed, rinsed her mouth and got into her nightdress. She thought of the little bottle of port she kept to calm her nerves before a show. A tiny drop would make her feel better now.

The tiny drop became two, then three. Not having eaten properly all day it went to her head, or as Mum would have said, to her legs, Mum swearing that was where it went to first, bringing on a sort of wobbly feeling. The thought prompted a silly giggle and she felt a little better.

Lying full-length on top of the bed covers she let the port send its warmth through her stomach, until a light tap on her door made her sit up sharply.

'Who's that?' she called.

The door was opening and she realised she had forgotten to turn the key. As Theo entered as if it was his every right to do so, Emma swung her feet to the floor, gripping her nightdress close to her neck, the warmth in her stomach from the port dissipating as she glared at him.

'What d'you want?'

He looked almost penitent. 'I felt I must apologise,' he began. 'I was so furious about being let down. It just is not done …'

'You've already said that.' She remained sitting on the bed, staring up at him. 'I'm tired, worn out by all that's happened today. I've tried telling you about that but you won't listen. You're interested in no one but yourself. Other people's problems just wash off you like ...'

He held up his hand to stop the angry flow, the imperious gesture somewhat spoiling his effort to apologise.

'Now that I have had an opportunity to recover a little and be alone to think, I realise I was wrong. Not wrong that I had to cancel my act but for refusing to hear your side of it.'

'It's a bit late for that now,' she snapped and began plumping up her pillow. 'I need to sleep. I'll see you in the morning.'

He was obviously not ready to leave. 'I've been remembering how it was when my wife died. I well recall going to pieces the next evening after coming off stage. I tried to carry on but I suppose I was numbed by shock. I felt her death was my fault. I don't want that to happen again.'

Emma gave a defiant lift of her chin. 'I'm made of stronger stuff,' she said but he wasn't listening.

'I wouldn't hurt you for the world, Amelia.' His tone had softened and he began to move towards her. 'You are too sweet to be saddened by my foul temper and my deepest wish now is for you to forgive me.'

What could she say before such a display of humility? This was so unlike him that she allowed him a tentative if tight-lipped smile. She was surprised to receive a similar smile in return, he who seldom did, except to burst into a roar of laughter at some party.

He continued to move forward until he was able to reach out and touch her arm gently. 'I am forgiven, then?' he asked quietly.

She conceded with a small nod. The touch on her arm was sending a small shiver of pleasure through her. She told herself it was because their differences had been settled, but that wasn't the whole truth.

He had sat down on the edge of the bed beside her. Leaning forward, he drew her gently to him and laid a kiss on her cheek, his trimmed beard softly caressing her skin.

'I loathe seeing your lovely face spoiled by anguish,' he murmured. 'You must always be adorable and never fade.' His arm tightened a little about her, drawing her even closer and she gave no resistance when his lips touched her neck.

'I have become ill with love for you, my sweetest sweet,' came the slightly dramatic whisper. 'Do you feel the same for me, just the slightest?'

She gave a barely perceptible nod of her head against his cheek and she heard him give a deep sigh of contentment. 'My darling,' she heard him say and felt herself gently but firmly borne back down on to the pillows. His hands were brushing lightly over her body, a caressing touch, slow and lingering, which felt so wonderful.

His lips pressing on hers, automatically her arm went about his neck. He had become a faceless lover for whom she suddenly yearned. There even came fear that he might pull away from her as he'd done before. But this time it seemed that his need for her was now strong enough for him to overcome his strange prejudice. There came another wild thought even as she felt him grow strong and hard against her: had he indeed quenched his anger just to have his fill of her?

It was that thought that made her begin to squirm, trying to push him away, half out of fear of being proved to have given in willingly and have him look at her in disgust the moment his urge had been fulfilled, and half in true fear of this her first time ever being taken by a man, and this man in particular.

He was ignoring her whimper of protest, his movements becoming urgent, almost selfish as he joined with her now, bringing sharp stabbing pains in her insides that made her gasp and cry out and frightened her even more. It felt almost as though he was taking some revenge out on her, all the time his head was buried in the curve of her neck and shoulder.

His movements were becoming even fiercer, the pain sharper, she heard herself crying out for him to stop, but he wouldn't, or couldn't. It was as if she were some thing on which he had to relieve himself, that she meant nothing to him but that, her feelings dead to him.

Finally he let his body collapse heavily upon her. Seconds later he'd flung himself away to lie on his back breathing heavily. That he was still clothed while her nightdress lay dragged up around her upper body, leaving her fully exposed, somehow made it all seem degrading and she heard her own distressed whimper, 'Oh, my,' tremulously uttered several times. Her mind felt numbed. For possibly the first time in her life she felt defenceless and vulnerable. It was as if she were someone else lying here and this man, someone she didn't know.

At the sound of her whimper, he turned to look at her, and leaning over her, took the hem of the nightdress and carefully drew it down to cover her, such gentle consideration after such violence that she turned her face from him with unexpected tears of shame trembling on her eyelashes.

'My dear.' He said no more

Turning from her, he got to his feet, his back to her as he adjusted his own clothing. Still without looking at her, he moved to the door to stand facing it without opening it.

'Are you all right, my dear?' he asked.

She found herself unable to answer. She felt damp and uncomfortable and distressed.

'I am very much in love with you, you know,' he added, then still without looking at her, opened the door and went out, leaving her full of disbelief at what she had let happen. And not once, after that initial tender embrace, did she remember him kissing her.

Chapter Twenty-Two

Despite yesterday's fiasco, Theo was greatly admired, and with his contract at the Oxford to run several weeks yet, the management was happy to see him back for both Saturday matinée and evening, continuing as normal.

Full of self-satisfaction these days, he said to Emma when she spoke about his being pleased, 'Without me, their takings would halve and they know it. They are fully aware that I am a draw.'

He was in a good mood. Last night with her had assuaged his anger about Friday and he seemed to be looking at her in a different light. As for her, it brought an odd sense of power over him that she'd never had before.

'I have to go and see how my mother is,' she told him bluntly in the hotel's breakfast room. To her amazement he put up no argument, and merely nodded as he continued eating his scrambled eggs.

'I promise to be back here before lunch, well before the matinée,' she conceded for good measure, as if he had in fact protested.

Despite the need for haste, she took a hackney cab to Whitechapel. A thick, pea-soup fog had descended in the early hours of the morning and was still lingering. Horses knew what they were about in fog, motor engines did not, and for once horse transport was quicker.

Her mother was in better spirits than she'd expected, and it came as no surprise to find that Ben had already settled himself in. In fact he'd been there since last night, now with a proper bed of his own.

'After you left, I went back,' Mum explained, a little apologetically. 'I know you put yerself out for me, but I couldn't leave 'im there. So I toddled back and found 'im still there and made 'im come back with me.'

She spoke as if he was still a kid in need of her protection. But, she supposed, Mum's first would still be her baby despite being twenty-one.

'Does Mrs Blacker know?' she queried. Mrs Blacker was no fool. If the two of them were being underhand, it wouldn't take long for her to find out and give them their marching orders. But she was being prematurely cross.

'I asked 'er before I went ter find 'im,' she was informed. 'I told 'er that after what happened he was 'omeless too, and she said it'd be orright but she'd want a bit more rent from us. So, well, I 'ope you don't mind, Em.'

'How much more?'

'Another three bob.'

Emma drew in a deep, slow breath, not to show her feelings. Nine shillings! She couldn't blame Mrs Blacker and in time the woman would realise that her extra charge had probably been too little once Ben started his tricks. How long would she put up with bawling and yelling when temper got the better of him along with a bit too much to drink? But Ben could put on the charm when he wanted, like he did with the girls, especially this one he called Clara. He'd probably keep on the right side of Mrs Blacker, knowing which side his bread was buttered – a nice place like this.

Emma let her breath out gently and nodded her assent. She could afford it, but it would have been nice if she'd been asked rather than told.

It was good to be back out of the damp but slowly yielding midday fog that would descend again by late afternoon, chill and clinging, but in weather like this even a hotel bedroom was acceptable. Mum's new place was already cosy by comparison – trust her to immediately turn three small rooms into a home.

Emma opened her door to Theo's knock and stood back for him as he came in, he assuming it to be his right. 'How is your mother?' he asked, surprising her. He'd never referred to her before.

'She's settling in,' Emma said as he went over to gaze through the window at the few horse vehicles passing below in Broadwick Street, growing more visible in the thinning fog. 'I think she'll be all right now.'

'Good,' he said. 'Then perhaps we can concentrate for an hour or two on my act without any interruption before we leave for the theatre.'

It was a sharp dig. Flexibility hadn't lasted long. 'I'll need to have lunch, Theo,' she said.

'Didn't you have something with your mother?'

'I hurried back here as soon as I could,' she said, 'because I didn't want to be late.' It was her turn to be pointed, but he ignored it.

298

'I'll have tea and sandwiches brought up. After the matinée we will have something more substantial and this evening I will take you to supper.'

That was it, he never asked – he assumed, he arranged. He made no more references to her mother's welfare and she volunteered none as he took her through those moves he considered required attention.

Once or twice he was needlessly sharp with her though she couldn't see why he should be – she'd made hardly a mistake. Nevertheless, she let it go. But when, as they finished, he remarked, 'Not too bad and I feel a little happier, but had you been here yesterday afternoon, we might have avoided doing it over again today,' her temper got the better of her.

'You're not going to let me forget, are you?' she pushed aside the plate of sandwiches he was now offering, her appetite vanishing. 'I thought you'd put it behind you.'

'I have,' he said, calmly helping himself to one of the neat little triangles of cheese and pickle though he did not lift it to his mouth.

'I thought that after last night,' she rushed on, 'after you made ...'

'Eat,' he said, pushing the plate under her nose. 'You're no good to me, Amelia, if you faint away from hunger during my act, and cause another disaster.'

'Another disaster!' She was on the verge of upending the plate but controlled herself. 'I'd say a disaster of your own making. I arrived a little late-ish, that was all, and we still could have gone on, but you'd already gone ahead and cancelled. There was no need for all that drama.'

'It's past now,' he said, putting the plate back on to the occasional table. 'You will drink some tea.' He began pouring it for her from a cream-coloured teapot, adding milk and sugar from the matching porcelain and even stirring it for her as though she was incapable of doing it for herself.

'I don't want any tea, neither.'

'*Either*.'

'I don't care!' As he stood watching her without speaking, she felt the blood rush to her temples in a fierce gush of rage. 'You enjoy tormenting me, don't you? It makes you feel masterful, don't it? All right, *doesn't* it. But I won't be some submissive little plaything of yours to have every last little error I make held over my head for the rest of my life while you go ahead enjoying your pleasure of me!'

She saw him frown. He put the cup down on the table and moved towards her. The intense blue of his eyes seemed to cloud over.

'The rest of your life, my dear?' His tone was low. 'I hope very much to be allowed to share the rest of your life with you.'

She wasn't to be fooled by that. Before he could touch her, she turned her back on him, snatching up her hairbrush from the dressing table to furiously brush her hair, the dragged-out hairpins making it fall long and heavy about her shoulders.

In the mirror she could see him come to stand behind her. His hands rested lightly on her shoulders. His eyes, now bright, regarded her in the mirror to hold her own with their hypnotic glow.

'You are so lovely, Amelia. Far too lovely to spoil it in pique.'

One hand had moved to fondle a thick lock of her hair, preventing her from continuing to brush it. 'I am too fond of you, my dear, to spoil what we have with argument. Forget yesterday and think of more pleasant things.'

Emma said nothing, her brush lying idle as he went on: 'You were so loving with me last night. I was over-whelmed. Say you are happy?'

Emma remained silent, refusing to fall into his arms, as he'd no doubt expected, not when his plea for her to be happy was so full of magnanimity rather than the other way around.

'Theo, I must start getting ready.'

He took his hands from her shoulders. 'First you must eat a little. At least for your own sake, if not mine.'

'I'm not hungry,' she said, huffy still.

'Then drink your tea.'

'I'm not thirsty.'

'As you wish.' He moved away. 'I'll come back for you later.'

'Of course,' she replied stiffly. But when he'd gone, she thirstily drank the tea, feeling a great need for it, still feeling the lingering, warm touch of his hands on her shoulders.

She poured another cup and drank that more slowly, ate a sandwich a little too quickly, then another, more thought-fully. Theo hadn't touched the one he had picked up. It lay beside the plate. Nor had he drank any tea. He would no doubt have another lot sent up to him. As with her, the act depended on him being one hundred per cent alert.

Their contract at the Oxford ended at Christmas. The Empire in Leicester Square was putting on *Aladdin* and had asked to have the Great Theodore as the evil magician, but he was having none of that.

'My work is above that sort of thing,' he told Jack Simmons.

'The trouble is, Theo, it's the panto season. It's a time for kiddies, and variety takes a back seat. What else can you expect?'

Theodore was emphatic. 'I'll not demean myself playing some damned pantomime magician, not after having now risen to top the bill at one of the foremost theatres in London. I will accept the Empire if they give me my own spot as an addition to their damned pantomime. But not to be *in* it.'

Jack Simmons pursed his lips and leaned back in his swivel chair. 'I'll see what I can do. But you can't start taking a back seat again now. You need to be working continuously.'

He leaned forward. 'I tell you what. I'll ask the Empire to think about what you ask for during the two weeks of pantomime. But it's the same everywhere at this time of year, especially in the West End. If they won't, we could look at Leeds possibly. Or Manchester.'

'I will not be fobbed off,' Theo said for an answer. 'Now as a leading performer I no longer run from one music hall to another, like some second-rate artist. My contracts must be for exclusive appearances at one hall.'

'The panto season's very short,' Simmons patiently pointed out. 'A couple of weeks in the provinces, and I'll make sure your fame is spread back to London and when you return they'll be clamouring for you, take my word.'

'I have taken this city by storm and he talks of Leeds,' Theo raged to Emma. 'I am virtually on equal footing with such names as Ellen Terry, Adelaine Page, Maud Allan, Henry Irvine, Albert Chevalier. It is crucial that

London does not forget me. I need to be here, not in some Godforsaken city like Leeds, Manchester, Liverpool ...'

Not listening to anything else, all Emma could think of was this string of provinces. She'd hated it that last time, always on the move, never in any one hotel for long. Not seeing her mother for the time being, though Mum had settled down nicely, could estrange them all over again. But maybe it wouldn't be too long before they were back in London.

It didn't look as though she'd see Mum even on Christmas Day, because Theo was taking her to a party, insisting she go with him. 'There are people you need to meet,' he said.

There had been quite a few social occasions these last weeks, society gatherings that people in the theatre seemed unable to do without. She'd grown to enjoy them, had made several friends, had begun to talk their language, laughed over the things they laughed at, understood their jokes, their witty asides, joined in to find herself popular. So she didn't recoil from Theo taking it for granted that she'd be with him on this occasion. Just that she felt guilty about Mum, and on Christmas afternoon rushed over to see her.

These days her mother was more amenable, enjoying an easier life. To Emma's relief she showed no animosity when told about the party.

'He's been invited by some friends,' Emma told her. 'But we don't have to arrive until eight-thirty tonight, so I can stay most of the afternoon.'

'I see.' But it didn't detract from her feelings of guilt.

'I'd sooner be here with you.'

'Why? It'd be too quiet for yer.'

Mum had never been one for social gatherings, not even when Dad was alive. Neither had family, Dad an orphanage boy, Mum's two brothers dying in infancy, her sister later in life, unmarried. Her mother, Emma's grand-mother, had been taken years ago with pneumonia, her grandfather a year after that. So Mum was used to quiet Christmases, never taking up offers from neighbours to join their extensive family parties. That Ben would go out enjoying himself didn't seem to bother her either.

'Won't he be here to keep you company?' Emma asked.

'I'd sooner 'im stay out if he's goin' ter come 'ome roaring drunk an' upsetting everyone,' she said. 'So far he's kept on the right side of Mrs Blacker. I don't want ter be turned out of 'ere now we've found a decent place ter live at reasonable rent.'

She seemed to have overlooked the fact that it was her daughter who'd found it and who paid the rent, but it wasn't worth bringing up. Instead she hoped that Mrs Blacker, realising Mum would be on her own, might ask her down for a glass of something – a Gentile Christmas no barrier to a bit of festive goodness of heart – along with the single woman in the two rooms below Mum and the couple occupying the basement, the ground floor, of course, being used by Mrs Blacker herself.

Emma refrained from mentioning that she could be out of London in the New Year.

It was so nice sitting here with her in this cosy room, enjoying tea and cake – Mum could afford to buy cake now. The room was large enough for Ben to have a proper bed, in one corner, partitioned off by a small screen for privacy and with a small wardrobe for his own use. The screen half drawn across, she could see he was keeping his part tidy, which was a surprise. Though much of it was probably due to Mum seeing his things put away and his bed made, the area swept and dusted, like the rest of the room. At last Mum could enjoy the satisfaction of tidiness without seeing it ruined by dirt and soot floating down like black snow from the railway to penetrate every corner and crevice of those old rooms she'd fought so hard to keep clean.

'I've got you a Christmas present,' Emma said, finishing her cake to pick up the grip she'd brought with her. From it she extracted two small, brown paper packages. 'One for Ben too.'

Mum took them as if they might burn her hand. 'I ain't got nothing fer you,' she said. 'Only you've got everything.'

Emma ignored what sounded like a sly dig at what she did, her mother's disdainful references to 'theatrical lady' always popping into Emma's mind. 'It doesn't matter,' she said evenly. 'I enjoyed getting something for you and Ben.'

She watched her mother look from the packages to her and back to them, turning them over and over. 'Well, go on,' she urged. 'Open the one with your name on it.'

The brown paper carefully torn off revealed a brightly coloured layer underneath. To Emma's urging it was slowly removed from the blue, flat box it covered.

'Oh, Em!'

There was a gasp of surprise and mild censure at having done such a thing as the lid was lifted and the blue, fine cashmere wool bed-jacket taken out to be held up by the shoulders in wonder, its fine texture felt. But the wonder had changed back to censure, this time not quite so mild.

305

'When am I supposed ter wear this?'

'When you're sitting in bed, of course,' Emma said.

'I've never 'ad the time fer sitting in bed. When I wake up I get up.'

'Now you have the time. You don't have to work any more. You've got all the time in the world.'

'An' it gets boring at times.'

Emma compressed her lips, her gift forgotten. She'd done her very best for her mother, these nice little rooms, a decent landlady, money for Mum to buy clothes, feed herself adequately, not have to scrimp and scrape any more, and all she could say was that she was bored. Emma bit back a retort that if she was all that keen on slaving for a penny or two, she could go out selling flowers again.

Instead, she said, 'You could join a women's club. Make friends. I think there's one around here where they have lectures, debates, sometimes dancing and singing, play dominoes and learn hobbies, or just chat.'

'What 'ave I got ter debate about?' Mum turned up her nose and Emma felt her temper getting dangerously shorter. Why was she always like this?

She had been reaching for another piece of cake, cake Mum could now afford. Withdrawing her hand, she got up from the table to leave before her temper really did get the better of her. She'd looked forward to spending several hours with Mum, had come with the best of intentions and now it was all spoiled, and none of it her fault.

'I've got to go,' she said briskly. 'Enjoy the present if you can. It might be useful if you're ever in bed with a cold.'

'You ain't been 'ere five minutes.' Her mother still sat there, looking up at her, the bed-jacket still held between her fingers.

306

The Flower Girl

'I've got things to do. And it's getting dark. And I've got this party to go to.'

Her mother sat where she was, surveying her with that discerning look she sometimes adopted. 'He says yer got to?'

'No ... I mean, well, he likes me there and I meet lots of his friends.'

'You used ter 'ave yer own friends, 'ere. The ones yer've left be'ind. Lizzie Wallis was once yer best friend, she still lives down the road.'

'I've made other friends. I don't suppose she wants to talk to me now.'

'She's got a young man now.'

Did it matter?

Mum's tone was quiet and deliberate. 'And you've got one of yer own, though not so young. Thought yer'd 'ave done better for yerself. A pretty face like yours, yer should of found a nice young man, not wasted it on an old one.'

Emma sat down abruptly. 'Mum, Theo isn't my fiancé. We work together, that's all.'

Her mother did not reply, but the look she gave her said it all. Emma could almost hear those disapproving, disparaging, condemning words as to where her daughter had gone to, where she was going to, and worst of all whom she was going there with. She could almost hear the accusation, 'Yer work tergether and I bet yer sleep tergether too.'

'I hope you get to like your present,' she said, getting to her feet once more, unable to keep the terseness from her tone. 'And that Ben likes his too. Tell him it's a cardigan.'

Her mother stood up too. 'Pity yer can't stay longer,' she said. 'But it was nice to see yer.'

She seemed to mellow suddenly, looking at Emma with an unusually soft expression. 'Enjoy yer party, Em.'

'I expect I will,' Emma said curtly.

'And have a nice Christmas.'

Emma was suddenly surprised as her mother came round the table and planted a kiss on her cheek, something she rarely did.

'I mean it, Em, 'ave a nice time.'

'I'd sooner be here, with you, Mum.' This time those sentiments were genuine, that one small kiss bringing moisture to her eyes and longing to her heart. If only she could take Mum with her to this party – a ridiculous idea, Mum would be like a fish out of water and she wouldn't thank her.

'I wish …' she broke off, not knowing quite what she wished. 'Will you be all right, Mum? You should have company at Christmas time.' Her mother smiled, another rare thing.

'There's an 'ouse-full of people 'ere. Nice people, decent. I've made friends with 'em, and no doubt someone'll look in. And I bet all the tea in China, Ben'll be 'ome soon as he's 'ungry. I've got a nice bit of beef ready ter cook in the oven. You go an' enjoy yerself, if yer can. I'll give 'im yer present.'

The Christmas party was being held by Mr Arthur Lloyd, an entrepreneur, shareholder in several London variety theatres, and friend of Theo's from many years back. The large Victorian rooms were crowded and stuffy and full of chatter and high-pitched laughter, through which a string quartet was having a struggle to be heard. Emma moved around talking to this one and that.

Someone she knew vaguely was signalling to her from one side of the room, the woman stretching her neck and waving for her to join the people she was with, no doubt keen on introducing her to someone. Emma began threading her way towards them as the woman turned back to the group.

Through a momentary gap in the mass of beautiful, flowing dresses and formal evening suits, she caught a glimpse of Theo. He was standing a way off and there was a pretty girl with him, her arms about his neck. He did not appear to be objecting as she brought her face close to his.

A stab of jealousy caught Emma, so intense that it took her by surprise. She was only half aware of the high and excitable female voice assailing her over the chatter.

'My dear! Amelia, my dear! I had no idea you were here.'

Turning towards the voice with its faintly Scottish ring, Emma saw an animated young woman skirting a small knot of people to reach her.

Marie Loftus was in her late twenties, an actress and music hall artiste with amazing powers of mimicry. Emma had met her at several parties and they'd struck up a friendly acquaintance for all Emma was some ten years younger. Marie would be playing Peter Pan at the Duke of York's Theatre come the New Year. Small and petite, she was suited to the part with her heart-shaped face, pert nose, teasing lips and dark, twinkling eyes.

'Aren't you with Theodore?' Marie was asking. 'I've just caught sight of him over there with some woman or other. I have no idea who she is. I thought you and he must have parted company. In fact I even got the idea that he was back working with that young man, Martin Page, who used to be with him. I did see Martin Page here earlier on, and assumed …'

Emma interrupted her with a light little laugh. Martin Page was here?

'No, Theo and I are still together. But he went wandering off a little while ago. There are so many people he knows and I lost him in this crowd. But I've just caught sight of him.'

She automatically looked in that direction. There he was, the fair-haired girl's slender arms draped around his neck. She looked like a chorus girl who had probably wheedled an invitation from someone aware of her obvious reputation, Emma thought with jealous vindictiveness. Marie's gaze had followed hers. She turned back, presenting Emma with a bright, reassuring smile.

'Oh, don't mind him, dearie. He has probably had a little too much by now. He can be quite the masher when he wants. He once made advances to me, you know. That was when his wife was alive. She quite caned him about it. They'd quarrel, you know, quite fiercely, but usually for the way she could attract the men rather than he attracting the ladies.'

'You said Martin Page is here?' queried Emma, changing the subject but finding herself unexpectedly interested in him.

Marie gazed about. 'He is here somewhere. He's usually to be seen skulking wherever Theodore goes. No, that's unkind. A handsome young man like that doesn't skulk, does he? Odd, the way Theo dropped him. I wonder why?'

She gave a rippling laugh, eyes already alighting on another quarry. 'If you'll excuse me a moment, dearie, there's Miss Gitana, Gertie, I simply must go and speak to her.'

Left alone, Emma found herself glancing around for any glimpse of Martin Page. What was he doing here? She gathered that he attended many parties, but was it only when Theo was there? Trying not to acknowledge a strange stirring of anticipation, she continued searching. Finally giving up, she looked back to where Theo and the girl had been standing, but the girl had gone. And so had Theo.

Emma made her way to where she had last seen him. Had he gone up those stairs that curved by a cluster of parlour palms to some room above? Previously unoccupied and silent after the noise down here, was it now being taken advantage of by him and that girl? Were they even now lying together on a sofa, its back concealing them from any interloper?

People came and spoke to her. She responded as sociably as possible, smiled brightly, frequently taking a glass of champagne from a tray held by a liveried servant. Warmed by the champagne and growing more light-headed, she watched the wide, curved, carpeted staircase as much as she could, and finally saw him. A tall, upright, commanding figure, he came down the carpeted steps at a measured pace, his eyes scanning the thronged room below. Of the young woman there was no sign.

It was then that she saw Martin, approaching her in the wake of a servant who with a tray of drinks was ploughing a pathway between the groups.

'Martin,' she said, as he reached her, while the waiter continued onward. Even as she spoke, her eyes were on Theo who had paused at the foot of the staircase to glance about. Martin too had seen him and when he spoke it was as if he were trying to get all his words out at once.

'I heard you and he would be here. I need to know if you are OK.'

'I'm fine,' she said

'I attended the Oxford a couple of times to see you perform. You're very good, very co-ordinated. He's taught you well. Is he treating you all right?'

'Yes,'

He was pressing a visiting card into her hand. 'If you are *ever* in any trouble, of *any* sort, here's my address. I've taken a flat in London, given up working for my father. Can't stand the tedium. Caused a bit of upset but I need the theatre.'

So it wasn't her welfare he was concerned about, it was to use her to speak to Theo for him.

'He may be treating you all right now,' he went on, 'but I'll be around if ever ...'

He broke off and she followed his gaze to see Theo moving towards her.

When she looked back, Martin had gone. She did not smile as Theo reached her, her mind imagining him and the unknown girl together, Martin forgotten.

'Where have you been?' she asked.

Theo ignored the question. 'I saw you with a young man.'

'Just one of the guests.' It was no lie, but it was prevarication. She saw him frown. He knew who it was and now it became a lie. She squirmed and hastily resorted to her earlier accusation. 'I asked you where you were.'

'If I have failed to be attentive to you, my dear, I apologise,' he said stiffly. 'I was talking business with someone.'

She couldn't help it. 'That being the girl I saw wrapped about your neck earlier,' she burst out. A man standing nearby looked sharply round at her then turned back to his companion. Emma lowered her voice to a hiss.

'I saw her. Who is she?' At least it had taken Theo off the scent. He was looking angry.

'Women are foolish,' he said, his eyes roaming the room, his height enabling him to see over most men's heads. 'I am well known and admired, you know that, Amelia. Women are apt to be carried away a little.'

He brought his eyes back to her, a smile causing his moustache to twitch upwards a little. 'If you need to know, my dear, I have been discussing business with Mr Charles Shirley of the Alhambra.'

The smiled broadened, making his short beard move too. 'My dear, did you think ... Are you *jealous*, Amelia?'

She remained silent. She didn't believe his story. All she could think of was Theo and that girl up there together, though it could never be proved.

She seethed silently, yet the image of him and the girl, true or not, had begun to arouse her, unnaturally so. She wanted him. More than anything else she wanted him – this sensual man at this very moment was overwhelming her as he stood looking down at her.

All thought of Martin Page was swept from her mind, as later that night proved to be the loveliest one she had ever known.

Chapter Twenty-Three

All the loving in the world, no matter how wonderful, couldn't erase the sight of Theo with that person draped around his neck, and Theo lapping it up.

Last night when he'd displayed his undying love in such a physical way, she had let it slip from her mind, but as she got up this morning, leaving him still asleep, she was more than sure he wasn't being honest. That reference to a business discussion, she didn't believe a word of it. She wasn't the assistant to a cunning magician for nothing. He might fool others but he didn't fool her. Yet how could she accuse him without proof other than merely seeing him with the girl? It could have been innocent. He could have been telling the truth.

In a show of defiance she scribbled him a note and went off early to spend an hour or two with her mother, glad of any diversion to smiling at Theo's lies and pretending she believed them.

Mum was in an unusually amiable mood when she got there, saying she'd had a very enjoyable Christmas.

'They're nice people 'ere,' she said. 'Made me feel very welcome and I 'ad a nice time with the Sullivans, what's got the basement flat. Very nice it was. I got ter bed about eleven-thirty. No sign of Ben. He was out until Gawd knows what time and I weren't sorry.'

Unusually chatty, she spoke of her evening with her neighbours, and of what Ben was up to these days, always with plenty of money that got Emma assuming it probably came from dubious sources rather than any she sent. Her mother seemed to be thinking likewise, saying darkly, 'Seems to 'ave made a lot of very unsavoury friends in Brick Lane. Not nice people.'

Her mother was no longer as alienated as once she'd been, though it was probably a temporary thing, this present congeniality brought on by her having had such a pleasant Christmas evening. She even asked how Emma's evening had gone, and listened with interest as she spoke of the fine dresses and rich food, the glittering venue, saying, 'Well I never' every so often.

Emma refrained from mentioning her suspicions of Theo, but at one time her mother looked quizzically at her. 'You are 'appy, aren't yer?' she said.

'Of course I'm happy,' she retorted, and no more was said, Mum going on to talk of her neighbours and the area. 'Some parts even 'ere ain't all that savoury,' she related. 'Still gangs of ruffians, y'know, just as bad as it was down our old place. Whitechapel Market's all right, decent enough people shopping after dark, though yer still 'ave ter keep an eye out fer tealeafs and pickpockets, but it's like that everywhere yer go. But them living in 'ouses like Mrs Blacker's is mostly decent people, certainly better than where we used ter live before the fire.'

It was astonishing – the hours couldn't have passed more pleasantly, leaving Emma to wonder if perhaps her mother had thought things out at last, except that the moment she spoke of the theatre, she closed up like a clam. When Emma was leaving, her mother took her confidentially by the arm, and said, 'He ain't been touchin' yer, 'as he, this bloke of yours?'

She'd tried hard not to colour up as she reassured her with the lie that it was no more than a working relationship. Whether or not Mum saw her cheeks colour up, she only nodded as if satisfied,

'So long as 'e ain't,' she said, adding, 'Only Ben's been asking. Keeps saying that if this bloke takes advantage of yer, he'll 'ave 'im. Ben is yer brother, Em, an' for all 'is faults, he do care for yer. Don't want ter see yer come to 'arm.'

'Tell him not to worry,' was all Emma could say, forcing a small, careless laugh as she presented her cheek for a peck from her mother.

'I know I can't make yer change yer mind, Em, about what yer do,' was her mother's departing shot. 'Yer grown up now and got yer own mind, but if ever yer in trouble, remember, I'm 'ere.'

'Of course I'll remember,' Emma said, feeling more comfortable with her mother than ever she'd been since leaving home. Yes, she was her own woman, and no one, not Mum, not Ben or Theo would alter that.

In a better frame of mind, she returned to the hotel to be informed by a hotel desk clerk that Mr Barrington was waiting for her in his room.

'I was worried by the wording of your note,' Theo said when she got there. 'It was so abrupt. Have I done something to upset you?'

316

'No,' she lied, taking off her outdoor things.

'If I have, please tell me.' He seemed almost entreating, and when she didn't reply, he continued, 'If you're still upset by that earlier incident, I apologise. If you wish to see your mother, I've no objection and shall never stop you or expect you to ask my permission.' He was being far too kind to be true and she assumed it stemmed from penitence at allowing his eye to alight on someone else. But his next remark swept that all away, rubbing at her already raw suspicions. 'In fact I intend to change many things.'

Change things? Did he have this other person in mind to take her place? Was that why the leech had clung to him, thrilled by his proposition? But what about last night – had he been trying to let her down lightly?

She turned on him. 'Are you trying to say you can do without me?'

Theo stared. 'Whatever made you think such a thing?'

'I don't know,' she said dismally. Seconds later she was in his arms.

'My sweet, you're tired,' he exclaimed. 'And probably hungry. That is why you are so tetchy. No more rehearsing for a day or two. We will have lunch and you will relax.' With a benevolent smile, he added, 'You'll feel much better once you have eaten and rested.'

And she did feel much better, but still uncertain. Over lunch she had to challenge him again, he and that girl disappearing after she'd seen her kissing him.

She was taken aback by his surprised smile. 'I have explained. The young lady having become over-amorous, I decided it best not to make a scene by pushing her from me but simply gave her no encouragement. She departed in a huff when Mr Shirley came up to say that he wished to speak to me in private.'

His grin widened. 'Mr Shirley's conversation with me proved very good news, my dear. I would have told you last night but that we had other things on our minds.' He chuckled then grew serious again. 'And this morning you were gone before I could speak to you. He has offered me top billing at the Metropolitan. From now on we will be performing alongside many other fine, well-known performers.'

He began reeling off a list of names. 'My salary will be two hundred and fifty pounds a week, the contract running for several weeks. And I shall command far more as we go on tour, five, six, seven hundred even. I intend to find us fine apartments here in London as our base. We shall live in style.'

Where moments ago there had been torment and dejection, a wave of elation swept over her. With that sort of money she wouldn't mind touring. And he said they would live in style. 'What about that house of yours?' she asked innocently, and seeing his confusion, made to elucidate. 'The house Martin Page said you own. I've never seen it. Is it nice?'

Rushing on in her enthusiasm, she forgot to eat, and even dismissed his frown. 'We could live in style there. Why don't you ever talk about it?'

It as then she saw that his earlier good humour had deserted him entirely. 'That's my business, my dear,' he said slowly, and now it was her turn to frown, her own joy diminishing.

'I think it should be my business too when you're sleeping with me,' she snapped waspishly across the table. 'As someone you sleep with, I think I ought to know everything about you.'

She should have known better. He continued eating and his tone hadn't risen, but it became dangerous. 'That's enough,' he said evenly.

'No, it's not,' she said, lowering her voice so as not to be overheard by others in the dining room. 'You think you can pop into my bed as if we was married, yet tell me hardly anything about yourself. I won't have you using me like I'm just your mistress and not worth being allowed into your private life. Even a mistress would get better treatment than me.'

'I!' he corrected, his gaze fixed on his half-empty plate.

She had heard herself falling into her old ways, but didn't care. 'How can you sleep with me, then virtually tell me to mind my own business?'

'You appear to welcome my presence in your bed readily enough.' His tone had grown savage. He still hadn't looked up at her. 'You take all that I offer,' he added, 'money, fine clothes, the best ...'

'I think I deserve it!' she returned equally furious.

'Payment for services rendered, is that it?' He looked up so suddenly that it startled her. 'As a prostitute might demand. Is it that your fee has gone up?'

Emma interrupted him with an enraged hiss, and before she could control herself, reached across the small, round dining table to slap his face for him, but before she could do so, he let the knife he was holding fall and skilfully caught her wrist in a vice-like grip, his reaction so amazingly swift and natural to one of his profession that she hardly saw it happening.

319

'Don't!' he warned under his breath. 'Don't make a fool of me here.' Her hand was released. 'Sit back,' he commanded, still in a whisper.

Chastened, she slumped back, looking about her to see if anyone had witnessed her show of temper. There were few people here. If any had seen the moment, they remained intent on their lunches, engaged in their own conversations.

'What is it that you want, my dear?' he was asking quietly, his voice steady as a rock. 'Marriage?'

Emma stared at him, his earlier exciting news now quite forgotten.

'Marriage?' she echoed, then, aware of what she took as a note of sarcasm, she drew herself up with dignity.

'Not until you tell me about yourself, I shan't *ever* marry you. I don't want you in my bed either. I won't have dealings with someone I don't know nothing about. I don't want you to touch me. I don't let strangers I don't know nothing about touch me.'

She was aware of slipping back into the old grammatical errors, her refined manners no more than a veneer, but although he made no effort to correct her, she knew she was letting herself down. For a moment he sat regarding her then slowly got up from the table. 'I am going up to my room,' he said. He came to stand over her, bending a little towards her. No one seemed to notice the move.

'To *my* room,' he emphasised. 'I shall make a point of not entering your room unless you request it.' He moved off, leaving her staring at her own half-eaten meal, her wine hardly touched, the bottle he had ordered still half full.

Guilt had begun to crawl over her like some foul insect – guilt and fear. Moments later she was up from the table and following him. He must have moved fast, must have taken the two flights of stairs to their rooms two at a time because he was already gone and the hotel's cage-like lift was still on its way down from the fifth floor. Nor did she wait for it, arriving at the second floor breathless from running upstairs in impeding skirts.

Gathering her breath, she tapped tentatively on the door to his room. She heard his voice saying, 'Come in,' as though having anticipated her, but she didn't pause to compare herself to some dog on a lead, as, unsure what to expect, she entered.

Before she could open her mouth, he said in a measured, almost resigned voice, 'I realise you have the right to know more about me. What do you wish to know? I shall try to answer as honestly as I know how.'

Now it came to it, what did she actually want to know? She found herself asking the only question that seemed appropriate to the start of any life.

'What you were like as a child?' Gathering momentum, she hurried on. 'What were your parents were like? Your education – anyone can see you were well educated – but what you were like as a young man, did you have many friends? And when did you decide to take up magic? What prompted you and what did your parents think about that?'

Emma tailed off, running out of ideas, and for a while he didn't speak. When he did it was with abrupt sentences, spoken in monotone.

'I was born in Surrey. The house I have was once my family home. My parents are dead, drowned at sea when

I was twenty-two. I did not grieve. I hardly knew them, being at boarding school from a young age, then Eton, then Oxford. My father was in the diplomatic corps, India. My mother went with him. The house knew little but emptiness. It stands empty now. I have no love for it, no fond memories. At university I made some friends, but no lasting friendships. I enjoyed sleight of hand and entertained them by it. At one time I practised hypnotism but did not pursue it after one ...' He paused as if searching for a word. 'Unpalatable incident,' he continued. 'I preferred the conjuring and it went well. I married, as you know, but my wife hated the house – too out of town for her. When she died I did not go back there. It is now run down but worth a good sum with the grounds. The rest you know.'

Listening to him was like looking at bones, a skeleton bare of flesh – solid but with no life to it. She had expected so much more. What sort of man was it that had gone through nearly half his life yet felt nothing for it, felt he had nothing to show for it, so much so that it wasn't worth enlarging upon. No reference to small moments of excitement, anticipation, passion, just bare statements. But she had asked her questions, had received his answers, and must be satisfied with that. He was no more known to her than before.

Suddenly he brightened and rallied, as though shaking himself out of a dream he would prefer not to have had.

'Now, we must discuss my good news. I have great plans, my dear.' It was as though he had never spoken at all of other things. 'I have in mind several new ideas that will much improve my act and stun my audience, but I will require two assistants.'

Emma's mind flew instantly to the girl she'd seen with him, as it had done too many times since the incident, accompanied by the expected pang of foreboding. His act did not call for two assistants. It was a ruse to have that girl near him. 'You've got someone in mind?' she asked as innocently as she could.

He shook his head. 'I have given some thought to it. My mind has been full of the many ideas I am considering. They'll be quite unique.' She could see he was not going to be drawn out.

'I shall tell you once it is clearer in my head,' he said, leaving her to squirm with uncertainty. She felt undecided too about his passing reference to marriage. Had it been a genuine proposal or just a taunt? Somehow she veered towards it being a taunt.

At the party on Boxing Day, he hardly left her side, almost as if to prove to her that he had eyes for no other. This was a more sedate party than the one for Christmas Day, the rich and famous gathered in yet another of those grand houses whose glittering chandeliers reflected off diamonds and emeralds as the light glowed down upon fine furnishings and rich gowns.

With Indian and Turkish carpet underfoot, liveried footmen bearing silver trays of alcoholic refreshments moved silently and effortlessly between groups, people moving off at intervals to pick at tiny delicacies from a table with a silver centrepiece of fruit and flowers. Emma joined in the polite conversation, had her hand kissed by those gentleman introduced to her and gracefully inclined her head in reply on being acknowledged by ladies more noticeably her betters on the social scale, and even curtseyed to a minor royal, recalling that the last time she had done so had been to the King himself.

Clutching a small, cream-coloured fan that set off a mint-green gown with flounced lace at her bare shoulders, her waist nipped in to measure a mere eighteen inches, leaving the skirt to fall smoothly over her hips into a generous flare of lace about her feet, it was not hard to feel quite special, and although the sparkle of her necklace and modest little tiara set on the piled auburn hair came from paste diamonds, they glittered and blazed in the light of the chandeliers as much as any genuine stones she saw around her.

For once Theo displayed no jealousy at the admiring glances of the men, rather he possessed a certain pride that made her wonder what he was was thinking. Nor did he show any jealousy at the New Year celebrations.

That was a far wilder affair, this time calling for fancy dress, she as a Southern belle – she'd have liked to wear something more daring, but Theo had other ideas – he more soberly as a Mississippi gambler, which did suit him.

Despite the gaiety, he seemed eager to be away when the first chimes of 1905 had hardly sounded. When Theo wanted something, it was hard to argue, though she made up her mind to display her displeasure in no uncertain manner at being dragged away from that glittering celebration, and was cold and distant as she was handed her wrap and he his cloak.

In the seclusion of a hansom cab bearing them back to their hotel, Theo took her hand. 'You looked so very beautiful tonight,' he whispered. 'Every man's eyes were on you.'

Hoping the old jealousy wasn't about to rear its head at last, she refused to reply, certainly not to demean herself in protesting any intention of drawing admiration.

'You know how I feel about you, my dearest, don't you?' he went on.

In the dim interior of the gently swaying vehicle, he lifted her hand to his lips, kissing each finger in turn. Now she knew the reason for the hansom – a conveyance of romance. A rattling, juddering motor taxi wouldn't have served his purpose. Well, she wasn't going to melt that easily after being dragged away from something she been so enjoying.

Her hand lowered slightly, in the darkness she felt the coldness of metal being slipped on to her third finger. She glanced down and, in what little light penetrated from a street lamp they passed, saw the brittle glint of diamonds.

As she gasped, his fingers tightened about hers. 'I want you to be my wife, Amelia,' he whispered. 'Say you will, my dearest. Say you accept.'

Astonishment made her gasp. Not herself for a second, she gave a half nod, aware that, even while with this small acknowledgment she was more or less committing herself, she wasn't as ready for this as she had thought. There was no reason for it – she'd dreamed of being the wife of the celebrated Great Theodore, and the wealth and security that came from it. Yet now it was being presented to her, she wasn't at all sure it was what she really wanted. But it was done. Engaged to be married. No retracting from it now.

Theo was elated. 'Our contract at the Metropolitan commences immediately the pantomime season ends,' he said. 'Just enough time, I think, to perfect the new illusions we've been working on.'

He now referred to 'our' rather than 'my', 'we' rather than 'I'. He had also decided to cease paying her a salary. 'From now on you will be having an allowance,' he told her, as though she were already his wife. He'd even made a will leaving all he had to her, waving aside any protest. 'You are virtually my wife, but for a ring, and should anything untoward happen to me, I could not have you lose what would be rightfully your inheritance as my wife,' he had said and would hear no more of her protests.

'These new illusions must be spectacular,' he was saying now. They really were spectacular, though even she could see that he would require two assistants for them, in time perhaps three or four. Some of the illusions looked dangerous, though he said that handled properly there was no risk. Others, known as black wash, had figures and objects appearing and vanishing within the empty space inside a frame, sometimes quite eerily.

'All done with carefully balanced and manipulated mirrors,' he told her. 'But the procedure has to be perfect, down to the smallest detail. For these new mysteries, we must have two assistants.'

His elation, however, was coupled with despondency. 'Unfortunately,' he told her, 'so much is happening so quickly that we shall not be able to marry as soon as I would have wished. Simmons informs me that I shall be in demand throughout the spring and summer, with hardly a break, and as I wish our wedding to be the finest yet seen in London for many a year, calling for much preparation, it will have to be put off until the autumn. I am so sorry, my sweetest. I hope you can wait that long. I too shall try to do so.'

Emma couldn't bring herself to tell him that it did not matter to her as much as he imagined, and in a strange way brought a small sense of relief, although she couldn't have told herself why. If this was how she felt, she told herself, then the longer it was delayed, the better. She needed more time to be sure of what he was and what she was doing.

Two days into the New Year, as they went up to their rooms after dinner, he said casually. 'I shall be going out for an hour or two this evening.'

Usually he took her wherever he went, seeming loath to have her out of his sight, so she was somewhat bewildered by this. There was no reason for him to see his agent and it was rather late in the evening to be doing so.

Curious, she paused by her door to ask, 'Are you meeting someone, then?' She tried to make the question casual, but grew concerned as he hesitated.

'It doesn't matter at this moment,' he evaded, immediately changing her concern to distrust.

'I'll wait up for you,' she said – like some old married woman – a wife sensing a husband's deceit. She cast the thought from her. Theo had put a ring on her finger, how could she fall prey to imaginings so soon after? Yet she kept seeing visions of that girl with lips lifted to his. But it was herself she couldn't understand: one minute this reluctance about marriage, the next filled with jealousy that his eyes could be roaming. It was stupid.

Even so, she nodded curtly, had him kiss her offered cheek and let herself into her room without returning the kiss. Hating herself, she waited behind her closed door, her ear to it listening until she heard him go past, taking the stairs, deeming them quicker even than the cranking, if modern lift. She waited a second or two then, scrambling into a warm coat, with just enough time to push a single hatpin through her hat, she hurried down the two flights, through the foyer and into the street in time to see him striding some way ahead. At least he hadn't hailed a cab. If he did, she was lost.

The freezing January evening plucked at her cheeks. She had forgotten gloves or muff or even a scarf. Already she'd begun to shiver. It was a relief to see him turn the corner without noticing her, going on into Kingsway, recently named for King Edward. She got to the corner then leaped back, her heart in her mouth. Theo had come to a halt and was standing in the glow from a hotel behind him, as if waiting for someone.

He would probably take the person inside, and after that? In her mind Emma could see the girl tripping up to him, her skirt hem, held clear of the damp pavement, revealing her ankles, see her as she reached up to kiss him, see him responding wholeheartedly. He would take her arm or even lay his hand around her narrow waist to guide her into the warmth of the hotel and some clandestine love nest. Had he been doing this since Christmas, the engagement ring he'd given her merely a blind? A man could marry and still keep a mistress, for secretive meetings often meant lovers were already married. But why bother to ask her to marry him? All sorts of things raced through Emma's mind. Feeling sick, she drew back and waited, occasionally peeping to see if he were still there. He'd begun pacing up and down, perhaps to keep warm. Emma herself was now shivering violently from the cold.

Emma noticed a tall, lightly built man on the other side of the road, skilfully dodging around the people thronging Kingsway and appearing to be in a tearing hurry, whereas most people were wandering and strolling as couples or in groups, which was probably why he stood out. She saw him sprint across the road, deftly avoiding the congestion of horse and motor traffic. He was coming directly towards her and Emma shrank back in dismay at being discovered lurking on the corner of this side street, perhaps taken for a beggar as he passed, she who'd once stood on kerbs and thought nothing of it.

But the figure went by without seeing her, gazing ahead. A gush of relief almost smothered her, not because she hadn't been seen, but that the man was Martin Page. He approached Theodore; they exchanged a word or two before going on into the hotel.

Why should she feel so chastened as she hurried back to her hotel that Theo's appointment hadn't been with a female? And why so glad to see it was Martin – not relieved, glad?

It had been strange, he and Martin sitting together at the hotel bar. Talking purely business, they'd skirted around things personal and kept to the point. He had been intrigued by Martin's letter asking to meet him and saying that he might be needing a second assistant, one who knew well the way he worked, saving him having to train up someone new.

Odd, how time blunts the keen edges of rage and revenge. Talking to Martin in the informal atmosphere of a hotel bar, Theo realised that he still had a tender spot for him. There had always been something about Page that had drawn his attention – not in the way some might interpret it, but a pleasure in looking upon the beauty of the young, the indefatigability of it, a little compensation perhaps for what he saw as his own wasted years. Martin had always been a naturally likeable person anyway, charming without effort, helpful without fawning, ever willing to see another's side of things. Perhaps that was why he'd walked out without a fight when accused of philandering with Eleanor – an unfortunate action that made him appear all the more guilty. Had he argued his corner … But some never do.

Walking back to his own hotel, Theodore found himself wondering, not for the first time, if he had mis-interpreted what was merely friendship. But knowing Eleanor's penchant for male attention, he'd assumed … but it was a long time ago now. All he could remember was the hurt – a terrible sense of being let down by the young man he had trusted. He wondered now, should he be blaming himself for what had happened, for leaping in without stopping to think, for allowing jealousy to control him and which he now felt had had no foundation except his own blind suspicion? Perhaps so.

Turning into his hotel, Theodore drew a deep, decisive breath, his mind made up. These new illusions: he, Martin and Amelia would make a marvellous team – he tall and commanding; Amelia compliant, at least on stage – she could be difficult other times; Martin matching her for height and slimness. On stage, one could easily be passed off for the other, the one vanishing to reappear apparently in seconds somewhere else. Removed from the audience, lights dimmed, who would spot the swap? It would work.

'I am taking you on again,' he had announced, his hand gratefully shaken by Martin, a gesture that made him tense as memories immediately flitted into his head, departing just as suddenly as he told Martin to be at his hotel at eight the next morning.

As Theodore mounted the two flights up to his room, his thoughts flitted through many differing emotions – excitement, misgiving, triumph, determination to put the past behind him. By the time he reached Amelia's room he had convinced himself that he could have been wrong, might have been unfair to Martin, that Martin could have been entirely innocent of encouraging Eleanor's leaning towards nice-looking men.

Theodore had begun to feel good about himself. He paused at Amelia's door, eager to tell her about his meeting. She had looked so mystified this evening, now he would enlighten her about the new act he had in mind. It would be an entirely different one, like no other in the country. It was rarely he felt this excited, and he needed to share it with her.

Taking the key he kept to her room, he opened the door, calling her name. The room was in darkness. She was already asleep. The only light came from a winter moon flooding between drawn-back curtains. She liked the curtains open, said it made her feel less closed in, at one time so used to them never able to completely meet across a window.

She lay on her back, one slender arm thrown above her head, visible beneath a gauze sleeve. The neck of her nightgown was open to reveal the delicate hollow of her throat and the gentle swell of her breasts. She looked so vulnerable that his heart thumped with longing, a feeling he hastily quenched. Martin would be coming here tomorrow morning and he needed to work on his new illusions, sketching them on paper, detailing movements, perfecting timings. It could take the best part of the night.

Tomorrow he'd begin ordering what he needed. Much of it he already had, but he had to have more metal straps and bars for his levitation illusion, and all the special equipment, the mirrors, the frames, for his black wash illusions.

He would still keep some of his old favourites like the Turkish basket illusion which Amelia did so beautifully, gracefully sinking down into the incredibly tiny mouth of the wickerwork basket, the lid she held above her sinking down on top of her, apparently impossible that she could fit even her slim, supple body inside an unbelievably tiny interior. Martin, dressed as a Turkish potentate, would trample inside it as though it were empty, the covering sheet pounded down into it too, then lifted for all to see while a sword was thrust several times with lightning speed through the wickerwork before the sheet was draped over it again, from which she would rise unscathed, her slender bare arms upheld as the sheet was whipped from her form.

Simple trickery, the tiny basket appearing to onlookers to be round but in reality oval, enough for her to squeeze inside, but from an astounded audience it drew tremendous applause after horrified gasps at the thrusts of the sword with which he had first sliced a piece of paper cleanly in half.

There were many such illusions and he revelled in the applause they brought. Soon his name would be spoken with awe. He was done with little tricks. The ones he had planned would cover the stage. It wouldn't take long to retrain Martin. Had he found someone else, they would have taken weeks to train, and he didn't have weeks. Martin had been the obvious choice and he must learn to bury the past. He and Amelia were a perfect pair, beautiful to look at, slender, lithe, almost the same height, Amelia tall and slender, and Martin topping her just by two inches, while he himself at well over six feet would tower over the pair as a magician should to complete the tableau on stage.

Quietly, he moved away from the bed, and, closing the door behind him, went back into his own room.

Chapter Twenty-Four

From London it was the provinces once more for several weeks, the name of the Great Theodore becoming even more well established with his amazing vanishing cabinet, his levitation acts, his mind-reading, and most of all his framed room illusion where complete suites of furniture, animals or persons would mysteriously disappear and reappear.

By April it was back to London again, making a name for themselves afresh. Emma was finding working with Martin a pleasure, so different from when there had been only Theodore. He was someone to run to when upset, and Theodore had an immense capacity for upsetting a person if he wasn't careful. Martin was sympathetic, understanding and gentle, and she was finding herself slowly forming a bond of friendship with him, though he was being very careful.

She too found herself being careful of detection, hating what seemed to her almost like deceitfulness. It shouldn't have been that way, but Martin didn't have to say much for her to know that his clash with Theo had started from innocent friendship too. 'I wouldn't want to upset the apple cart again,' was all he said, but it spoke volumes. Yet how could people work together properly without being friends?

She had come to realise just how accomplished an assistant Martin was. Theo must have been quite lost without him, but at that time he'd been lost anyway, he and his strange attitude. She could never take her problems to him. Martin with his quiet wisdom made up for it, yet it was still Theo who took command of her, overwhelming her when making love to her so that she forgot all else. Sometimes she wondered why she did not fall pregnant by him, but surmised that she must just have been lucky so far. Work had got in the way of most things, including plans for marriage. 'In the autumn,' he promised her. 'The second we have a let-up.'

But there was no let-up. They were living in style and he was loath to spoil it. She too. At present she was having the best of both worlds. Not only would Theo frequently indulge her with any piece of jewellery that caught her eye, but she now had savings in her own account, which she wouldn't have had a few years ago.

One day in early May, he returned from seeing Simmons after having received an urgent message from him. Theo's normally unimpassioned face was wreathed in a wide smile, his strong, large, regular teeth unfamiliarly stark against his trim beard.

'We are going to America,' he announced, facing their astonished expressions. 'Jack Simmons is arranging a three-month tour of the East Coast for us.'

Emma's stare was apprehensive. 'But I've never been abroad before.'

Noting her tone, Theodore gave a brief bellow of a laugh. 'There's nothing in the word "abroad" to bite you, my dear. I have spent some time in France in the past, and I understand Martin had been on the Continent when he was a boy.'

'But America's a long way off,' she insisted, and saw his smile fade.

'It's not the moon, my dear!' He could sometimes make that term of endearment seem like one of censure. She hated it when he did. 'Many of our now top artistes have toured the United States and consequently made their name, as have many who come here – a two-way exchange. We must begin making preparations.'

It wasn't easy telling her mother what was in store, as her mother saw the money Emma sent coming to an end. 'Of course it won't,' Emma told her. 'I'll be sending you a regular money order for probably a lot more than I'm giving you now.'

'You'll be so far away.' The forlorn reply was music to Emma's ears, proof that Mum did care.

'It's only for three months, Mum.' She comforted her happily, hardly able to believe that she, a girl who had imagined her whole life would be one of struggle and poverty, lording it in America. It was like a dream. Where she was, and where she was going from now on, would always be *the* place to be. She couldn't be happier. Better still, Martin was included in this trip. If Theo upset her, she would still have him to turn to. It was like a dream, a magic dream.

*

Like a dream it had all passed so quickly. Already the middle of September and they were on their way back home, back to dull old Britain where people were staid and on coming upon anyone famous seemed afraid to acknowledge them lest they be laughed at, as withdrawn as British weather itself.

In the States people had been so open, so ready to come forth and make themselves known, inhibition hardly recognised. In fact, Emma loved every moment of it. But it was the pace that had got her down, that and Theo's unbounded energy. America had been tiring: New York with its bustle and its noise, fast-talking New Yorkers, loud, clamorous, often too clamorous, Theodore's rapidly expanding act well acclaimed. And the long train journeys to places spaced as widely apart as Boston and Philadelphia, train journeys that went on for ever and diminished those of England to a mere jaunt.

All she wanted now was to relax, slow down, although she knew that the moment they reached home, Theo would cash in on his fame and hardly give her any breathing space. Her only compensation was that he might still be too busy to find time to arrange their wedding just yet. She found herself hoping so. These past months she had grown closer to Martin, running to him when the pace got too much for her. Theo, seemingly tireless, expected everyone else to be the same. It was Martin who calmed her and introduced those few moments of sanity into the hectic life at which Theo expected her to excel.

She was making the most of this voyage home to be totally lazy, so long as Theo didn't get too obsessed with working on yet more ideas. If only the voyage could go on for ever, she thought as she lounged under a parasol on the promenade deck of the *Victoriana* and watched the distant flat cloud that was the coast of Ireland grow steadily clearer. If only the ship could be taken up into the heavens to drift for ever in the same mist that seemed to be covering that shadowy coast. It was what lay in store for her once they got to England that was lowering her spirits.

Once home there would no longer be hotel rooms, except when on tour or a need to stay overnight in London. While abroad, Theodore had arranged to have the house he owned in Surrey restored. In fact he had telegrammed home to commission builders, decorators, gardeners, so that it would be ready for when he came home, his initial idea of renting a luxury apartment for him and Emma put aside.

'I sincerely hope it is all finished by then,' he'd said as word of delays came in reply to his many telegrams. That he was now setting his heart on living in the place had been all due to her, trying to be prudent.

She had no fancy to live out in Surrey. For one thing, she would be a long way from her mother; for another, when Theo had taken her to see the house before leaving for America, she had shuddered at the mausoleum it appeared to be with its peeling wallpaper, faded curtains at dusty windows, bare floorboards, forlorn furniture and overgrown gardens, but she'd made the mistake of smiling, for his benefit, and saying it could be lovely once done up. He interpreted her smile as one of enthusiasm.

Emma sighed as she watched a bevy of white gulls wheeling overhead against the blue September sky still warm from summer. Yesterday she had asked if she would be having her own bedroom at The Manse, as his house was called. She'd seen him frown then heard his answer, 'By the end of summer you shall be my wife.' But he had consented to her having a room of her own though she knew he'd be more in hers than his own.

Emma adjusted her parasol to her other shoulder as the *Victoriana* swung a little to starboard, and narrowed her hazel eyes at the faint blue haze of land, her mind wandering to other things. She was eager to get home but it brought problems that she'd been able to put behind her so far: there were times when she'd noticed Martin looking at her in a way that made her feel uncomfortable. She found herself needing to keep him at arm's length. If Theo got a hint of even these mild attentions, it could become difficult. She liked Martin very much, even found him attractive, but it was Theo who could turn her to jelly when he came to her room at night. The last thing she wanted to do was to jeopardise that. But it was too lovely a day to be thinking, the sea as calm as a millpond, the *Victoriana's* fast-moving bows making a rhythmic hiss. Mixed with the ocean's briny taint came the aroma of coffee and lunch from the first-class dining room.

She was beginning to feel hungry. The sea air promoted a good appetite. Already those who had been sharing the promenade deck with her were vacating deckchairs one by one, lethargic conversation now broken by animated chatter.

Still a little reluctant to leave her small haven of peace, Emma finished the last cool dregs of lemonade in her glass and got up to follow the others.

Halfway down the companionway from the first-class games deck, Martin paused as he saw Emily come into view. Theo insisted on calling her Amelia but it was Emily she'd been christened. She seemed more like an Emily, a lovely name for a lovely girl and just as down to earth. She walked slowly as if in a world of her own. She looked so relaxed. She'd not looked like that for ages, but here she wasn't being so harassed by Theo. Theo could harass anyone. Martin smiled tightly. Theo had interrupted him from an enjoyable game of deck quoits to go and look for her and inform her that it was time for lunch. She didn't need telling, the gong having announced it moments later.

Why did she put up with Theo? But he knew why – for the same reason he did, to trade in an otherwise dreary life for the excitement offered by the stage. In his case it had been a wish to quit a dull future in an office in his family's business, for her, a chance to escape a life of unending grind and poverty. Her chance had come from colliding with him in a winter fog, then helping a sick man back to his shabby home. His had come from a huge charity garden fête on a warm, sunny summer day when Theo's wife had smiled at him and he had smiled back.

Before he knew it, she had glided across the lawn towards him. Falling into conversation with him, she'd told him she was married to a professional conjuror. He was invited to see them perform at a local theatre and he had gone backstage afterwards. Theo had enraptured him with small sleight of hand tricks and he had slowly become involved until, seeing his worth, Theo, who had at that time been well into enjoying his success, had suggested he join him. It had been an exciting time, until things had gone awry, which he preferred now to forget.

He had gone back to his family, determined to face up to the reality of life, and fortunately his father was a forgiving man and had been glad to see him come to his senses. But dull routine brought back yearnings for the limelight and he'd disappointed his father yet again. But in tracing Theo, he'd found Emily, and Emily was beginning to attract his gaze at every turn.

He stood watching her pass below him. She looked stunning in a pale blue summer dress, its hemline fluttering like tiny wavelets about her feet in the breeze from the ship's progress, the smile hovering on her lips as though from amusing thoughts. Pert lips, they were, with a hint of stubbornness about them. Everything about her was stunning, from the luxurious auburn hair to the way she carried herself, and that mischievous sideways flick of the hazel eyes towards a person, enough to make the heart almost collapse. How could she love someone like Theo? Obsessed only with himself and his work, Theo didn't appreciate how tired she sometimes looked.

When he mentioned it once, Theo's reply had been, 'When she and I are married, we shall honeymoon in the south of France where she will be able to rest to her heart's content and return refreshed.'

Martin doubted it.

He let her go on some way ahead before continuing on down the companionway to follow at a distance amid others moving in the same direction.

Theodore was already at their table when Emma reached it. He didn't rise for her or even smile. 'You are late,' was all he said.

'Hardly,' she said. 'Martin's not here either.'

A waiter drew out her chair for her. She inclined her head to him and sat down while the waiter flapped her napkin open and placed it across her lap. She smiled up at him, but addressed Theo.

'They've not started to serve yet. People are still coming in.'

'Nevertheless, it is courtesy to be on time, Amelia.'

'If I'd been any earlier I'd have been sitting here on my own!' she snapped as Martin arrived. He looked from one to the other but said nothing as he sat down while their waiter did the honours with the napkin.

Theo didn't acknowledge him, irked by her sharp rejoinder. Her lips were compressed, a strained atmosphere was already making its presence felt. She'd been so content out there on the deck. Why did Theo have to go and spoil it – and without reason? Unless he thought she should have been with him.

The soup course being consumed in silence, Emma stared about the spacious dining room with its lofty, domed, gilt and plaster ceiling and its chandeliers; the tall, draped windows were elegant and the expensive pictures around the silk-papered walls were in the art nouveau style. In one corner a grand piano was being discreetly played. All around came the soft buzz of conversation interspersed by the clink of cutlery against crockery, while the gentle thrum of a transatlantic liner's engines as it ploughed effortlessly and steadily through calm waters went unnoticed by the chattering passengers after days at sea.

Their plates being taken away, she turned her gaze on Theo. There was a distant look in his eyes. Probably dwelling on some new illusion, or was he sulking? Theo was very good at sulking – he did it thunderously. She looked away.

'Did you hear what I said, Theo?' Martin was saying, as if from a distance.

Theodore came to himself with a start, the sounds around him leaping back into his hearing – of dishes being collected following the first course, uneaten food scraped on to used plates, subdued chatter, a voice or two lifted a little above the rest, a laugh here and there breaking the smooth flow of conversation.

He had been miles away. This morning Amelia had excused herself from his company, saying she needed a few moments to herself on deck to read and doze. He had indulged her, but had been lost without her. By lunchtime he'd been on edge, had found Martin and because he was on edge had curtly told him to go and find her, damned if he would demean himself by looking for her.

Martin had gone off at his bidding and he too had made to depart but noticed that Martin had paused at the top of the companionway and was gazing at something below him as if mesmerised. In curiosity he leaned over the rail, looking in the direction of Martin's gaze, and there was Amelia below them, walking slowly. He had switched his eyes back to Martin. The young man appeared fascinated and Theo had felt the rancour rise up in him. Had he been right all along about Martin?

Brooding now as they ate, he'd glanced at the sea through the large dining hall windows and an entirely random memory had crept up on him uninvited, probably from the sight of that smooth blueness.

It had been smooth and blue that day. He'd been nineteen, only just becoming wrapped up in his new interest in magic. It was distancing him from his college companions and many of them had noticed. He was in fact standing on the cliff top with one of them, Delham, aware of his nineteen-year-old companion's slow taunting tones. 'You're all puff and wind, old man. You've not the first idea how to hypnotise a chap.'

He'd made the mistake of saying he could hypnotise anyone. Studying it, he'd found it easy to do and had afforded several willing victims a bit of fun. Delham, though, was a know-all and sneeringly refused to take part. But now he had him alone and he would show him.

Already, with his parents in India, his father expecting him to follow him into the diplomatic corps, he had ideas of his own. He had found his niche. He would take command of people's minds, hold an audience in his hand by the power of his will. He would perfect a mind-reading act, and with magic would hold them spellbound, and even more with hypnotism. People would stand in awe of him instead of ridiculing him as Delham did. He would start with Delham, his main tormentor, while they were alone. He would frighten the living daylights out of him. Delham would never again dare scoff. If it didn't work he didn't want witnesses to laugh at him. But it would work. He had absolute faith in his powers and would make this idiot smirk on the other side of his face.

It was a bright, balmy day, a breeze ruffling the clifftop grasses, the blue of the English Channel some five hundred feet below the chalk cliffs of Eastbourne's Beachy

Head. He and a few companions were there on holiday, and it was the high summer of 1886.

'You think I can't?' he queried at Delham's sniggering challenge. 'I will prove I can. And if you dare to laugh I will really put you under never to come out of it.'

That of course was impossible but it sobered the other one as, fixing him with a steady gaze, he lifted his hands to shoulder height, palms facing his subject in a slow, mesmeric gesture. Delham's expression growing blank, eyes following the movements, he succumbed easier than expected, but it was not the time to be amazed or pleased with his own powers. The know-all would receive the biggest scare of his life on waking up to find himself gazing down at the sea with a single step between him and the pebble beach hundreds of feet below.

In sonorous tones he told Delham that he had a sudden fancy to walk back into Eastbourne; that he would turn and walk along the paved road leading him there; that on hearing a single, sharp handclap he would change his mind and wake up. He was planning to allow Delham to walk only a few steps along the cliff edge before waking him but decided to let him go a yard or so more, savouring the moment when his victim would come to with a start, realising where he was. He was in control, and as expected, Delham came to a halt to the sound of the single hand-clap, his body stiffening as he looked down. There came a gasp of terror. His body teetered, bent forward from the waist. There was a sharp cry, then a shriek as he plunged.

Theo could still see those arms waving helplessly, hear the protracted scream, see the body slowly turning over and over, the terrified scream cut short as the body crashed on to a chalk promontory, to bounce, limp, off other outcrops.

He had never used hypnotism again. But that moment in his youth came back to him on odd occasions and to plague his dreams from time to time, a sensation of being transfixed in disbelief as though it were he who had been hypnotised, he who was falling ...

'Theo, did you hear what I said?' came Martin's voice.

Theodore recovered himself and turned towards the voice. 'I am sorry, Martin, what did you say?' he asked in as steady a tone as he could muster.

'I asked if you wanted more wine. Your glass is empty.'

He didn't recall drinking the first glass but it didn't matter. He nodded and glanced at Amelia, more to take his mind off his previous thoughts. She looked stunning and his heart raced at the sight of her.

'You look very pretty, my dear,' he told her amiably as the fish he had ordered was placed before him. 'So I shall forgive you for being late.'

She did not smile at his forced little joke and he couldn't blame her. He must remember not to be too hard with her. Were she to know that he'd been directly responsible for another man's death, virtually murder, she would never smile at him again.

He felt he could be forgiven for the argument that had led to Eleanor's death. But Delham's? He did regret his part in that death but the man had been an insufferable fellow and he couldn't summon up any great sorrow for him. He hadn't forced Eleanor to do what she did in the way he'd compelled Delham. For all his jealousies, he had loved her deeply. But now he loved Amelia. As for Martin, he like any man would find her captivating. It didn't mean he was about to snatch her away. And after the last time, innocent or guilty, Martin must have learned his lesson. All the same, though he had vowed to lay the past aside, he would watch Martin more closely from now on. Just in case.

Thinking this, he nodded his assent to his wine glass being refilled. At the same time, to prove his ownership of Amelia, he reached out and laid a hand on her arm, gratified to see her smile at last.

Chapter Twenty-Five

Those Theo had engaged to restore his old home during his absence had done wonders to it.

As the carriage bearing him, Emma and Martin turned into the short, newly laid drive between late flowering shrubbery with not a weed in sight, it presented an impressive spectacle. It wasn't exceptionally large but it was still grand and all spruced up, so different from when Emma had last seen it. Even so, she experienced a sinking feeling. It still retained that remote look.

It was obvious that Theo was rightly pleased with the results. As they alighted from the carriage and went on through the door between a pair of now scrubbed, and shining white, fluted stone columns supporting the old portico, and into a wide, somewhat echoing hall, he positively strutted.

'I will show you your room, Amelia, my dear,' he said, conducting her up the wide, central staircase. 'It will be yours should you ever wish to be alone.'

It was a pointed remark but she smiled with assumed gratitude. There was a bedroom she was expected to share with him but which he would use should she prefer not to at other times, though it was expected that he would come to her if so inclined.

Martin had been given a room further along, separated from them by two others and a bathroom, making it obvious that he was to be segregated from Emma and Theo.

Emma stared in amazement as she stepped through the door to what was to be her private bedroom, her little haven of escape, as Theo put it. With the woodwork all of rosewood, the decor in pale lavender, it was the loveliest room Emma had ever seen. She almost burst out, 'Is this all mine?' but quickly curbed any show of exuberance because fundamentally the house, for all its impressive beauty, still held some indefinable something that made her shiver. He might take it as a wish to live there permanently.

She moved across the room to the bay window that overlooked the gardens, now with restocked rose beds, well-cut lawns and a wealth of what in spring would be small flowering trees. The house stood on high ground, allowing her to see for miles, the whole vista framed by slender Surrey pines. Theo had told her what they were, as she, having lived her whole life in London, was unable to tell one tree from another.

'We will be staying here this week,' he announced. 'You will be able to rest here before we go back to London.'

Emma accepted that with as much good grace as she could muster, grateful that even he couldn't justify rushing from Surrey to London and back between shows, as they were already engaged to appear at the Pavilion at Piccadilly Circus. It was a great relief to know. To a London girl, the open countryside had a strange, uneasy affect on her, as if all that vastness might reach out and engulf her, body and soul. She needed the hubbub of London as a fish needed water.

Theo, with more money than ever before, could now well afford to splash out on a rented luxury apartment in town for them both. In a rush of apparent generosity, he had rented a single flat across the hall for Martin.

'I must have you on hand when we need to rehearse,' he told him, and, like Emma, Martin nodded compliantly. With Theo's tendency to awaken in the dead of night to rehearse something that was on his mind, he'd only need to knock on Martin's door.

'I could have found my own place,' Martin said to Emma in private. 'And a blessed sight cheaper.' Theo's generosity wasn't so magnanimous that he didn't expect Martin to fork out two-thirds of the rent himself. 'Still,' Martin shrugged amiably, 'I'm in the money now, thanks to him, so I suppose it's only fair. And at least I can close my door when I want.'

Emma tried to let it wash over her but she couldn't help feeling envy. Yes, Martin could close his door on Theo's world, if not very often. She would have no such freedom, with Theo assuming that he and she would live in this apartment together and finally be wed. Why such creeping reluctance at this coming marriage, she had no idea, yet it was growing more pronounced with every passing day.

The apartment had only two bedrooms, one a mere box-room for storing stage apparatus. The rest comprised a bathroom, a tiny kitchen with a hatch through to the small dining room and lounge that looked down on busy traffic. Theo had engaged a woman to come in to cook and clean for them.

At least they were in London. It was nice too to go down to the foyer and step out on to a street full of people passing to and fro about their business. Emma dreaded the end of this present engagement when she would be dragged back for 'a rest' in the country with its lonely birdsongs and its vast sky and its looming, open spaces. This was her home, this noise and bustle, dodging traffic, horse-drawn vehicles now vying with the odd motor-powered one.

Theo was talking of buying a motorcar. She hoped not. It would mean being able to get in and out of London easier, spending more time at his house. She didn't think she could stand that.

The Wednesday after settling into the apartments she at last had an opportunity to see her mother. 'After all this while away, I must,' she said as she got herself ready. He wasn't pleased.

'There are certain moves I need to perfect,' he said. 'The Pavilion is an important engagement – our first since returning to this country.'

'They're always important,' she snapped back. 'Tell me one that isn't. And just for once I want to go out!'

'I need you here to rehearse, Amelia.' It wasn't an appeal, it was a command, and it was the last straw. She rounded on him.

'I'm sick of rehearsing! It never stops!' She was already donning her hat, rearranging veil and feathers with agitated energy borne of irritation. She saw his lips tighten at her sharp tone. She *was* sharp these days, but she felt justified. He was making love to

351

her and treating her generally as if she were already his wife, so why shouldn't she express her feelings? There could have developed a fierce argument but he suddenly mellowed.

'I planned to take you out this evening,' he said. 'Covent Garden Opera House is staging Puccini's new opera, *Madama Butterfly*. A little treat.'

Treat! Didn't she see enough of theatres? But it would be a novelty to be the other side of the footlights for once. She knew she should be grateful, and she was, and she would enjoy it, but all she wanted was a few hours away from him. 'I'll be back by midday,' she said, securing her millinery with a hatpin. 'Is Martin coming with us tonight?' she asked.

'No.'

She looked at him narrowly. Why had he said that so abruptly, as if she'd touched a sore point? She shrugged – probably just Theo being Theo.

Emma looked at her mother as if she must be lying. 'What do you mean, he's been in prison?'

Having asked Mum how she was as she came in, and being told, 'I'm orright,' in a flat tone, her next words were to ask after Ben as she prepared to settle down for a morning's chat, perhaps tell her mother about America, taking it that she'd be interested. Now, taken aback, all she had to say was being blown away.

Her mother's expression didn't alter from its grim look. It was almost as though she blamed her for whatever had happened to Ben. Perhaps for not being on hand when whatever had occurred, happened.

'Like what I said. Been in prison.'

'But why? How? Why didn't you tell me?'

'You weren't 'ere ter tell, were yer?'

Yes, that was it, still regarding her as gallivanting off, no matter what she said or did. She sat down with a jolt on the edge of one of Mum's elbow chairs, leaving her to continue standing, as if that would add more weight to the remark.

'You could have written to tell me,' she accused, jerking the hatpins from her hat to take it off and lay upon the seat of one of the nearby dining chairs. This visit promised to be longer than she'd thought, as Mum was required to explain what had happened during her absence and this involved discussion on the why and wherefore.

'What did he do to be sent to prison?' she repeated. 'How long for?' Hopefully it would have been a couple of weeks or a month for affray and disturbing the peace. Knowing Ben, it was very easy for him to disturb the peace.

'Got three months fer burglary,' her mother said. 'The other bloke got two years, fer being the one caught with the money he stole still on 'im.'

Her tone grew bitter. 'He should of been the one ter get two years. It was 'im what planned it. But he got some other silly bugger ter do 'is dirty work for 'im. But yer know Ben, wriggle out of anything.'

'What made him do it?' She knew Ben was a tealeaf, but he certainly couldn't have needed the money. 'I've been sending money to the both of you, regularly. And it wasn't small amounts either. He didn't need to steal.'

In fact she'd been so well paid in America that she'd been sending more money than they'd ever had in their lives, even when her father was alive. They should be living in comfort, the pair of them. The fact was that she could see by glancing about her and at her mother, that Mum didn't look a bit as though she was living in comfort. She was no longer all that well dressed, and while the place was neat and tidy, there was no sign of any new bits and pieces. Maybe she was tucking it away for that 'rainy day' she was always worrying about, unable to believe this sort of money could go on.

Emma had sent the money over by a sort of money order, leaving her mother to sort it out, no doubt getting the kindly Mrs Blacker to put it through her bank into English money. Mum had no idea of banks. Perhaps it was all in savings, Mum spending nothing on herself. Mum turning into a miser? No excuse for that. Emma felt mildly irritated.

'What have you been doing with all that money I've been sending?'

With a weary gesture, her mother sat down on one of the tall-backed, upright chairs and Emma noticed for the first time how tired and drawn she looked, as if all the stuffing had been knocked out of her. Yet her tone was still angry as she answered Emma's question.

'It was all that money you was sending 'im what probably started it.' So Mum *was* in a way blaming her for Ben's shortcomings. It was unfair. 'Yer know what he's like. Seeing 'imself in the money, spendin' it like water, throwing it around, gambling, and when he lost, borrowin' it off mates. Yer know what gangs around 'ere are like, what he's got in with?'

She paused and Emma nodded, saying nothing as she continued, 'Got inter debt and couldn't pay it back and they came after 'im for it. He came 'ome 'ere all beaten up one night around the end of April. Said they'd threatened ter do for 'im if they didn't get their money.'

Mum fiddled for a while with the bit of trimming on her black skirt. Emma waited in silence.

'I couldn't give it to 'im,' Mum went on at last. 'I ain't got that sort of money. Not even with what you send. 'Undreds it was. I suppose that's why he went nicking, 'im an' this other mate. Goin' ter halve the takings down the middle.' She continued fiddling with her skirt trimmings. 'I s'pose Ben was lucky none of it was found on 'im. He just made off, but the other bloke got caught red-handed with all this rich geezer's stuff on 'im. Place up West. He blabbed on Ben, but Ben didn't 'ave no money on 'im, so they let 'im down lightly. Gawd knows why. But he can talk 'imself out of anything, charm a bird off a bush when he so needs to. Came out last week.'

She gave a little sigh. 'I've been all this time tryin' ter pay it back to the blokes what he borrowed off. I still ain't done. They want interest now. I just can't do it.'

No wonder Mum was looking worried. 'You let me go on thinking you two were all right and all the time you've been struggling like this?' Emma said in disbelief. 'You could have written, Mum. You should have warned me and I'd have been able to sort him out.'

But of course, Mum wouldn't have known about it until Ben came home knocked about. But she ploughed on. 'I might have been able to stop him doing what he did and going to prison. Why didn't you write to me?'

Instantly she was aware of the way her mother's back went up. As soon as she'd spoken, Emma realised that she already knew the answer. She'd need to tread cautiously in order not to humiliate her mother further.

'I wasn't goin' ter air me dirty linen in public,' came the stiff reply. 'Yer washed yer 'ands of this family when yer went off with that bloke of yours. I know yer've always seen me orright, but I ain't one ter go cryin' ter outsiders fer 'elp.'

'I'm not an outsider, Mum, I'm your daughter, and it is my business to see you all right. You and Ben.'

She knew why Mum hadn't written and the excuse she'd given had nothing to do with not wanting to air dirty linen in public or anywhere else. It was the writing – she was not totally illiterate but unable to spell and with hardly any knowledge of grammar as there was so little schooling for the children of the poorer classes. Mum, being the eldest, had been needed at home to look after the younger ones. Her only tuition had been later in life and she still felt the humiliation of partial illiteracy. It was better not to try to write than to risk ridicule. Mum had always been a proud woman. It was why she had been so adamant about her own children not missing school.

'Just a line or two would have done,' Emma said inadequately.

Her mother shrugged. 'Well, he's out now, so it don't matter no more.'

'It does when you're paying back his debts for him,' she said. Already she had pulled a book of cheques from her reticule. She was at ease with banks and cheques these days. 'How much does he still owe?'

There was an obstinate silence. Mum had to be prompted again before Emma was told, reluctantly, and even she gasped at the amount. When Mum had said hundreds, she hadn't exaggerated. Tightening her lips, Emma wrote out the sum and handed the cheque to her mother. 'I could get it out in cash myself,' she said, 'but I don't think I'll get the time and you need it urgently. Ask Mrs Blacker to cash it for you. She'll oblige.'

Her mother looked uncertain. "She'll think I've come inter money.'

'Does it matter? Explain to her.'

Her mother's thin lips became even thinner. 'I ain't tellin' her all me business. Besides, she thinks Ben went off ter stay with someone. She even put me rent down again. Now he's back she'll put it up and when she sees how much is 'ere, she'll wonder. Might even think of asking more rent. I ain't explaining where he went to.'

Emma could understand that. 'I'll cash it and bring the money round to you tomorrow,' she promised. Tomorrow was going to be a problem, Theo with his eyes on her all the time. The Pavilion looked to be taking up his whole time, all their time, but this was urgent.

'Make sure Ben gives it to the people he owes it to,' she warned. 'And not sink it on the odd rum that'll become three or four, or more gambling.'

Her mother looked sly, colluding with her. 'Don't worry, love, I don't think he wants another bashing like that one he 'ad. That put 'im on the right track about 'imself and 'is big ideas. I just 'ope he'll settle down now.'

Emma was back next day with the money, despite Theo forbidding her under pain of virtual death.

'She's got a bit of a problem on her hands,' she told him, 'and I'm sorting it out.'

She hadn't told him what the problem was. If he knew he would hit the roof. Theo was generous with her, never stinted her with money, bought most of her

357

clothes for her and made sure she wanted for nothing. He also felt it his duty to keep an eye on what she spent, and had taken it upon himself to look into her savings now and again, concerned about her financial wellbeing, questioning her about anything that seemed to be amiss. That he could do this irked her. But they were engaged to be married and he took it as his right to protect her, much as a husband was expected to protect and guide a wife. But he wasn't her husband yet.

'I've got a duty towards her,' she said firmly.

'You have a duty to your profession,' he thundered back. 'You have a duty to me.'

'I'll be half an hour, Theo,' she snapped. It angered her that while he demanded she consider him, he considered only his own self, so it seemed. 'Anyone would think,' she continued to mutter, 'that the theatre would collapse without me being here every second of the day, going over and over all the things we've been through hundreds of times before.'

'*I* shall collapse without you,' he echoed, his voice becoming gentle.

Hers did too. She knew what he meant. 'You won't be without me, Theo, I promise.' But when she touched his arm he pulled away.

'I'll be as quick as I can,' she said abruptly, hurrying off before he could say anything more. What could he say beyond telling her to leave and not come back, and he wouldn't do that. He was deeply in love with her. Her worry was that she wasn't sure she felt exactly that way about him.

*

The Flower Girl

There was no sign of Ben at her Mum's. Keeping out of the way. Mum must have told him about the money, but Emma had never seen her so grateful as when she clasped the handful of large white five-pound notes to her bosom.

'I'm taking it to them so-and-so's meself,' she announced. 'I don't trust 'im with this. Ain't been 'ome not much more'n a week and drinkin' already. He could booze it all away and be back where he started, an' I've just about 'ad enough of 'im!'

Emma felt her fear for her clutch at her heart. 'You can't go having dealings all on your own with people like that,' she said, but her mother gave a grim smile of determination.

'What can they do ter me, an old lady?'

She wasn't old, and with her washed-out hazel eyes alight with fiery intent, her tall thin figure stiff as a weather-dried stick, she looked a match for the devil himself.

'If they try anything on me, they'll get what for. Besides, no matter what sort they are, they've all got mothers. They won't 'arm me.'

Looking at her, Emma had to agree.

It was a week since she'd last been to see her. She was aching to find out how everything had gone, but Theo was so wrapped up with his act, and so much was expected of Emma and Martin, that she could hardly go off just when she pleased. He was after all the source of her success. Without him she wouldn't be where she was today, she would be still in the slums, probably thinking of marriage to some struggling, pasty young man instead of into the wealth and security assured by this now celebrated and powerful man. She owed everything to him. There would be other opportunities to see her mother, and after all, she told herself, as Theo put her and Martin through their paces endlessly, Mum had done far less for her than she'd done and was still doing for Mum.

She rested on the trust that Mum must have successfully handed over the money, though there was not a peep from Ben, not one word of gratitude. Knowing him, she hadn't expected any, rather he was probably grudging her the ability to bale him out, seeing himself as belittled, indebted to her, a woman, his little sister doing for him what he failed to do for himself.

It was three more weeks before the end of their contract would allow her some brief respite to hurry off to see how her mother was.

She found her barely able to hold herself together. And again no one had told her.

'We've been asked ter leave,' Mum said in a small, brittle voice when Emma had hardly come through the door, before she'd even had time to take off her outdoor things.

'Why, what's happened?' she asked, disturbed by the sight of her mother.

'It's Ben,' came a defeated reply.

Emma stood in the centre of the room. 'What's he been up to now?'

'Everything.' Mum wandered past her, crossing the room to plump up the cushion on the elbow chair and returning to reposition a vase on the small sideboard, remaining there staring at it with her back to Emma as if to face her would have crumbled her efforts to hold herself together.

'Prison's changed 'im,' she said. 'He knew when we first came 'ere to mind 'is p's and q's or we'd be asked ter leave. I told 'im, no matter if he was drunk, he wasn't ter bring his ways back 'ere, and he listened. I don't know what being in prison did. Still got that swagger and all that big talk what makes the ladies fancy 'im. He'd even twisted Mrs Blacker around 'is little finger when he put on the charm. But now ...'

She paused, knowing she must admit yet another failure, another problem to her daughter, Ben's shortcomings always at the root of all her problems.

'Since coming out,' she continued still with her back to Emma, 'he's back on the drink. I know we've lots of drunks and troublemakers round 'ere, but now he's coming home in the early hours of the morning, soused to the eyeballs, waking up the other people 'ere who've complained to Mrs Blacker. To give the woman her due, she didn't say much at first, but it was only a matter of time.' Emma said nothing.

Her mother's voice sounded small, which was so unlike her.

'I 'ad a go at him and it caused such an uproar, 'im bellowing and throwing things, a fire iron he threw hit the wall with such a crash. Mrs Blacker came up and called for the noise ter stop. But she didn't do nothing. She was worried more about me.

'Then last Saturday week he came in at one o'clock in the morning, banging on the door she'd locked, shouting out about what he was going to do to the bleeder what floored 'im with a foul punch and doing 'im out of 'is winnings and what he was going ter do to that crooked referee what 'ad been paid ter turn a blind eye, and yelling that he'd split their eyeballs for 'em both, calling 'em bleeding crooks, and worse words as I can't repeat. It upset everyone to 'ear such words, them being decent people in this 'ouse.

'Mrs Blacker 'ad ter let 'im in before the police turned up, and he 'ad a set to with 'er, insulting 'er and calling 'er names, an' swearing something chronic. The next day she gave fair warning that any more disturbance and she'd 'ave ter ask us ter find somewhere else to live, that she couldn't have her other guests upset this way. She said I could stay if he went but if he wouldn't, the two of us would have ter go. She was sorry, she liked me, but 'ad no choice. And I do understand that. I wouldn't want this sort of thing if it was my lodging 'ouse.

'I tried telling 'im, but all he said was, "If we get slung out, Em'll 'ave ter find somewhere else for us." He said, "She might find us somewhere even better. She's got the money, ain't she?"'

Mum turned to face her, her expression bleak. 'I told 'im, I wouldn't take a penny off you what you didn't give of yer own free will. But he just smirked and said so you ought, because you get plenty, showing yer legs on the stage and being kept by this magician bloke, and that's what you was, a kept woman.'

She didn't wait for Emma to protest, her daughter's angry gasp going unheard as she said that this Saturday he had upset Mrs Blacker again.

It seemed that Mrs Blacker had put a polite note under everyone's door saying that due to the rough element in the neighbourhood she'd be obliged to bolt the front door after midnight and she apologised if it might cause any inconvenience but all landlords were adopting the same procedure and she thought it best to follow suit. She gathered everyone was in full agreement and was confident that as self-respecting people they would abide by the rules and find it no serious inconvenience to them.

'I got the same sort of note,' Mum said.

Sighing, she went on to say that two days after the note, Ben had come home rolling drunk again at two in the morning, and finding the place locked had hammered on the door until the police had been called by a neighbour, but Mrs Blacker had got him inside before they arrived.

Mum's face went deep red as she described how Mrs Blacker had said almost apologetically said this couldn't go on and she would have to give her a week's notice for the sake of her other tenants, and although she was a good woman, her son was not welcome, and that she was deeply sorry.

'So at the end of the week,' she finished, 'I've got ter leave. I've been so comfortable and happy here. I've been dreading telling you, Em, but I 'ope yer see 'ow I'm placed.'

Back to finding Mum a place to live; her money would soon find her somewhere nice. The problem was always going to be Ben. If only he'd find a place of his own, but he knew where his bread was buttered, didn't he?

There was some hope that Mum might be free of him. Before Emma left, she told her that Ben had apparently got a girl into trouble – a girl called Clara who he'd been going around with – at least going around with

Chapter Twenty-Six

Theo was holding out her savings book to her as she came into the bedroom.

'What is this?' he asked, his tone tight and level, which always denoted controlled anger, penetrating and wounding anger. She wasn't so much alarmed by it as thrown off balance, incapable of maintaining self control. She didn't know which was the more preferable, a good open row with shouting and bawling, things said that shouldn't be, or this silent hostility.

'What is what?' she asked insolently. She knew full well what it was, and could imagine him having been standing there for ages, still fully dressed, simply waiting for her. How dare he pry into her private things? Yet she couldn't say it was none of his business when it was he who gave her an allowance, and a generous one.

He'd been fine earlier on. They spent the evening sitting at ease in the lounge, she and Martin reading, Theo at his desk writing, no talk for once of rehearsals, just passing the time pleasantly. Martin finally finished off his brandy and went off to his own apartment, murmuring goodnight. These days he seemed to be spending more time in Theo's than his own. Whether Theo approved, Emma wasn't sure, though he could hardly tell him not to come in of an evening when at any time day or night Theo would be summoning him for yet more rehearsal. Anyway, she enjoyed Martin's company.

The moment Martin left, Theo went off into their bedroom, leaving her to follow at her leisure. He never did until Martin left, perhaps imagining he might take advantage of Emma if they were left alone. Emma knew that even the casual admiration from those stage-door Johnnies made him edgy. But with Martin, perhaps he had a point? On several occasions she'd caught Martin studying her, and as their eyes met, he would smile and look quickly away. He had a nice smile, and its warmth seemed to flow over her like morning sunshine, making her feel suddenly alive. She felt different in his company than in Theo's. There were moments when she real-ised how she'd changed since being with Theo, her old naturalness insidiously sacrificed for what he preferred her to be, sophisticated, aloof – a goddess. Martin was showing her that under the veneer, she was still what she had always been. She liked it.

Now she faced Theo's cold censure, glancing dispar-agingly at the savings book and back at him, her gaze glacial. 'You've no right to go through my private things,' she said as coolly as she could.

'This is not private,' he said gratingly. 'This is the allowance I give you. For your own needs, not those of feckless hangers-on.' She leaped on the implication. 'My mother's not a hanger-on!' He was looking down at the savings book again, his scrutiny slow and deliberate.

'There is hardly anything left in here. You told me she and your brother were being evicted and needed to find somewhere else to live. I do not complain at your helping them with that, so long as it does not interfere with your work. But this ... this is a huge sum, Amelia! What have you been doing, buying Buckingham Palace for them?'

'I'm not *buying* anything,' she gabbled, gradually losing control. 'I'm letting her have a sum of money so she won't feel beholden to me any more. I know she hates it. She's an independent-minded person and she can now put some away and live on the interest, perhaps find employment enough to supplement it. It's what she'd want.'

'In the meantime she will allow that feckless son of hers to bleed her of every penny, proving that whatever you give to her will be thrown down the drain. I do not recall your asking my opinion on whether you should spend your money in this way. I recall your having told me the sort of person your brother is. Yet you, Amelia, woolly-headed little fool that you are, continue to use what I allow you in order to support these people. In other words, it is I who am supporting your family! Yet you behave as though I have no say in the matter.'

'That's unfair,' she cried. 'You *give* it me. It's mine to use as I please.'

'I beg to differ, my dear.' She hated him calling her 'my dear' – not a term of endearment these days, but usually heralding censure. 'I'm extremely upset at your having kept this from me. I will be your husband before long and responsible for you and all your actions. It's not a good start and I am not at all pleased.'

'Neither am I,' she burst out. 'I'm not a child, but you treat me like one, then expect me to be a woman when I'm in your bed. I won't have you ...'

He closed the book quietly. 'Kindly lower your voice, Amelia. Martin will hear us and think we are quarrelling. The whole apartment block will think we are quarrelling.'

'I couldn't care less,' she said, but lowered her voice anyway. 'And we *are* quarrelling.'

'Then let us do it quietly,' he suggested, so evenly that she was at a loss how to carry on the argument.

Perhaps she shouldn't blame him for being annoyed, but she blamed him for snooping into her business. That she'd settled her mother into her new home would come out eventually; she was biding her time to tell him in her own words without it seeming as though she was being underhand with him. She'd waited a bit too long – three weeks too long.

In a way it had been a bit sneaky, but like her mother, she was independent by nature, and though she would be Theo's wife, she needed to remain her own person. He, like many, expected a wife to be guided by her husband in all things. Little wonder those suffragette women selling their newspaper on street corners and parading so as to recruit more supporters thought they had a point. They wanted the right to vote, and questioned women's subservience to men who thought they needed protection and guidance to be told what to do and how to behave. By law the man was also responsible for his wife's debts and possibly Theo was thinking of that too. But it was this thinking that trapped a woman in marriage, and with such a forceful man as Theo she again had qualms about it.

'I do what I like with my own money,' she said sullenly but with a certain edge of determination, and began undressing for bed, ignoring him.

She was relieved as he put her savings book back into the drawer where she kept her undergarments with no more being said. Not until after he had made love to her and they lay side by side in cosy reverie, when he turned his face to kiss her lingeringly on her cheek.

'I love you so very much, my sweetest,' he whispered against her ear. 'And I am concerned for your wellbeing and safety and feel a need to protect the one I love against the impulse to spend unwisely. You allow me that, don't you, my darling?'

When she nodded silently, he added, 'I feel it my duty to look after you, nothing more. You are my whole life, sweetheart, and soon we will be married.'

The fond kiss became another, then another, growing passionate once more until he took her again with his usual immense energy, leaving her utterly breathless.

'I would marry you tomorrow, were it possible,' she heard him say as they lay side by side. 'But sadly it is not. We will be working until well into the new year. Simmons has several engagements lined up for me.' His appetite satisfied, instead of being ready for sleep he seemed inclined to talk on, while she wanted only to relax and doze off.

'To think how my life has changed since we met, Amelia, my sweet, in three short years. It will soon be 1906, and we have our whole lives ahead of us, as husband and wife.'

Every now and again she made little sounds of agreement though only half hearing, his voice lulling her close to sleep. It was becoming hard to keep awake.

She vaguely heard him say that there would be a break from work in May and that this would be a good time for the wedding. 'I'm sorry it can't be sooner,' came his voice, as if from a long distance away. Her breath caught in a snort deep in her throat. Instantly he turned to her.

'But I am keeping you awake, my dear,' he said quietly. 'I'll talk no more of our wedding, and let you sleep. But you do agree, the month of May would be a good time?'

The last she remembered was trying to offer an assenting grunt and wondering vaguely why she should feel strangely glad that there was still plenty of time before then.

After all these years, Mum had her own front door once more – no more living in other people's houses. She had a small apartment on the ground floor of a three-storeyed block of flats in the heart of London in one of the small roads behind the Tiv, as the Tivoli Music Hall in the Strand was known. It was a moderate walk from where Theo's more splendid apartment lay, and by going through the back turnings Emma could pop in to visit any time she pleased and still be on hand when Theo needed to practise the dozens of illusions he devised. And so the months to Christmas passed smoothly enough.

She made a point of spending Christmas afternoon with Mum before going off to a party that she and Theo had been invited to. She found Mum in good spirits. In fact she had never seen her so bright.

'You go off ter yer party,' she urged. 'I'm off out too. Been asked ter spend the evenin' with Mr and Mrs Copeland and their son and daughter-in-law. They're me new friends what I've made, what live just along the street.'

Listening to her, she was the mother Emma remembered when Dad was alive, still of a distant disposition, never kissed or cuddled or touched her, but cheerful and optimistic, a real mother. Widowed, impoverished, forced out of her home, she'd grown gaunt both in stature and attitude. Now the Maud Beech of old had returned. Emma felt gratified, at ease.

'How's Ben?' she asked. Ben must surely be behaving himself or Mum wouldn't have smiled the way she did.

'Oh 'im! He's getting married.'

'Getting married?' Emma echoed. 'Who to?'

'That girl he got in the family way. That Clara. You remember – the one he said whose baby he swore wasn't 'is?' She gave a smirk. 'It's due mid-January, and he's now admitted that he must be the dad.'

'Why the change of mind?' Emma asked. Her mother shrugged.

'I think he had a real scare over that prison business. He probably needs ter settle down and she's handy, baby or no baby. I think he's secretly proud of being a dad. Twenty-two now, and he's feeling 'is responsibilities.'

'And somewhere to live?' Emma queried. Again her mother shrugged.

'We've got two bedrooms 'ere. They'll 'ave one of 'em. He might find a place later but I don't mind 'em 'ere. Because it's 'appened sudden like, them getting wed in two weeks, 'er so near to 'aving the baby. Ben did the banns as from last week. They'll just be in time before she 'as it.'

'So long as it's not at the altar,' Emma commented.

Her mother didn't laugh. 'I 'ope not. She'll be 'aving it 'ere. Her own mother's ill and her dad's a drunkard and they've umpteen kids. This place will be a little 'eaven for 'er, and I don't mind. I'll be glad of some excitement in me life. An' me a grandmother.'

It was exciting for Emma too. Ben settling down at last, she could hardly believe it. It would be very quietly done, Mum said. In her obdurate way she had put her foot down at inviting any of Ben's mates. 'Not a nice sort, and I won't 'ave any of 'em 'ere!' she said. 'Just them two and me, and me new friends as witnesses – I asked and they agreed. I told 'em of 'er condition but don't know what they'll think, seeing 'er so way out in front.'

She gave Emma a narrow look. 'And there's you. You'll be there, won't yer, Em? Won't be too busy?'

'I shall be there, no matter what,' Emma vowed, ignoring the sly dig, and turned to more social chit-chat.

Spending the whole of Christmas afternoon with Mum had been rather against Theo's wishes. They were off to a big party that evening, every bit as good as the one last year. Theo was receiving more acclaim than ever, able to fill a theatre twice over, making his theatrical agent a happy man into the bargain.

He tended to see Emma as basking in his glory, but she was aware that it was her own glory she basked in as well. The beauty he'd made of her, turning men's heads and filling women with envy, still seemed unbelievable to her at times. But while he was pleased to see the girl he planned to marry so well admired, she often noticed the sidelong glare he would give any who admired her too much, and it was this that also brought her vague unease, hardly sure of what she wanted. She told herself it was probably some sort of premature premarital nerves. After

372

all, they were living together, as much husband and wife as they could be without a ceremony, and whatever she wanted he provided. That he loved her intensely went without question, but it was a possessive love, she knew that too, and there was that dark and smouldering side to him, and the unnatural ability to control his temper, somehow far harder for her to combat than if it had been an explosive temper. Once married, she would be compelled to live with it for the rest of her life, and that worried her.

'Theo says we're getting married in May,' she told Martin in February, as their four-week engagement at the Empire in Leeds came to an end and they prepared to go back to London.

She had just about managed to fit in Ben's wedding to Clara before being whisked off up country, anxious that Theo would insist on going that one day sooner than he'd planned and she'd be forced to break her promise to Mum. But he had been kind to her, seeing how much she needed to be there. The whole thing was over in four hours, just the ceremony and a bite to eat in Mum's apartment, the Copelands departing soon after drinking the champagne Emma had brought. They, along with everyone else politely tried to look as if they liked it, and Ben said more crudely, 'Tastes like cat's piss ter me!' while Clara, with her stomach larger than she was, laughed.

As from next week Theo would be at the Strand, and straight after that, the Metropolitan in Edgware Road, but for the time being there were a few days' respite, something Theo could now well afford.

It was a Saturday morning. Theo was at his agent's. Martin had joined her in Theo's apartment – as he casually said, 'No point me sitting alone in mine.' He was relaxing with the morning paper while she read a magazine, but she was not as relaxed as she tried to make out.

The nearer this wedding came, the less happy she was feeling about it. There was no one to confide in. Mum would have advised her to marry and make a respectable woman of herself. Clara was still a stranger to her, and wrapped up in her new baby whom they'd named Jack in honour of his deceased granddad. Martin was the only one she could talk to. From time to time she'd glanced up at him, weighing up how to approach him with what was troubling her, to have his opinion.

Martin was a listener and a sympathetic one; he was kind, and lately she had felt herself being drawn more and more towards him, able to talk to him about most things that worried her, but that was when Theo was out of hearing.

There was something else disturbing her, and this she wouldn't tell him. The thing was, she'd missed her last period and that was unusual. It might not be anything at all, but with her next period due any day she was on tenterhooks awaiting its arrival. Once it did, she'd feel easier. There was only three months to go to the wedding and if she were pregnant it wouldn't be a problem except that it would make marriage inevitable. So far she still had a choice, or so she told herself, but if she were carrying, there'd be no choice at all.

'There'll be no time for weddings until after the Met,' she said to Martin, who looked up from his paper at the sound of her voice. 'So it'll be at the end of May.' She was trying to sound casual. 'Theo says we're going to the south of France for our honeymoon.'

Martin laid his newspaper on his lap to look questioningly at her, no doubt detecting the dejection in her voice. 'Has he asked if that's where *you* want to go?'

'Where I want to go?' she echoed. Why was Martin being so difficult?

'Yes.' He folded the newspaper and sat forward in his chair. 'Has he asked your opinion on all this?'

'Well, he says ...'

'Damn what he says! What do you say?' She had never seen him so impassioned.

'I'm quite happy.'

'Happy? *Are* you happy?'

'Yes, of course.'

He was scrutinising her face. 'You don't look happy to me.' Her back should have stiffened defensively, but she felt suddenly, oddly, weepy, as if all this time her body had been supported by a metal rod which had suddenly collapsed, leaving her limp and weak. She wanted to be held, to be taken in his arms and be soothed. She let her head droop forward.

'No, Martin, I'm not happy. And I'm not sure why.'

'I know why,' he said. Getting up, he came to crouch in front of her. Reaching forward, he laid both hands on her arms, so strong, steadying, comforting. He'd never touched her before apart from accidental moments when shoulders touched. 'Because you don't love him. I can see you don't. You never look at him in the way a woman in love would look. You behave as if he is God's gift, but never as though you adore him.'

Emma tried to pull away, but he held her firmly, gently but firmly.

'You know you're not in love with him, Emily.'

He was right. She could never talk to Theo the way she could talk to Martin. She tried to tell herself that it was because they were closer in age than she was to Theo, who, when truth was told, made her feel she was always talking to a superior. That wasn't the way lovers should be. Over these few months she and Martin had grown closer; chatted a lot, when they could; discovered similar interests; found they shared the same sense of humour.

Theo had no sense of humour. His laugh was more a bark than a laugh, never lingering with amusement. Sometimes Emma had caught him glowering at them as they laughed over something quite silly.

With Martin's hands on her arm, their warmth penetrating even the lined sleeves of her blouse, she found herself wondering, foolishly, what it would be like being made love to by him. He'd be gentle. Theo seemed incapable of being gentle when making love, his passion possessive.

Last night he'd taken her in his usual way, never asking how she was, afterwards assuming she needed no further attention as he turned over to fall asleep, while she had lain awake wondering how it would be if it had been Martin lying beside her, trying to imagine it, in the darkness imagining him gazing anxiously into her eyes for signs of any discomfort afterwards. She had tried to imagine the soft tone of his voice crooning the sort of words a fond lover might use – that he loved her so very much and needed to hear her say how much she loved him. She'd imagined his arms cradling her, the two of them cuddling close to fall asleep in each other's embrace, next morning rising to laugh together as they set about the day's business.

This morning, as Theo got out of bed and without a word to her, donned his bathrobe and went off to the bathroom, there had come the realisation that she could be in love with Martin. Looking at him now, she knew that she was.

The revelation brought no joy with it, only a deep sense of stunned dismay, as of some great void waiting to engulf her in a marriage she now knew she no longer wanted and yet could not escape. One did not escape Theo easily. She was trapped.

Martin had his arms around her. Without her intending it, tears began welling up. As her head fell on to his shoulder, she let them flow unhindered and soon this unspoken misery had become great gulping sobs while Martin's arms tightened still further about her.

Martin's single apartment had no bathroom, but each floor of this building had a communal one. It was there that he made his way the following morning, his mind on what had transpired the day before. He'd held Emily close, she in tears, his own emotion at discovering just how much he loved her all but overwhelming him too. The day had been a surreal one, with both of them trying to behave normally, Martin hoping that they wouldn't betray their feelings just by trying too hard not to look at each other.

Reaching the bathroom, he paused as the sound of running water told him it was already occupied. Making to turn back, he caught another sound – someone crying. He recognised the sound immediately. Unable to stop himself, he tapped on the door. 'Emily,' he whispered. 'What's wrong?'

There was no reply but the crying ceased abruptly. He waited, hoping Theo wouldn't emerge from his rooms to discover him there. He could just imagine his thoughts. He'd been on the disastrous end of such thought before. He didn't want it happening again.

He was about to move away, to return to his room, when the door slowly opened a fraction and Emily's pale, wan face appeared.

'Martin, what do you want?' she whispered tremulously.

'I heard you crying. Is there something I can do?'

'No,' came the reply.

There was a pause, as if she'd caught her breath and couldn't let go of it. She seemed to partially collapse, seeking the door's support as it opened a fraction wider to hold her. Words, almost incoherent, poured from her in rapid whispering, mixed with dry sobs.

'Oh, Martin, I'm so upset. The way he treats me. As if I'm only here for what he … I mean … I sometimes feel I mean nothing to him, except for what he wants. I mean …'

She became less distraught, humiliation and discomfort taking over, but he knew what she meant. Certain things a woman couldn't explain, personal things, things too embarrassing to put into words to anyone, much less a man, and a man she didn't know all that well either.

He saw her cheeks had grown hot. She was trying to close the door, but he held out a hand to stop her. Of course she didn't want him here seeing her at her very worst.

'I'm sorry, Martin,' she said quickly. 'There's nothing really wrong with me. I suppose I just feel a bit out of sorts, that's all. You'd better go before Theo finds us.'

For a moment he hesitated, then lifted his hands and took her face between both palms. Before she could pull away he'd leaned forward and pressed his lips against hers, leaving her stunned and breathless. He hadn't done that even as he held her yesterday, feeling it not appropriate then as she sobbed against him. Not long after that, Theo had come back and by then he was back in his own rooms, with Theo ignorant of what had transpired.

'If you need me, Emily,' he whispered now, 'I shall be here, because I love you.'

Daring not to look at her again, he turned and went quickly back to his own rooms, closing his door quietly behind him. For a while he stood with his back to it. He knew full well what he'd done. He had opened a floodgate and no will in the world could return that flood to the place where it had once been, still and silent, behind its barrier.

He'd hurried back there, not because he was frightened of Theo but because the consequences could be too awful for her. Worse still, Theo could be quite capable of ordering him to pack his bags and leave. It would make no difference that he was a necessary cog in this present act – Theo's jealousy could be utterly blind. It had been so once before, when Theo was convinced of intrigue between him and Theo's first wife.

That time Theo's accusations had been unsubstantiated. This time, there was every reason for him to be jealous. If Theo ever got the slightest inkling of how he felt, he'd be rid of him in a second, and she would marry that man. His life and hers would never again entwine.

Emma too crept back into her rooms. Theo was still in his own bathroom. The reason why she had sought the communal one was so as to have a good cry in private. Now her tears were dry and all she could feel was the touch of Martin's lips against hers, which had sent such a wave of joy through her that she'd had to resist an urge to draw him into the sanctuary of the room where she had been weeping only a moment ago.

She knew now. She was in love. For the first time she knew she was. But it was Theo she was promised to and there was nothing she could do about it. To reject Theo now would be for him to banish Martin. So now, joy turned once again back to earlier despondency and despair. But worse, what if she were pregnant? How would she expect Martin to react? She would wait. It was all she could do.

The time for her next period came and went, and there was nothing. She was sure now, and it terrified her. She was trapped, and the nearer the date of the wedding approached, the more foreboding she felt.

Now came the testing time. She had to keep her distance from Martin and he from her, avoiding each other's eyes, hardly daring to speak to each other. Yet there were times they had to touch, during rehearsals and on stage, and it was becoming hard to concentrate on what she was supposed to be doing. Instinctively, she knew it was the same for him.

Chapter Twenty-Seven

Before answering the knock on her door, Maud Beech glanced hastily around the living room for anything out of place.

It was becoming hard work keeping this flat as she would like. With Clara and a baby, tidiness had gone out of the window. Ben was still the same, dropping his stuff everywhere, hardly washing, his turning over of a new leaf very brief indeed. Clara was proving to be of the same ilk, raised in the mess and confusion produced by a drunken father, a slovenly mother and a horde of siblings. But she was a friendly young girl, so it was hard to reprimand her. If she did, Clara would smile her sweet smile and promise faithfully to clear up – as soon as she got little Jack down for his morning nap or his afternoon nap and had a sleep herself, for he fair wore her out. But nothing was ever done, leaving her mother-in-law to do it all.

Opening the door, Maud was surprised to see Emma standing there. The girl looked woeful.

'You orright?' she asked automatically. 'I thought yer was the rent collector.' She saw her daughter's wan smile at the comment and moved back for her to enter. 'What's wrong? Yer don't look all that well.'

Ushered into the living room, Emma sat down on the edge of the settee. Maud came to sit beside her, taking one of her daughter's elegantly gloved hands between her roughened ones. 'What's the matter, luv?'

She saw Emma's eyes begin to glisten. 'I've something I've got to tell you, Mum. Something I need to ask you. There's no one else I can tell or ask what I should do.'

Maud Beech had only to look into her daughter's eyes to know exactly what the girl had to say. There wasn't long to wait before Emma burst out, 'Mum, I've got myself in the family way.'

After a short pause, Maud said slowly, 'It ain't you what's got yerself in the family way. It's 'im.' Emma said nothing, gazing down at the hands still holding hers.

'How could yer let 'im do it?' Maud prompted, and her daughter looked up, sharply defensive.

'He's asked me to marry him – in three months' time. But I can't ask him to bring it forward with so much work on, and make him angry.'

Maud ignored that. 'So you thought it orright ter take chances?'

'It's him – he's never taken precautions. It's amazing that it hasn't happened sooner. But now it has.'

'Em!' Maud cut her short. 'Yer should of stopped 'im. A girl ain't got ter to do what a man wants, not when it comes to 'er well-being.'

'It's not easy. It'd cause a row.'

'Then bloody cause a row! Better'n you coming ter me now with yer troubles after the thing's done.'

'You don't know him. He can be ...'

'I know what a woman ought ter be when a bloke thinks only of his own needs. You 'ave ter push 'em off, not beckon 'em on, lying back like some slave.'

She could see by Em's face that this had not been possible, that her daughter was virtually under that man's thumb. Emma used to have such a will of her own. What had happened to it? What sort of man was this to change her so? Maud felt slow fury mount within her against this man.

She let go of Emma's hand and got up to remove a baby's vest Clara had carelessly left on an armchair, absently beginning to fold it neatly.

She had never met this man. She'd seen the posters outside theatres. The artist's portrait had made him look quite terrifying – a penetrating gaze and a set mouth behind the trim beard. She had attributed the mesmerising expression to the artist's licence in emphasising the way the Great Theodore could command the awe of his audience.

Was that how he commanded her daughter? If so, the girl hadn't a leg to stand on. Thoughts of veiled threats of violence if she refused to comply came to mind, and the mother in her sought only to fight for her child's chastity. It was too late now of course – the damage was done. So long as he kept his promise to marry her, that was all.

Still unfolding and refolding the baby vest, she came back to stand in front of Emma. 'You should of tried,' she said ineffectually.

'I'm not worried about that,' came the reply. 'It's just that when I tell him, he'll bring the wedding date forward. So I've nothing to worry about, except that ...'

She broke off, fiddling with a fold she'd made in the garment, running the material between thumb and forefinger. Maud stared at her in disbelief. The girl was refusing to meet her gaze.

'You mean you 'aven't told him,' she said, nodding at the confirming statement. The fact that Emma hadn't told him made him even more an ogre in Maud's eyes – she was a girl too terrified to tell the man she slept with that he was to be a father.

'It's just that I'll have to marry him now, won't I?'

'You mean yer've got doubts?' She saw Emma nod miserably.

'Him with his pots of money and a big country 'ouse?' Emma had told her this on one occasion. 'Yer'd be secure fer the rest of yer life, which is what every girl dreams of, but yer don't love 'im.'

'I'm not sure.'

Maud dropped the vest on the settee, her tone grown sharp and loud. 'Then what've yer come 'ere for?' In the next room her grandson was starting to whimper. 'If I was in your place,' she went on, 'whether I fancied the bloke or not, I'd think about the comfort he could provide and ...'

She broke off. Would she indeed do that? Comfort and money couldn't provide happiness if the source of it sprang from a loveless marriage.

A voice broke through her thoughts. 'So she's up the spout, is she?'

Ben stood at the door to his and Clara's bedroom, his bulk filling the doorway, his face dark as a thundercloud.

In none too clean combinations he too didn't look all that fresh and clean, his thick, dark hair tousled and last night's stubble dark on his cheeks. His shoulders were hunched forward and his chin was belligerently thrust out. He presented a huge body of a man, enough to frighten the life out of anyone.

Behind him stood a fair-haired, mild-faced young woman, about nineteen, their baby in her arms. She looked about as tousled as Ben.

Emma turned to face him without fear or awe. She'd had to deal with Theodore's ominous fury too many times to be worried by confrontation with her blustering brother. She threw him a sneer as she adopted the language he understood. 'Been listening at key'oles, have yer?' she challenged.

'Couldn't be off it,' he growled. 'Us trying ter get a bit of kip. Now yer've woken up the kid neivver of us'll get any bleedin' peace till she feeds 'im.'

Marriage hadn't changed him at all. And it seemed his Clara was just as slovenly by the look of her, even though sweet-faced. He was looking Emma up and down, his gaze coming to rest on her narrow, corseted waist, as though expecting to see her stomach already bulging.

'So, he's put yer in the club at last. An' you looking down yer nose at me and 'er.' He jerked his head towards the petite Clara. 'At least we got married. When do you expect 'im ter marry yer, then? Sometime never?'

'We might not get married.' It came out before she could stop herself, the thought that had been playing at the back of her mind for so long.

Ben's eyes narrowed. 'Don't want yer, now yer pregnant, is that it?'

'I didn't mean ...' She was cut short by his deep bellow as he lunged forward, leaving Clara still standing in the doorway.

'I ain't gonna see my sister put up the duff by some stuck-up bleeder wot thinks 'imself better'n people like us just because he's got money.'

He stood glaring down at her, and as she tried to rise, thrust out a fist and pushed her back down on the sofa.

'Well, I'm tellin' yer one thing fer nothing! If 'e thinks 'e can treat me own sister like this, he's got anuvver think coming. He's gonna 'ave me ter reckon wiv, and I'm gonna knock 'is block orf, that's what I'm gonna do.' He already looked as though he was facing Theo, his hands curled into fists, eyes blazing, shoulders hunched forward ready to do battle. 'I'll bash 'is bleedin' 'ead in, don't yer think I won't!'

Emma summoned up a show of defiance, forgetting she'd intended to say she'd be getting married in May. 'And get yourself arrested for assault and battery? You've been in prison once,' she reminded him hotly. 'They'll have you back behind bars again, quick as lightning.'

'It'll be bloody worth it,' he swore, undaunted. 'I'll get 'im one dark night and bleedin' shove 'is bleedin' lights out for him. You see if I don't! And don't go thinking I ain't capable of it!'

Ignoring his mother's order to mind his tongue, he towered over Emma as though to physically show her what he was capable of. The last time she had come up against him he hadn't seemed half that large. In that time he'd grown even taller; had broadened out as males after twenty-one usually do. Boxing had given him biceps as large as some men's thighs. Yes, he could be terrifying. And yes, he could do Theo damage, lots of damage.

'Listen, Ben.' She reached up and touched those bulging muscles. 'I know what you could do. But there's no need. I'm happy with Theodore and I'm happy about having his baby. We're getting married in May. We might have to get married a bit earlier, that's all. So don't go looking for a scrap. There's no need.' She gave a sharp little laugh. 'I don't want my husband-to-be going up the aisle all bruised. And by the way, you'll all be invited to the wedding.'

Tension melting, Clara came forward to present her baby for Emma to admire. But still feeling tense and with nothing solved, Emma had to fight to bring herself to comply, not only because her visit had been unfruitful, but also because the little mite struck her as quite unpalatable. Obviously put to bed last night without a wash, the remains of his last feed had stuck to the corners of his little lips, and the shawl he was wrapped in could have done with a wash. She was surprised Mum had allowed him to be left in this state and guessed that as soon as she got her hands on her grandson after Emma left, she would put to rights that which his parents had found unnecessary to do.

Ben pushed through the grubby swing doors of The Huntsman, gazing about for the face of a mate or two to have a drink with, and Wally Cartwright in particular, whom he'd become great mates with.

It was too early yet. There were just a few old lags around unable to keep out of pubs, a few jobless with just enough pence in their tattered pockets to help drown their sorrows, a couple of old soaks who'd no doubt be kicked out once the regulars came in, and they'd begin begging a drop of beer off one or two of them.

Despite being so close to the rich and fashionable of London's heart, the back streets remained seedy, run down and unsafe for any other than its own doubtful denizens to walk alone in.

This was where Ben felt comfortable. This was where he could hold his own against any ruffian, as he'd always done. Used to East End gangs, the streets behind the brightly lit West End were no different. In shadowy courts and yards, the houses built in the middle of the last century leaned towards each other, hid thieves and murderers and the poverty-stricken as much as any back street in London did.

Ben moved towards the bar, lounged against it and turned his body slightly to enable him to watch the door. Sooner or later some of the mates he'd made since arriving in this area would come in and join him. By that time the place would have filled with men's voices, becoming slurred, raised in guffaws and song as drink began to deaden the miseries of their world. He and his friends would down a few pints, form a school of pontoon, have a laugh with a few girls, and finally he'd stagger home to his wife and baby to become husband and father again and as a husband claim his rights. Clara was a very willing wife in that direction. It didn't worry her that they shared his mother's home, and that the next morning, after Clara had given full voice to their love-making, Mum would go around the flat with a long, disapproving expression. Clara knew that her own sweet disposition would soon put a smile back on her mother-in-law's face, until tomorrow night's repeat.

But since his sister's revelation, Ben was having continual visions of Theo doing the same thing to Emma as he was doing to his wife and it made him feel unaccountably sick and outraged. He vowed as he propped up the drink-stained bar of The Huntsman that he wasn't going to let that pig she'd taken up with get away with it; dirty old sod, looking for a bit of young meat bleeding magician or no.

Interrupting his vicious reverie, the barman came to ask what he fancied, taking his order for a pint of his favourite porter, the best, dark and bitter, and a shot of rum, shaking his head as Ben asked if he'd seen Wally Cartwright.

'Not so far,' came his reply. 'But he always comes in here; maybe in half an hour, perhaps less.'

Ben already knew that, and satisfied that the man he had recently befriended would appear soon, he leaned with his back to the bar, elbows supporting him, and surveyed the half-empty pub with its smoke-darkened wood panelling and faded pictures, and its not too fresh scattering of sawdust on the floor. The barman wiped the bar top, skirting around his customer's elbows.

'You're Ben Beech, the boxer chap,' he commented, continuing to wipe the same dry place. Later the surface would be awash with beer, and his cloth more necessary. Ben nodded briefly and continued to sip his porter, his back still to the man.

His name was getting around. He experienced a tingle of pride. Wally, who also boxed, had found him a proper manager, getting him proper bouts, proper training.

Thanks to Em he had money to train, and boxing had now become a serious business. He intended to get somewhere in this life – once he'd put this magician bloke to rights. But he'd bide his time first, see if he intended to marry her and make a good woman of her. If not ...

Last night Theo's lovemaking had been so vigorous that, despite being used to his buffeting, she feared for the life she felt sure she was carrying inside her. He could damage it, she thought fearfully. She would have to tell him soon so as to make him more gentle with her. She would tell him today.

She found herself starting to want this baby even though it would mean her future being mapped out for her from now on. Theo, the father of her child, would be her husband, and drawn though she was to Martin, she'd have to be stern with herself. His kiss the other morning was proof of how he felt towards her, and it must stop. She needed to speak to him too.

There was no chance to tell Theo next morning. He had risen early as usual and was already talking to Martin about some matter or other, and she had to leave for her regular appointment with her hairdresser. She'd tell him on her return when she had him to herself for a few minutes. It was certain now – she was pregnant; there was no going back. But he would be pleased with this ultimate token of his love.

She arrived home to find him not there – no note to say where he'd gone. Going across the hall, she knocked tentatively on Martin's door.

'Do you know where Theo is?' she asked as he opened it.

Martin was scrutinising her. 'He said to tell you that Jack Simmons telephoned him.'

Theo had installed a telephone recently, keeping abreast of the growing fad for them on the part of those who could afford them. Telegrams arrived minutes after being sent; a letter posted in the morning with three or four posts a day could arrive that same afternoon; but telephones were becoming the rage. Emma hated theirs. She hated its jangling summons, fearing to be alone when it rang. It had happened once. She had unhooked the earpiece from the instrument on the wall to hear a distorted, disembodied voice asking for Theo. She'd said no one was at home and had hung the thing back on its hook before the voice could reply. Afterwards she had hated herself for being a coward, vowing to be different next time. But since then Theo had always been here.

'He's only this minute gone out,' Martin was saying. 'He could be gone all morning.'

There was a note to his tone as he spoke, and Emma knew that her immediate change of expression had already been interpreted. Not stopping to think, she found herself in the little square hallway of his flat, fully aware of what could happen, wanting it to happen yet knowing that it mustn't. It would bring with it impossible circumstances. She would have to confess her love for him to Theo, but what about the baby? Would Martin understand about the baby? Would he still want her when she told him? But if he did and they were found out, he would be made to go and she would never be able to follow, a woman pregnant with someone else's child. This had to stop, now, before it got out of hand. Her head was filling with awful thoughts – how could Martin bear to make love to her knowing she was carrying Theo's baby?

391

'Martin ...' she began. It must have been a look in her eyes, for he moved back a little from her, lowering his gaze.

'I know,' he said lamely.

Shock ran through her. 'What do you know, Martin?' she gasped.

'I know how hard it is for you.' He was looking at her, his eyes full of love. 'I know you're promised to Theo, but I can't lose you, Emily, not after yesterday. I know you feel the same about me.'

The relief was almost a pain. He knew nothing of her condition. She put out a hand to him. He took it and held it to his lips. With no will to pull away, she stood with her hand to his lips. 'I'm to marry Theo,' she said ineffectually.

He kept hold of her hand. 'You don't have to. You can marry me instead.'

'You don't understand,' she said desperately. If only Theo hadn't got her pregnant. She was suddenly filled with hatred for him – his selfishness, his lack of consideration for her, his assumption that she would be his wife, no matter what she thought about it. But she had never yet told him what she thought about it. And if she did so now, would it be typical of Theo's perverse nature to insist she be his wife, she and his child? And Martin? With this baby on the way, there was nothing she could do. Hatred of Theo, of herself, of fate, gnawed at her as she stared at Martin. 'If he knew about us,' she said tremulously, 'he'd kill you, and me too, for encouraging you.'

Martin became resolute. He even grinned at the histrionic touch. 'The worst he can do is tell me to leave.'

Seconds later, he sobered at a thought. 'He'll make sure I never see you again and he'll make your life a misery.'

She wanted to say, then I'll leave too, but she couldn't. The baby was preventing her. Her own honesty told her that she couldn't deceive Martin in that way. She stood in silence.

What option had she but to stay with Theo? An unmarried woman with a baby, alone in the world; she had no choice. It made no difference how strong she was, her future would be living hand to mouth, begging for her child's food, her only recourse to prostitute herself for her bread – it happened all the time. A man could father bastards with no repercussions, but a woman, pregnant, unmarried and alone … She wouldn't ask Mum for help – she had her pride. The only answer was to make the best of a bad job and marry Theo.

There was a strained look of longing on Martin's face. She was aware of that same look on her own face. Not wanting him to see it, she turned and made for the door.

He was there before her, barring her way. Holding her upper arms in a vice-like grip, he drew her to him and planted his lips fiercely on hers. With no more will of her own, she let him hold her, her kiss suddenly as hungry as his. Her body pressed against the door, her response was instinctive: reaching up to clasp him about the neck, she felt the desire to have him make love to her numbing all other thoughts, as he was lifting her to carry her into his lounge.

From somewhere inside her brain came a sharp stab like an electric shock at the sound of a key being turned in the door of Theo's apartment, and the door opened then closed.

The two of them had frozen into immobility, Emma still in Martin's arms.

'Darling!' Emma hissed in horror. 'I have to leave.'

'He doesn't know you're here,' he whispered.

'He could come and knock,' she said, terrified now.

'I'll hide you.'

'No.'

The word forced itself from her. She couldn't be found crouching behind a sofa, trembling behind curtains. Her love for Martin had to be above all that.

'Put me down, Martin.' Her voice was sharp with embarrassment. 'I have to go.'

He seemed to know how she felt. Perhaps he felt the same way. Gently, he stood her back on her feet. 'You'd best tidy yourself,' he said, defeated.

Praying that her burning cheeks would not be noticed, Emma let herself out of Martin's apartment and taking a deep breath, straightened her posture, and let herself into her own apartment. Theo came into the hall from the lounge. She gave him a smile. 'Hello, darling.'

She was acutely aware that he did not reply to her light salutation, and she tried again.

'I'm sorry, Theo, I was a bit longer in the hairdressing salon than I intended to be. I got into conversation with someone I know there and had to hurry back.'

That would account for her flushed look and unusual breathlessness.

It seemed to convince him. Yet she was uncertain. There was an odd glint to those brilliant blue eyes as he said abruptly, 'I have some things to go over for tonight. I need both you and Martin here. Perhaps you would go across the hall and fetch him.'

He leaned towards her, pecked her cheek and, turning away, went back into the lounge and his desk to sit with his back to her, leaving her to wonder what interpretation she should put on it all, if any. Or was she merely falling prey to her own guilty feelings?

Chapter Twenty-Eight

The comic singer at present on stage, Sam Mayo, popularly known as 'The Immobile One' from his lugubrious expression, was having the audience in fits with 'She Cost Me Seven and Sixpence'. From the wings, Theo watched without even the semblance of a smile.

His equipment was already in place, hidden behind the traveller curtain that would be drawn back at the same time as he made his dramatic entrance, the lights suitably dimmed. Amelia would be on his arm, Martin entering to stand to one side until called upon.

He licked his lips. They were strangely dry. He was seldom edgy prior to going on but felt unusually so this evening. He stole a glance at Amelia standing beside him in the wings. Her gaze was on the comic, her lips tilted at the corners by Mayo's hilarious song.

She looked dazzling: her profile with its up-tilted nose, softly mobile lips and the smooth line of the chin was perfect, the gentle curve of her neck sloping down to the low décolletage revealing the gentle rise of her breasts; exquisite. Her piled-up auburn hair held a single, green-tinted osprey feather secured by a cluster of emeralds, stage jewellery set in imitation gold. She wore a shimmering green dress. Green on stage was often viewed as unlucky by theatre folk, but it was the colour he favoured on her, bringing out even more the colour of her hair. The dress clung to her figure like a second skin except where the skirt fell to a flare at the hem. It would be divested, following the audience's appreciation of it, to reveal legs clad in the black tights needed for the contortions of the performance. It also afforded an audience, seldom treated to the sight of ladies' legs, the pleasure of their shapeliness.

It was not her appearance, however, that drew his sidelong glance but what he had noticed today: the way she had glanced at Martin when he'd answered that summons, a glance full of wariness, when she otherwise seemed to be making a purposeful effort to avoid him. What was going on? Suspicion stirred and seethed in his veins as he stood in the wings, silently going over his entrance. This was how it had begun with Martin and Eleanor. She had hotly denied it in a display of indignant fury, with Martin professing shock and distress. He'd never really got to the bottom of it and still felt the embarrassment of the lack of real evidence and for allowing passion to overrule self-possession. But he should not jump to conclusions so quickly this time. Eleanor was one thing. Amelia was entirely another, far too sweet to countenance the overtures of some other man. For her sake and his own peace of mind, he needed to trust that Martin had indeed been innocent all that time ago, that he'd done the right thing in re-engaging that man's invaluable skills, and he was sure that history would not repeat itself; it was just he himself being over-sensitive after that first time.

Theo came to himself as the gales of laughter from out front followed the singer's final lines, and prepared to go on stage, growling to the other two to make themselves ready. For all his resolve, from now on he would keep an eye on the two of them, watching for every turn of the head, interpreting every glance that might pass between them.

It was urgent that Theo should hear her news as soon as possible. It was the only way she could push Martin away for ever, for she'd not find strength to do it any other way. After the show Theo took her to supper, asking Martin to return home on his own or go on elsewhere if he chose.

Theo was being unusually quiet. There was something on his mind no doubt, probably his act. They might be alone at their table but it was hardly the place for conveying something so personal while eating, and with so many noisily enjoying supper and the small orchestra playing.

They returned home around midnight. There was no sign of Martin. Theo spoke about being weary, though not so weary as not to make love to her before seeking sleep. Afterwards he lay with his back to her while she stared up at the ceiling, fully awake.

'Theo?'

He gave a faintly irritable grunt.

'I've something to tell you,' she persisted.

'Can it not wait until the morning?'

'No, not really.'

He turned irascibly to face her. 'Amelia, we've had an exhausting evening at the theatre. And I am not pleased.

Martin failed to respond as quickly as I needed during my curtained door illusion.'

'I wasn't aware of anything wrong,' she said sulkily, hating the change of subject. 'Not until you just pointed it out.'

'He will have to improve before our next engagement.' The next was at the Royal Holborn, virtually their last before the wedding.

'You were sluggish tonight,' he said, coming more awake. 'Any slower and they would have seen through my swivel box trick. As for mind-reading, you hesitated far too long with your responses. You unnerved me. A certain hesitation is necessary, but that was ridiculous. Tomorrow we will go over the whole thing, beginning to end. There is no slickness to this act any more.'

He turned his eyes to her with a suddenness that made her nerves jangle. 'Is there something making you tired, Amelia? You *and* Martin?'

His keen gaze was boring into her, the question full of innuendo and she felt a tiny stab of warning. Praying that the darkness afforded by the thick curtains drawn against the glow of the London street lights wouldn't let him to see her discomfort, she returned to her initial quest in a frantic rush.

'Theo, I'm going to have a baby.'

The silence seemed to go on for ever. She couldn't see his expression but when he finally spoke the tone wasn't at all as gentle.

'What did you say?'

'I'm having our baby,' she said, hating the timidity in her voice.

He sat up sharply. 'Oh, no, you are not!'

Stunned, she too sat up. 'What're you talking about, darling? I am. I've got all the signs. It's true. I'm not mistaken.'

'You are mistaken.'

'No, love. I haven't seen for two months, and my body feels different. I was sick yesterday morning, for the first time.'

'No doubt something you have eaten.'

'No.'

'I say it is.'

'Theo.'

'I wish to hear no more about it, Amelia. You're mistaken and I am tired. Go to sleep.' He lay down, but she wasn't to be fobbed off. Surely a man would be pleased at such news with the marriage already arranged. It could be brought forward so there'd be no stigma.

'Theo,' she begged again, and found her plea viciously cut short.

'I am not interested!' He'd sat upright to lean over her in an almost menacing posture.

'Listen, Amelia.' His deep voice growled above her. 'I need to put this to you bluntly. In our profession, with you as my assistant, we cannot deal with a child. I have never had a wish for children and am not prepared to change my mind now.'

Her protest sounded stupid to her ears, weak and ineffectual. 'You could train up another assistant as I get ...'

'*You* are my assistant. I want no other. As for this business, I know of a certain person who will be able and willing to help you rid yourself of it. It will be quick and painless. I will arrange it tomorrow. Within a week you will be back to your old self.'

'Rid? Rid myself of it?' she stammered, appalled and confused. 'No, Theo, I won't do that.'

'Then have it!' He threw himself back down on to his pillow. 'Leave the act. I will cancel our wedding. You can go off on your own and give birth – on your own. I will have nothing to do with it, or with you. In fact, go now. Leave this bed. Leave this apartment. Pack your things. Take whatever you wish. I shall not lay claim to anything you feel you need to take with you. Whatever you take may help towards the cost of having your baby.'

So savage were the words that she cringed. 'I can't go, Theo. Where would I go?'

'I don't care where you go. But as long as you keep that thing inside you, you are on your own.'

'But it's our baby,' she squeaked in disbelief. 'Ours. I can't leave!'

She found the plea ignored as he continued. 'And once you have sold what you take away with you, I shall not provide for you, do you understand me?'

'I shall starve.'

'Go to your mother.'

'There's no room. And I can't expect her to keep me. She couldn't afford to.'

Without what he gave her, there'd be nothing. With Mum unable to pay the rent, losing her home, they be reduced once more to practically begging for their bread, she with a child born out of wedlock and no hope of marriage. Where would she end up? Martin must not hear of her plight. How could she put that burden on him? All this flashed through her head in the seconds it took for her to gasp out those last words.

'Then do as you please,' came the reply.

All at once, his tone moderated. 'Don't you see, my dear, in a few months you will be bloated and ugly and quite useless as my assistant. I have no intention of finding a replacement. It was you who helped me return to where I am today. Without you I am lost. We complement to each other. If you do as I say, you know you will never want for anything. We'll marry and your future will be assured.'

He was gazing intently at her.

'Which do you choose, Amelia, to go back to selling rubbish with a tray around your neck and an illegitimate child at your skirts or to enjoy a life of society with beautiful clothes, fine jewellery, others hanging on your every word – for that is where I intend to go, my dear – and a full life and a secure marriage?'

He paused for her answer but when none came, he said in a sad voice, 'What has happened should never have been allowed to happen. How could you have let such a thing occur? It has ruined everything.'

For a moment Emma couldn't believe what she was hearing. Anger rose up inside her. How dare he put the onus on her, he who'd always had his fill of her without once exercising the least precaution. It was his duty not hers to see that she didn't fall pregnant.

'If I were to go,' she said softly, 'and you refuse to take on another female assistant, what will you do?' He had never worked with only Martin, as previously his wife had helped too.

'I shall leave the stage,' came the unemotional reply. 'I will not come after you, Amelia, nor see you again, and I shall never forgive you. I shall simply disappear.'

Such strange words, yet heart-rending. It almost rang of some suicidal intention that made her feel suddenly afraid for him.

She wanted to say that she wouldn't be blackmailed into submission. Yet the dreadful choice she was being given took the heart out of her. Once living in the gutter had been all she'd known and had accepted, but she had tasted the wine and honey of fine living, and to return to the dregs of life after that would make it bitter beyond measure. She had to stay. At the same time her breast filled with intense hatred for this man. Faced with these alternatives he'd put before her, what could she do other than comply with his dictates? Even now the full impact of what he was asking of her had not quite hit her.

It did, however, and with full force, a few days later.

Emma let Theo help her out of his fine Austin York Landaulette, just as he always did, always the polite one. But this time she was in too much of a daze to support herself, needing to lean on him like one stricken by illness.

'This way, my dear,' he was saying, taking her arm as he closed the car door behind them. 'Don't be afraid. It will be over before you know it.'

He had dispensed with the chauffeur he often used these days, taking it on himself to drive here. Of course he would. He wouldn't want people to know his destination, even to the point of coming here after dark.

Before them stood a dark, shabby, two-storey building, one of several, hardly discernible in this ill-lit back street, and Emma felt her insides contract. He could have chosen a more salubrious place. He could afford it. But of course, it wasn't the money that had made him select this place – it was his reputation. He didn't need this sort of thing being broadcast.

'All you have to do, my dear,' he said gently, 'is to relax. When this is over we can resume our life. We will be married in May and I promise I will make you happy. You are a brave girl.'

She didn't feel brave as she gazed, mesmerised, at the dingy door in front of her that stood open to the street. With Theo holding her around her waist, his free hand gripping hers and to which she was holding tightly as if she would fall without it, they entered. Inside was a flight of rickety stairs leading up to a second door. That too stood open, and in the light from the room she could see a frowzy, middle-aged woman in a black skirt and blouse. Instinctively, Emma drew back. She felt Theo's grip instantly tighten around her waist, his grip on her hand strengthen.

'It's all right. There's nothing to be frightened of. She is very good. I have checked. I wouldn't bring you here otherwise.'

Coming here, she had said not a word to him. Now she found her voice. 'I can't, Theo,' she managed to whisper. 'I can't do this. I want to go back home.'

'That's impossible, my dear,' came the reply. 'It's too late. The money has already been paid.'

He had made this decision for her, taking no notice of her protests, ignoring her rage when he refused to heed them. Finally she had succumbed in the knowledge that she was indeed trapped. Yet there still remained a spark of her old spirit, but an unreasonable spark, knowing she had nowhere to turn, faced by what would lie in store for her were she to refuse to do as he said. Misery had torn at her very bowels. There had been a mad moment when she had thought of ending it all, of throwing herself from the roof of their apartment block or going off to drown herself in the Serpentine or the Thames, but the instinct for self-preservation had prevailed, and now she was here, hating that cowardice, unable to take her fate into her own hands as she should have.

Theo was helping her mount the bare, wooden stairs. She could hear their feet scraping the boards. The woman in her sombre dress was coming nearer, her frame seeming to diminish as they mounted higher.

Emma was aware of unpolished boots peeking out from under the skirt, though why they should be so important she didn't know, that and the fact that she was smaller than Emma had first imagined.

They had gained the landing. The woman was reaching out a hand to her. Something inside Emma seemed to snap and she let out a shriek of protest.

'No!'

Pushing away the outstretched hand ready to draw her into that dreadful room, she wrenched herself free of Theo's hold, lashing out at him.

'No!'

With him not holding her, she took a step backwards. Her foot met empty air, then crashed down on the step below taking her off balance. The next thing she knew, with a shriek of terror she was falling backwards, an attempt to clutch at the unsteady banister sending her body tumbling over and over.

Bruised and battered, she hit the floor with a thud that knocked the breath from her body. The world spinning, she was dimly aware of feet hurrying down towards her, of her head being lifted on to someone's lap, of a man's voice saying, 'My God! I think she's been knocked out,' followed by a woman's voice, sounding impatient, 'I can't deal with her now, not like this, you'll have to take her home.' And again, 'My time's been wasted, I don't give money back!' Theo's voice again, saying, 'Surely you can give her something. This has to be done. It's imperative. I'll pay you double.'

There came a moment of silence, then, 'Very well.'

'She won't feel anything, will she?'

'She won't know a thing about it,' came the reply through a fog that seemed to be surrounding Emma.

There was more movement. Her head was being lifted a little, a spoon being eased between her flaccid lips. She tasted liquid, aromatic yet slightly bitter – laudanum. A second spoonful followed the first, making her choke against it, but despite that, yet another. How many spoonfuls were fed to her she had no idea as she felt herself sinking into that soothing darkness of oblivion.

When she regained consciousness it was to find herself lying in her own bed. Theo was holding her hand, his eyes gazing down at her, his expression troubled.

'How do you feel, my dear?' he asked as she focused on him through a drugged haze.

'What happened to me?' she mumbled wearily.

He leaned closer. 'Everything is fine now, my sweetest. You had a fall.' Yes, she remembered. 'You were lucky – a few bruises, nothing broken. Being light-framed and supple as you are, you fell lightly, otherwise you might have been seriously hurt. But you lost the child.'

She stared at him, not quite comprehending. 'I couldn't have – not as quickly as that.' The fall could only have been a few hours ago and even she knew that one wouldn't lose a baby so soon afterwards.

'Nevertheless,' he said softly, 'it is gone. You are as you were. You are no longer pregnant, my dear.'

Now she remembered, in her half-dazed state, the distinctive taste of that laudanum, not one dose but several, slowly reducing her to jelly, to sink into oblivion. She looked at Theo in horror at what had crept into her mind.

'Did you ... .' It was hard to say it. 'Did she ... that woman ... while I was ...' she couldn't go on. But she saw him bow his head.

'You've nothing more to worry about, Amelia. It's over and you are fine. In a few days you will be on your feet, as right as rain, with this far behind you. Now, you need to rest to regain your strength.'

He patted her hand and rose to go while she continued to stare at him in shocked disbelief at what she now knew had been done to her while she was without any will to protest.

Disbelief slowly began to change to cold hatred, hatred that seemed beyond words.

'I'll leave you to sleep now,' he was saying, entirely unaware of what was churning in her breast. 'This has been an ordeal for you, but when you awake you will feel much better. There is a good fire in the grate so you will be quite warm and cosy. Anything you want, just call. Martin and I will not be far away.'

She didn't know why she asked except that it seemed imperative. 'You haven't told Martin about this?' She had even managed to keep her voice steady.

He paused at the door, looking back at her. 'He knows nothing,' he said as though this were a conspiracy.

'I told him you had a slight tumble, nothing more. I said you might also have a slight chill coming on. It's as well that tomorrow is Sunday, and Monday hardly matters. He and I will manage the act between us. I will reorganise and modify it. Sleep now. We will be in the lounge.'

Emma blinked as he went out. The act! The bloody act! All that had happened to her, all that had been done to her without her consent, and he could think only of his bloody act!

For a while she remained staring at the closed door until she became aware of tears trickling from the corner of her eyes, to make rivulets across the bridge of her nose and her temple, wetting the pillow beneath her cheek. Slowly she turned her face into it to muffle the sound of weeping, numbed of all feeling except one: the hatred that remained and, she knew, would remain for ever, dulled maybe by time, but never entirely to leave her.

Chapter Twenty-Nine

'How are you feeling, my dearest?' Theo asked on coming into her room on Tuesday morning.

He'd slept on the sofa these two nights, allowing her the bed to herself, for which she was deeply glad. Having him next to her would have sickened her. Even now, her hatred awakened at the sight of him, knowing what he had done to her for the sake of his act, his fame, his ambition.

She pulled herself up on the pillows piled behind her. 'I feel weak,' she replied, wanting to say as little as need be to him.

She was in fact feeling somewhat better. He was right, her suppleness had saved her from worse injury. Her shoulders felt a little stiff, that was all. She was still tender elsewhere, still having to wear a towel, though the blood loss was now a mere brownish staining.

Lying in bed, her meals brought to her by an attentive Mrs Hart, who was employed to come in to cook and clean, she'd felt a little better by yesterday morning, except that attempting to get up to visit the bathroom she'd been overcome by giddiness, making her sink back on to the bed. No doubt it was because of all this immobility. All she'd done so far was to get out to use the chamber pot, which Mrs Hart quickly covered and carried away to empty, reassuring her, 'Don't be embarrassed, pet, I've got a bedridden mum what lives with us and I do this for her all the time.' But her brow had furrowed seeing the stained water with its shreds of red matter.

'I've had a very bad period,' Emma said, which seemed to satisfy Mrs Hart.

This morning, before anyone was up, she had gone to the bathroom on her own. Ignoring a certain stiffness of limbs, she'd crept along the hallway, holding on to the wall for support, glad to sink down on the polished wooden toilet seat. Creeping back had meant a supreme effort to be quiet in case any sound of her progress alerted Theo. The last thing she'd wanted was having him touch her.

He sat here now, talking mostly about his concern for his act if she didn't get on her feet soon, his hand on her forearm gently smoothing the skin. It was all she could do not to pull away.

'I'm tired,' she sighed, hoping he might take the hint and leave. 'I've not long woken up.'

'Did you have a bad night?'

'Restless. I think I might need to get in a bit more sleep.'

'I expect you miss my company beside you. Perhaps I will join you tonight. I shall be glad not to sleep on the sofa any more.'

Emma bit her lip to prevent herself saying she didn't want him in her bed ... his bed.

'Perhaps leave it a few more days,' she said instead.

'No, my dearest.' He was all concern for her. 'I shall stay with you tonight. You will feel much safer and sleep far better. But I will let you rest now. I have to go out for a while. I shall come in later to see how you are. You might be feeling somewhat stronger by then, my dear.'

Five minutes after he'd left, she heard Martin's voice at the door and her heart leaped. She hadn't heard his knock. Mrs Hart, having got breakfast for her employer, had been on the point of leaving to get her own husband's meal. Now Martin's voice in the hallway came like a hospital whisper. 'It's all right, Mrs Hart, I know Mr Barrington is out. I'll keep an eye on her.'

'Oh, I'm glad, Mr Page,' came the woman's voice. 'I don't like leaving her on her own, though she said it's all right. But I do have to see about me own family. You know.'

'Of course,' came the soft reply. 'You trot along then.'

'I'll be back about eleven to do lunch.'

'Fine.'

The voices faded. Emma heard the door click, then came Martin's tap on her door. 'Emily – can I come in?'

She sat up with an effort. She'd not seen him since Theo brought her home that night. He had obviously been told very little. Theo wasn't going to reveal the truth. Now as he crept into her room at her bidding, Martin looked anxiously into her face.

'I've been so worried for you,' he whispered.

411

He leaned down to kiss her lips but for some reason that she couldn't understand, she turned her face away, at the same time shattered by her own unexpected reaction.

He straightened up and she could hear the perplexity in his voice. 'Theo said you had a fall. He said it wasn't that bad, but he wouldn't let me see you.'

He was talking so formally, like a stranger. She had hurt him, turning her face away like that. Emma felt tears begin to gather. She needed so much to have his shoulder to cry on, to be held in his arms and be released from this lonely prison she was in. Why, when she loved him as she did, had some strange fear clouded what should have been her natural response? Was it that she dared not tell him the reason behind her accident, certain that if he knew she had initially consented to what had been done to her, even though she'd attempted to back out, it would send him from her in horror? She couldn't have borne that, and this sense of complete helplessness was overwhelming.

She wanted to reach up and pull him to her as he now bent to kiss her lightly on the forehead. Tears of desperation had begun to course down her cheeks. Seeing them, he drew back a little, his expression full of concern and a need to comfort.

'Darling, what is it? You look so washed out. Theo keeps saying you've also had a chill. Why hasn't he had a doctor to come and see you, with that fall and all?'

'I didn't need a doctor.' She was trying not to break down. 'I wasn't really hurt, just shaken. I'm over it now. Martin, I love you so much. I just couldn't bear to drive you away from me.'

He was looking bewildered. 'Why do you say that? Nothing's going to drive me away from you, certainly not the fact of you being ill. It brings me closer to you, in fact.'

He was being so loving, so tender, so concerned that she could no longer hold back her feelings.

'I hate him!' she burst out. 'I hate him for what he's done to me – for making me greedy enough to do anything he says – for making me hate myself!' Tears were flowing unchecked down her cheek. 'I loathe him with all my soul and I don't know what to do.'

Martin gathered her up in his arms. 'My sweetest, what's been going on? What's he done to you?'

'I can't say,' she sobbed. 'All I know is I just want you here to hold me.'

She knew she mustn't say more. Theo would keep quiet about what had gone on. Yet Martin would always wonder. If ever he found out, either he'd be so appalled that his love for her would dissolve, or he would take it into his head to seek out Theo and thrash the daylights out of him. The outcome of that was numbing – Theo would have him for assault, he'd be prosecuted, sent to prison. Could she stand up for him and bring herself to say what she'd allowed to be done to her?

She knew she would – for Martin's sake, but it wouldn't save him and she'd be left to face the world alone, because Theo would have no more to do with her either. He was capable of it even while professing to love her. She knew him by now as a man who wouldn't flinch to exact his pound of flesh for any slight to himself.

She recalled being told of the drunk who'd gone for him with a knife in an alley after he'd been shown up in

413

front of a music hall audience. Theo had seen to it that his assailant had been committed to a lunatic asylum, and no doubt was there still while Theo himself had forgotten the incident. His scar hidden by an impressive, well-trimmed beard, he had climbed to heights far greater than before with no thought of the one whose brief drunken act was still regarded as that of a madman, locked away for ever.

And what of Martin? Could Theo also make him out to be insane? A brief spell in prison for assault was an alarming prospect, but to be locked away in a madhouse for ever? It didn't bear thinking about, and she'd be consumed by guilt for the rest of her days at having been instrumental in doing this to him. Life without Martin would be the worst punishment she could imagine. And could Theo force her to marry him? At this moment, fantastic though it seemed, he could quite easily do that.

'I'm sure he suspects something, Martin,' she said. 'That's why he hasn't let you come near me. You know how jealous he can be.'

'He can't suspect. We've been careful.'

'Tm sure he knows more than we think.' A sudden premonition took hold, and she broke away from him.

'Darling, you mustn't be found here with me. You shouldn't even be in the flat. But I feel a lot better for seeing you. It's all I wanted. I shall get up tomorrow, but now hurry up and go, my love.'

He lifted her hand and kissed her fingers, seeming to sense that anything more would cause her to recoil. He seemed to understand her better than she did herself, and she loved him for that.

414

'We'll sort this out in time,' he said gently. 'But you can't marry him.'

'I know. But I'm scared of what could happen when I tell him about us. One day he'll have to know.'

'He doesn't scare me. I'll face him. He can't make you marry him.'

But she knew he could – what had happened albeit without her consent or knowledge, but which couldn't be proved as such, could be held against her. Theo would be well aware that she wouldn't want Martin to know about it and he could very well blackmail her into marriage. Either way she would lose Martin. Coming from Theo it would sound vile. He could make it seem as if it had been all her doing, and that he'd tried to stop her, that he was devastated at what she'd done – all sorts of things, making it so convincing that he could turn Martin's mind round completely.

Emma went cold at the thought of what Theo could achieve. 'He can be devious,' was all she could say, but saw Martin's loving smile.

'Don't fret, my love,' he said confidently. 'I shall straighten him out.'

Emma clutched at his arm. 'No! Let me do it. I need to bide my time. Please, Martin, don't say anything to him just yet. Promise me!' He looked a little mystified, but nodded.

'Now go!' she urged, pushing him from her. 'Go on, darling, before he comes back and finds you here.'

Martin nodded reluctantly and gave her hand a gentle squeeze. 'I love you, Emily,' he said simply, and left her.

*

415

Theo reached the top of the flight of stairs to his second-floor apartment in time to hear the door to Martin's rooms click shut.

Theo stopped abruptly before going on more slowly to the now closed door, where he again came to a halt, and surveyed it as though looking for it to talk to him.

Why should Martin have been going into his apartment at that precise moment? The door *was* speaking to him as surely as if it had a voice. It was saying to him that if its owner had gone out of this building on business and had only just returned, he, Theo, would have seen him enter, being only just behind him. But there had been no sign of Martin. So where had he been, he asked the door, and the door said, 'He has been in your apartment, knowing you were out.'

He had indeed mentioned to Martin that he was going out. 'You are a fool,' said the door, 'to tell him how long you'd be out. He timed Mrs Hart's leaving so as to get into your apartments and see Amelia. He didn't reckon on you returning so soon and he must have seen your vehicle draw up and made a bolt for his rooms.'

'That has to be the answer,' Theo muttered to himself. Coming to a decision, he knocked on the door, now eager to see what reaction he would get from Martin.

It was opened after quite a pause. A sign of apprehension, he thought with perverse satisfaction. A glance at the dark brown eyes revealed them to be wider than they should be, with a feigned look of complete innocence. He smiled to himself – he wasn't a professional reader of minds for nothing, and it was not entirely all trickery – he knew people. It was what had made him the magician he'd become. Innocence, guilt, honesty, mendacity, it was there in the eyes. And this man was being devious.

He could be devious too. 'Ah, Martin,' he began, making his tone jovial. 'I shall have need of you before lunch. Things I want to go over with you.' That was true. 'Just a few small things.' True again.

Relief showed in the young man's eyes, and he went on, 'As Amelia will not be well enough for a day or two yet, the act needs to be modified, not too much. Have you seen her?'

The question was shot out of the blue, and yes, there was a startled look, veiled and vanishing in seconds but there all the same.

'You said she hasn't been out of her room,' countered his victim, and again Theo smiled inwardly – an astute evasion.

'Well, if you're not doing anything particular at this moment,' he went on, 'I'll go over those details with you now, then we can start properly after lunch.'

Already he was retreating almost imperceptibly towards his own door, one shoulder tilted just a fraction in that direction, compelling the man to make a decision – the one he sought from him. Almost hypnotism. 'Perhaps you'd like to come in?'

Martin hesitated. Fear – the villain reluctant to revisit the scene of his crime. Theo laid a hand on Martin's shoulder. 'Good man,' he said giving no more opportunity for a change of mind. But Martin was in his pay. He couldn't protest.

With Martin following, he let himself into his apartment and with leisurely care laid his homburg on the hall table, placed his damp brolly into the umbrella stand, and

417

with equal slowness took off his chesterfield and hung it neatly on the hall stand. He kept his back to Martin, but his ears were alert for the inflections he sought in the man's tones. 'So you haven't seen her at all?' he queried casually. 'You don't know how she is?'

He heard the hardly perceptible intake of breath. 'I'm, sorry, Theo, I don't,' Martin said.

'But you are concerned for her?'

'Of course, but not unduly so. You said she'll be better in a day or two.'

'And what does she say about it?' Theo turned sharply to look at him. He saw a blank stare and read into it what he wanted to. 'What did she say, Martin?' he repeated. 'When you visited her?'

Strange that he should be enjoying this when what he was mostly feeling was anger and a sense of betrayal. It was all starting up again. He should have known he could never trust Martin. He saw his adversary's lips tighten but gave him no chance to construct another lie.

'If you were not *unduly* concerned, why did you not ask to see her – why wait until I was out?'

He could see the hostility creeping into Martin's face. 'Because you made it plain you had no intention of letting me see her.'

Theo refused to allow emotion to show on his face. How many other times while he'd been out had she and Martin been together, Martin creeping from his rooms to come in here? Had she tried to push him away, not daring to tell anyone, or was she happy to accept him? She was being very cold towards Theo himself but he'd put it down to her condition. Not cold towards Martin, it seemed. The child she'd been carrying, was it Martin's?

That was taking matters too far. Had it been Martin's, would she have been so pliant about getting rid of it? If he faced her with all this, might she not up and run off with Martin? The idea wasn't impossible but it was unthinkable.

Eleanor – he had driven her away from him, not into another's arms but to her death. Such a thing must not be allowed to happen again. This time he'd be careful – watch and wait, and if proved wrong, no harm would come of it. But if he were proved right, he must make a plan, a careful plan.

In spite of this, he couldn't keep the sarcasm out of his tone. 'So you chose to go behind my back instead.'

He knew immediately that he hadn't kept control of himself as he would have wanted as Martin suddenly raised his voice.

'What is all this about? Whatever it is you've got on your mind, say it and have done with it!'

With Theo refusing to respond, he turned and strode for the door, calling over his shoulder, 'You can think what you like as far as I'm concerned!'

Trying to master his tension as the door closed with a sharp, angry click, Theo moved towards the bedroom. Amelia must have heard Martin's raised voice. She was sitting on the edge of the bed, a robe over her nightgown. She was gazing bleakly at him but he ignored the look.

'You are up,' he said, forcing himself to speak quietly. 'I take it you are feeling better.'

She nodded. 'I thought it was time I got up.'

Theo studied her closely. Had she been enjoying that man's company, yes, she would feel better. But her gaze, though troubled, held such a look of innocence that he was already beginning to doubt his earlier conviction. She could have repulsed Martin and was now reluctant to say anything about it, or perhaps Martin hadn't been here at all and he had misconstrued the whole thing, reading things into something quite innocuous, because he had wanted to.

He spoke gently now. 'I'm glad you feel better. Mrs Hart will be back soon to prepare lunch and we will have it together, all three of us.'

He had hoped lunch would be its normal relaxed meal, with earlier strained relations having calmed, but Amelia, now dressed and reclining on the sofa, remained quiet and withdrawn. At lunch she spoke only when spoken to. He tried to dismiss it as Amelia still not feeling quite herself, but when Martin too, when he joined them, had little to say, he was forced again to read something significant into it. More significant still was that there wasn't even an exchange of smiles between her and Martin where usually they would chat, sometime to his displeasure that she never chatted to him that way. True, Martin had always been easy to converse with and ready to talk, but this lunchtime they could have been total strangers.

'When do you think you will be well enough to return to the act?' Theo asked her, with a need to break the silence.

He saw her tense but ignored it. 'It is very difficult with only myself and Martin.'

Her eyes flashed, her words came sharper than usual. 'Did you really expect me to get up straight after ...' She caught herself in time, throwing Martin a quick glance.

Obviously she hadn't told him. 'So soon after such a silly accident?' she finished.

'I hoped,' he went on, ignoring the small show of anger, 'that now you are up, you'd be feeling well enough to at least come to the theatre this evening, if only to watch from the wings. I have had to drop those illusions that I devised purely for you, and had to resort to part of a routine Martin and I once did; it's old stuff, and it cannot go on indefinitely.'

He busied himself in cutting into his lamb cutlet. 'Our present arrangement is not going down well with the audience. If it goes on for much longer, we will lose out to that ridiculous conjuror, Chung Ling Soo, at the Pavilion. Twice nightly he is putting on his Boxer Rebellion, a bullet-catching routine set around an execution, and is playing to a packed house. I cannot afford to lose my audience to him. I know how it is done, an easy trick, a mechanism in the rifle that retains the bullet in the muzzle. The rest is mere sleight of hand.' He knew he was talking far too much and too unnecessarily, but needed to fill this silence.

'I would not lower myself to imitate such cheap tricks, which to my mind are downright dangerous were the mechanism to fail to operate. But should he come to a sticky end, I should be the last to mourn his passing.'

He paused at last to help himself to more vegetables. 'You are not eating,' he said, looking up to see them both merely picking at their food. Surely only the guilty would be unable to eat except with effort.

Nevertheless, be they innocent or guilty, he was going to marry Amelia, and soon. He would bring the wedding forward and to hell with a huge reception. That done, he would rid himself of Martin and there would be little she could do about it. He would take on another assistant, maybe two, maybe a whole host such as Mr Chung Ling Soo had, and like him have a complete show based on one splendid illusion, twice nightly, taking it around the country, around the world.

Chapter Thirty

'You shouldn't be going there tonight,' Martin hissed as Theo locked the door to their apartments.

Emma gave him a secret smile. 'I feel fine,' she whispered back.

'You don't look it.'

Any more was cut short by Theo coming to take her arm, waving Martin ahead of them down the stairs to where his car sat waiting complete with chauffeur, Theo living up to his growing name and bank balance.

Despite opposition from the Pavilion, the illusionist there purporting to be Chinese but as Western as anyone could be, according to Theo, the Great Theodore was still the talk of the town, filling the Palace of Varieties twice nightly. When this ended he was booked for a three-month engagement at the Oxford at a salary far exceeding that which he was now commanding.

He gently helped Emma into the back seat, getting in beside her, thus compelling Martin to sit in the front with the chauffeur. There he put an arm about her, drawing her close to him with a firmness that prevented her pulling away from him.

They were at the theatre in plenty of time for his appearance, as always, allowing time to go over any move in need of checking and to be sure his apparatus was where it should be.

In the dressing room Emma hadn't felt too bad, installed on the chaise longue Theo had had brought in for her. But later, sitting on a chair in the wings at his insistence, she was feeling the effects of being out for the first time. Fighting down a wave of weakness, all she wanted was to be taken home and put to bed to sink down under the soft warm covers. It was always cold backstage, more so in winter, and she was shivering.

Theo's face was dark as they came off, even though it was to huge applause.

'This is no good.' He glared at Martin as the curtain fell and stagehands rushed to clear away his apparatus. 'They are applauding, but what they want is my mind-reading act. The whole thing is useless without it.'

Emma squirmed. Surely he wasn't expecting her to go on stage so soon. She remained silent.

Theo was pacing in the wings, ignoring the next act to go on, finally turning abruptly and making for his dressing room. Martin helping her to her feet, the two of them followed.

'Amelia should be at home,' he said as she sank down on the chaise longue. 'She doesn't look at all well.'

Theo glanced at him through the small dressing-table mirror and for a moment his reflected expression was tight with hate. 'And you would know about that, would you?'

He broke off, but Emma experienced a prickling of foreboding that he knew more about her and Martin than was good for them. They had been careful not to let their feelings show, but he saw more than people thought – it was his stock in trade, after all.

'I only know that she doesn't look well,' Martin was saying.

Theo had turned back to his reflection. 'Very well,' he conceded. 'Go and tell Robins to bring the car and take her home, then come back to wait for us.'

He hadn't once offered her any sympathy, nor as she was assisted away by Robins did he wish her better or bid her farewell.

He arrived home earlier than she had expected, coming straight from the show. Normally he would have gone on to supper somewhere, to meet friends and drink well past midnight. Perhaps he hadn't felt so inclined without her there, or perhaps he was anxious to get home and see how she was, sympathetic for once. But he didn't ask her how she felt. He merely got into bed beside her, his back to her, without even bothering to murmur goodnight.

She hadn't expected him to. Her eyes tightly closed as he came to bed; no doubt he hadn't wanted to disturb her. In fact, it was a relief. Even having his back touch her made her muscles tighten with loathing

The following morning, feeling a lot better, she rested all day in a loose tea gown, not even dressing her hair. Her wish now was to visit her mother, who was probably wondering why she hadn't been to see her, but she would have to take things gently for a few more days yet.

Lunch was again taken in relative silence, Emma avoiding Martin's eyes, and he hers. He went out just after lunch. So did Theo. Mrs Hart would be off soon, having washed up and tidied.

'Will you be all right on your own, dear?' Mrs Hart asked. 'Is there anything I can do for you before I go?'

Emma nodded her head to the former, and shook it to the latter, which appeared to satisfy Mrs Hart, who took off her apron, donned her hat and coat and departed with, 'I'll be back at five,' to which Emma again nodded.

Left alone, she felt much stronger and sat by the window taking in the busy Friday going on below the wide lounge window. It was then she heard a key turn in the front door lock. Mrs Hart must have forgotten something. But it was Theo who came into the lounge, his voice shattering her earlier peace. He studied her as she looked up at him, wishing it were Martin standing there, and she felt her cheeks glow at her thoughts of him. Theo saw immediately, and seemed to take it as meant for him. He smiled. 'You seem much better, my dear.'

Emma managed to produce a smile, presenting her cheek to him to kiss, hating the touch of his hands on her shoulders. 'I think I'm over the worst,' she said obligingly.

'I am glad.' He went to stare out of the window, his hands behind his back. There was something menacing about that stance. 'I'm glad because I must have you back in the act, my dear. I thought about it last night. You slept well and I can see you're recovered at last. You seemed more your old self this morning. I think you are ready to take your place once again.'

Emma stared at the broad, perfectly still back. 'Theo, I can't, not just yet.' His turning made her jump, it was so immediate. From his height his blue eyes bore into hers.

426

'And how long do you think it will be before you deem that you can?' It was a challenge rather than a question. Her voice came out small.

'I don't know, but ...'

'So my dearest doesn't know,' came the caustic interruption, each word carefully measured. 'Then I shall enlighten her. To me she looks well enough recovered to appear before our audience this evening and enliven their interest with her glittering presence. I'm being asked from all quarters when you will be with us again. There is some fear you may have left us altogether. But that's not the case, is it, Amelia, my dear?'

Emma shook her head, angry with herself for doing so. She should have fought him but she'd lost the strength, and the will.

'Fine,' he concluded, interrupting her as she made an attempt to protest. 'So tonight you will make your entrance.'

'Theo ...'

'I take it you haven't forgotten all you have been taught concerning our mind-reading act? Don't worry, my dear, you have the rest of today to relax. I will make sure you are not interrupted.' She was left stunned and aghast by the man he was becoming and by this new and overpowering hatred she now had for him.

Martin came back later, unable to speak to her for Theo's constant presence. There was now one thought in her mind. She would recover from this, go on stage, and tonight she would shine, but not for his benefit. Then she'd tell him she would never marry him even if he threw her out.

*

Theo was right – she did feel well enough to be on stage. To give him his due, he was being considerate, the routine moderated so as not to tax her too much, using Martin in her stead for moves requiring the contortion of a body to fit into small, cramped spaces; the agility used in making swift disappearances or reappearance seeming miraculous.

The mind-reading routine went without a hitch. Her few days' rest seemed to have improved her memory, if not her physical self, which still felt a wee bit shaky. Seeing her perfect performance, Theo took heart.

'I think you are up to the levitation on the scimitars,' he said quite suddenly after their first appearance, and despite her protest, considered it reintroduced in the next act later that evening.

'We will surprise them tonight,' he announced. 'We'll delight them.'

'Theo,' she begged. 'I don't think I'm strong enough yet.'

It was no good. Try as she might, he was adamant, eyeing her slim body up and down and saying she would be fine.

She watched, numbed, as each turn went on stage and came off. Theo was hastily supervising setting up the necessary equipment backstage. This illusion had always been spectacular, holding the audience spellbound and gripped by fear as the girl slowly levitated and came to rest over the three gleaming scimitars, her body lowering itself at his command on to their apparently deadly sharp points. The audience had seen how sharp they were, as one had previously been shown to slice cleanly and without effort through a sheet of paper before its point was thrown down to cruelly pierce a block of wood, leaving its steel blade to shiver dramatically. Yet the scimitars miraculously failed to pierce the tender flesh of the girl supported on a single one by only her neck as the other two blades were removed.

Would she have the strength to hold her body rigid even on the thin, slender, steel sheet that, unseen by the audience, supported the rest of her body?

She'd been trained to hold still and rigid and had always done it to perfection, her body strong; and the stiffness from the fall had quite gone. But those days of rest had made the muscles weak. They should have been worked on. Not only that, but her heart was no longer in it and strength of mind counted for a lot in this game.

She no longer had strength of mind, nor the will, and indeed, was beginning not to feel well. The thought was turning what strength there was in her muscles to water as she watched him go about his preparations behind the scenes. Perhaps it would go well so long as she concentrated on what was required of her.

Martin, watching the procedure, touched her arm. 'You can't let him make you do this. One false move and you could be badly hurt. Can't he see you're still not fully recovered? If you move just slightly and if that steel support slips ...' he didn't finish that sentence. 'Why are you letting him do this to you? You could refuse.'

His words brought unexpected determination. She wouldn't let Theo see her fear. He had put her through enough over the abortion, seen her at her weakest and had ignored it. He wasn't going to see it again, ever.

Once it was over and they left the stage to a thunderous applause, she would tell him that she was leaving

– leaving him, leaving his act, she and Martin together. Martin need never know what Theo had made her do. He loved her. He had as good as said he wanted to marry her. They'd go away together and put all this behind them.

That Theo was in love with her was beyond doubt, but it was a selfish love, a need to possess. He'd be devastated at losing what he'd assumed was his, and she would revel in it. She had money saved and Martin wasn't hard up, coming from a well-to-do family who would be only too glad to have him leave this profession and rejoin the family business. Even if they did not see her as the proper wife for their son, Martin had said she was the only one he wanted and in time he'd get them to come round. Whatever, it would still be wonderful to live her life with a normal human being after Theo.

She more or less knew the true reason he had sought to team up with Theo again. 'I was drawn to you the moment I saw you,' he'd told her some time back. 'But you were so young then. When I saw you again, you'd grown up and I was swept off my feet by the sight of you. Do you think I'd have put up with him if it wasn't for you?'

He'd said how devastated he'd been when he found that she had consented to marrying Theo. 'I had no idea you loved me,' she'd explained, filled with regret. 'Nor was I sure then of my own feelings.'

She gave Martin a smile as the orchestra began building up for Theo's dramatic entrance. As ever, striking a theatrical posture, he drew delight from his audience, waiting for such a one as this. The lights slowly dimmed to an eerie glow, a single spotlight concentrating on his impressive figure in its sombre evening dress and cloak.

In a moment he would extend a dramatic hand towards the wings and she'd emerge, the dim light making her gown of shimmering green appear ethereal against his almost satanic image, but she'd reach out one slender arm and touch his face with a tender, loving hand. The audience would clap their appreciation and with the applause dying away a strange atmosphere would settle over the auditorium.

'I shall be fine, my dearest,' she whispered hastily to Martin as Theo held out his hand towards her for her entrance. 'I love you.'

'And I love you,' Martin whispered in return as she moved away. As Theo received her apparently loving gesture, Martin too would come on stage to take up his place to one side as the back curtain slowly lifted to reveal the sinister props used by the Great Theodore.

The first part went well, as always: the many sleights of hand; now including a fiery container and the sword piercing in which Martin took part, then the mind-reading at which she and Theo so excelled and which this evening brought the usual gasps and awed cries.

The clapping died away, as did the music, and as Emma left the stage to change hurriedly into her diaphanous costume with its flowing skirts, Theo announced in deep, sonorous tones, that with the return of the delightful Amelia Beech to the stage, he was reintroducing the dangerous and sensational three-scimitar scene.

With a back curtain of his own design, an Arabian scene, descending, preparations were made, the table covered in rich gold cloth brought in, the scimitars introduced, one of genuine steel and now embedded in a block of wood where he had thrust it to more gasps from the

431

audience. Emma in her floating skirts came on stage, barefoot and with a veil hiding her nose and mouth.

'Don't do it!' Martin had pleaded, now in an identical costume to hers, the trick being to appear from the wings seconds after her vanishing, to complete the illusion.

'I promised,' she'd gasped and he reached out to catch her arm but let it slide through his hand. Whether Theo saw it from where he stood, he gave no sign and she came out for this final dramatic illusion.

She was having to fight against a wave of nausea. It had been a long evening and she was becoming almost too worn out to deal with this. Hardly out of her sick bed, she was a fool to agree to it. But she hadn't agreed, Theo had just assumed.

The lights dimming again, she stepped into the circle of the spotlight. No one applauded, everyone tense and waiting. Gracefully she would approach the narrow table, cross her arms over her breast and, apparently hypnotised, sink back into Theo's arms to be laid upon on the table, face upwards.

The strong, supporting metal sheet, hidden from the audience by her trailing skirt, would lift her body slowly and theatrically, seemingly under his influence, its single upright support concealed by his cloaked figure. A hoop would be skilfully passed around and around her suspended figure with the use of clever misdirection to prove that no visible support held her aloft.

He would take the scimitars and again strike the edge of one of them clean through the paper to show its sharpness. Then, with the hilts balanced in their slots on the table, the points upwards, he would bid her rigid form to sink until only her crossed ankles, the middle of her back and the nape of her neck, rested on the points, appearing to be her only support. The one at her feet he'd remove with dramatic gestures, then the centre one, leaving her still rigid, apparently supported by that one single point at the nape of her neck, a miracle in itself. He'd then shroud her with a white silken cloth.

Seconds later he would bring both hands up and strike downwards on the concealed form with both fists and with such force that some in the audience would leap up in terror as a piercing scream was torn from her throat to echo around the theatre. A patch of blood would appear on the white silk, bringing more cries from the audience.

Then with a flourish, he would rip away the soiled silk to reveal the single scimitar standing on its hilt, the body gone. Instantly, Martin in an auburn wig, yashmak and Eastern costume would appear from the wings, with a low curtsey, his head lowered, and then retreat, so giving Emma time to regain her breath after running the length of the backstage to the wings to take her place and come out to receive her encore by a relieved and ecstatic audience. Theo would take her by the hand and parade her back and forth before a rapturous audience, Martin too, hurriedly divested of his disguise, would come out to take a bow also.

The stunning illusion had been performed many times these past months, but tonight it didn't happen. As she approached the table, the stage and its spotlight began to waver before her eyes. Desperately she fought it, but her physical weakness began to win.

'Theo!' she gasped. 'Give me … one minute. I …'

The words fell away as her breathing seemed to give out. She was falling, slowly, powerlessly, the stage rising to meet her, a hollow, rushing noise in her ears obliterating all other sounds.

She regained consciousness in a hospital bed with Martin gazing down at her. While Theo spoke to the doctor, Martin told her that the curtain had to be brought down on the act and she herself taken off.

The manager, going out front to calm a frantic audience, had told them in full and flowing terms that their beautiful, favourite and much acclaimed idol, Amelia Beech, had only that evening bravely returned to the stage after an illness – had left her sickbed prematurely and had fainted away.

Amid prolonged applause well-wishers had yelled their hopes for her swift recovery, identifying with her for even daring that fearsome levitation.

With Theo out of hearing, Martin managed to whisper to her that he had been beside himself with fear for her safety.

'What if it had happened while you were up there or jumping down off that support? I love you so much, sweetheart. I couldn't bear for something to happen to you. I want so dearly to marry you.'

Before she could respond, Theo was stalking back, having been told that her collapse had merely been a faint.

'You have made a fool of me, Amelia,' were his immediate words. She saw Martin grow tense.

'How can you talk to her like that?' he exploded, sending fear through her that he might so easily betray them. 'She didn't do it deliberately. Can't you understand she's been ill? You made her come back too soon, and all you can think of is looking a fool! Haven't you any decent feelings?'

434

'I know that my finest illusion has become a laughing stock.'

'And that's all that matters to you.'

Theo's piercing blue eyes glittered. 'I take it that your concern for Amelia is purely a polite one? It could lead a person to imagine you have more than a passing concern for the woman who will be my wife in a couple of months.'

Please! The prayer ripped through Emma. Please, Martin, don't say any more. We mustn't give ourselves away, not yet.

Was Theo aware how close to the truth he was? So dangerously close. Her eyes sought Martin's, beseeching him to keep his temper.

'I'm sorry I ruined the act, Theo,' she blurted. 'I have to blame myself for thinking I was a lot stronger than I was. Please, my dear, don't be angry with me.'

To her relief Theo's indignation melted like ice cream before her abject plea, as he probably saw in her the pliant, vulnerable woman ready and willing to become his obedient wife. She cringed inwardly at what she could descend to, but it had its desired effect of allaying a dangerous situation.

'Of course, my dear.'

He bent and dropped a kiss on her cheek, his beard which had once felt soft against her skin now causing a disagreeable sensation that made her think of the hair of some dead creature. How could she have ever thought of that touch as pleasant?

He straightened up, confident of his forgiveness. 'Rest now. You'll be home by tomorrow afternoon, my dear. As for myself, I must go and see what damage has been done. Martin, we will leave her to rest.'

She watched them go. With Theo marching ahead, Martin turned back briefly to mouth a furtive kiss towards her. She in turn blew one back, made happy by the thought of those two air-borne kisses meeting halfway, like secret lovers. That's what they were, he and she, secret lovers. But not secret for much longer, she hoped.

She was being made to stay in for another day while the cause of her illness was diagnosed. Frowned on by starchy nurses in their stiff aprons and caps, and presented with the expressionless face of the doctor, the only bright spot was visitors' hour. Theo having announced he would be unable to come owing to some business, she had Martin all to herself. Her last chance before being sent home tomorrow morning, and her heart rose at the sight of him among the ingress of visitors looking for their sick relatives.

As he sat in the black, tall-backed chair beside her bed, she held out her arms to receive him with no danger of interruption from Theo. His kiss sweet on her lips, his words, 'I love you so much,' spread contentment through her whole body like warm honey. If only it could go on for ever.

He came in through the glass doors on the heels of the last trickle of visitors. Amelia's bed was at the far end of the long, narrow ward, beds lining each side, each occupant with a visitor, the ward echoing to subdued chatter.

Amelia too had a visitor. They hadn't seen him, but he'd seen them. Martin's hand on her arm, their lips so close they might have just parted from a kiss. From here he could have mistaken close conversation for a lovers' kiss, but he knew he hadn't.

His expression impassive, he approached, saw them spring back from one another as they spotted him, like children caught stealing.

Martin's voice was loud. 'So you hope to be out tomorrow morning.' He glanced at Theo in feigned surprise. 'Oh, hello, Theo, old man. You said you wouldn't be here today. So I thought I'd pop in, see how she was.'

Amelia too was smiling, her smile strained, but that could still be from weakness. He presented both of them with a reciprocal greeting, revealing teeth that to him felt like the fangs of a stalking tiger.

'I didn't think to see you here, Martin. Did you not think to tell me that you had decided to visit my intended bride?'

Not waiting for Martin's answer, nor expecting one, he leaned over and dropped a kiss on Amelia's cheek. It was flushed and felt far too warm. He was only too aware of the cause. But tomorrow it would flame to his own caress. That she'd transferred her affections to someone else would make no difference. He would bring her back to him with or without her consent. He must marry her as soon as possible, woo her if needs must. And she would be his wife whether she wanted to or not. As for Martin …

Even as he sat on the chair Martin had vacated for him, he was hatching plans – weighing them and their consequences. To tell Martin he no longer needed him in the act meant that Amelia would leave too. He needed a better thought-out solution, one that could be executed without losing Amelia. Something final. It needed a good deal of thought.

Chapter Thirty-One

Her collapse on stage had only enhanced Theo's reputation and brought audiences flocking to see an act that had so terrified his female assistant that she had passed out from fear, or so the press wrote, their natural instinct to disparage but in fact merely recruiting the curious.

The Palace's manager said he'd never had it so good. People were forsaking the Chinese conjuror at the Tivoli to swarm to the Palace Theatre to see the Great Theodore.

Despite Martin's misgivings and her own better judgment, Emma was back working the next day. The two days' rest in hospital and one at home had helped, that and her own willpower. The scimitar illusion went without a hitch that first night and continued to do so. Theo was being deeply attentive and loving towards her, and considerate of her still delicate condition as he put it, and she could almost forgive him. Martin he mostly ignored.

Despite all Theo's efforts, there was still a side of him she had begun to silently loathe, his amorous side. Tonight he was far from happy with her.

'When *do* you think you will feel ready to receive me, my love?' he muttered when yet again she said she wasn't ready as he lay beside her.

'It takes time,' she explained. 'I'm still very sensitive there.'

It was true to some extent – she was not exactly sore but the fear of any interference to her still tender parts made her flinch from his touch.

'You have had more than a week to get over this, Amelia.'

'I know, and I expect it must seem a long time to you, Theo. But to me it still feels like only yesterday.' She didn't think she'd ever get over it, would ever again be able to accept his touch in that region.

It would be different with Martin. He was the man she loved and who loved her and whom she knew would be considerate of her feelings. Slowly he was restoring her confidence in herself with understanding and patience. With Theo, she knew that would never happen, not after what he had made her do.

Even now, ignoring her plea, his hand was wandering over her body. 'I don't know what you mean, my dearest,' he was saying seductively.

No, he wouldn't know. He never would. His voice carried the slow, smouldering tone that she hated. 'But I will help you, my darling.'

He would talk at length, ignore any protest, then take her whether she cried out against it or not. His sole aim in life had always been to have his own way and tonight would be no different. Her body now lay under his as he droned on in that deep and awful calm tone of his.

439

'I shall soon be your husband and you my wife, and for a long time now we've been married in all but name.' The voice grew harsh. 'I don't think it is your parts that are sensitive, my dear, but yourself.'

'No.'

'I feel your affection for me has faded a little.' His weight was pinning her beneath him.

'No.' The lie trembled on her lips.

'Then you are merely a little wound-up, my dearest, and not sure what you want. I shall help you relax. I shall be tender and respect your sensitivity, but I do have the right since we are virtually husband and wife. Enjoy my love, my darling wife, let me into your secret world.'

Her secret world – was he talking of her body or what lay in her heart, her love for Martin, his love for her?

His weight made it hard to breathe. She began to fight against him to try and regain her breath. Suddenly his hand was at her throat, the other dragging up her nightgown, her legs being forced apart; all the time he was crooning in her ear that he would make her feel better again, would help to return her to her normal self, that from now on they'd be so much closer and more loving to each other, and that he planned to bring the wedding to next month instead of May, and have done with waiting.

She had never seen him this harsh, savage. Almost stifled, she was given no consideration, no tenderness or respect for her sensitivity as he had promised, his needs all that mattered to him, and even as she hurt, she stifled her cries lest he lose his temper with her and grow even more savage.

*

Neither he nor Martin saw her leave the next morning, Martin in his own rooms, Theo enjoying his ablutions. She could hear him singing – a deep, quite melodious voice, but she derived no joy from it, except as an indication of his remaining there for some time yet.

She rose, dressed hurriedly, listening for any sign of his leaving the bathroom. With her winter coat over her arm and the small, unobtrusive hat she'd chosen in her hand, not even daring to answer nature's morning call, she hurried out of the apartment, for once praying not to bump into Martin opening the door of his apartment. It would mean explanations, and she couldn't have borne to have him see her eyes swollen from crying. She was thankful at last to be down the stairs, having not been discovered by either.

Theo, coming back into the bedroom, would find her gone. Thinking her still asleep, he'd leaned over to brush her temple with his lips, before going out of the room. It had been all she could do not to wince, and when he'd gone, she had taken a corner of the bed sheet, wet it with her tongue, and had viciously scrubbed the spot his lips had touched.

She didn't care what he might think when he found her not there. He'd demand to know where she'd been and, being told, would ask if she had said things to her mother that he'd rather not have her know, but she no longer cared. She'd not seen her mother since that terrible business, and Mum was now the only person she felt she could turn to.

In the foyer of the apartment block, donning the hat and coat, she was acutely aware of needing to pay a visit, but there were public toilets not far away, by the crossroads, steps leading down to below street level. In the seclusion of a cubicle, she dissolved into a bout of weeping, unable to help herself. Recovering, she washed her hands and face at a basin, ready to walk through the back streets to where her mother lived.

It wasn't too far and should have been a pleasant walk, a sunny March morning giving a touch of spring. But she felt nothing other than the need to get to her destination.

She was welcomed in a way she'd become used to of late, Mum at last appreciative of what had been done for her. Her miseries behind her, she looked brighter, younger, gazing out on the world with more hopeful eyes, and all while Emma's own outlook was becoming more and more miserable.

This morning it showed. Mum took one look at her and almost pulled her in through the door.

'What in God's name ... Em, you look awful! What's 'appened?'

Emma almost fell into her arms. Mum, never a demonstrative woman, was taken somewhat aback.

'Oh, Mum,' she burst out. 'I can't take any more.'

Led to the settee, she sobbed out last night's ordeal and everything leading up to it. Mum, sitting beside her, listened in silence to the end. When she spoke it was in the tone of an outraged parent but which sounded to Emma to be directed solely at her.

'First yer let that dirty old bugger get you pregnant, then yer let 'im make yer get rid of it. 'Ow can yer be such a bloody, silly little fool?'

'You don't know 'im!' she sobbed. 'And I didn't get rid of it – I told you they done something while I was unconscious.'

'But yer went along with it up until yer took fright.'

Emma stared at her mother in disbelief. 'Ain't yer got just one kind word ter say to me, Mum?' she asked, imploring tenderness in a way that seemed now to come naturally. To her astonishment she found herself enclosed in her mother's arms, her mother's tone softening though dark with anger.

'Luvvy – I *know* what some men can be like. Not yer Dad – the salt of the earth, yer Dad – but what neighbours 'ave told me of bein' browbeaten by their men. But I thought yer was made of stronger stuff. I brought you up ter look after yerself and you ain't no child no more. Why didn't yer keep legs tergether and tell 'im ter keep 'is whatsit to hisself? You ain't even married to 'im.'

'He's not the sort of man you can tell what to do,' Emma said against her mother's shoulder in this unaccustomed embrace.

Her mother gave a disparaging snort. 'Yer should of left 'im a long time ago. Oh, my poor Emily!'

It was rarely Mum called her Emily, said only on occasions that called for sympathy, like when she'd hurt herself as a child. 'You should of come ter me first, luv,' she crooned. 'Faced with a choice like that.'

'I couldn't. I was so ashamed.'

'Ashamed? After all yer've done for us, me and Ben – this nice place, you coming ter see us against that vile sod's wishes? He may be famous but he ain't in my eyes. Man like that don't deserve to live. I'd like ter kill 'im meself, I would. Em, yer've got ter leave 'im.'

The door to Ben's bedroom opened. He had obviously been listening to all that had been said. She should have known. This time though, there was no sarcasm. He was filled with fury, his eyes blazing. His voice grated like a knife against stone.

'So! Showing 'is true colours at last, is he? So much fer them what thinks they're a cut above the likes of us! You an' yer fine living.'

Emma felt too humiliated to retaliate, but her mother glared up at him. 'Shut up, you daft bugger! She's had enough ter put up with, without you sticking in yer two-penn'orth.'

'Someone 'as to,' he said, coming into the room. 'It's someone like me she needs. Someone what can defend 'er. Seems she ain't got no one and I ain't standing 'ere and see 'er treated like she ain't worth the likes of that bleeder's spit.'

He closed the door on Clara, who had made to follow him out of their bedroom, and turned back to Emma. 'This is between me an' 'im now. And this time I mean it. I'll show 'im he can't abuse me sister like he's done and think he can get away with it. I've been up ter some tricks in me time, but, Gawdstruth, I've never treated a woman like he's treated 'er. And I'll get 'im for it, if it's wiv me last breath,' he vowed darkly.

Clara had opened the door again. 'Git back in there. This ain't none of your business!' he yelled at her.

'I'm family too,' she shot back at him, her small face tight. 'I ain't goin' ter be 'prisoned in me own bedroom.'

'Christ Almighty!' Ben bellowed. 'It's all bloody women in this bleedin' place. A man can't air 'is feelings without some woman puts 'er spoke in. I'm slinging me 'ook out for a bit o' peace.'

Pushing past Emma, he grabbed his jacket and flat cap off the back of a chair. Shoving the cap on his head as if owing it a grudge, he turned back to Emma. 'I'm goin' ter get 'im, don't you worry. I ain't seeing 'im ill use yer. I'm gonna do fer 'im, I promise. This time I will. Gawd strike me dead if I don't.'

As he lumbered past, the front door slamming behind him, Clara came quietly forward and touched Emma's arm with her free hand.

'Don't mind him, Emma. He's all wind and you-know-what.'

But for once Emma was only too gratified to have a champion, if only her brother, confident that when confronted by Ben's hulk, Theo would be the most subdued man anyone could imagine. So long as Ben didn't forget all about those brave vows in the next pint of porter.

There had been a sense of satisfaction in the way he had subdued her, the way she had submitted to him. Theo smiled. In three weeks, long enough for banns to be called, he'd have all the marriage arrangements in place. It would be a splendid wedding, taking place in one of the best of London's churches, a host of celebrated names invited, the reception at the Savoy. He would find Amelia the most fashionable and costly wedding gown, and champagne would flow like the River Thames. No expense would be spared on this.

When she saw all that he had done for her, she would love him and him alone, seeing at last the wonderful life he would give her. She'd forget this silly affection for Martin Page, who thought he could lure her into some dreary, humdrum life, which was all he had to offer, whether his family had money or not. What the Great Theodore would give her would be a life of excitement, a host of society friends, endless parties, constant change and a thrilling existence. What more could a girl want?

It was Martin he needed to concentrate his thoughts on – Martin, who had tried to turn her head as he had caused his first wife's head to turn. He was a womaniser and the world would be better off without him.

No good informing him he was no longer needed. The way Amelia had looked at him in the hospital, if he left she might follow. The only way to rid himself of the wretch would be by some fatal accident. With Martin out of the way she'd soon forget. They would be married and her life would be sweet and contented. He'd buy her the world if need be. He was going to the very top of his profession and she along with him. But no more talk of babies, and no more Martin.

He felt very good as he made his way down the hall to their bedroom, a smile of contentment on his face. He had the means to rid himself of Martin easily enough. The scene hovered before his eyes: the Sword Cabinet, basically a square box raised off the floor by four legs, containing two hinged mirrors and slots for inserting fifteen swords, shown to the audience as being hard, genuine steel and sharp-pointed, capable of stabbing through human flesh as well as piercing the displayed wooden block.

Somehow it must be arranged that Martin take Amelia's place the night it would be done. The mirrors of the cabinet folded out of sight, Martin clearly seen inside the small box – the front being closed, he would pull the mirrors together in front of himself, concealed behind them so that a number of swords inserted would be reflected as twice that many by the mirrors as the doors were opened to show an apparently empty cabinet but for the mass of blades, the other four inserted with force behind the hidden man.

His plan would be to make one of the slots at the rear slightly wider than the others to allow a blade, driven with extra force, to be directed and driven through the heart. He would need to rehearse this most carefully.

The doors opened, the cabinet magically empty, the blood on the stage seen as a prop, who would suspect? Closing the doors and withdrawing the swords, he would cut the illusion short by not opening them again to reveal the young occupant unscathed. At the end of the act, with the curtain closing, the accident would be discovered, he himself pale with shock, comforting a weeping Amelia, beside herself with horror.

Could anything be more convincing? And once the police investigation was over, he would soothe away her grief and she would turn to him in her hour of need and they would be married. With all the things he could give her, she would soon forget.

But it must be gone over very carefully, and the sooner the better. He would get to work on the cabinet, enlarging one slot enough for a blade to be manoeuvred where he wanted, no room for mistakes – merely wounding him would have her running to his side, and there would never be another chance. No, this had to be carefully rehearsed.

He would tell Martin that he did not consider her up to contorting her body into such a small space as the Sword Cabinet so soon after her illness. Martin would be more than willing to see her excused.

Going back into the bedroom, he was surprised to find Amelia not there. Nor was she in the kitchen. Theo felt his chest tighten on him. She could only be with Martin. Striding across the hallway, he hammered frantically on his door, to have it answered by the startled young man holding a half-completed letter, quite obviously having been interrupted in the middle of writing it.

'Where is she?' Theo bellowed, blind rage destroying all reason. 'I know she's in there.' His eyes alighted on the notepaper. 'Who's that for?'

Martin blinked. 'I'm writing to my parents.' He was offended and annoyed, forcing Theo to take a deep breath to calm himself.

'Amelia is not in the apartment.' He was damned if he'd apologise to a man whose end he was planning.

'Then she must be out.' Martin's tone was still angry. The man was too confident. Had they planned to meet somewhere later? His scheme must be put into operation much sooner than he would have liked. An idea came to him. Why not have the accident happen here? Amelia being out could be fortunate – foolish not to take advantage of the opportunity. It was fate.

'I wanted to go over a part of our act this morning,' he said. 'I needed her. I have to go out this afternoon. I need to perfect something urgently. If she isn't back in half an hour, you will have to stand in for her.'

Martin compressed his lips but nodded his assent. 'I'll come through when I've finished writing this letter to my parents,' he said pointedly.

Theo smiled grimly as the door closed. Things were all going his way. He returned to his own apartment in a fever of excitement, still wondering where Amelia could have gone to, and why. But his mind was more on the next half hour. Before Martin appeared he must enlarge that slot in the sword cabinet, test where the sword would pierce and make sure the false back of the cabinet stuck to prevent escape, the occupant's mysterious disappearance.

Ben sat at the bar of the Duke's Arms in a grubby little side street. It had been open since early morning as were most pubs all over London and other big cities, catering to the thirst of night workers cleaning streets while others were asleep, and that of other working men.

This time of the morning it was pretty full but he sat alone. He needed to be alone, to think. He sat over his pint of brown ale trying to form a plan, but all he could see was Emma's ravaged expression, her face all stained with tears, her eyes staring. Not the self-assured Emma he'd always known – the sister who stood up to him, or anyone for that matter. Where had that girl gone? That bleeder had taken that girl away and replaced her with someone he no longer recognised.

His blood seethed as he gulped his beer. Revenging her had become a wasp buzzing and stinging inside his brain. Yet it would be stupid going into this blindly. The way he was feeling at the moment would make any plan useless. Revenge, on his or anyone else's part, needed to be cooled before being carried out, with a cool head and in cool blood. As in boxing, coming in blind just asked for trouble. It had to be thought out before climbing into the ring.

He'd bide his time until he'd cornered the scum in some dark alley. There he'd beat him to a pulp or within an inch of his life – a lesson he'd never forget. First though, follow him, mark where he went, wait for him outside where he was living, not the theatre – too many people about. Then, bash-bash-bash! Maybe with a good strong cudgel to back up the fists.

It must be done soon, before March got too well under way and the evenings stayed lighter.

Two blokes be knew had wandered in. Cheering up, Ben bought them a drink. For a moment or two he toyed with the idea of asking them, one a hefty Irish road mender named Frank Mahoney and handy with his fists, and the slighter Dick Diamond who knew of lots of geezers ready to do anything for a few quid, to come in on this plan of revenge. But that would be sort of broadcasting his intentions, so he put that aside for a while to enjoy a few more beers before going home to Clara and Jack.

Emma finished the cup of tea Mum had made, feeling more comforted, but with no appetite to touch the biscuits she'd put on the table. At the back of her mind was the likelihood of Theo's annoyance that she had left without saying she was going.

'I'd best be off, Mum,' she said, putting the cup back on its saucer and getting up.

'Yer ain't been 'ere all that long,' came the statement, her mother too getting to her feet, a little stiffly, not quite so agile these days.

'I've been here over an hour,' Emma reminded her.

In that time, without Ben to interfere, she'd told her about Martin and how they'd fallen in love with each other, how sweet and considerate he was, and that he didn't really want for money.

'Then why does 'e work fer this Theo?' Mum had asked.

'I think it's because he's always been smitten by the stage.'

'Well,' had come the disparaging remark. 'It ain't much of a job fer a young bloke with people what's got a good family business. He'd be better off puttin' 'is mind ter doin' what 'is Dad wants rather than mucking about on a stage. I should think 'is family must be very disappointed in 'im. But if you feel like that about 'im, my advice is to leave yer fancy man an' go off and get married ter this Martin.'

Sympathy on learning about Martin had changed to vague impatience even before Emma decided to leave.

'It's simple enough. What annoys me is you comin' 'ere with yer tears, tellin' me yer let that brute talk yer into getting rid of what was 'is doing, then telling me there's a good man just waitin' ter take yer away from all that. Trouble is, yer don't know what side yer bread's buttered, do yer?'

'Martin doesn't know about me being pregnant and getting rid of it.'

'Then I should tell 'im if I was you.'

'I can't explain that sort of thing to him.'

'Then don't tell 'im. But if yer don't, it'll 'ang over yer, there in the background ter plague yer marriage.'

She appeared to assume that her daughter would leave this Theo bloke and marry this Martin chap.

'One day it'll all come out, maybe in a bit of a row or somethink and he'll never forgive yer for not ever 'aving told 'im. Best always ter be open an' honest.'

One thing about Mum, she had always been open and honest, too often to her own detriment, getting on the wrong side of people by revealing exactly how she felt and what she thought.

'But if I cross Theo,' Emma had wailed, 'he might tell him and Martin won't be able to bear to look at me ever again. I know just what Theo can be like.' Her mother had given her a shrewd look.

'I don't think this Martin will see it that way. If this Theo is like yer say 'e is, then this Martin will see through 'im and take your side – if he loves yer that much. But yer won't know until yer find out, will yer? Well that's my advice, anyway.'

After that she'd not shown much interest in Emma's troubles, shrugging her shoulders as if already solved when Emma tried to pursue the matter. Finally, Emma got up to leave.

At the door Mum tilted her cheek for her goodbye kiss and closed the door the moment Emma turned to go down the status, not waiting with a farewell wave. That was Mum all over. But Emma wasn't upset, her mother's good advice was being slowly absorbed.

Chapter Thirty-Two

It took a time for Theo to regain his composure after having embarrassed himself before Martin. He now made ready to summon Martin for the short rehearsal. He would apologise for his outburst, saying that he'd been worried at Amelia going off without so much as a by your leave. Martin knew where his bread was buttered, would do as he was told. By the time she returned home it would be all over. He found himself almost gloating. She would find him in shock, the police already called, and they would break the terrible news.

The strain was making his heart pump inside his chest as though it were a drum. This was no light thing he was embarking on. That business on the cliff edge all those years ago had been unforeseen, a prank gone wrong. This would be deliberate, only made to seem accidental. The tension was making the muscles of his chest feel tight and even brought a dull ache to the arm muscles too.

Talking to Mum had made her feel a lot better. Letting herself into her apartment, she was full of determination.

Some time in the week she and Martin would creep away together, go as far away as possible and never come back. But first she must explain about the baby and pray that, understanding though she knew him to be, he would find just that bit more understanding, enough to forgive her.

She felt a certain satisfaction in knowing Theo would be left high and dry. Even though his was a selfish love, it was still what he saw as love and there would be such an emptiness left inside him. Would his career falter as it had once before? Next time there might not be someone to help him pick himself up. Would he find someone else willing? In truth, she didn't care; she only hoped that he wouldn't be down for long and might not be so tempted to seek revenge and spoil her life with Martin.

Theo wasn't in. A note said that he had gone to see his agent and would be back around lunchtime. She felt a prickle of anger. The fact that she had left this morning without saying a word to him hadn't apparently bothered him – no reference to it in his note – nothing. Perhaps just as well.

Letting herself out of the apartment, she went to Martin's door and tapped lightly on it. 'Are you there, darling?' she whispered.

Soon, she thought as Martin answered her call, she wouldn't have to do this any more.

Theo's mood was thunderous. With Amelia safely out of the way, he had gone to summon Martin, but this time had received no reply. Anxiety deepened into fury as it dawned on him that this had been pre-planned: they had arranged to meet somewhere.

Of course, Martin would say that he had slipped out to buy cigarettes. He'd even mentioned last night having only a couple left in a packet – a good ploy but he wasn't fooled.

Biding his time, he knocked a little while later to find Martin had returned. Asked where he'd been, he said he had indeed been out for cigarettes. Liar! came the silent accusation as he blandly informed Martin that he was off to his agent and would be back around lunchtime. Too late to carry out his previous plan today but it would cement his decision if returning earlier he caught them together. When he did return, Amelia was alone in the lounge, sitting by the window reading. Yet the glow on her cheeks betrayed her. They had been together. He'd been just a little too late.

After lunch, which he always insisted all three ate together, he curtly told Martin that they wouldn't be rehearsing this afternoon.

'I do not wish to tire you, Amelia,' he said to her across the table. 'I need you to be strong again. I shall not be using the Sword Cabinet on stage for the next couple of performances. After that we will use you, Martin, for that illusion. It will allow Amelia more time to regain her suppleness.'

More to the point, he needed to spend time in the spare room where his props were, working on the aperture that would perfectly direct the sword to where Martin's treacherous heart lay beating so joyfully at this very moment.

Their next three performances continued as usual in all other aspects, but his plan was becoming an obsession, watching the two of them, making certain they were never left alone together, that he was with one or the other.

He was unable to sleep. The moment Amelia slept, he would creep off to examine his Sword Cabinet for any flaw that he might have missed. But it was perfect. All he needed now was the opportunity. Would it be better to carry it out here in privacy while rehearsing, or on stage in full view of everyone? It would give him witnesses to this horrific *accident,* where here, foul play might more easily be suspected.

Swinging between the one idea and the other was making him nervous and that stood no illusionist in good stead. This had to be done soon. Perhaps it should be done here after all – less publicity. If he could get Amelia out of the way ... to exonerate himself in some way, and out of concern for her, he didn't want her present for him to witness her horror as she saw the blood. She must be out of the way and then gently told of the tragedy.

'You look pale, sweetheart,' he told her after another two days of nothing yet accomplished. 'Why don't you meet a friend or two for coffee?'

She had many friends, most of them theatre folk, many well known, among them the beautiful Victoria Monks, Gertie Gitana the only slightly less pretty but charismatic comedienne, one or two girls from the Tiller troupe – Nellie Whiting and Nellie Turner, Cissie Loftus, the bubbly impersonator who had been a friend for a long time now. There were others whom she'd met at the parties she'd been to with him, but try as he might she remained ensconced in the apartment.

'At some point you must begin socialising again,' he urged her, frustrated and increasingly edgy by the end of the week. 'I know you have been unwell, but you need some recreation away from all this. You cannot stay in day after day. It's unhealthy.'

'We have to be on stage every evening,' came her cold reminder.

She was sitting, stiff and very upright, on the extreme edge of one of the armchairs, her fingers fiddling agitatedly with the corner of one of the linen antimacassars protecting the chair arms. Everything about her betrayed unfriendliness. He needed to be gentle with her.

'But you need fresh air and sunlight, my darling,' he said as tenderly as he could. 'You should be taking advantage of this spring-like weather while it lasts.'

He was forcing himself not to pace around and let her see how stretched his own nerves were

'It worries me to see you so pale and lacking energy. You're becoming too cooped up. For your own sake, why not telephone one of your friends to meet them for an hour or two, maybe a walk in the park? You would enjoy it,'

'You know I hate the telephone,' she parried.

'That's ridiculous, my dear.'

A touch of anger was creeping into his tone. He fought it. 'We live in modern times. You should be completely at ease with it by now.'

All she did was shrug, as she often did these days, leaving him even more frustrated and at a loss.

To combat his frustrations he had taken to going out for ten minutes or so after returning home from the theatre. A stroll through a few of the back streets, ill-lit though they were, served to settle his mind, grateful for a little solitude in which to contemplate the task ahead of him, and think of the day when he'd have Amelia to himself once more.

Once rid of Martin, he would expand his act in competition with people like Mr Chung Ling Soo. With female assistants only, Amelia would have no temptations. After his first wife, he hadn't dreamed it could all happen again. The quicker he got rid of Martin the better. What he was about to do was the only way to keep her for himself.

This evening he walked slowly, deep in thought, savouring the silence, the darkness, the stillness, far preferable to the brilliance of the main thoroughfare with its hustle and bustle of people and traffic. No one queried these brief, lonely walks and Amelia didn't seem to care where he was. She was no longer the starry-eyed young person he'd first met. This business with Martin had dulled her eyes to a brooding sullenness.

After a glorious day tonight was chill with promise of an early morning frost. The dark street was even more deserted but for one person who passed him with head bent. His mind clearing, he was ready to return home. He had been out longer than usual. While Amelia slept, he would make use of a couple of hours going over again and perfecting what he knew must appear to be a pure accident. It would happen tomorrow evening. He had but the one chance and nothing must go wrong. It must be foolproof.

He took in a few deep and regular breaths to help him relax. All was quiet. The theatre crowds had long since departed, on their way home or on to a restaurant for a congenial supper with friends. Only some distant sound of singing from some pub or other wafted on the still air.

He turned slowly for home, pausing first to light a cigarette, flicking the match into the gutter. For a moment he gazed after it lying there, a thin, pale thread among the ancient mud and old muck that was hardly ever disturbed

– only the more important streets of London were cleaned nightly, the dim and dingy back streets and their denizens largely forgotten much as the rats in the sewers were.

He drew in a lungful of sweet smoke and gazed contemplatively up at the stars, in this unlit street, bright as diamonds in that black and moonless sky.

Tomorrow evening, on stage in front of everyone – he'd decided at last that it would be better that way, appearing more as an accident – his worries would be over. He would choose the second performance, so that the police would not disrupt the theatre too much when the accident was discovered.

Flicking the half-smoked cigarette from him, he adjusted his scarf, pulled the collar of his warm ulster further up around his neck and moved leisurely off. He'd go to the main road tonight then turn into the road to his apartment. He felt more at ease with himself than he had been for days.

Soon, life would be sweet again. Once Amelia had got over the shock of Martin's death, and with his gentle help finally put her grieving aside as all must do in getting on with life, yes, everything would be sweet again.

Some way ahead lay Charing Cross Road with its lights and distant din, making this street all the more dark and lonely – too lonely. An sixth sense of something not being as right it ought to be sent a shudder through his body and he quickened his step a fraction.

With the light from the busy main thoroughfare plainly silhouetting his figure, behind him a silent shadow began to move forward, stealthily but swiftly narrowing the gap between itself and its quarry.

*

For two evenings Ben had watched Theodore Barrington. Hanging around outside the splendid, three-storey apartment block where he and Emma lived, in a fine street off the Charing Cross Road, he thought of the poverty that lay hidden just behind this finery – grubby streets, dirty yards, as degrading as anything in the East End if not so extensive, people living hand to mouth.

Behind every fine façade such pockets of poverty lived cheek by jowl with the rich – a place to ambush a bloke, if he could get him to go down just one of those streets. Hoping for a sight of his quarry and buoyed up by more than just a pint of porter, Ben agreed with himself that the whole bloody lot wanted knocking down, clearing away, got rid of. Maybe one day it would be. Wealth hiding squalor, it was like that Charles Dickens bloke wrote about around fifty years ago. Not that he'd read any of it, but Emma had, and had told him. She was the clever one, but look where that had got her – in the bed of some rich geezer who had abused her, put a kid in her and then made her get rid of it. Ben prided himself that he wasn't a forgiving man and he could champion someone like his own sister when in trouble.

This was the third night he'd hung around here, wondering how the hell he could waylay a geezer who was always with other people. He had decided against enlisting help – if he couldn't do this on his own, he was no sort of bloke! But this was getting bloody boring. Perhaps Barrington never went out alone. When he did appear it was with Emma and this other bloke she'd taken a fancy to. They'd come down the steps to the street, Barrington holding her by the aim as if frightened to let go, the other man following. The first night it had been to get into a taxicab, and last night it had been a fine-looking motorcar with a chauffeur.

That first night Barrington had come out on his own after coming back from the theatre he was playing at Ben was on the point of leaving, it being an overcast night with a nasty bit of drizzle and very uncomfortable, when he saw Barrington descending the few broad steps to the street. He saw the man look up at the sky before going back up the steps again to disappear. Last night he'd gone a few yards along the street away from Charing Cross Road, walking slowly, but just as Ben made to seize his chance, had turned and hurried back.

This evening while they were at the theatre, he'd whiled away the time in a nearby pub with a couple of nips of gin and a couple of pints of beer to lessen the growing chill of a frosty night. But though he was still steady on his feet by the time the theatres turned out, he was seeing this waiting lark as a sheer bloody waste of time. And he wanted a pee. Lolling behind the public letterbox across the road from the apartment house, waiting for them to appear, made trying to hold his water none the easier. A few pints did that to a bloke.

Bursting by the time they'd gone inside, he went up against one of the red sides of the old-fashioned pillarbox. Another pee not long after, and a movement across the road caught his eye – someone coming down the steps.

Ben moved hastily back behind the fouled pillar-box, recognising the figure of Barrington. He was alone. Unable to believe his luck, Ben curled his large hands into even larger fists, aware of his biceps bunching beneath his jacket. But how far would the bleeder go before turning back? Ben felt he had just about had enough.

Barrington turned away from the main road, was walking slowly and leisurely towards the turning that led to the darker back streets. This time he did not retrace his steps. It couldn't be more perfect, an opportunity not to be missed; the man would be sorry he ever left home tonight.

Ben tweaked the peak of his cap, pulling it low over his eyes. Lurching forward, he was instantly aware of not being as steady on his pins as he'd have liked to be. One glass of beer too many, stupid sod, when he knew he needed to keep a cool head for the job in front of him. But he wasn't exactly drunk, just slightly unsteady. Following at a distance, stopping when his quarry stopped, slipping into the shadows when he turned to gaze up at the frost-brilliant stars, Ben slowly began to gain on Barrington.

The streets the man was walking formed a block, dark, with only the glimmer from a spluttering gas lamp on a bracket at the first corner. Ben grinned.

If Barrington were to turn back now, he'd leap out, block his path, bring his fists into play and when the man was down, get the boots going. That bugger wouldn't get up again for a long time.

If Barrington carried on round the block that would eventually lead him to the brighter main road, he'd put a spurt on, catch him up before he got there. Then, bash, wallop! Pummel that face to a pulp. No need for a cudgel – he could use his fists to deadly effect when he wanted, drunk or sober. And again the boot, leaving him bleeding in the gutter for someone to find in the morning if he hadn't dragged himself back home, a long way for anyone in the state he'd be in to drag themselves.

Lurking in the shadows, he saw the brief flare of a match, the flame extinguished as it was tossed into the gutter, the small brief glow from the gasper as Barrington drew on it. Then he saw him turn towards the main road. He'd have to act now or be too late.

Ben had been as silent and stealthy as several pints allowed, but like a lion provoked into action by its fleeing prey, he leaped forward to narrow the gap, to catch him up before the man was aware of him.

Barrington saw him too late. Ben saw him raise his hand to defend his head, his hat flying off. Ben let out a roar, took a wild swing. The man ducked, more athletic for someone his size than Ben had imagined. In the ring he'd have anticipated such a move, but in the dark ... *And* he was a bit drunk.

Enraged at having missed, Ben let out another roar of fury, but before his huge, boxer's fists could find their target, the man was already running for his life towards the safety of the bright main thoroughfare. Made furious by his failure, Ben pounded after him, bent only on avenging his sister.

There was a pain in Theodore's chest, but he kept going. If he could reach the safety of the busy major road and make it across to the far side, his unseen assailant, whoever he was, wouldn't dare to follow him.

Running blindly onwards, he burst out into the safety of bright street lighting, bright shop windows, people passing to and fro, and the glorious rumble of traffic. Certain he could feel his attacker's hands grabbing at his

shoulders, he bounded across the road. He didn't hear the man yell out to him. Nor did he see the motor omnibus.

Emma alighted from Theo's handsome, shiny black Austin York Landaulette and stood in the warm August sunshine gazing at his country mansion, still as forlorn as ever, for all the work that had gone into it. Soon it would be sold. The money it would bring would buy something far more cosy.

Nearly six months since Theo's accident. She remembered how she'd felt when the police came in the small hours, waking with a start to their knocking on the apartment door. Realising Theo wasn't beside her, she had flung on her robe and staggered to answer the door, seeing Martin coming from his room, he too awakened by the knocking. Stunned by what the bobby was saying, unable to take it in, she remembered reaching out to Martin.

It was August now. The day planned for her wedding to Theo had long since passed. And now she gazed at his country manor before smiling up at the man whose arm she held.

'I don't think I could have borne to live there, ever,' she said fervently.

'I know how you feel,' came the reply. 'We'll find something nearer London so that you can see your mother more easily. In fact, she must have a house of her own and let's hope she won't be plagued with your brother any more, as he has his own place now and can live as slovenly as he wishes.'

Emma hugged the protective arm. How things had changed since the accident. Ben had confessed to her, only to her, what he'd been about to do. The law had no idea of the hand he'd played in it. But Ben had been well shaken. He would never change, but he'd certainly changed her life for her that night.

'I think he will always be a problem,' she smiled wryly, still gazing at the empty windows of Theo's mansion.

'He'll be all right,' replied Martin. 'With the money you've promised him he'll have something he's always wanted, his own boxing booth. That should be enough to give him a sense of responsibility. And he's married now too.'

She felt Martin gently squeeze her arm, the gesture full of love. 'Just as we will soon be, darling.'

As she cuddled against him, her smile faded a little. 'I hope it will be with your family's blessing. I know they don't approve of me.'

He was looking reflectively into the far distance. 'It'll take time. My father desperately wanted me back in the business and I told him that so long as I've got you why should I want to go elsewhere.' Martin gave a little chuckle. 'OK, call it a bit of blackmail, but I think it hit its mark.'

Listening to him, Emma was sure he was right. They were doing all the proper things. She was back living with her mother, Ben and Clara having found a flat of their own. Martin was back with his parents. She and he met a couple of times a week and at weekends, like proper courting couples do. All was above board and respectable and as he said, it was only a matter of time before he talked his family round to accepting her. And even if they didn't, he would marry her anyway.

Her life had changed so abruptly and though she did feel sad at the terrible way it had, what would her life have been like if it hadn't? Visions of leaving Theo and

Theo coming after her still caused bad dreams despite the knowledge that she was free of him for ever. It would always play at the back of her mind. She needed to cling to Martin to dispel it, but would he be there for her if she told him the truth about herself?

That also constantly played on her mind, that she was still unable to bring herself to tell him about the baby. She tried to convince herself that with Theo gone and the threat of exposure gone with him, she would never need to tell him.

For the benefit of appearances, she had affected to put on a brave face regarding Theo's untimely death. His act, of course, had come to an abrupt end. Shocked at a gifted and famous figure being torn from them by such a tragedy, crowds had attended his funeral while she, feeling hypocritical at having to hide an overwhelming sense of relief, had made a great show of honouring him by generously giving him the best funeral money could buy, able to afford to be generous, as he had left everything to her, fully believing they would soon be mamed.

Yet there still remained her secret. There was no Theo any more threatening to expose her, but might she one day expose herself, say a wrong thing, utter a thoughtless word?

The vision of Martin's face as it all came out, maybe in years to come when they had a family of their own, haunted her. She must tell him, tell him now. Yet what if he looked at her, appalled? She could see herself running frantically after him as he walked away. But though the man she'd come to know wouldn't do that, the look on his face would haunt her for ever. To tell him would prove the hardest thing she could ever imagine doing.

She turned from the cheerless house, at the same time pushing away the moment that had nearly occurred and glanced up at him.

'I don't think I really need to look around it,' she said, which they had first intended to do, to see if there was anything that needed to be taken prior to the sale. 'Let it stay as it is.'

Let everything stay as it is, came the thought. 'Perhaps the people buying it will throw out what's left, cheer it up and bring it back to life.'

'Maybe what's left needs to be thrown out,' Martin mused, and spoke one more single word. 'Sad.'

He shook his head, then brightened. 'Come on, darling, let's go.' He put a hand over hers. 'Leave it to itself. We have a life to look forward to.'

Emma couldn't laugh with him. It hit her that she couldn't do this, couldn't live a lie with him for the rest of her life. Whether she lost him or not, she must speak. But oh, dear God, she didn't want to lose him! He looked so happy and she was about to destroy his world, both their worlds.

'Martin.' She pulled back as he turned towards the car. Her tone made him pause. He frowned. 'What is it, my sweet?'

'I've something to tell you. I have to tell you now. Something you must know about me. Something you have to know.'

Giving him no time to interrupt the way she was gabbling, she forged on, the words falling from her lips giving the true reason, the whole reason, for her faint on stage. When she'd finished, he stood looking at her, unsmiling, and she felt sick. She had lost him.

When he spoke, his voice was low-pitched and steady. 'I had a feeling something like that had happened,' he said slowly. 'I never said anything. I felt I had to wait for you to say it and I'm glad you did.'

There was another pause that drew itself out until she wanted to cry out to him, asking what he intended to do about it. But he spoke first, again very slowly, almost proudly. 'It must have taken a lot of courage to tell me.'

She was looking at him through a film of tears that made him seem as though he was floating in water as he continued. 'And now we can put it all behind us.'

He glanced past her at the grim edifice. 'Just like that house, and all that it represented. Come on, darling.' He took her arm again and began leading her towards the Austin.

Without a word, he settled her in the passenger seat. Walking round to the driver's side, he got in and pressed the starter button.

As the engine roared into life, the brake and the gear stick released, he briefly laid a comforting hand on her knee under its heavy skirt, giving her a broad smile before transferring his gaze back to the road they were about to take.

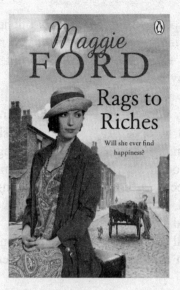

In the 1920s, nobody is safe from scandal...

Amy Harrington leads a privileged life out in London society. Her maid, Alice Jordan, lives in the poverty-ridden East End. But when a disgraced Amy is disowned by her parents and fiancé, Alice is the only person she can turn to...

Forced to give up her life of luxury, Amy lodges with Alice's friendly working class family. But while Amy hatches a plan to get revenge on her former love who caused her downfall, Alice finds herself swept into the glittering society her mistress has just lost. And when Amy meets Alice's handsome older brother Tom, they can only hope that love can conquer all...

Will the two girls ever lead the lives they dream of?

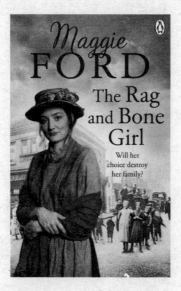

What will she sacrifice for love?

Growing up in London's East End with six siblings, Nora Taylor has always been close to her younger sister Maggie. But when she meets Maggie's fiancé Robert, they are immediately drawn to each other. Forced to choose between her family and her heart, Nora decides to marry the man she loves – even if it means losing her sister.

When the First World War breaks out, Nora must fight to hold her family together through the challenges and tragedies to come. As her children grow up they embark on their own adventures, but another war will threaten all their hopes for the future. Can this broken family survive the dark days of wartime?